THE BUS PASS

Ian Cullingham

Copyright © 2015 by Ian Cullingham.
All rights reserved. No part of this book may be reproduced in any manner without written permission except in the case of brief quotations included in critical articles and reviews. For information, please contact the author.
ISBN-13: 978-1515302827
ISBN-10: 1515302822

All characters appearing in this work are fictitious. Any resemblance to real persons, living or dead, is purely coincidental.

ACKNOWLEDGMENTS

I would like to thank my wife, Kath, for her help and patience in proofreading my manuscript at every stage, without which my work may never have made it this far.

Also, for the support and encouragement of my daughters: Beth, for her unwavering conviction that the book should be published, and Amy for critiquing the story in every draft.

Finally to Val Cooper, my debt for her honest evaluation.

It is said that every person has the capacity to write one book.

This is mine.

PART ONE

CHAPTER 1

Henry's Dilemma

"Hi Dad, how are you? I thought that you would be feeling low today, so I decided to give you a call."

The sound of his son's voice down the telephone, all the way from Sydney, leaves Henry Long with conflicting feelings of excitement and loss at the same time. Obviously he knows the reason for the call from Richard, and appreciates his sensitivity on this day, the fourth anniversary of the death of Isabel, his mother and Henry's wife. At the same time he is reminded of his loss, that even after all this time, Henry has still not come to terms with.

"Hello son, it's lovely to hear from you, I was just getting ready to take flowers to your mother's grave." replied Henry, the thought of which brought a catch in his voice. "I'm doing fine," he lied, not wishing to cause his son to worry about things that he could do nothing to resolve.

Richard understands his father very well and sensing his feeling of depression, says, "Well, part of the reason I rang was because of Mum's anniversary, but also to remind you of my offer for you to come over and live with Janet, me and the boys. You remember we raised the subject with you when you came to visit eighteen months ago. We are concerned for your welfare and you are not getting any younger, you know! Anyway, it would be good to have you here, and it would give you the opportunity to watch the boys growing up. We have plenty of room and you could even have your own rooms with separate facilities, which you could use if you wanted your own space and privacy. Now that Penny and her family are probably coming to live here in the next few months, it would mean that we could all be together, so what do you say?"

It is 25 March 2008, and the sky overhead is heavy and leaden, the morning mist just beginning to lift. It seems, to Henry at least, to have been a very long winter, and although not particularly cold it has been damp and dreary, making the short winter days seem even shorter.

Henry, sitting in the bedroom which he has converted to use as a study, looks up out of his window, down to his back garden, with its patio leading down to the lawn with evergreens, hydrangea and laurel shrubbery in flower beds with early daffodils looking for all the world like a band of trumpeters blown hither and thither by the cold March wind, resplendent in their yellow uniforms. As Henry raises his head higher to see past the shrub beds, he can see the rose arch which Isabel had tended so lovingly, until finally at the extreme end of the garden, to the pergola covered with wisteria waiting for the first rays of spring to show its beautiful purple blossom, which looks for all the world like huge bunches of grapes.

This is a far cry from how the garden looked when the children were young and where they had spent so many happy hours. Then it had on many occasions been the venue for The Football World Cup, or High Wycombe versus Manchester United, in which invariably Richard was playing centre forward for England or Wycombe and without fail, would always score the winning goal. Or perhaps it would be a Hospital or a Ladies' Hairdressers usually run under the strict auspices of Penny. It also served as a jungle where children could hide or a place where treasure hunts could be held.

Unfortunately The Ladies' Hairdressers was short lived, because one day when Penny was about eleven years old, the mothers of several of her school friends came knocking on Isabel's door complaining that Penny had gone from playing to actually doing hairdressing, and one by one they produced their offspring, whose hair in most cases was in clumps of varying lengths, with a few small areas of baldness in between. It transpired that Penny had taken one of Isabel's pudding basins down to the shed at the bottom of the garden, which she placed on the victims' heads and proceeded to cut round with scissors from the kitchen, with disastrous results. Isabel, although horrified, found it difficult not to laugh, but quickly admonished Penny and banned hairdressing forever.

THE BUS PASS

Mini Olympics were also held in the garden, with Richard winning most of the men's events (Henry made a point that he at least won one or two), and Penny the female events with Isabel managing to win the occasional egg and spoon race, so honour was satisfied. Thus it continued for several years until the garden became too small to contain the children's activities, when the local leisure centre then became the new hub of their lives. For a fleeting moment Henry sees it all again in his mind's eye and lives again the sheer joy of those wonderful years.

His eye then comes back to the desk that he is sitting at, to the photograph of Isabel, his beloved wife of some thirty-eight years - the photo that had been taken before her illness had ravaged her beautiful looks. Here she was smiling at the camera (as Henry recalls vividly), on the point of breaking out into peals of laughter that characterised her sunny disposition and attitude, that said life was to be lived to the full, both in good times and in bad. She had lived the mantra, only succumbing at the end when the drugs and chemotherapy had made it impossible.

Months before she died, her consultants had told her that her condition was terminal and that her life expectancy was probably no more than six months. She took the prognosis with remarkable calm. After all, she had already suffered the humiliation and indignity of surgery for a mastectomy some eighteen months previously, fighting the dreaded breast cancer; at first it had gone into remission, but returned with a new malevolence which destroyed even her massive resolve.

About eighteen months before Isabel died, Henry gave up his work as a graphic designer to be with her, initially while she was still able and fit enough to do some of the things that they had both wanted to do, and had promised each other when they retired, and then later because of necessity to take on the role of carer..

Henry comes out of his reverie with a start as Richard says suddenly, "Are you there Dad, can you hear me?"

"Oh yes son, I can hear you," says Henry. "I have thought of nothing else since I came back from Oz."

Henry was in fact still far from sure that a move to Australia would be as idyllic for him as his son thought. After all, he still had a few people that he could call friends, and he had always loved

England's verdant panorama, something that he particularly looked for from the aeroplane window when returning from Australia, or any other country for that matter. Both Isabel and he had always loved England, and it was a constant source of regret to Henry that they had not been able to see more of its ever changing beauty before Isabel died.

He realises with a start that if he does emigrate, he will miss England and its heart-warming idiosyncrasies, and he almost chokes as a lump comes to his throat at the thought.

No, the basic problem is that he just cannot make up his mind; on the other hand, now that his only other child, Penny, and her family were contemplating also moving to Australia because she was offered promotion by her employers to open a Sydney branch sometime within the next few months, a new dimension had entered the equation. Penny's company specialised in interior design, mostly for corporate clients, and after only ten very successful years in the UK were looking abroad for other areas to expand and bring their expertise.

Henry also knew that if he did decide to take the plunge, once the decision had been taken and the move made, he doubted very much if he would be able to return to England, even if he wanted to, because he realised that life moves on, and those few people still involved in his life who were very precious to him would inevitably, slowly become less and less so, once he made the decision to emigrate.

He also suspected that Richard, although the offer he was making was perfectly genuine, could possibly regret it after a decent length of time had passed. Living in each other's pockets in Henry's experience very often caused irreparable damage even to close relationships such as theirs.

Finance was another big stumbling block as far as Henry was concerned. Retiring early had meant that he had been unable to clear his mortgage completely, which in turn meant that if he sold up now in a market which was slowing perceptibly as each day passed due to the dreaded 'credit crunch', his available capital would be very limited, bearing in mind that it would have to last him for the rest of his days. Although both Isabel and he had taken several trips to see Richard and his family over the years, he was not fully aware of things like health cover and qualifications for residency which Australia imposed on people wanting to immigrate to her shores - particularly for people of retirement age or over.

Rather than commit himself to Richard just yet, Henry prevaricates and says, "Well son I really appreciate your very kind offer, and it's certainly true that it would be wonderful for me to be able to watch all my grandchildren growing up, and to be with your and Penny's families. In fact the thought of remaining here in England without you all doesn't bear contemplation, but I need to be sure and we need to be honest with each other. I have seen and heard of similar situations with other people over the years which have progressed, but in due course things have deteriorated leaving families broken and destroyed forever. I would not want that to happen to us. I love you all too much and the thought of losing you in that or any other fashion makes me cautious. Before I decide anything, I need first to examine your end of things to see just what the conditions of entry to Australia are - I also need to discuss the whole thing further with Penny, to see how she feels about it all."

At this point Richard interrupts saying, "I already have some bumf from Australia House which I will send you, and I will get some more covering the points that you have raised and send them to you. We can discuss them once you receive them. With regard to Penny, I have already spoken to her several times and her opinion is the same as my own, that you would be better off here with all of us. In fact Penny went further, saying that she would feel guilty as hell coming over and leaving you behind. I respect your comments, Dad, about the thought of things possibly going wrong between us, but it's just not going to happen. Both Janet and I are determined on that. We appreciate that although you will be able to see us and be together, and that will be great, but that you also will be losing a way of life. But we all love you all too much, and we will ensure that there are enough things to do, so that you will just not have time to think about Good Old Blighty."

"All right son, let's leave it there for now. See if you can get the information to me and I will also try this end. I will in the meantime speak to Penny and find out just how far down the line her arrangements are. I will get back to you in a few days, even if not with any news, just to speak to you and the children, bye for now, love to you all."

"Bye Dad, same to you." Richard hangs up, leaving Henry looking pensive and tired.

After a few moments he picks up the phone again and dials his daughter's number.

"Hullo, Penny love, how are you? I have just been speaking to Richard and he is urging me to move to Sydney again, which you are no doubt aware of. How are things looking with your proposed move?"

"Oh Dad things are pretty hectic just at the moment. Mark is away on a training course with his company this week and I have to drop the children off at school every morning, although I am managing to get them picked up by one of the other mothers in the afternoons. As yet, there have not been any further developments with the Sydney office, the company are still jumping through the Australian legal loops, but providing all that goes through OK, everything else should follow quite quickly."

"That won't leave you much time to clear all your arrangements up this end." said Henry. "Things like selling the house and looking for property in Sydney, although I suppose Richard could help you with that from his end. What about schools for the kids and alternative work for Mark? Presumably that won't be a problem, him being a research scientist. I am sure that Australia will bite their hand off to get him."

"Well Dad, things are still very much in the air as you will appreciate, but I would just like you to know that both Richard and I are as one in our wish for you to move to Sydney, where we can all be together. We have put the house on the market, but as you know things are very sluggish because of the credit crunch at present. Mark's situation, as you say, is good, and when things are more finalised, he is proposing to talk with his bosses to see if there are any vacancies in any of their subsidiaries in OZ. When things are a little clearer, my company intends that we could fly out for a couple of weeks, prior to the final move, so that we can suss out things for ourselves."

"Well love, I told Richard that I would find more information about the possibilities of my moving as well and I will let you both know when I have done that," says Henry.

"That's lovely Dad, do that and we can discuss it further with you. By the way, I am aware that it is the anniversary of Mum's death today, and I would like you to know that I am thinking of you. I am intending to bring the family over to you on Sunday, and if you agree, perhaps would could all go out to lunch?"

"Thank you, that would be very nice, I look forward to it. Perhaps with any luck, I will have more info then. Well, I had better go if you have to do the school run. See you on Sunday, bye love."

"Bye Dad, take care."

As he returns the telephone to its cradle, Henry cannot help but marvel once again of the speed (at least how it seems to him) at which his children have grown from toddlers to adults, with families of their own. He feels almost robbed of the period between their childhood and parenthood, with very few memories of the time in between, and wonders constantly just how it happened.

CHAPTER 2

Richard and Penny

Henry and Isabel were living in a poky little two bedroom flat in High Wycombe High Street when first Richard was born in 1967 and then Penny three years later, after which it rapidly became obvious that space was a huge problem. They put both children in the second bedroom for a couple of years, but it was apparent to both of them that this situation could not last for very much longer.

Fortunately, because their rent cost was relatively small, they had managed to save some money towards a deposit for a house, and Henry's parents, because he was their only child, managed to make up the shortfall.

After looking around for some time to find property within their limited price bracket they managed to find a house which although modest, met most of their criteria in Downley, just outside the town, which was high up overlooking High Wycombe, which nestled in the valley below. It was also close to Downley Common, which had large areas of grassland and woods which they could use for recreation as a family. Even better from Henry's point of view was that the pub on the common, The Kings Head, was only just up the road, within walking distance. But the added factor was that it also served wonderful real ale and pub grub. All of this fitted Henry's own perception as an ideal local, useful for both him and Isabel to go for a reasonably priced meal out on those occasions when they managed to get a baby sitter.

They eventually managed to purchase the house, and here it was that Isabel and he raised their family and watched their children leave the nest, only for them to return briefly on the saddest day of all their lives four years ago, for Isabel's funeral.

THE BUS PASS

But it was also here that the children grew and developed. Isabel had given up work when the children came along, so money was very tight, but they managed; sometimes Henry got part time weekend or evening work in a bar or cleaning cars for local garages, whatever was available, while Isabel helped stretch the money by doing things like sewing clothes from material bought from High Wycombe market and using vegetables and fruit grown from their garden. Her ingenuity knew no bounds and was a constant source of amazement and admiration to Henry.

They did usually manage to take at least one holiday a year, which due to cost restraints were of the camping variety, usually in Devon or Cornwall, which seemed to somehow give them all a feeling of independence.

Once Richard and Penny started school, they took to the learning process like proverbial ducks to water. Although distinctly different in temperament, Richard being quiet and reserved while Penny was effervescent and bubbly and in-your-face, full of fun.

Looking back, Henry could see that Richard's temperament was more like his own, which he mentally unfairly described to himself as 'steady and dull, with occasional doses of humour.' On the other hand, Penny had more of Isabel's attributes, both being 'live for the day, because this is not a rehearsal, so let's have fun' sort of mentality, which was part of the reason why Henry had fallen in love with Isabel in the first place.

As time went by, Richard proved to have a voracious appetite for learning, with an inquisitive mind that questioned everything that he was taught. The tools he used were 'What, Why, How, When and Where', and once he had applied them he usually found that for which he had been searching. But Richard was by no means just a studious swot. On the contrary, he loved most sports, in particular cricket, rugby, and football, all of which he played at various levels at school, making many friends along the way in the process. He was extremely popular; his contemporaries enjoyed his company but above all trusted him implicitly.

When the time came, he had no trouble in getting very good A Level grades in English, maths and history, but could not decide what to do with them. Finally he took a two-year course in media studies at the local college and then applied to London Weekend

Television in a response to an advertisement for trainee camera operators. This would have been the mid-1980s, and Richard found the work fascinating, so quickly learned his craft, only to discover within a few short years that most television channels switched from employing individual camera operatives to contracting out programs to a host of new companies which a few individual entrepreneurs had set up for this for this very purpose.

The end result was that most of the cameramen began to work for the new innovative companies, but strictly on a self-employed basis. Generally, this meant that the better operators found suitable employment, with the less adaptable being unable to stay in the industry. Conversely, the benefit from operating in this fashion meant that the new companies could offer ideas and products to more than one television channel, ensuring that the quality of the most innovative could not only survive, but also prosper.

Richard himself prospered under this regime, until eventually, through contacts in the, industry he managed to obtain contracts on an annual basis televising golf tournaments for satellite television, mostly in Europe, but also some Asian countries, which he was totally responsible for organising. This meant hiring camera crews and equipment and arranging for everything to be available and ready to go wherever and whenever.

Once this was established, Richard and Janet - for by this time he had met and married and had two young children - were enjoying a very comfortable lifestyle. However, the constraints of the job did mean Richard being away for frequent periods, sometimes for up to two weeks at a time.

Although they had both agreed that they wanted to continue to enjoy the standard of living which this work brought them, Richard also knew that it put an intolerable strain on Janet who still worked part time as a nurse, while managing to bring up two young children and running the family on a day by day basis. The only support Richard was able to offer was usually over the telephone, which could be from literally anywhere in the world.

Just as he was thinking that he ought to try and rearrange his work schedules, an old colleague whom Richard had worked for on a number of occasions contacted him from Australia, offering him a senior position in a company he had set up producing programmes for television. Not only would he have a senior management role, but there was also the promise of a fifty per cent equity holding in the company after two years. Both he and Janet talked the matter over endlessly in the next forty-eight hours, and eventually both of them agreed that it was a fabulous opportunity, but also that if for any number of reasons they decided to take it and it didn't work out, then they were still young enough to return to the UK and start again.

Henry and Isabel were heartbroken when Richard broke this to them, but tried desperately to not let their feelings show, because they too realised the huge opportunity which had been offered to their son and his family, so they smiled and congratulated them and wished them well, and kept their tears to themselves until they could be alone.

Henry mused to himself that it must have been some eight years since Richard's family had moved to Australia, which had proved to be a complete success for them, and although he and Isabel had made a couple of visits to them in Sydney in between that time, they both, as it seemed to them, mourned the loss of their son and his family, which was accentuated every time that they returned home to the UK after visiting them.

Henry's thoughts turn to Penny and to all the pleasure that she had brought to both him and Isabel over the years. She was, in short, a treasured bundle of joy from the very first day of her birth, full of mischief and laughter, an antidote to those moments when those around her were feeling low. She was quite simply irrepressible, a source of confidence and positivity that left her parents floundering in her wake. With her fair hair, laughing blue eyes and infectious smile, she captivated all who came into contact with her.

One occasion that Henry recalled as he sat and mused, which still made him laugh, was one year that the four of them had gone camping in Cornwall. This would have been when Penny was only some nine or ten years old. On the first evening they had all gone down to the beach, and after a while watching the sun set in a blazing ball of red, which seemed to sink and be enveloped into the sea.

Penny suddenly turned to them and said in a very knowing and world wise way, with her head on one shoulder, "It's very dangerous here isn't it, because there are some very bad *cherries* aren't there?"

Feeling totally bemused and not understanding her, Henry ventured to ask, "What makes you say that Pen?" to which she replied in an almost haughty manner, almost questioning his right to ask her, "Because it says so on the board as we came down to the beach."

There was total silence for what seemed forever, until suddenly the penny dropped and Henry clapped his hands together in sheer joy, and began to laugh uncontrollably.

"Oh no Pen, the board is a warning to swimmers not to use the beach when the red flags are showing because there are very bad *currents* when the tide comes in."

He quickly stopped laughing when he saw Penny's face pucker up, the tears filling her eyes, consoling her by saying that he was proud of her for noticing the sign and for pointing out the dangers.

As she grew, she continued to sweep all before her, or rather gather things and people to her, like a snowball gathering speed downhill, picking up everything in its path. Being of open countenance and manners she made friends easily, almost unconsciously. They were, as Henry described them, 'sucked in, like moths to a flame'.

She had from an early age shown an interest and talent for the arts, in particular painting using various applications, but she also had a flair for fashion and interior design, so both children's interests and how they attained their goals followed a familiar pattern of the arts and creativity.

Like Richard, Penny showed a natural flair for learning; academic subjects were achieved readily, although she had no particular interest in applying things like maths, English and the sciences eventually in a work environment. Nevertheless, when she was eleven she managed to obtain a pass to a local Grammar school where she achieved three A Level passes in maths, English, and design. Like Richard too, Penny did not seek academic qualifications, so turn instead to college where she took a three year sandwich course in design. This she did over four years, the third year being spent at an interior design company's offices in London to get experience on the job.

The company had liked her and her approach to their work and when she completed her college course, they had offered her a permanent position with them. From the very first day Penny had taken to her job like a duck to water and over the next few years had progressed up the promotional ladder, which she enjoyed not so much for the monetary rewards that they brought, but rather as a means for her to express herself and her designs.

She accepted that starting on the bottom rung meant that she would have to assist other more senior designers and interpret their thoughts, but as time went by she began to have more freedom to do her own designs, giving her a great feeling of worth and accomplishment.

These feelings were indeed reflected in her work and the definitive style of her own that ensued from them. Not only that, but Penny's work was sought after by many clients, mainly because she interpreted their half-formed thoughts into beautiful designs which, once implemented, gave added value to their businesses. Quite simply, they loved both her approach to their problems and the practical but effective and stunning manner in which she solved them.

But Penny was so much more than the sum of her parts.

She was now also a mother and wife, having met Mark at one of the many corporate parties for existing and potential clients that she was involved in. Theirs was an explosive meeting of minds (and bodies, as Mark was quick to point out) which was fuelled by similar tastes in humour and attraction.

Within weeks they were engaged, and wed after another year; they were so sure of their feelings, again Henry was reminded of Isabel's gospel. 'don't waste time, let's get on with living', which her genes had so obviously passed on to her daughter.

CHAPTER 3
The Bus Pass

"Morning Henry, how are things this lovely day?" called Madge Nugent, as she lets herself in. "Is there any shopping that I can get for you? Because I have to go to the supermarket this morning."

Madge and Rob had been neighbours to Henry and Isabel forever; the two women had always got on famously and both families had children of similar ages which meant that they had all grown up together. Rob Nugent was probably Henry's closest friend, a drinking pal and confidant for many years. Although their interests were not really similar, apart from the drinking, the differences only seemed to strengthen their friendship.

Henry's pursuits were more ethereal and consisted of watercolour painting, gardening, and more recently, family history. His love of painting was a lifelong hobby, and was something that early in his career he would have liked to pursue as a way of earning a living, but he quickly realised although he had a talent, it was not good enough to sustain a family.

Rob was more practical and enjoyed nothing more than doing car repairs for friends and family. He was by profession a qualified air mechanic working at Heathrow, but had recently retired. He, like Henry, had a wonderful sense of humour, but also an indefinable presence that drew people to him. He could always be found in the centre of a crowd, telling jokes from his never ending repertoire. At parties he would not call attention to himself, preferring to find a quiet corner with a pint, but inevitably within a few minutes, he would be surrounded by people paying homage. He was just likeable. Henry could never identify why exactly, but was proud to count him as a friend.

"I seem to have everything I need just at the moment, thanks Madge, but while you're here can you remind Rob that it's our night for The Kings Head, tonight?"

"As if he would forget." replied Madge. "He keeps telling me drinking is a skill, and the only way that he can improve is to practice," replied Madge, laughing. "Oh, by the way, here's your post that I just picked up."

Madge calls in most days to check on Henry; in fact, she always called in regularly, even before Isabel died. She is a very caring, motherly person, always ready with a smile and a willingness to help, which Henry has had cause to be very grateful for, both before and after Isabel's untimely death. When a young woman, Henry remembered her as a rare beauty, whose dark natural complexion and elegant, slim figure turned many men's heads, but she was unaware of any of their glances, being completely besotted by Rob, the sole benefactor of her attentions.

Indeed, the years had been very kind to her, thought Henry, and although her appearance was more matronly these days, her facial bone structure ensured her lasting visual beauty.

She still manages to work part time as a clinical receptionist in the local doctors' surgery, and although now she is over sixty, neither she nor the doctors want the arrangement to cease.

Being such a social animal, Madge herself, like Rob, has a large repertoire of anecdotes that she regales to Rob in particular, but also to Henry to a lesser extent. The difference between Rob and Henry's reception of these daily notations is that Rob finds them to be about people he has never heard of, or in fact, wants to hear of, so he tends to switch off when they are being told, whereas Henry by comparison, although finding most of them boring, listens intently, because he knows from previous experiences that occasionally they are very funny, not just because they are intended to be so, but simply because of the manner in which they are told.

Today is one of those days when it is worth listening, as Madge launches into her latest diatribe, saying, "You remember I told you that my friend Daphne usually calls in to see me on a Tuesday morning at the doctors' surgery for a chat and a cup of tea? Well last week, she didn't come in because she felt a bit under the weather. The doctor, who was aware of this arrangement, came out of his consulting room and enquired why she hadn't come in to see me, so I had to tell him that she was feeling very unwell and so had decided to stay at home."

Henry immediately sees the funny side of this little verbal epistle, and not wanting to upset Madge, decides not to ask her why someone could visit the doctors regularly on a weekly basis for non-medical purposes, but then was incapable of visiting it the one week that she actually needed to.

Madge left, leaving Henry quietly smiling to himself once she had gone.

Regaining his composure, Henry decides to open his morning's post; the first two are bills for water rates and credit cards, but the third and last is a new bus pass from his local council, replacing an older one. The significant difference is that the new pass can be used for travel anywhere in England, providing that it is used on local bus routes commencing at eight thirty in the morning within his own local borough, but after nine thirty on any other borough services.

Henry has not realised it just yet, but he has just received the tool which he can use to give him the freedom to see those places in England, either which he has not yet experienced, or which he has already visited and would like to see for one last time. However, once implanted, the realisation will grow and grow and become all consuming, but it will take his oldest and best friend Rob to spot the opportunity when they go for their weekly constitutional to the pub that same night.

Rob, of course, is aware of Henry's dilemma, between his children all moving to Australia, leaving Henry to have to choose between either also moving with them or staying put in England. It is something that makes him feel extremely sorry for his friend, who is going to have to make such a momentous decision.

When they arrive at the pub, they continue their usual discussions, in which they catch up with world events that have occurred since their meeting the previous week, such as Madge's incredibly boring conversations, the lowly position of Wycombe in the football league and the humungous amounts of money that football players now receive in the Premier division.

THE BUS PASS

They next turn their questioning minds to lesser topics, like the state of the country politically, the financial situation (specifically, generally, and personally), the quality of this week's guest beer, and as always, the quality of the last week's television programmes, the verdict of all of which was inevitably 'rubbish'.

This then is the usual pattern, which is, as always, interspersed occasionally by a game of darts or crib. The only difference this night is when Henry remarks in passing that he has received his new bus pass and explains the significant difference between this and the previous one.

Rob, who is very perceptive, thinks for a moment and says, "You mean you can use it anywhere in the country," which Henry confirms, only for Rob to say excitedly, "There's your answer then, you can use it to do your Grand Tour and visit all those places that you have wanted to see. In fact my own pass should also be due anytime now, and although I wouldn't like to leave Madge for any length of time I wouldn't mind joining you for some of the time. What do you think?"

Henry's reaction is in turn one of complete astonishment and growing excitement, followed quickly by one of complete scepticism, as he immediately throws back verbally to Rob all the negatives that would make such a journey impossible.

"But it could take months travelling this way to visit all those places that I would like to visit, and how am I supposed to carry enough supplies of clothes etc. to last me all that time, because it would be impracticable to cart a suitcase for any length of time, and how the hell would I find guaranteed accommodation exactly when I needed it? No it's not possible."

"Hold hard Henry, old mucker," says Rob, laughing. "Just think about it for a moment; sure you could be away for some time, although you don't have to do it all in one go, and as for carrying clothes and other necessities, all you would need would be enough for one or two days, and once you had decided on an itinerary you could book accommodation in advance and arrange for fresh supplies to be sent on. I am sure that Madge can do that for you."

Rob was by now in full flow and was not going to let his argument be denied. "All you need to do is prepare a list of places which you would like to visit and then put them in a logical order, deciding how long you would like to stay at each place. You can then look at accommodation locally and book it in advance, although perhaps not until you have reached your previous destination. It's easy peasy."

Rob's enthusiasm Henry finds very infectious, and soon he is throwing out place names that he could include in his itinerary. This could work, he thinks. *I must consider it in more detail in the morning when I can think more clearly.*

"Hi Granddad," cry Penny and Mark's two children, Joshua and Oliver, in unison. "Will you take us up the park after dinner, and then afterwards can we play cards and watch *Robin Hood* on TV."

"Hold on a minute boys and give Granddad a break," says Penny, bustling in with a bottle of wine and a bunch of flowers. "We are going out for lunch soon and we will see what time we have to do other things, if any, after that."

It is now the following Sunday morning, by which time Henry has had time to think further of Rob's idea of travel by use of a bus pass.

"I have booked a table in town for lunch, and there is something that I would like to discuss with you and Mark when we get there."

"That sounds rather ominous, Dad," replies Penny. "You have got us really intrigued, hasn't he Mark? We had best go now, because I just can't wait to hear what it is all about."

While Mark drives to the restaurant, Joshua, who is four years old, is sitting in the back seat with Henry and his brother Oliver, the latter now eight years old and much more thoughtful and serious than his younger sibling. The radio is playing an old tune which Henry remembers from many years previously, and starts to sing.

Suddenly, Joshua says, "Stop the dance, Granddad," to which he replies, "I'm not dancing, I'm singing."

Quick as a flash Joshua retorts, "Well don't sing the dance then."

Henry is stunned by the reply for a moment and then dissolves with laughter. He loves Penny's children with a rare passion. They have filled a small part of the hole left by the loss of Isabel, but at the same time he wishes that she were still with him so that she could enjoy them too.

After settling themselves and ordering food and drinks at the restaurant, Penny starts the ball rolling, saying, "Well Dad, what's this great mystery you want to discuss, no don't tell me, and let me guess. You have met a thirty-year-old, leggy model who is besotted with you and wants to elope with you to Jamaica. No? OK, has one of your watercolours been selected for an exhibition, or, even more important, has The Kings Head given you a silver tankard in recognition of your attendance record?"

"No, none of those unfortunately," Henry replies with a rueful grin, recognising Penny's efforts to keep the mood light. "It's simply that I received my new bus pass this week, which didn't mean anything to me at the time, but once I mentioned it to Rob he got very excited, and said that the new one can be used almost anywhere in England on local bus routes and that I should consider using it to visit all those places that I have wanted to, or already seen and would like to see again one last time." Henry then goes on to explain the discussion that he had with Rob, and finishes by saying, "So I have given it some thought and would like to give it a shot, what do you think?"

Penny, suddenly realises the huge pressure that Henry is under because of her families proposed move to Australia, and her immediate reaction is to encourage and support her father, who is so torn between upping sticks and moving to the other side of the world to be with his family, or staying in the country of his birth which he loves so much, without them.

Quickly controlling her emotions to hide the tears which were just below the surface, she replies, "That sounds a fantastic idea Dad, I think that you should do it, and I am sure that Mark agrees with me, don't you?" to which Mark nods his agreement vigorously. Henry silently pays homage to Mark for his support; he and Mark have always got on very well, although they didn't have too much in common, but Henry knows that Mark loves Penny completely, and her wellbeing is his number one consideration. Because this is also very high on Henry's list of priorities, it means that he and Mark, in a strange sort of way, bond, and although no words are ever spoken they both accede to her needs whenever they can.

"Anyway," Penny went on to add, "Have you had any ideas or made a list of places you would like to see? If so let's have a look."

"Well, yes I have Penny love," says Henry, pulling a crumpled piece of paper from his pocket. "But the list is so long that it needs to be rationalised. I can't possibly cover all of them, but I will read them out in no particular order. The only categorisation that I have done is to put them down in sequences of those places which your mother and I visited and loved, sometimes with both you and Richard, which I have called Memory Lane. After that I have listed those places that we would have both liked to see, but unfortunately never had the time, which I have headed 'Wish List'.

"Oh! Then there are those places which I visited with Rob and a couple of the other lads at the pub, when we went on our fishing trips, some of which I have very happy memories, some of which I suppose could come into the Memory Lane category, but which I have chosen to call 'The Fishing Trips', for no other reason than at the time they were a form of escapism from the pressures of work. In the main these concerned eating and drinking, some sight-seeing and walking, games of cards and very little fishing.

"However, I have not yet thought the logistics of sequence, time and place," said Henry, and proceeded to produce his list, and read it out to Penny and Mark.

MEMORY LANE

1. Bridport, West Dorset, and the surrounding area, because your mother and I loved it so much.

2. Glastonbury Tor, Somerset, with its mystical, ethereal qualities, which your mother and I both visited, and which I would like to see again for just that reason.

3. The stretch of coast between Porlock and Barnstable in Devon, which is just exquisite.

4. The Totnes, Dartmouth, Slapton area of South Devon, where we used to take you and Richard as children. Also the South Hams including Bigbury and Burgh Island.

5. St. Ives in Cornwall, with its narrow winding streets and bustling community.

6. Fowey, on the south coast of Cornwall.

7. Truro, a small but enchanting county city.

8. St. Agnes on the Isles of Scilly. Probably the most wonderful of all the places that we visited together, and with you children of course. A really hallowed place for all of us.

9. Bristol, to see the 'Great Western', Brunel's and the world's first steel ship.

10. Alnwick and Holy Island, Northumberland.

11. Wastwater in the Lake District.

12. Durham City, to visit the wonderful Cathedral.

WISH LIST

1. Canterbury, to see the cathedral, with its connotations of where Archbishop Becket was slain.

2. Sutton Hoo, Suffolk, to see the Viking burial site.

3. Chatham Kent, to visit the Naval Museum.

4. The Eden Project and the lost gardens of Heligan.

5. Minack open air Theatre in Cornwall, to see a play being performed.

6. The Oval cricket Ground, South London, to see Surrey play a County Match.

THE FISHING TRIPS

1. Christchurch in Dorset, the site of our first fishing trip.

2. Westward Ho and Appledore on the North Devon coast.

3. Whitstable in Kent.

4. Toller Porcorum in Dorset, a place we visited for many years and which was the source of so many hilarious experiences.

Penny looks thoughtfully at her father as he passes her a copy of his list, which she and Mark proceed to examine. After some little time she observes, "Well Dad, this is certainly pretty comprehensive and ambitious. My first thoughts are that it is going to be very difficult to achieve in one go. If it were me, I think that I would break it down into areas, say for instance the South West, the South East, and then all other points North. I think if it was done in this fashion you could return home after each part to recover before attempting the next. Have you considered a time frame to achieve all this?"

Henry was taken aback for a moment, but then suddenly realises that Penny's agile brain has quickly analysed the list and assimilated the best way to solve it logistically.

"Well, no love, I can't say that I have given it much thought yet, but your idea of breaking it down to areas certainly makes a lot of sense. I can't think why it never occurred to me. As for the amount of time it would take, I think that would depend how well the travel and places that I visit go. If I find somewhere that I like and there are things to see and do, then it will obviously take longer than if I just moved on to the next location. So it could take anything from say a couple of weeks to three months I suppose, but taking our good old English weather into consideration, I certainly would not want to start before, say, the middle of May."

Penny nods her agreement and then says unexpectedly, "If or when you find your Shangri La, let us know, and perhaps we could come down and join you for a few days. I still have fond memories of some of the places on your list that we went with you and Mum as children. Does that sound OK to you?"

For the second time in a few moments, Henry is overwhelmed by emotion, and unable to breathe without it showing, nods his head in acquiescence.

"That's great Dad, now all you have to do is decide on the area you would like to cover first, and then those local buses you need to catch, where they leave from, what time they go, and the time that they arrive at your destination. You should be able to find most of them on the internet, also accommodation when you decide where to stay. That should keep you out of mischief for a while Dad, and oh, by the way, you would find it easier to keep in touch with everyone if you took your laptop and mobile phone."

"Point taken Pen, I will start searching next week. Now let's take the boys to the park or they will never let me forget it."

They walk to the park, the boys trying to hurry them along. When they reach it the boys produce a football and demand that the adults all get involved in a game, which soon tires Henry, so they put him in goal and rain shots at him mercilessly. Eventually, the boys themselves tire, their little faces red with perspiration, so activities are transferred to swings and roundabouts.

On returning from the park to Henry's house, they get are settled down with the Sunday papers and steaming cups of coffee.

While the children watch the television, Penny suddenly says, "Did I tell you about Joshua's latest escapade last week Dad?" at which Henry shakes his head, so Penny continues. "Well, both the children were at home one afternoon last week, busily playing games on their PlayStation, which demands great concentration on their part. In fact they hate interruptions of any kind. Meanwhile, Louise, the cleaner who comes once a week for a couple of hours, decided to use the vacuum cleaner, which is quite old and makes a hell of a racket. Louise told me that nothing happened for several minutes, until suddenly, Joshua appeared in the doorway, and putting his head on one side, said, as if talking to a naughty child, 'Louise, would you like to take that upstairs to play?'"

As Penny finishes relating her tale, Henry, who knows his youngest grandson very well, can picture the scenario, and begins to laugh in unison with Penny and Mark.

Yet again, Henry is reminded just what he would be missing if he decides not to emigrate to Australia. The thought of not seeing his grandchildren growing up, with their image of their grandfather fading with every passing day, is almost too much for him to bear.

After Penny, Mark and the children have said their goodbyes for the day, Henry is unable to settle down. He has so many wonderful thoughts of them, and wishes once again that Isabel could be here to share them with him. From this point his thoughts move onto Penny and Mark's response to his ideas of travel using his bus pass. It is so like Penny to not only to approve of his suggestion, but also to encourage and support it as well.

Thus the seed is well and truly sown and the green shoots will soon be growing as Henry develops his itinerary.

CHAPTER 4
Departure

Several weeks have elapsed since Henry and Penny's discussion, and it is now mid-May, during which time Henry has decided and firmed up, not only on his itinerary, but has also researched the bus routes, local to the places that are necessary to achieve his objectives. Many hours have been spent searching the web and making phone calls to various bus companies, however this information could only be assimilated after many intense discussions at The Kings Head with Rob, who by now has become as interested as Henry on the project. Madge has also contributed by offering many more common sense suggestions, such as what clothes to take, and the system of returning them to her when they need cleaning; also the type of low cost accommodations to look for and a myriad other tips, for which Henry is suitably grateful.

Finally the date for 'Operation: Bus Pass' is set for Monday 19 May. Accordingly, Henry, Rob and Madge wend their way to The Kings Head on the eighteenth for a farewell dinner- cum-bus travel ceremony. Steak and kidney pies with mashed potatoes with vegetables are consumed, along with numerous pints of real ale.

Henry realises it is time to go when Madge starts to giggle and to tell everyone who will listen that the beer 'has gone to her legs', a euphemism that Rob and Henry know from previous experience means that she is becoming inebriated, which will probably need the two of them to help her home. This proves to be the case (not for the first time, as Henry can testify), so they make their way laughing and joking about nothing in particular, but with a deep feeling of togetherness, construed from many years of friendship and experience in each other's company. For the first time in a long while, Henry goes to sleep and sleeps solidly, waking refreshed at seven o'clock ready for the first day of his journey.

His itinerary for this part of his pilgrimage will take him to Dorset, and then on to Devon and Cornwall, but this, his first day, will hopefully take him to Dorchester, where he has arranged one night's accommodation in a local pub.

Suitably attired in casual clothes, a short-sleeved shirt and jeans and heavy duty trainers, Henry walks down the steep hill from Downley to High Wycombe Bus Station, carrying a backpack in which there are two changes of clothes and a light weight waterproof, some sandwiches, fruit, and canned cordial. Finally his laptop and mobile phone are packed carefully in his bag.

It is with mixed feelings of trepidation and elation that he boards the first of what will hopefully be many local buses at eight forty a.m. which will take him to Reading town centre, arriving at nine minutes past ten, via Marlow, Medmenham, Henley on Thames and Binfield Heath. As Henry is soon to discover, travelling by means of local services is relatively slow, but the length of the journey in the time taken is more than compensated for, because of all the small villages and places of interest that they go through. The bus, the Arriva No. 800 from High Wycombe to Reading, begins its journey on this slightly overcast but dry day in May.

Henry knows the area very well, but never ceases to be amazed at the sheer beauty of the countryside, which is now becoming a riot of colour from early flowering rhododendrons, magnolias, and also the bright green foliage from plants and trees which are just beginning to become established. In two or three months' time the green colours will dull and become tired looking, but for now they are so bright that they almost dazzle Henry's eyes if he looks at them too long.

As the bus passes through some of the small villages, it picks up an assortment of people who are mostly elderly women or couples, together with a number of young mothers, presumably all making their way to Reading to shop.

Henry soon becomes aware that quite a few of them know each other very well from the greetings they receive, as they climb aboard the bus. After a while their cheery banter, combined with the steady throb of the bus begins to have a relaxing soporific effect and Henry finds it difficult to stay awake. It is with a sense of relief that the bus reaches Forbury Street, Reading on time,

THE BUS PASS

giving Henry forty minutes to get to Gun Street, where he needs to catch a Newbury bus service, leaving at ten forty-six, which gives him plenty of time to grab a coffee and a daily paper en-route.

The trip to Newbury is uneventful, the bus being virtually empty; the route follows the A4, passing through Theale and Thatcham, eventually arriving at Newbury bus station at eleven fifty-two. So far, so good, thinks Henry, who knows that today will be one of the longest days for bus travel in his itinerary. When considering his route he could have spread the journey over a couple of days, but preferred to try to get to Dorchester in one day, because of the number of places that he wants to visit in the locality.

The value of Henry's research holds him in good stead as he continues on his journey; first, the Stagecoach service x20 takes him from Newbury to Andover, arriving at the bus station at one thirty three p.m. Next it is another Stagecoach service No 8, which delivers him to Salisbury Station in Endless Street at twenty-nine minutes past three. It is finally here that Henry's luck runs out on this his first day, as he goes to queue for his connection to Blandford Forum.

There is a notice on the time table explaining that the connecting service has been cancelled and that the next one is due at four minutes past five, arriving in Blandford at eleven minutes past six. This means effectively that he will be unable to make a connection from Blandford to Dorchester today, and with the realisation, Henry's mood of elation and self-congratulation dissipates like fog on a windy day.

After gathering his thoughts, he sits and consults the internet on his laptop, and then phones a pub in Blandford and makes a reservation for a room that night. The information that has enabled him to do this is from a list that he has prepared (one of Madge's invaluable suggestions, god bless her). Once this has been achieved, he cancels his accommodation at Dorchester, the place where he was hoping to get to.

The later departure time means that he has time to get to a café where he orders coffee and surreptitiously eats the sandwiches that he has brought with him for the journey. Feeling suitably refreshed Henry duly catches his last bus for the day, for the final leg to Blandford.

This route is more heavily boarded, and he finds himself sitting next to a school boy of about twelve years of age, as far as he is able to judge. Time goes by, with Henry doing a crossword in the daily paper, while the boy fishes out various work books from his satchel, before sighing deeply and returning them to from whence they came. The boy is obviously distressed, and suddenly turns to Henry and says, "I have been given some homework which has to be in to school tomorrow, and I don't know how to do it, can you help me please mister?"

Looking at the boy properly for the first time Henry sees a fair-haired lad with large blue eyes that are filling with tears. He is wearing the obligatory school uniform of navy blazer, grey trousers and a white shirt, the latter of which is by now being worn outside his trousers, although Henry is pretty sure that when the boy had left his home that morning it would have been suitably tucked in. The top two buttons of his shirt are undone and his school tie has worked its way half way round his neck, giving him the appearance of someone being hung.

Being unable to resist such an appealing request, Henry asks him which subject he has for homework, at the same time making a silent prayer that it isn't English, or maths even, for that matter.

"Well, it's history, and my teacher wants us to write about what life would have been like for people living in Britain during the Second World War. The trouble is that I could look some of it up on the internet, but we don't have a computer at home, and I don't have time now to go to the library either."

Henry heaves a silent sigh of relief, and although only a baby when the war started, he does remember living and experiencing the atmosphere during this period.

The next thirty minutes Henry spends explaining what life was like at that time, the sound of the air raid warnings going off like banshees at any time, night or day, the sound of German bombers droning overhead almost every night, the rush for the Anderson shelter in the garden, which invariably was flooded in a foot of water, explaining why the shelters had to be covered with turf, to stop them being targets for German bombers, and that in London, when air raid warnings were sounded, people made their way to the underground and spent their nights on the platforms for safety. He

THE BUS PASS

also told Jack of the period later on in the war, when Germans started using pilotless V-1 bombs (called Doodlebugs by the British, because of their distinctive droning noise) which were jet propelled, of how when they were running out of fuel over their target, the droning noise that they made suddenly cut out. This for the people living under the flight path was the most stressful time, because the silence meant that the bomb was now heading down its destructive path to wreak huge damage to life and property.

Henry then goes on to tell of food rationing, caused primarily by German U-boats sinking so much of our merchant shipping and the food that they contained.

The boy - by this time Henry has discovered that his name is Jack - is busily making notes as Henry speaks. He continues to he asks questions and is becoming more relaxed. As he looks up and out of the bus window, Henry realises that his stop is coming up and that he has to get off. Explaining this to Jack, to his amazement he is met with howls of anguish, crying, "Please don't go, please don't go."

Henry hurriedly placates him, explaining to Jack that he should now have enough information to complete his homework, but that he has no choice but to get off the bus, so why did he want him to stay? Jack, calming himself, finally says in an awestruck voice as Henry prepares to disembark, "Because you old people don't arf know a lot of stuff."

Alighting from the bus, Henry's mood is lifted by the boy's comment and he allows himself a quiet chuckle before waving to Jack as the bus moves away.

A quick look at his watch reveals that the time is now ten past six and Henry moves briskly to find his accommodation for the night, the Jack the Lad in Florence Street, which by good fortune is only a couple of hundred yards from the centre of Blandford, where he is now. Florence Street is north of the centre and Henry can see the inn sign at the far end of the road. However the road is on a steep incline, so by the time that he reaches it Henry is breathing heavily.

Pushing open the door to the saloon bar, he is agreeably met with the smell of food coming from the kitchen. The saloon bar also appears to act as the dining room and is comfortably furnished with matching deep red fabric settees and chairs at one end, with tables and chairs at the other and the floor is covered by an Axminster type carpet, making the overall effect one of comfort and warmth. But the clincher for Henry is the log fire in the dining area, its heat throwing out its welcome while its flames cast mysterious flickering shadows into the room. There is only one couple in at present, and they are eating, but Henry realises that it is still early for evening meals to be served, but nevertheless, he suddenly realises just how hungry he feels.

At this point a portly man of about fifty years of age appears behind the bar, who Henry correctly assumes to be the landlord, a.k.a. the person that he has made a booking with for that night's accommodation.

With introductions out of the way, the landlord, William Whelan ("Call me Bill.") shows Henry to his room, and in response to his request about eating time, says, "You can come down any time, there's a copy of the menu in your room, but there are some of today's specials in the bar downstairs. Breakfast is between eight and nine thirty."

Looking round his room, Henry is pleased to see that it is clean and presentable, with a double bed, wardrobe and chest of drawers, on top of which there is a small television. Additionally there is a shower and toilet in an adjoining room that leads off the bedroom. Because he only intends staying for the one night, Henry is not too worried about the standard of the room, but is agreeably surprised just how good it is, considering the low cost.

With hunger stabbing at his vitals Henry returns to the bar where Bill greets him with a "What will it be Henry?" to which Henry asks him which beer he would recommend, and after the first taste of his pint of Tanglefoot, he then orders liver and bacon with veg and mashed potato.

While he is waiting for his meal, Bill asks him how and why Henry comes to be there, and after some hesitation Henry explains his situation about the likelihood of all of his children and grandchildren moving to Australia, which means in turn that they would like him to move there also so they could all be together. He then goes on to relate about him visiting various places by means of his bus pass.

THE BUS PASS

As he progresses with his story, Bill's chubby and jovial countenance becomes more serious, until at last as Henry finishes, he says, "Well oim blowed, and you be doing this all on your own then, be you?" to which Henry nods.

"Where you be going to next then?"

"Well, tomorrow I am going to Dorchester, and then on to Goderston, which is an old stomping ground for my old fishing trip with some old chums. I hope to stay there for a few days and then move on to other places in the Bridport area."

Fortunately for Henry his food arrives at this moment, so the matter is not pursued any further. As he eats Henry can hear men's laughter and banter coming from the public bar next door, and suddenly feels strangely lonely. He realises that his pilgrimage will inevitably mean that he will encounter situations like this, and so, once he has finished his meal he makes his way to the public bar. As he pushes open the door, he sees florid faced man who is holding court standing with his back to the bar, waving a pint of Dorset best bitter to emphasise his words to several other men, who he obviously knows well.

"You remember I told you that old Bert had moved in with Sadie, who he claims is his niece, well, if you believe that, you'll believe anything. I'll tell you what, I'd like to holler fire, and see which rooms the heads come out of." As he finishes, there is a roar of laughter from the rest of the company, most of whom turn their heads to see who has entered and invaded their sanctuary.

Henry casts his eye round the room, taking in several of the men, who appear to be a mixture of labourers or agricultural workers, tradesmen, and also some who would appear to be younger professional blue collar workers.

For what seems to be an eternity to Henry, but in fact can only have been a couple of seconds there is complete silence, which is broken by Bill's entry behind the bar. He introduces Henry to the assembled throng, saying, "This is Henry, who I told you about, who says that he is a dab hand at darts and challenges all comers to a game."

Henry stands flabbergasted as Bill speaks, having never even discussed darts with him, but quickly realises that it is his host's way of making Henry's presence welcome to the regulars.

He quickly denies saying any such thing, but the florid man comes up to him, saying, "I'm Joe, and I have a small farm locally." And then pointing to each of the rest of them in turn, "This is Martin, then Norman who we call Sparky, 'cos he's an electrician, then there's Phil who runs a local newsagents, Fred Cole, nicknamed 'King', and finally Bert Prosser, nicknamed 'Tosser'."

Joe's narration continues and takes in all of them, with Henry trying desperately to remember names. When he has finally finished, Joe explains that they are regulars, who got together once or twice a week for a beer and social evening, a natter and game of darts, dominoes or pool.

"So, what about this game of darts then Henry?" says Joe. "We are just going to have a knockout between ourselves, and we have you on the oche first against Phil - best of three games of three hundred and one, start and finish on a double. Phil shouldn't give you too much trouble. With his eyes he can hardly see the board."

Henry, protesting the fact that Bill has told them all that he was good at the game, and that in fact he definitely wasn't, is lead unceremoniously to the oche, and winning the toss, threw first. It soon becomes apparent to everyone that Henry has not been lying, and after a titanic struggle, at one point which threatens to take the rest of the evening, loses to Phil by three games to two.

However he is not left standing around too long, because the rest of them who are not involved in darts, are either playing cards, or as Henry prefers, dominoes, and he joins a threesome who are looking for a fourth person to play doubles at which he proves himself more adept, winning three games with his partner, and then going on to see off all comers.

During a lull in the proceedings, Joe asks why Derek, obviously another regular, has not arrived, only to be told that he isn't coming, because he has no money.

Joe seems to take exception to this explanation, and says, "It's not because he's skint, but because he's mean - in fact he's so mean that he'd steal a dead fly from a blind spider," at which point the bar becomes alive with a mixture of ribald laughter and comments, agreeing with the sentiments expressed about Derek's financial acumen.

As the evening goes on, Henry begins to warm to them all, enjoying their humour and strong sense of comradeship. As he does so, he suddenly becomes aware of how tired he is after his long day travelling, so with regret makes his farewell and thanks for their enjoyable company.

Before leaving, Joe asks him where he is next heading, to which Henry replies, "Goderston, where I am hoping to stay at the White Swan for a few days," to which Joe replies, "Then maybe we will see you again, because this pub is due to play the White Swan at skittles on Friday."

With this revelation and their good wishes ringing in his ears, Henry makes his way back to his room, and before settling down to sleep, gets out his laptop and sends emails to Penny, Rob and Madge and Richard in Australia, informing them of his travel and experiences so far.

Lying back on the bed, Henry feels warmed by a sense of accomplishment and good will towards the happy band of men he has befriended in the bar. With these thoughts filtering through his mind, he falls contentedly to sleep.

Waking to the sound of pigeon's cooing on his windowsill at half past eight, Henry hurriedly dresses and finds his way to the dining room for breakfast, where Bill and his wife Betty greet him.

"Oih thought you were never going to get up," Bill says jokingly, before taking Henry's order for a full English breakfast.

"Sorry about that," Henry replies. "But I think that I was mugged by a combination of good food, Dorset bitter and great company, which I thank you for most sincerely. I haven't slept that well for a long time."

"Glad you enjoyed it, now don't forget that our skittle team will be playing at the White Swan on Friday, so if you are still there, we'll see you again. Any-road, if not, try to drop in and see us on your way home, whenever that is."

Henry assures him that he would like that, if possible, and by now suitably fed and watered, after settling up with Bill, Henry takes his leave to start day two of his journey.

CHAPTER 5

Dorchester

Making his way back downhill to the centre of Blandford, Henry is drenched suddenly in a shower of rain, which gives him no time to seek shelter. Arriving at the bus stop thoroughly wet, Henry mentally revues his objective for the day. In fact, he only has one, namely to get to Goderston, which is a small picturesque village that lies between Dorchester and Cerne Abbas, so he first has to get from Blandford to Dorchester, then change route.

He arrives at Blandford at half past nine, well in time to catch the Wilts and Dorset service to Dorchester, which leaves promptly on time at nine forty. The bus is nearly full of people who Henry assumes are going to Dorchester which, being the county town, has a larger selection of shops, particularly supermarkets, which are not to be found in any of the small villages locally.

The journey continues with Henry being lulled almost to sleep by a combination of the soft swish of the bus wheels as they negotiate the narrow Dorset lanes, and the sun streaming through the window, all signs of any rain showers by now having dissipated.

The only thing to break this soporific sensation is the sound of idle chatter between the passengers. Suddenly he is made aware of two elderly people with raised voices sitting in front of him.

The first begins, "You remember that Wendy Lewis I told you about, who I used to work with when I was nursing at the hospital, well I saw her yesterday for the first time in ages. What I didn't tell you was that when I worked with her on the same ward many years ago she was caught stealing from the patients' personal belongings."

"Oh, what happened to her?"

"Well, you will never believe it, but they suspended her at first and then transferred her to another ward after several weeks."

"Get away with you, that can't be right, which ward did they transfer her to?"

"The blind ward."

Henry, smiling gently, is lulled once again to a state of drowsiness, until at last the bus arrives in Dorchester at seven minutes to eleven. The sun is now high in the sky and has burnt off any rain that has fallen.

Although Henry has been through Dorchester on a number of occasions, he only stopped off once many years ago. Realising that he has time to kill until his next bus departs at twelve thirty, he decides to be a tourist for a short while. So, finding the local tourist office, he selects a number of pamphlets which he thinks might be relevant.

He is aware of the author Thomas Hardy's links to Dorchester - that he was born in Bockhampton, a village a few miles away, in 1840, but eventually moved to Max Gate on the edge of Dorchester, which he had built in 1885. Hardy was and is Dorset's most famous son, but another character who Henry knows had an infamous reputation and connection, although not belonging to Dorchester, was Judge George Jeffreys. He became known as the Hanging Judge, because of the punishments he gave to the supporters of the Duke of Monmouth as the result of the failed rebellion.

Henry read that in 1685, Judge Jeffreys came to Dorchester and lodged at 6 High West Street (now the restaurant Judge Jeffreys). The bloody assizes were held in the Oak Room (now a tea room) of the Antelope Hotel on the fifth day of September in that year. From his school history lessons Henry knew that dozens of people were executed, and hundreds more transported from Judge Jeffrey's court. Those executions were carried out in towns and villages close to Dorchester.

Almost every time Henry has been through Dorchester by road, the route has taken him past both the restaurant, Judge Jeffreys, and Hardy's statue at the top of the town. He has also visited Hardy's birthplace at Lower Bockhampton, a beautiful cottage on the edge of a wood, where Hardy no doubt obtained the inspiration to write a number of his books.

There is one place, however, that Henry has never visited, but has always wanted to see. That place is Maiden Castle which lies just a short distance from the outskirts of Dorchester.

Isabel, wonderful wife that she was, had never been at all interested in history or archaeology. In fact it was one of the rare differences between them. Her attitude had been 'what is gone is gone. Let's look forward to the future.'

Henry, however, is fascinated by history, which over the last few years has been increasingly brought to life by archaeologists using the latest hi-tech equipment, and he is an avid watcher of documentaries like *Time Team*. Maiden Castle is one such place which has been featured in several documentary television programmes, so now that he is here he thinks that it would be a good time to see the site.

Another quick calculation tells him that he will be hard pushed to walk to the site and see as much as he wants, and then walk back to town all within the time he has available, so he decides to take the leisurely approach. He will get himself some victuals locally, which he can consume when he gets to the castle, then have a good look around and return to the town in time to catch a later bus at four o'clock to Goderston.

Now that the decision has been made, Henry finds the local Marks and Spencer, and after getting appropriately stocked with salmon and cucumber sandwiches, a chunk of Victoria sandwich and a soft drink, commences to walk to the castle, which takes a shade over twenty minutes.

Although he knows that Maiden Castle covers a large area, he is still unprepared when he sees its huge earthen ramparts, with its steep array of ditches that tower high above him as he goes round the road that circles the site, until he finds the entrance. Here is displayed a summary of the history of the site, which explains that it was the largest hill fort in England, extending to some forty-five acres and was first occupied around three thousand years BC by the Durotriges tribe.

In AD 43, the Romans attacked the inhabitants of the town, who lived at the top of the site, inside the wooden ramparts, and a hard, vicious battle was fought, the local inhabitants knowing that if they lost, their lives would almost certainly be forfeit. The battle focused towards the eastern entrance, where, led by Vespasian, the Romans would have found it very difficult to overcome the steep array of ditches before they could defeat the inhabitants of the castle.

As he climbs on up past the entrance, in his imagination Henry can hear the sound of battle, and see the Roman foot soldiers in close order, with swords and spears at the ready, and shields held out before them in a solid line, supported by cavalry on their flanks as they met the tribal warriors in close combat. He can imagine the terror felt by all the combatants. The noise and jostling of the horses, their eyes showing huge and white in terror, their flared nostrils flecked with foam and their flanks covered with a sweaty sheen. Only the noise of harnesses and soldiers armour clinking, and the striving of both men and horses straining to climb the steep incline, can be matched by the noise of the tribal warriors at the top, who are armed with much less sophisticated weaponry, but filled with a burning desire to defend their people and territory. Above all else the tribesmen would have realised that if they were defeated, the Romans would almost certainly massacre the remaining members of their families still alive on the top of the fort.

They would already have witnessed some of their families and comrades being crushed to death by the Roman ballistas which could throw a fifty pound stone over five hundred metres, or by their scorpions, which worked like a fixed crossbow, and threw large javelins. It was feared for its accuracy, which could wreak huge damage and injury to the villagers taking refuge on top of the fort.

By contrast the biggest advantage that the inhabitants had was the fact that they were at the top of the site and had probably gathered an assembly of large rocks and scalding hot water, which they could use to throw down the hill at the Romans who were precariously trying to climb up to attack them.

The blood and fearful injuries caused by such brutal weaponry must have caused unimaginable injury on both side of the conflict, and climbing up the steep slope where the sun has not yet reached, a shiver runs through Henry and he can almost smell the fear conjured up by such a cataclysmic battle.

As he reaches the top of the ditches, he is met by a large area where the tribe would have lived in their round, wooden framed huts, the walls of which would have been framed with wattle and daub (a mixture of mud and cattle dung). The roofs would have been thatched with reeds with a hole at the pinnacle, to allow smoke from the fire in the centre of the floor to escape.

On top of the fort the sun is now directly overhead, and its heat begins to warm Henry, who suddenly realises that he is hungry. Finding a suitable spot he sits down on the grass where he consumes his sandwiches and soft drink, which leaves him feeling strangely unsatisfied. Thinking why this could be, made him realise that he would have preferred either a cup of tea or coffee with his meal, and he determines to purchase a vacuum flask as soon as possible for just such a purpose.

As he sits there he is struck by an association of ideas which remind him of a joke about an Irishman, Pat, who met his friend Murphy, who was carrying a vacuum flask. So Pat says to Murphy, "What's that you have there, Murphy, and what's it for?" to which comes the reply, "It's a vacuum flask, and it keeps hot things hot and cold things cold."

Pat is very impressed by this explanation and says, "That's marvellous, so what have you got in it?" To which Murphy replies as quick as a flash. "Soup and an ice cream."

Henry, his spirits lifted by a combination of the sun and his own thoughts, lies back and a feeling of lethargy comes over him as he falls contentedly to sleep with his head resting on his rucksack. He wakes with a start, before spending another half hour walking round the top of the fort, before deciding to make his way back to Dorchester for the last leg of his journey to Goderston.

Returning to Dorchester, Henry catches the D12 Nord Cat service, which will pass through Goderston before arriving at its final destination of Cerne Abbas. Surprisingly the bus is almost empty, a situation that becomes completely empty after a few stops, as all the other passengers get off.

Finding himself on his own apart from the driver, Henry, who is sitting nearly opposite him, starts to make idle conversation by asking him about his job, how long he had been driving buses, what sort of shift patterns does he work.

The driver, Peter, who is obviously pleased to have another person to converse with, talks readily about his job, which he loves with a passion, explaining about the long hours and some difficult customers, although he hastens to add that most of them are wonderful people and regulars who he has known for a long time.

In turn Henry also talks about himself and explains how he comes to be on this particular bus, then asks Peter if he has ever experienced any unusual situations while doing his job. The driver thinks for a moment before replying.

"Well there is a very strong camaraderie among all the drivers, who love a good laugh, but sometimes they overstep the mark."

Only a couple of weeks previously he had found himself in the driver's rest room in Dorchester, waiting for his next change over, when suddenly he saw one of the other drivers who he knew very well being led by the arm by a third driver out to the bus that he was due to take out. However the significance of this was that the driver being led was wearing a pair of dark sunglasses and carrying a white stick. As he reached the bus he fumbled around for the driver's door handle, then hoisting himself up into the cab, calmly laid the white stick on the floor beside him, took off his sun glasses and started up the engine.

The passengers already on the bus had viewed these proceedings with a mounting state of apprehension, which reached full blown terror by the time the bus started up, at which point they decided to leave en masse, fighting each other to get to the exit.

They took a lot of placating by the bus company officials, together with an apology from the driver concerned before they were fit enough to resume their journey.

"I think the driver thought the episode well worth the apology, because the escapade had made him almost a sort of folk hero among his contemporaries at the bus depot," finishes Peter. "Anyway, Henry, this is your stop, thanks for your company."

THE BUS PASS

As the bus has been travelling, Henry has noted the gradual transition from the more built-up areas surrounding Dorchester to the softer, greener landscapes that he knew and loved so much. On his right hand side now are hills, which climb steeply away from the road, on which sheep graze. A stream fed from the hills meanders its leisurely way along the side of the road, upon which several species of duck are perched, bobbing up and down looking for all the world like targets at a fairground. On his left hand side Henry notes that the landscape is flat and some of the fields were being cultivated. He could see some type of wheat or maize being grown, as well as rape seed, with its stunning bright yellow canopy, a vista that could make the world seem a brighter place even on the darkest and stormy of days.

Bidding farewell to Peter, Henry gets off the bus, a mounting sense of excitement growing within him now that he has finally reached Goderston, the place which holds so many happy memories for him.

CHAPTER 6

Henry and Isabel

About one o'clock on 19 September 1964 is a date and time etched indelibly on Henry's mind forever.

It was the heart stopping moment that he saw Isabel for the first time, a view that took all the oxygen from his lungs and left him breathless. The first impression that Henry noted was not just her beauty, which was obvious, rather her sheer vivacity and animation as she passed him with several of her classmates, chattering and laughing as they made their way from their classroom to town in their lunch break.

Henry took in a fleeting glimpse of a woman of above average height, of pale complexion and fair hair - not so much blonde, more straw-coloured - which was long, flowing half way down her back. A quick glance at her face revealed light, blue-green eyes, which danced mischievously as she talked. A freckled snub-nose, together with a laughing mouth that was the cause of - or the response to - her sparkling eyes, was enough for Henry to know instantly that he wanted to get to know her better.

At this time, they were both attending High Wycombe College, Henry being in his third and final year, studying graphic design, with a view to finding work in a graphics studio locally, while Isabel was in her second year taking a course in advertising and marketing.

Unfortunately for Henry a suitable opportunity to meet Isabel again did not present itself until the College Christmas Dance, toward the end of term that year, by which time Henry was completely infatuated with her, thinking of her constantly, and even worse, worshipping her from afar, but incapable of asking her out, or at least frightened by the fear of rejection.

However, the night of the dance came and Henry, supported by a few of his friends who knew of his feelings for Isabel, together with the buffer of a number of beers to give himself Dutch courage, found, or at least thought he had enough confidence to ask her to dance, which hopefully might lead to getting to know her, and who knew, further meetings.

To his amazement however none of his carefully constructed plans were necessary, because when his "Ladies, excuse me," was announced, Isabel suddenly appeared before him, saying, "Shall we?"

As they took their first hesitant steps, Henry tried desperately not to tread on her toes, while all his pent up feelings for her, seem to be released, and he said, "I was just about to ask you to dance, in fact I have been trying to pluck up courage to ask you out a number of times, but never been able to actually quite do so."

Henry was conscious of Isabel's beautiful pale green eyes focusing on his, as she told him, "I know, I have noticed you many times and hoped that you would ask me, but you never did, so I thought that I would take the initiative."

It was this moment when Henry heard Isabel's mantra for the first time, when she told him, "Life is for living, and every moment is precious, whether good or bad, so let's not waste any more time," something that she continued her best to do for the rest of her life.

This then was the starting point in their relationship, at which time Henry was twenty and Isabel nineteen.

Henry spent most of that Christmas with Isabel at her parents' home in Aylesbury, and they remained virtually inseparable from this time until Isabel's death nearly forty years later.

They had both been involved in other relationships before, but from this moment their love was irrevocable. They were married two years later, by which time Henry was working in a graphic design studio, and Isabel had just started working in the advertising department of a furniture manufacturing company, both of which were based in High Wycombe.

Through friends at work, Henry managed to find accommodation in a flat over a shop in High Wycombe High Street at a peppercorn rent. This was just as well, because the space was little more than a garret, with two bedrooms, small dining-cum-kitchen area, with a separate miniscule toilet and shower.

None of this mattered though because they were deliriously happy here.

CHAPTER 7

The White Swan, or the Mucky Duck

Henry pushes open the door of the saloon bar with mixed feelings of trepidation and elation, because he is so looking forward to seeing Toby and Avril again, but fearful that the rapport and bonhomie that they have always enjoyed will be diminished somehow due to the death of Isabel.

After the fishing trips had finished several years earlier as the four of the 'fishermen' got older, Henry preferred to spend more time with Isabel once the children were grown and independent.

However, there was still a small part of him that missed the camaraderie with his life- long friends and the places that they had visited. Consequently, Henry eventually persuaded Isabel to accompany him on a number of pilgrimages, of which Goderston was high on his agenda.

To his complete amazement, Isabel had loved the place and the area, and they had stayed at the pub a number of times, captivated by Toby and Avril's hospitality, going for long walks in the surrounding countryside, visiting Bridport on market days, then going back to 'the Mucky Duck' in time for a lovely evening meal before retiring to bed, both physically and mentally exhausted.

He could remember the very last night they spent here with aching clarity.

At dawn when he woke, Henry stared at Isabel sleeping, looking so beautiful with her long hair spread across the pillow. Seeming to feel him looking, she awoke and smiled at him.

Her sheer beauty and vulnerability gave Henry a feeling both of wanting to protect this wonderful woman, and to want her at the same time.

Recognising the look in his eyes, Isabel said in her best Mae West imitation, "Why Henry, is that a gun in your pyjama's, or are you just pleased to see me?"

Henry, laughing at her wit, replied, "Am I that obvious, you little minx?" and before she had time to reply he kissed her with all his pent up passion, his tongue seeking to enter her mouth, with Isabel corresponding by parting her lips, her own passion mounting rapidly under his mouth and touch.

He paused just long enough to lift her night dress over her head, while still marvelling at her still slim figure that had always excited him from the very start of their relationship.

Then, cupping her breasts, he brought his mouth down to her rose-coloured nipples, slowly running his tongue round each in turn, encouraging them to become hard and erect in his mouth.

Isabel responded with a low moan and lay back to receive him. Feeling her wetness he entered her quickly, but Isabel slowed and soothed him with words of love.

Now they could enjoy the exquisite pleasure as Henry moved deeply inside her, withdrawing even more slowly which aroused Isabella to hold him inside her, until she could contain herself no longer and whispered to him, "Come on Henry, I think it's time."

Their bodies were now synchronised and the momentum was mutually raised to a frenetic level, until both of them climaxed simultaneously in a flurry of murmured sexual releases and endearments of love.

After a few moments Henry rolled away from her and as they both lay relaxing in a post coital haze, Isabel, suddenly seeming to foresee the future, said, "You are a good man Henry Long, both as a loving husband and father, and you are all that I have ever wanted," to which he replied, "You know I love you Bella," which was the name he had always used for her. "I know that sounds daft from an old fart like me, but it's always been that way."

Years later, in retrospect, Henry would often recall her comments, which had been such an unusual thing for her to say. Personal declarations of love between them were not often spoken, because they had never been necessary. They both knew their love for each other was irrevocable.

It was almost as if she was trying to tell him that changes were coming that neither of them could control, but her feelings would never change, no matter what.

It was only a few months later that Isabel's first breast cancer diagnosis was made.

Lightening the moment, Isabel said with a smile, "We must come back more often; this place does so much for both of us."

But they never did!

His thoughts are brought to an abrupt end as they are interrupted by Toby's large, booming voice crying, "Henry, you old bugger, so you've made it at last, I have given you room six, overlooking the common - your usual, in fact."

Peering through the gloom, Henry sees Toby just coming into the bar, presumably directly from the butchery next door, because he still has on his butcher's apron.

Although Henry had written to Toby and Avril explaining Isabel's death, this was the first time that he had visited since that, and he was, to say the least, a little apprehensive about how they would react.

But he has no need to worry because Toby, after yelling for Avril to come and see who has arrived, claps a huge hand around Henry's shoulder and, hugging him, says, "We were so sorry to hear about Isabel, she was such a lovely lady. Both Avril and I often talk about the two of you and reminisce about the times we all had. You should have come back sooner, Henry. We couldn't have stopped you mourning, nor would we have wanted to, because that would have not been natural, but we would have been here to talk to, to fill some of those interminably long silences, when you can only sit and ask yourself why!"

Just as Henry is about to reply, Avril comes hurrying in, saying, "Why Henry, it's so wonderful to see you again, we often talk about Isabel and you, don't we Toby?"

Henry is overwhelmed by these two kind people, who both Isabel and he had come to love so much.

Floundering for an adequate reply for their concerns, he mutters, "Well it's really great to see you both again, and I shall need the room until at least Sunday, possibly longer, because I understand that you are playing the Jack the Lad pub from Blandford at skittles on Friday, and I would like to be here to watch that."

Henry then goes on to explain how he had stopped at Blandford the previous day and the warm welcome that Bill and Betty and the others had shown him.

Hearing this, Toby exclaims, "That is typical of they two, I've known them for many years and they are the salt of the earth."

While they are discussing Henry and the reason for his being there, he thinks that it is right moment to explain about his journey and the reasons for making it. Toby and Avril hear him at length, and when he has finished there is a silence for a brief moment before Toby ventures, "What a terrible decision to have to make Henry, I hope everything works out for you. In the meantime let's all enjoy the time that we have before you leave for the next leg of your journey. Why don't you go and freshen up, then come back down and we can all have a chat and a pint before we eat. There's a quiz night tonight which you might like."

Henry, who by now desperately wants a lie down, thanks Toby and says that he will be delighted to join the quiz later on, something that he and Isabel had enjoyed and done often with Rob and Madge at their local Kings Head.

With the thought of Toby and Avril's welcome ringing in his ears, Henry makes his way to his room, feeling relaxed and happy, which no doubt contributes to the fact that as soon as he lies down on the bed he falls into a deep sleep, waking with a start on hearing the church clock strike half past seven.

Quickly washing and changing, he returns downstairs, apologising to Toby for being so long, which the latter laughs off, saying, "I didn't really think that you would be down again very soon because you looked knackered when you arrived." Henry props up the bar for a while chatting and drinking with Toby about old times, until Avril appears and says, "Well Henry, I think that we had better have a bite to eat, because the Quiz starts in the bar at half past eight and we'll need the tables to be cleared by then."

Henry, who has suddenly realised just how hungry he is, orders a steak and chips and all three of them sit and chat some more, until Toby, suddenly noticing that it is now ten minutes past eight and that a number of people are beginning to arrive for the quiz, rises and says to Henry, "We usually have teams of four people at each table playing as teams, so we will have to see if there two or three people who need to make up a team that you can join. If not you can always play on your own, but it's much more fun if you can play with others. Is that OK?"

Henry assures him that it is. Within a few minutes the bar is almost full, with most of the tables being taken up by locals who obviously play together as teams and Henry is beginning to think that he will have to play on his own.

Suddenly Avril is beside him, saying, "Right Henry, three of my friends have just arrived and they will be happy for you to join them, to make up a team." Dragging him across the room he arrives at a table where two women and a man sit. Both women appear to be aged in their mid to late fifties, with the man perhaps a little older.

As they rise to be introduced Henry notices that the first woman is tall and has a large angular framed body. Her hair is dark brown, perhaps a little more brown than nature provided originally, which is short cropped. Her eyes are also brown, the colour of milk chocolate, which makes her look like a downcast spaniel under normal circumstances, but her face is transformed when she smiles, and welcoming, as it is now, as she introduces herself and her companions.

"I am Megan Chaplin, and this is my husband Alistair (indicating the man in the party), who is usually known as Charlie, although why I will never know, because he's not in the least bit funny - and this is Kate Challis, who has been my friend for all my life. We were born and both grew up here, went to school together, married our partners, had children here who have grown up and left the nest. Now we are growing old together."

Henry shakes hand with each in turn, and he takes stock of the other two as he does so. Charlie, as he is known, is tall and painfully thin, and indeed looks as if he doesn't laugh very much, but as Henry is to discover in the course of the evening, looks can be deceiving, because 'Charlie' has a very dry wit, and is very sociable company.

Turning finally to the third member of the party Henry's gaze is met by Kate's clear blue eyes, which he finds strangely disturbing, and which seem to laugh at the same time she laughs. She is not tall, about five feet five inches he guesses, with a slender figure as far as he can judge, underneath a jumper and jeans. Her hair is silver grey, which makes her look distinctive rather than old, and falls to her shoulders in what appears to be an orderly tangle. A short snub-nose and high cheek bones, complimented by a wide mouth obviously used to laughing, completes the picture.

Thinking back to Megan's remark about Kate and her growing up together, Henry can only wonder at the difference between them. Kate only appears to be in her early to mid-fifties, but old Father Time had not been so kind to Megan, who Henry now realises, must be of an age with Kate, but looks considerably older.

As they all sit down, it is Kate who opens the conversation, saying, "Well Henry what brings you to our little village? Avril said something about a bus journey?" Feeling slightly embarrassed Henry relates his story again, explaining about Isabel and her death, then going on to describe his dilemma about moving to Australia to be with his children. When he finishes, Kate goes on to ask how long he intends to stay in the village and where he will be headed next.

All three exclaim their dismay at his predicament, but before they are able to continue further, Toby calls for attention so that the quiz can start.

Toby has given out papers, for subjects to be answered on a variety of subjects, and as they are called out Henry is delighted to find that he can make a useful contribution to the team's efforts. Although they have all said that they only play for fun, and for a social night out, Henry can sense that they all have a competitive streak, which they relieve by laughing at themselves when they are wrong or do not know the answers to the questions.

After a series of ten questions each on five different subjects, there is an interval for liquid refreshments at the bar, so Henry buys a round.

THE BUS PASS

Before proceeding further, Toby comes around to see who wants to partake in the quiz jackpot. At a small cost of one pound per ticket everyone can be involved by writing their name on a slip of paper, which is put into a hat, which is then drawn, and the person or team selected have to try and answer one question. The first answer is the only one that can be accepted. The money collected, is put into a pot, and paid out to anyone giving the correct answer. However, if the team or person concerned gives the wrong answer, the money will then go forward to the next week's draw and will be added to any other money that also has not been claimed.

On this particular evening the prize money stands at seven hundred and eighty-seven pounds, which is to be played for in two lots, the first amount being for five hundred pounds and the second amount is for the balance of two hundred and eighty-seven pounds.

This is because once the prize money reaches five hundred pounds it is put into a separate pot and money built up in subsequent weeks goes to build a second prize.

There is a hush in the bar as Toby's assistant (one of the barmaids) draws one of the slips of paper that they have all filled in, which is handed to Toby for him to announce.

This he duly does, saying, "The table selected for the five hundred pound question is 'The Dorchester Angels'."

As this is announced there is a sudden increase in noise volume in the bar, some people muttering, "It's a fix," others clearly relieved that they will not be called upon to embarrass themselves by trying to answer a difficult question correctly, but by far the loudest noise comes from directly behind Henry's table. The Dorchester Angels are obviously delighted to have a crack (incidentally they are all men).

After calling for hush, Toby asks them the question. "Can you tell me who Queen Mary the first married? You have thirty seconds in which to do so."

The Dorchester Angels go immediately into a huddle, whispering behind their hands to each other, as indeed do the rest of the contestants at their own individual tables.

At his own table, Henry, whose strengths are sport and history, thinks that it was a French king, perhaps a Louis, but he doesn't know which one; Kate, though, thinks that it was a Phillip of Spain, but here again she is not sure which one.

Megan and Alistair, not being the least bit interested in history, have no solution to offer.

The seconds finally tick away, until Toby asks The Dorchester Angels for their answer.

Their spokesman who has been volunteered by the rest of his colleagues stands up and says, "We are not sure, but we think it was Phillip of Spain," only to be met by Toby's withering reply, "Yes, but which one?" This throws the team into turmoil once more, until after hurried discussions the spokesman announces, "We don't know but we are guessing it was Phillip the Fifth."

Before Toby can reply, Kate suddenly says conspiratorially in a hushed voice to the three others on her table, "I think that's wrong, I think it was Phillip the Second."

A few seconds later Toby confirms her answer by saying to The Dorchester Angels, "Sorry folks, good try, but it was Phillip the Second, at least it says so on my piece of paper, so the five hundred pounds jackpot will be carried forward until next week."

Hearing this, a mixture of groans and cheers go up in equal measure, during which Henry congratulates Kate for getting the answer right, even though they can't win anything.

Toby proceeds with the second half of the quiz, but not before saying that they will all get a chance to win the second jackpot draw of two hundred and eighty seven pounds at the end of the evening.

So the evening continues, with drinks, laughter and groans being consumed in equal measure. There is no time to discuss anything other than the quiz with each other, but Henry still has time to ask himself why Kate has not brought a partner. She wears a wedding ring, so he can only presume that her husband either can't make or didn't want to join the quiz. It seems to Henry that it is important that he should know, and realises with a start that this woman, with her twinkling eyes and ready laugh, is beginning to stir emotions in him like no other since Isabel.

THE BUS PASS

As the evening progresses, Alistair comes into his own, evidently being a buff on geography, while Megan excels in all sorts of music questions from Led Zeppelin to Chopin. Now that the questions have been completed, each table passes their quiz sheets to the nearest table to them for marking, as Toby calls out the answers.

Once this has been completed, Toby asks each table for their final score. To their utter amazement they have managed a close third, winning a lottery ticket each for the second draw for the second jackpot.

So the draw procedure has to be gone through once more until finally Toby calls out "The team that has to answer this draw is 'The Three Musketeers Plus One'." This is the name that Kate, Alistair, Megan and Henry have decided on for themselves, so they give a great shout in unison, leaving Toby in no doubt which team they are.

Again once the room quietens down as Toby poses the final jackpot question of the night by asking, "Can you please tell me the middle name of the television character Reginald Perrin, played by Leonard Rossiter in the television series of the same name?"

Suddenly a huge smile engulfs Henry's face, which causes the other three to look at him with a mixture of hope and anticipation.

Unable to bear the suspense any longer, Kate says, "What is it Henry? Do you know, because the rest of us haven't a clue - you must do, because you look like the cat that's found the cream," to which Henry replies, "They could have asked me a million other questions to which I would not know the answers, but way back, the *Reginald Perrin* programme was one of my favourites and I was a real anorak about it. So yes, the answer is Iolanthe, which I remember so well, because it made the initials of his name, R-I-P."

At the end of the allotted thirty seconds, Toby asks them for their answer, which Henry duly gives. There is a heart stopping several second pause, which to Henry at any rate seems to last a lifetime, until Toby, in his most booming, theatrical voice, announces the answer as correct. Suddenly the bar goes wild with joy and other contestants start coming up and slapping them on their backs, and crying things like, "Mine's a pint of best," or, "Can you lend me a quid?"

Toby brings the winnings to their table, which Henry proceeds to split four ways. Seeing this, the other three all declare, "No, we can't take that, you answered the question, we didn't have a clue what the answer was." However, Henry has none of it, saying, "That's why we play as a team, so we win and lose as a team. Tonight we won," and insists that the others take their share.

Within a few minutes the bar has virtually emptied, but Henry is enjoying his team's company, and not wanting them to go, he orders another round of drinks. Kate and Megan decide on coffee, but Alistair joins Henry in a double whisky as they all adjourn to sit on stools at the bar.

Wanting to know more about Kate, but not knowing where to start, Henry finds the situation turned on its head, when she suddenly asks him, "What work did you do before you retired Henry?"

"I trained at Art College, and eventually worked for a local graphic design agency based in High Wycombe as a graphic designer. The agency had a good reputation and we worked on packaging and point of sale designs for national and international clients. Apart from having a career as a watercolour or oil painter, there was nothing else that I really wanted to do with my life, so I was really lucky, because I spent my life doing one of the things that I really enjoyed, which made it more like pleasure than work."

Hearing this, Kate looks at him quizzically before asking about his work in more detail, which Henry does, being only too happy to explain something of which he is so proud. As he finishes, Kate changes the subject by asking him, "So how long do you think it will be before you will be moving on, Henry? I am sure that we will all miss you, we have never won anything at a quiz night before, have we?" to which the others both re iterate, "Never!"

Henry tells them that he is not sure how long he is staying in Goderston, but he certainly intends staying until after the next weekend, partly to see the bowls match between the Jack the Lad and the Mucky Duck on Friday.

Seeing the look of utter bewilderment on their faces, Henry hurriedly explains the reason for the nickname for the White Swan, and just how it had come about, which they think is a hoot, and somehow he thinks that they too will never quite see the pub in the same way again.

He then goes on to tell them that Toby had told him that Netherton, a village only a couple of miles away, were due to play Goderston at cricket on the common on Sunday, as well as challenging the Mucky Duck to an annual tug of war which takes place across the pond outside, which is won by the team who could pull their opponents into the pond.

Now that he is feeling more relaxed, and seeing an opportunity during a lull in the conversation, Henry dares to venture to ask Kate, "So where is your husband tonight Kate, could he not make it, or does he not enjoy quizzes?"

As soon as he speaks, Henry sees a stricken, helpless look cross Kate's face, giving her the appearance of a vulnerable child, and he immediately backtracks, apologising for any offence he has unwittingly caused her.

Before either of them can say any more, Megan interjects on behalf of her lifelong friend, and, turning to face Henry tells him in a quiet, reasoned voice, "I know you meant no offence Henry and there is just no other way to tell you this, but Kate's husband Mike was involved in a traffic accident ten years ago and was killed instantaneously, returning from a business trip to Manchester."

Henry's world, and more importantly his evening, which has been so wonderful up to this point, dissolves into a quagmire of depressing emotions, as he remembers his own loss, leaving him with a feeling of inadequacy and foolishness.

Hurriedly murmuring his apologies for his insensitive and crass behaviour, Henry's mood is lifted somewhat as Kate recovers her composure by saying, "No, you mustn't blame yourself Henry, you weren't to know - it's just that although I have been a widow for so long, I have never been quite able to take off my wedding ring. It's as though I would be betraying Mike's memory if I did. Can you understand that?" Henry, who suddenly realises that he too still wears his own wedding ring for much the same reasons, agrees that he can, by pointing it out to her.

Not wishing to cause any more unpleasant moments, the conversation returns to more uncontroversial topics. Megan asks

Henry what he will be doing until the weekend and he tells her that he has no specific plans, other than to take some walks in the surrounding countryside, weather permitting.

From scraps of conversation garnered as the evening progresses, Henry realises that Alistair, a.k.a Charlie, is retired, having worked all his life in H M Customs and Excise, and that Megan, also now retired, had been a schoolteacher. Feeling more on safe ground he asks Charlie, "Where were you based when you were working?"

"Well I ended up at Poole in the customs house, but I worked at a number of places, mostly where Channel ferries docked. I could be asked to cover at any given moment. I even spent some time at Heathrow and Gatwick Airports, which meant staying away from home from Mondays to Fridays. But I can't complain, in truth I loved almost every minute of it, which not a lot of people can say about their working lives. It was a constant source of amazement to me, the lengths Joe Public would go to in order to avoid paying excise duty. In fact I am seriously considering writing a book about some of the stunts that I saw."

"Oh don't start him off on his favourite hobby horse Henry, or else we will never get home tonight," laughs Megan. "I am sure there will be other evenings this week he can bore you lifeless with his stories of Daring Do."

On this note it seems to be the appropriate moment for the evening to draw to a close, much to Henry's disappointment, because he has enjoyed all of their company - Kate's in particular.

"Does that mean that you will all be coming to the pub another night this week?" he asks plaintively, only to be reassured that they will indeed, because they invariably have a meal together at the pub one night a week, and sometimes a light bite at midday on another.

As they say their goodbyes, Kate says, "Thank you for joining us tonight Henry, I have had a lovely time," and then rather more mysteriously, and with a mischievous twinkle in her eye, "I am sure I will see you again soon."

With her words ringing in his ears, Henry makes his way to his room, feeling tired and excited at the same time. Fighting off the urge to sleep, he quickly emails the usual suspects on his list, updating them of his progress and events so far. As he turns out the light the thought suddenly strikes him that it will be useful if he records his adventures, by way of a day to day diary on his laptop. If he does that, then he can produce a record of his happenings for the future which he could refer to in years to come, perhaps when he is living in Australia. In any event he could give his children copies.

He would make a start first thing in the morning, while the last two days were fresh in his mind!

CHAPTER 8

Kate Challis

"Hey Madge, did you see the email from Henry?" inquires Rob as they sit at the breakfast table the next morning. "He certainly seems to be having a good time. I quite envy him staying at the Mucky Duck in Goderston, it's such a beautiful little village. He seems to be enjoying his travels. I had thought that I might have to go and spend some time with him if he started to find the travel and meeting new people difficult to deal with, but he seems to be having a whale of a time. If I sense that the whole thing is going pear-shaped for him, I will join him straight away. What do you think?"

"Well, on this occasion I agree with you Rob," said Madge disconcertingly. "I just hope he doesn't wear the few clothes that he took with him for too long."

This remark is followed be a lull in the conversation, which Madge quickly fills by saying, "You remember that woman that I told you about a few weeks ago, you know the one that was a sister at Wycombe General, well she came into the surgery yesterday and during our little chat she told me a story of something that happened recently when she was admitting a woman to the hospital. In fact two women had turned up, presumably the second to comfort and assist the first.

"The sister went through the whole admittance process with one of them, which took her some thirty minutes. When she was finished she asked the woman if she knew why she was being admitted. The reply when it came was devastating, as the woman replied, 'Oh it's not me that's being admitted, it's my friend over there.'

The sister, sounding very annoyed, said, 'Well, that being so, why didn't you say something to stop me, instead of letting me go on?' only to hear the reply, 'Well, you were doing so well dear, that I could not bring myself to.'"

While this little monologue is going on, Rob tries his best to look interested, and as soon as the story ends, laughs, and stands up and says, "Well, I had best get out to the garage if I want to finish the service on Jeremy's car from up the road."

As he makes for the door, he hears Madge call out, "Wait a sec, don't you want to hear what else she had to say?"

Rob continues toward the door, calling back over his shoulder at the same time, "Sorry love. I must get this car finished. Jeremy needs it for work tomorrow and I have agreed that he can pick it up tonight. Tell me this evening."

When Henry wakes the next morning he finds the sun streaming in through the windows. Quickly checking his watch, he sees to his horror that it is nearly nine. Hurriedly doing his ablutions he dresses and goes downstairs to the dining room for breakfast. To his surprise there are three other couples doing just that already, who have obviously stayed overnight.

His newfound confidence gives him the courage not only to wish them all good morning, but to enquire how long they are all staying, where they are from and where they intend going after their stay finishes in Goderston. He finds much to his pleasure that his forthright approach is rewarded, because their own reserved, shy composures break down under such a direct attack, and they are soon talking to him and each other with a fervour not usually associated with the British.

They come from various places - Bristol, Birmingham and Tunbridge Wells, but all of them come for the same reason. They are all retired and are taking time to visit places of interest out of school holiday period, because it is cheaper and the roads are less congested. Much the same reasons as he himself, thinks Henry.

The couple from Bristol are staying another few days, but the remainder are moving on, so, wishing them all the best, Henry returns upstairs, determined to write up his diary on his laptop, before contemplating what he will do for the rest of the day. Once he has started writing, it soon becomes clear to him that it is going to take more than just a few minutes to record all his experiences, but he perseveres, finishing at eleven o'clock.

Looking out of the window across the common, he can see that it is a glorious summer's day, and for some inexplicable reason finds himself wondering just where Kate lives - and Megan and Charlie, his conscience reminds him, but not very convincingly.

Finally, he returns downstairs, after deciding that he will take a walk to Cerne Abbas across the fields, which will be a shorter route than following the road, and safer too, because the small country roads do not have any footpaths, making walking precarious to say the least. When he gets there he will then find himself a pub or café to get a light lunch and, depending on the time available, either walk back or catch the bus.

As luck will have it he bumps into Toby as he leaves the Mucky Duck and seeing an opportunity, thinks he will try and find out where Kate lives. However, rather than ask the question directly he decides on subtlety and cunning and asks as casually as he can.

"Morning Toby, I am just off to Cerne Abbas, I thought a walk would do me good," and then pensively, indicating the various buildings that followed the crescent shaped road fronting the pub. "These buildings must contain the major places that the village needs to be a viable self-serving community. What are they and who lives in them?"

Toby looks thoughtfully at Henry, and, turning to face the buildings, indicates from left to right which they are.

"The first is the Post Office and General Store, which sells everything from food and drink to papers, candles and lottery tickets. Next is the village hall which was built relatively recently, thanks to contributions from lottery funding, replacing an older version that had become unviable because of the constant cost of repairs and maintenance. Here villagers gather through the year to hold meetings to decide on parish activities, to play table tennis and pool, and to host the WVS meetings. It also acts as changing rooms for cricket and football teams, and also the place where the teams are fed and watered after fixtures."

Additionally, Toby explains that the hall is the place where dances are held throughout the year. Oh yes! The village hall was an absolutely indispensable part of life for its inhabitants.

To the right of the hall another row of old cottages stand, built of stone and thatch construction, originally for farm labourers, but which now house Jenny Wright, an elderly widow, and her younger spinster sister Molly Arnold,. Next to them lives Graham Gardener, known as 'Digger', who was a potter and ceramics maker. 'Old' Matthew Higgins comes next. He has spent his life as an odd-job man, mending fences, gardening, decorating, and sometimes doing agricultural work for local farmers, or even doing a bit of poaching on the side. He is also involved in other nefarious dealings and can often be found in the pub, selling articles of dubious origins.

Finally there is a young couple, Norman and Sharon Druce, who have only been married for a year, and live here because it is the only place that they can afford. They came originally from Dorchester where they both still work.

Next to the row of cottages is the rectory, where the young vicar lives with his wife and two children, both girls. Like so many ministries today he works a circuit of several village churches locally, alternating services, marriages, funerals and births as required.

The church, St. George the Martyr, is next, and is of Norman design, built sometime in the thirteenth century. Although attendances have dwindled over the years, there is still a hard core of active members in the congregation, whose volume is increased at the Christian festival periods of Christmas and Easter.

Ironically, next to the church is what some members of the congregation regard as a 'den of iniquity', but which even more villagers regard as a place to relax and meet friends, namely the village pub i.e. the White Swan - or the Mucky Duck, as Henry prefers to call it.

Opposite the pub, across the road on the common is a small pond, which has an island in the middle, upon which mallard ducks and some moorhens nest with their young. Around the pond are a couple of benches which have been donated by villagers at various times. This area is used throughout the year; in the summer villagers picnic on the grass, running to and fro to the pub for liquid refreshments, and in the winter parents take their young children to feed the 'quack-quacks'.

Completing the semi-circle in front of the common is a number of larger houses which have been built as late as the early twentieth century, the occupants of which would have been considered as outsiders by the villagers, even though some of them had lived here for many years.

Beyond all these buildings is a heavily wooded area of beech, oak and sycamore trees, access to which can be got to by means of a pathway running beside the church.

Apart from the usual benefits of walking dogs and children playing hide-and-seek, these woods are the source of a ready supply of logs for some of the villagers' fires, which they consider as a right, handed down through the generations.

As he finishes speaking Toby says with a smile on his lips, "Oh yeah, and Kate lives over the far side of the common, over the bridge... number fifty-six."

Henry, who is left stunned by Toby's perception, replies, "Am I as transparent as that then Toby?" whose only reaction is to nod, confirming the fact. Suitably chastened, Henry makes his way across the common, turning left and following the road to Cerne Abbas before crossing after a mile or so and branching out across a field.

It's not too long before he is confronted by the image of the Cerne Abbas Giant, a huge figure cut out into the chalk of the hill in the form of a man holding what appears to be a club. However, the most amazing thing about this chalk cutting is that it is naked, showing a huge erect penis. As far as anyone knows the figure is some two and a half thousand years old. According to folklore, the figure is a sign of fertility, but just how true this is nobody appears to know.

Resolutely marching on up to the top of the hill, Henry can see the landscape before him stretching out for miles. Cutting down the far side means that his course is shorter than the road, which follows the contour of the hill at the bottom. At the bottom of the hill he picks up the footpath marked 'Cerne Abbas 2 miles'. The path runs parallel with the edge of the field at this point, and is flanked both sides by hawthorn hedges which are covered with a mass of mayflowers, looking almost like snow, incongruous on an early spring sunny day.

Henry marches resolutely on and reaches Cerne Abbas at half past one, before he immediately looks to find somewhere to eat and slake his thirst, because the walk has given him a huge appetite.

Making his way to the Red Lion rub, being aware of it from previous visits, he orders a ploughman's salad with a pint of Dorset bitter to wash it down. Unusually the pub is quiet, so Henry leaves, and feeling a little tired after his exertions buys a daily paper and heads for the nearest place to sit, which he finds when he comes across a bench in a park not far away.

It is still a gorgeous day, and sitting on the bench, Henry contemplates with pleasure his last two days. The mixture of quiet contemplation, sun and food conspires against him and he knows no more until he wakes with a start having nodded off. As he does so the church clock strikes four o'clock and gazing up through the sun dappled leaves of the trees under which he is sitting, the thought of walking back to Goderston is too much even to consider.

Knowing that the bus to Dorchester leaves at five, Henry thinks that a coffee will wake him up a bit and fill his time until it is time to catch the bus, so he returns to the centre of this lovely picturesque village one more time, until he finds a café. But instead of a coffee he decides to get a cream tea and sit outside, where there are a number of tables with colourful parasols on the pavement, until it is time for him to get the bus. The journey is uneventful, and the driver is different than Peter the previous day.

Reaching Goderston at half past five, he negotiates the common and makes his way wearily into the bar for a quick snifter before going to his room.

There are a number of people already ensconced in the bar, several of whom he saw at the quiz the previous evening. After ordering his pint Henry makes his way back to one of the unoccupied tables. He has just sat down when one of the men at the bar makes his way to Henry's table and introduces himself, saying, "Hi! My name's David and I gather from Toby that you are Henry." Rising to his feet, Henry shakes the outstretched hand extended to him, while at the same time appraising the person offering it.

What he notes in the fleeting moment before he replies is a man in his mid-thirties, of open countenance, with yellow hair swept back, ending just above his collar. His eyes are piercing blue and are obviously accustomed to smiling, if the laughter lines which form creases (vaguely reminding Henry of someone) are anything to go by. This is confirmed now by the broad smile hovering on his lips. He is about five feet nine inches tall and of slim build and wears a dark navy, double breasted suit with narrow white stripes, a yellow tie and matching handkerchief, with what Henry recognises as black Gucci shoes completing his apparel.

"I am afraid you have the advantage of me David," replies Henry. "We have not met before have we? I feel sure that I would have remembered."

"No, not at all, it's just that I was talking to Toby just before you came in, and he told me a little about you and the things you were hoping to do. I hope that you are not offended and that I have not got him into trouble."

"Of course not, I have known Toby too long to be offended - in any case what I am doing is of no world shattering consequence, except to me that is, and I am only too aware of things that are discussed in pubs (having been the recipient of many such juicy pieces of information) to be in any way put out."

"Thank God for that," replies David, laughing. "It sounds a fantastic journey and challenge, and I wish you well in it, but one other topic came out of my conversation with Toby, which interested me very much."

"Oh and what was that then?" says Henry, not a little bemused.

"Well, Toby also mentioned the fact that you are now retired, but you were a graphic designer working in an agency in High Wycombe all your working life. The reason I mention it is because I run a small graphic design agency of my own in Dorchester, and not to beat about the bush, I am looking for someone with suitable experience to help me for a short period. My own background is very similar to your own, but the problem is that the studio is quite small - there are only three other designers and myself, but practically all my time is spent on the road drumming up either new or expanding existing business. Before you say no Henry, let me explain my problem a little more fully. Of the people I employ, the youngest is a junior who is attending an evening and two day release design course at the local art college, and with the best will in the world does little more than make tea. The second is a mature woman who is very good, providing that her work is monitored, because she does not always keep to the job spec, tending to - how can I put this? - lose sight of the objective.

"My final employee has been employed by me or the company for many years, starting in fact when designs were drafted by hand onto boards. With the introduction of computers, in particular Apple Macs in the late eighties, unfortunately he has not been able to make the transition to the new technology and to tell the truth Henry, I only employ him for old times' sake.

"The effect on all this for me is having gone out and got the business, I then have to come back and do most of it myself. After that, I then have to monitor the remainder that the staff has worked on as well. All this has been aggravated even further recently, because I recently won a fantastic order for a whole range of repackaging from a client for tinned fruits.

"I realise that you are retired and I understand the mission that you are on, but we both know that our skills do not suddenly disappear, neither does our desire to use them.

"Before you ask, yes I have been looking for a suitable person and have advertised for several months now, but the problem is that ours is a small provincial agency, and the big city boys take their pick of the crop when it comes to recruitment, and reward them more financially accordingly. It is impossible to poach from the big boys, and in any case if any of them are any good they usually try to start out on their own, although in truth, the law of averages dictates that not many of them make it.

"Take your time Henry, but in broad terms only, what do you think?"

Henry, who has sat through this monologue in what can only be described as amazement, finds his jaw dropping with every revelation.

Gathering himself he says, "But you don't even know me or what I can do," only for David to hold up his extended arm and say, "That's perfectly true, but I do know that you worked for Armstrong, Blitz and Merchant because Toby told me, and I am aware of their work and have been for many years. The industry knows them and they are considered to be as good as any of the London agencies, which is reflected in their client list, all national and international brands. The fact that you were employed by them for all that time leaves me in no doubt of your capabilities Henry."

As David talks, the implications of what he has been saying begins to percolate through Henry's mind, and he suddenly feels a warm feeling of what he can only describe to himself as gratitude. The fact that this young man going on such little knowledge could appreciate his skills is very gratifying and little short of miraculous.

On the other hand, Henry considers, David is right in his assumptions. He had been good at his job… bloody good in fact. By the time he left to retire he was, and had been for many years, the design studio manager and was involved with the work from the time that it had been won by the account director, after which he then he discussed with them the strategy to achieve the objectives, within the necessary time allocated.

But by far the most important factor when this had all been done was to ensure that the time allocated was kept to, and this was where Henry played his major role - allocating the work and monitoring its progress. If it looked for one moment like not hitting the time target, Henry would use all his wiles and experience to make sure that it was brought back on track, either by changing a designer if they were experiencing a mental design block, or by using his vast experience and sitting with them to iron out problems. The achievement of a good product within the time allocated, of course, was key, but the former was taken for granted or the company would not have remained in business.

Coming back to the present, Henry says, "Thank you for that David, and although generally I am not given to blowing my own trumpet, most of your observations are pretty accurate," and then suddenly remembering. "It has just occurred to me that I have my laptop upstairs in my room, which has a number of my projects on that I kept for old times' sake. If you can wait a minute I will go and get it."

THE BUS PASS

"Well that will be great Henry, I would certainly love to see them, but make no mistake my offer stands unconditionally, and I do not have to see them for you to justify yourself."

"Thanks again, but I would still like you to see them." Saying which Henry goes to his room and returns shortly with his laptop.

Propping it up on the bar table, he calls up the files he is looking for and David pulls his chair alongside so that they can both look at the screen.

"Here's one that I prepared for a major international client for a brand of kitchen cleaning agent called ZIP, which was hugely successful both in the UK and in Europe. As you can see the concept was very simple, but very in your face as well, which is necessary when your product is on a supermarket shelf, fighting for recognition with similar brands."

Calling up the next design, Henry says, "This next one was a redesign for a food manufacturing company based in the North of England who wanted to increase their market share within supermarket chains. As you can see the product has to appear mouth-watering and irresistible to the punter. This design improved market share by some eight per cent for our client, although it dropped back after some twelve months, as inevitably happens when other competitive brands redesign their product range."

Henry goes on to point out the rationale behind these designs and others, and finishes by saying, "I have many other examples at home on disc, as mementos you might say of my career."

David is enthralled by this impromptu presentation, and as Henry finishes, he tells him, "As I told you just now, I didn't need to see these, but having done so, it makes me realise even more how much your skills could be utilised if only for a short period. My company has not worked with anything like the class or type of client that you have just shown me, so what do you say?"

"Well David, thank you for your kind words, but I would really like a moment or two to gather my thoughts. I really need to see if I were to take it on for say two weeks, how my itinerary will be affected. Having said that, it's pretty fluid, rather more a list of places which I might or might not get to."

Listening to this, David, who has returned his chair to be opposite Henry again, looks thoughtful, before his face suddenly clears as he says, "Tell you what, why don't I get us both a meal and have a chinwag about it, during which I can explain the role in more detail," and showing Henry the menu, he goes on, "What do you fancy?"

Before Henry can reply, a woman's voice from behind him which he vaguely recognises, breaks in, saying, "That sounds wonderful David, can I assume that you are including me in your invite?"

David, on looking past Henry's left shoulder, smiles, saying, "Of course you can, Mum, let me introduce you to Henry Long… but I think you have met already, haven't you?"

Henry, half rising from his chair, turns, only to look into Kate's piercing blue eyes as she laughs at his obvious amazement at seeing her.

Kate, addressing Henry, continues, "I think that I owe you an explanation Henry. You see, when you told me that your work before you were retired was in graphic design, the connection with my wonderful son here (indicating David) seemed to be almost fate. If I can explain further, you see, my late husband Mike started up the studio some twenty years ago and when he was killed, David, who was already working with him, developed it further. My other son Geoffrey was not artistic in that way and showed no interest in it. He has subsequently taken up various arts and crafts, some watercolour paintings, also Batik work, which is just beautiful, together with some ceramics, and now lives and works with his family near Beaminster. So I took the liberty to get the information about you out of Toby on the phone this morning, and I then told David. I hope that you do not feel that I have betrayed you or made you feel antagonistic toward me, but I know David's situation well because I spend time every week at his studio, doing the books and keeping up with his paperwork. I know that he is at his wits' end, and after meeting you last night saw a possible answer to his problems."

There is silence for a moment before David asks them what they would like to eat, before returning to the bar to order food and get a round of drinks, leaving Henry and Kate to discuss the situation.

THE BUS PASS

Henry starts by saying, "Of course I don't feel angry about you using your initiative, Kate. In fact I am very flattered, and it's given my confidence no end of a boost." And before he can stop himself, he goes on to add, "I really enjoyed your company last night. It's been a long time since I spent a lovely social evening out like that," to which she replies, "Oh I'm so glad. This way if you decide to take David's offer up, we can do the quiz again next Tuesday, because I enjoyed your company too."

Henry laughs and says, "That sounds a bit like blackmail to me, but if so I can only say I like being blackmailed by you," while thinking to himself at the same time, *What are you talking about you silly old fool, you are acting like a teenager courting a girl for the very first time.*

Before any more can be said, David returns and proceeds to overwhelm Henry with his sheer enthusiasm. He is like a whirlwind, never giving Henry time to consider his position, which only confirms the latter's view that David is one hell of a salesman.

Terms are discussed and offers made. A very attractive salary rate is agreed and areas of responsibility discussed. The position is for two or three weeks, depending on the situation Henry finds when he starts and how long it will take to implement procedures to improve performance. The question of transport is raised by David, who says that he himself lives at Netherton, and has to pass through Goderston every morning to get to Dorchester, so he can pick Henry up on his way, unless he needs to visit clients, in which case he might not go into the studio first thing.

Kate, in turn, then offers that in the event of this happening she would combine it with the time that she needed to go to the studio, and take Henry in with her.

"Right then, that's that, I will pick you up on my way in the morning," says David, and rising suddenly before Henry can say any more, kisses his mother on the cheek, saying, "Good night, I had best be getting home or my lovely wife will be putting out a gone missing broadcast on me."

"Good night, son," said Kate. "Love to Gina and the kids."

After David leaves, Henry emits a long low sigh, before turning to Kate and saying, "Well you're a dark horse, why on earth didn't you tell me about David last night, although thinking about it there was little time with so many people here. Anyway, I want to hear about it now, and you as well come to that. After all, it's only fair, because you know lots about me."

"That's fair enough I suppose, but there's not much to know. I was born and brought up here and thanks to a little luck, hard work and some wonderful teachers, managed to get to Bristol University, where I graduated with a degree in business studies. Life in Bristol in the late sixties was exciting to me, a country girl from a small village in Dorset. I loved the pace and the vibrancy of Bristol at that time, which was still rebuilding from the effects of the bombing from the war. Large parts of it were brand new, with shops, bars, and restaurants springing up everywhere, while still retaining buildings from the sixteenth century, like The Landogger Trow pub, just off Queens square, or the old market, where you could get almost anything you could imagine. There were many churches and cathedrals that were a thousand years old as well."

Kate continues. "But more than any of that there was a great feeling of togetherness at uni; it was the time of revolution, of things changing, not all for the better, but nevertheless changing. Flower power, Bob Dylan, Carnaby Street, Mary Quant and Biba were all the result of the first generation after the war, pushing for change, and I was one of them. I first met Mike at a uni party (there were lots of them going on all the time), although he was there as a guest of someone else. He was several years older than me and was working in a design studio just off Park Street, which is close to Bristol Uni. Our courtship, if you can call it that, was like life itself at the time, a heady whirlwind, from which there seemed to be no shelter. Mike had an old Morris Minor eleven hundred which took us to places that I had only ever heard of. At weekends we would pack a picnic and go to the North Devon coast, or to Somerset, sometimes just the two of us, or occasionally with other couples. Money was tight, so we would quite often sleep over in the car, or if we were feeling flush we would try to get into a youth hostel. But none of our tribulations mattered because we were deliriously happy.

"Eventually I graduated and the next problem we faced was what we were going to do about our relationship, which we both knew was strong.

"Mike had only just finished his time at Art College on day release, although still working for a design studio, so he was very much a junior, and paid accordingly. It was imperative that he stayed working for the studio, at least until he had gained more experience, and I would have no trouble finding work in Bristol, so it was decided that we would try and find accommodation there, until Mike had more experience. Mike was a Bristol boy, born and bred, and so using his connections he managed to find us a one bed flat in the Hotwells Road. By this time I had met his parents who were very supportive, but he had yet to meet mine. This was not because I thought that my parents wouldn't like Mike, but because I knew that we could not afford to get married at that stage, not having yet earned any money to speak of.

"No, the overriding reason I was reticent was because I needed to break it to them that we intended living together until such time that we could afford to be married. Although I have said that the sixties was a time of great change, most of the change applied to people of my generation, but it had not necessarily happened to my parents' generation. Only a few short years before, they survived a world war, with all the deprivations and hardships that had entailed, and were not yet quite ready to accept free love or flower power, or whatever. At that time, living together was classed as 'in sin' and was simply unacceptable. Young couples in those days got married and lived with one set of parents until they could afford to rent or buy somewhere of their own. In practice this caused huge family rifts and hardly ever worked without family relationships being destroyed, sometimes irreparably. If children came along in the meantime the percentage failure of marriages surviving were even higher.

"Eventually I plucked up courage and Mike and I went to see my parents to explain our situation. We stayed for a week with them and had a wonderful time. It was so nice to return to my home and meet all my friends and neighbours and spend time with them. My parents took to Mike straight away and he to them, but it was not until later in the week that I brought up the subject up of us living together.

"There was a prolonged silence when I told my parents the news, which my father, God bless him, eventually broke by saying that although they would have preferred for Mike and me to wait until we could afford to marry and get a place of our own, he at least was glad that we had told them. He then went on to say that rather than lose me completely, both he and my mother gave us their blessing and were quite prepared to pay for our wedding breakfast and my dress when we chose to marry, providing we did intend to get wed eventually.

"The notion of Mike and me not getting wed was, I must admit, a new one, because I had always assumed that to be the case. However, thinking about it, I realised that marriage had never actually been discussed between us.

"I hastily reassured my parents that marriage was indeed our intention as soon as funds would allow, but I made a mental note to raise the subject with Mike as soon as we were on our own.

"To my utter amazement when I confronted Mike, I discovered that marriage was not in fact on his agenda. Reasons such as that we were too young and that we should experience more of life before settling down were given, which I found somehow inadequate and quite frankly inexcusable. I in turn felt that we had known each long enough to be sure about our feelings and that we would experience other things together as we went along, and that if he did not feel as I did, then perhaps we should not consider living together either."

As Kate pauses, reliving her memories of those days, Henry, who feels that she has probably reached a critical period in her story, asks simply, "That must have been a very emotional time for you. How on earth did he respond?" By now Kate's eyes have filled with tears, and seeing this Henry adds, "Look I don't mean to upset you, so if you had rather, would you prefer to stop now?"

"I am sorry Henry, but I need someone to hear my story - even my lifelong friend Megan has never heard it in its entirety. I have always felt ashamed somehow, although there is no reason why I should. For some unknown reason I just feel able to talk to you. I trust you and respect your honesty."

Henry, who by this stage is treading uncharted waters, says, "Well why don't I get us another drink to anaesthetise the pain a little?" at which Kate gives a laugh, saying, "Why Henry Long, if I didn't know you were an honourable man I would think that you were trying to get me drunk for some nefarious reason known only to yourself."

Henry smiles in turn and goes to the bar for refills with a strange warm feeling. He likes this attractive woman and enjoys her company very much. He also feels that she is at least partly right when she intimates that he harbours more than thoughts of just friendship.

As he sits down again, Kate continues. "Well, I am sure you must be wondering what happened, because you know that Mike and I were married, but it was not just as straight forward as that. No, when I challenged Mike, his response to my bitter disappointment was to tell me that if I felt that way, then we had best finish our relationship. Hearing this spoken in such cold terms I was absolutely devastated and felt that I had no option than to comply, although I loved him with every fibre of my being, but obviously his feelings for me were not reciprocated in quite the same way.

"So the decision was made, and Mike returned to Bristol while I stayed at home with my parents, who were as always completely supportive; in some ways I suppose they in their wisdom had crystallised the situation between Mike and our relationship.

"However, there it was, and I just had to get on with it and make another life for myself, so I applied for a job as a legal secretary in Dorchester which I managed to get and found really interesting.

"Things went along much as usual for several weeks and although I still could not forget Mike, I was able to lessen the pain slightly by becoming more involved in work and village activities. That was until I began to notice subtle changes in my body. I was suddenly aware that my breasts were becoming tight and swollen and worse, that I was beginning to have bouts of sickness and vomiting.

"Casting my mind back I calculated that it had been probably six to eight weeks since I had my last period, although I this was not an unusual situation in my case because they fluctuated wildly and I had not given it a second thought until then. Eventually I became so afraid of the symptoms that I made an appointment to see my family doctor who quickly confirmed my worst suspicions.

"Apart from living in sin in those days, the other huge social stigma was to have a child out of wedlock, so one way or another I was going to become a big disappointment and embarrassment to my parents, which was my immediate concern. At first I didn't know what to do or where to go. I feared that word of my pregnancy would come out by accident (as it would inevitably very soon).

"After a lot of thought I decided that it would be better if I moved back to Bristol. From university I already knew of a number of houses occupied by students who were always looking for more people to spread the costs of the rent, so I contacted some that I knew and was assured that it would not be a problem.

"The hardest part was telling my parents that I wanted to return to Bristol to live, but I just could not bring myself to tell them the true reason for my sudden change of mind, and left them to assume that I was missing the buzz of city living, that a small village life could not begin compare with. How wrong they were, because Goderston from birth to the present has always been my Alpha and Omega. Even in those periods that I have not lived here it has always been in my thoughts.

"However, I digress, so I duly moved back to Bristol, even managing to get a transfer to another branch of the Dorchester solicitors where I was currently working.

"Several weeks had passed since breaking up with Mike when I again returned to the flat to collect personal items. I had spoken to Mike first to make sure that he would not be there, because the pain of us parting was still a raw ugly wound to me, but when I arrived I found him waiting for me, which I found almost unbearable. I had no intention of telling him of my condition, but before I could say anything he took me completely by surprise by telling me he still loved me and that he was unable to forget me and that he regretted the fact that we had parted. This was the last thing that I expected and my resolve crumbled like wheat before the harvester.

"Before I knew it we were in each other's arms crying and laughing and yes forgiving each other. In between kissing and holding me Mike murmured in my ear, 'Let's get married... soon.'

"Hearing this brought me to my senses with a jolt, and taking a huge breath I told him about my pregnancy. To my utter amazement after several seconds when I could see the news initially written like a cloud across his handsome face, his countenance changed completely and a huge smile enveloped his handsome features. Holding me to him he whispered, 'That settles it then, move in here and we will get married as soon as.'

"My joy was of seismic proportions. Of course I was delighted, but there still lingered a thought at the back of my mind that Mike was willing to get married because he thought it 'the right thing to do', which as far as I was concerned was not enough. I pleaded with him to only consider marrying me provided he loved me and he assured me he did. It was only several years later I realised that it wasn't necessarily the case. Oh, he did love me, but it was not unconditional, nor confined just to me, but I am getting ahead of myself again.

"Anyway to cut a long story short, we soon told both sets of parents, and although they must have been surprised to say the least they were delighted for both of us. I can only suppose that they guessed the reason for the hurried wedding, but this again was not unusual in those days. If a woman became pregnant before marriage, the stigma was not carried forward providing she married before the birth.

"The wedding was held in Goderston, with the reception in the village hall. My parents were as good as their word and supplied the wedding breakfast, my dress and the photographer, and made a financial contribution towards our honeymoon. Whenever I think of the sacrifices they made to make my day a happy one I feel almost ashamed. The whole of the village seemed to be there, and overwhelmed us with their love and generosity. We finally left for our honeymoon to the Channel Islands, stopping over in Poole overnight, before getting on board the Ferry the following morning.

"I won't go into the details any further Henry. Suffice it to say that I was very sick on the sea journey, almost inevitably so, I suppose, when you consider that I was being sick regularly anyway, coupled with the fact that I am not a good sailor. We had a wonderful two weeks on Jersey, a place that I absolutely love. The sheer beauty and isolation of those islands totally captivated me to such an extent that I have returned again and again over the years.

"On returning to Bristol we started married life in the flat and everything was perfect between us. Mike was by this time making great strides in his job, not only designing but also visiting prospective clients to sell them his vision of their products. His skills rapidly became recognised and he was rewarded accordingly, so much so that he was head hunted on a number of occasions, but decided to stay where he was.

"Our first son David was born some six months later, which must have made relatives and friends search for their abacus to establish the date of conception. But no matter, the birth was relatively plain sailing, so to speak, at least as these things go, and our son was born in the Bristol Royal Infirmary to an overwhelming welcome of love and good wishes.

"I had finished work at the solicitors some four weeks before the birth. They all seemed genuinely sorry to see me go as indeed did I them, because I had not only progressed very well with them, including getting involved with conveyance matters which I loved, but also had made a number of firm friends, some of which I keep in contact with to this day.

"We stayed in the flat for another two years and then decided that we would have to find something larger and if possible something of our own. With only one bedroom, space was becoming a nightmare.

"The other factor which would not go away was that by this time Mike was becoming disillusioned at work. His rise through the echelons of the company had been meteoric to say the least. In some ways this was the problem, because he was starting to think that if he had his own studio he could not only make more money, but also he could be more independent. The problem was where to start such a business - leasing costs were prohibitively expensive in Bristol.

"You can probably guess what happened next Henry.

"Of course, Dorchester happened. The costs were only half those of Bristol, and it did not really matter where Mike operated from because potential clients could be found virtually anywhere in Britain, so extensive travelling would inevitably be involved no matter where he was based. After much searching, we found the ideal premises that we were looking for, on a small trading estate on the fringes of Dorchester, some fifteen hundred square feet with some internal partition walls divided up into offices. We retained some of the walls to give us three offices and pulled the rest down to give us a large space suitable for a studio.

"Capital equipment costs were a problem, but this was solved by Mike buying some second hand cabinets and boards from his previous employers. When he first started, it was very much a make do and mend situation, and Mike did everything himself for the first nine months, but it was probably the most exciting time of our lives. I helped to decorate the place and we both worked like slaves to make the business happen.

"We would work non-stop from dawn to dusk and then return home to my parents where we were living until such time as the business made enough money to enable us to buy somewhere to live. Mum and Dad looked after David during the day to give us time to establish ourselves. By this time I was doing the book keeping for Mike so my days were pretty full too.

"When David was just over three and a half I fell pregnant again with Geoffrey, but I continued to work with Mike in the business, until I could no longer go into the office - but even then Mike would bring me the paperwork home, so I managed most of it that way.

"Mike employed another designer after a year, Malcolm Manners, who still works for the company. You will meet him tomorrow. He is an older man whose experience was doing work by hand and eye onto graphic boards, but unfortunately he has been unable to adapt to computers. I am not quite sure if that is strictly the true situation, or because David has been unable to spare the time necessary for him to learn. He certainly appears intelligent and having been in the business all his life, he is a steady hand when David is unable to be in the office.

"The studio went from strength to strength, but it took Mike some three years to build up the business enough to gain a credible portfolio. He started by doing point of sale material for clients, then gradually finding more rewarding work from larger clients. He was making good money, most of which was poured back into the business, and after three years we both felt able to look for a home to buy, and where better than... you've guessed it, Goderston.

Houses rarely come up for sale in Goderston, as you can imagine, but old Mrs Goddard who lived only across the green from my parents died suddenly, leaving her house to her sister, who lived in Wiltshire. Having no use for the house, she put it up for sale.

"Mike and I jumped at the chance - I, obviously because I had lived here virtually all my life, but also Mike had also started to love the place. In any case it was a practical solution as well, because my parents could continue to look after David and then later Geoffrey as well, while Mike and I worked. The village had a primary and nursery school, so they could manage them if necessary until they were eight years old."

"So that's how you came to be living back here then," says Henry. "Your story sounds a triumph of spirit over adversity. I can understand now why you miss Mike so much, after all your experiences."

Taking a sidelong glance at him, Kate continues. "Well on the face of it and what I have told you so far, I suppose you would come to that conclusion, but as you know things aren't always how they appear. The truth is that we did have a wonderful marriage for several years, Mike and I, in particular when times were tough and we were struggling, but things started to change once Mike became more successful. Oh! They were only things of no consequence at first, seemingly anyway.

"But gradually a different Mike began to emerge. Social drinking increased and he became snappy with the boys and indeed with me as well. We started rowing for virtually the first time - up until this time we had never had time to row. Because things were hectic and he was away regularly pitching for business all over the country, I assumed stress was the cause of his irritability.

"But things between us didn't improve. I did my best to make allowances for his attitude and behaviour. We would go out in a foursome sometimes with Megan and Charlie who we had been friendly with for a number of years, but suddenly he would start talking down to them, almost as if he thought that now that he had become relatively successful, they were beneath him.

"I could not let that happen to my friend who had been there for me all her life, so I would take issue with him when his rudeness began to ruin our evenings. These issues would surface when we got home, leading to prolonged rows.

"Gradually Mike would stay away for more and longer periods, and what was even more worrying was that I began to suspect that he was seeing other women. No one thing made me suspicious, rather a series of little things, which like a dripping tap pointed in that direction - sometimes his clothes would smell of perfume, or he would ring me from say a hotel in one town, but when I checked the number it would be from somewhere else nowhere near it. Eventually I tackled him and he denied everything, having excuses for every occasion, but of course his excuses could never be verified, but seizing his chance he tried to turn the tables on me, saying that I didn't trust him and what right had I to check up on him.

"Matters got very heated and by now Mike was so incensed at my effrontery to confront him that unable to contain his temper no longer suddenly verbally lashed out at me saying words to the effect that he had only married me because I was pregnant and that I had trapped him into a loveless marriage.

"My world crumbled around me at that point, because for all his faults I never thought for a moment that he had never loved me, because you see, I had always loved him. He had always been everything to me and the shock of hearing his confession left me bereft and unable to say anything more.

"I think it was my silence that brought home to Mike the enormity of what he had just said, and he tried to backtrack, saying that he didn't mean it and was sorry.

"We patched things up then and for a while things were different between us. Mike was the old Mike that I loved, the man who I had shared endless laughter and obstacles which we had climbed together. Even his drinking was brought under control, although not completely; his travelling became less and we found more time for the children. Suddenly life was good again, and yet I couldn't quite forget what he had said although it was never mentioned between us again.

"We began to socialise again and all seemed well between us for several years. But the business continued to grow and we were at this time employing something like six design staff and two more account directors, as well as me helping with admin. Then in the early nineties there was a recession and businesses started to cut back on our clients promotional, advertising and PR budgets. Work was more difficult to obtain, so Mike had no alternative than to eventually do what they would today call downsize.

"We could no longer afford account directors or some design staff because the market had shrunk, so we were back to the days of a smaller operation and more stress.

"To my dismay I watched Mike slowly reverting to the bad old days. Travel was back for even more regular and longer periods - drink, too, was again part of the mix. I watched, helpless to do anything positive to help as my husband plumbed his own personal depths. Of course I tried to help, pointing out the situation to him, but he was unready or unable to listen.

"My suspicions that he was seeking solace elsewhere eventually surfaced again - the smell of perfume on his clothes and hurried telephone calls at home which were quickly discontinued if I appeared, and worst of all were the sympathetic looks I got from some of the staff when I went to the studio. This time I suffered it all in silence. I no longer wanted to raise the subject with Mike, because I feared that if I did it would lead to a breakdown in our marriage. It was cowardly of me, I know, but you see, as I have said before, I still loved him.

"I suppose to the outside world, Mike must have appeared a considerate, loving husband, and in many ways he was. We didn't row and the boys were unaffected, but I felt wretched more or less until the day Mike was killed in that terrible car crash.

But there was even worse to come, because shortly after the funeral, I received a letter from a woman in Manchester who admitted to being Mike's mistress and went on further to tell me that his death was largely my responsibility. Her deranged thinking had led her to this conclusion for two reasons. The first was Mike was travelling too fast, hurrying to get home, having said that he would be home to me several hours prior to his accident and did not want me to be suspicious. The second was even more blatant and abhorrent to me, because she blamed me for not giving him a divorce, even though he had promised her a future."

THE BUS PASS

As she sits back, finishing her story, Kate says, "So you see Henry, when you asked me where my husband was the other night, the memory of all that came flooding back to me as it always does and the tears you saw were for what might have been, rather than for what actually were."

Looking at her again, Henry notices the distress on Kate's face and leans forward to cover her hand on the table with his own, saying, "Oh, Kate, what a dreadful thing to do. How can writing to you in such a manner have helped either one of you? What did you do - did you reply?"

"No, I never saw the point. I didn't even show the boys, but just kept things to myself and I never heard from her again. In truth I felt ashamed, unclean even, and it was several years before I regained even a small measure of confidence that allowed me to meet people on a regular basis. Megan, of course, was everything that you could wish for in a friend. She was there for me whenever I needed her, and boy did I need her, but she never knew why I was so depressed, she assumed it was because I had lost Mike, when in fact I had lost him years previously.

"So that's my sorry tale Henry - thank you for listening to me. Just talking to you seems to have lifted a weight off my shoulders, you kind man."

The rest of the evening is spent talking of more pleasant subjects. Henry tells Kate more of his life with Isabel and the children. And also the fishing trips which explains how he came to be here.

For her part Kate listens and laughs at his stories. Henry can see that she is recovering her composure and she joins in by telling him little anecdotes about the village and various inhabitants. Henry does not want the evening to end and suddenly realising the fact stole a quick look at his watch. To his dismay it was now eleven o' clock.

Kate has noticed however, and says, "Well, I had best be going, we both have to be up in the morning and I don't want you to be late for your new job," to which Henry replies, "That will never do, that new boss of mine looks a stickler for good timekeeping. By the way, did you bring your car or walk across the common?"

"Oh no, I rarely use my car when I come here; it's not far and not worth risking my driving licence, although I am usually with Megan and Charlie, so it's not a problem."

"In that case let me accompany you to your door, I would never forgive myself if you were to have an accident."

"That's very kind of you Henry. I would be delighted to accept your offer."

So, they leave the pub together and make their way across the common laughing and joking in each other's company. Henry is reminded of the last time he went with Madge and Robert before he left Wycombe, so much so in fact that he tells Kate all about them. She listens enthralled as he tells her about them and explains just how much they mean to him. "I suppose they fill a similar role to me as Megan and Charlie do to you." Kate can understand this and tells him if they were half as good to him as her two friends were to her, then he was much loved.

There is a full moon and a cloudless sky which helps them to see their way, and suddenly looking up Henry notices a number of what appear to be birds silhouetted against the light He is just about to point them out when Kate suddenly exclaims, "Look at the bats Henry, I haven't seen so many for a long time. They have a colony in the church steeple." For a few moments they both watch fascinated to see the bats swooping and diving to catch midges, moths and other flying insect life.

As he looks higher to the heavens Henry is once again amazed to see with perfect clarity, hundreds or even thousands of stars, set out against the dark blue backdrop of the sky. It is always a sight that makes him catch his breath and one that almost always occurs on cloudless nights away from urban areas, something that he always looks for when in the country.

Chatting and trying to tell each other all the things that they suddenly remember, they cross the bridge at the other side of the common and turn left. Within a few short yards Kate stops and says, "Here we are, this is my place, thank you so much for a lovely evening Henry - thank you also for agreeing to help David out for a couple of weeks. I feel so relieved, because I have watched him being dragged down with the weight of it all. I hope we can do something again soon." And reaching up, she kisses him lightly on the mouth, and before he has time to reply she is gone tripping up her front garden path.

Whispering good night, Henry turns round and crosses the bridge.

Making his way back to the Mucky Duck, which he can see from its welcoming, tiny, coloured lights all around the front, he spends a few minutes with Toby and Avril.

After bringing them both a drink Toby says, "Did you agree to help David, Henry?" And when the latter confirms it, he goes on to add, "I am so glad, he is such a lovely person and he deserves all the luck in the world. After his father's death he took the business over, even though he had only just finished his course doing graphic design at college. He has worked hard to make a go of it, while managing to look after his mother at the same time. They are very close as you have probably gathered, so if you help one you are helping both." To which Henry has to agree.

Being extremely tired, Henry makes his excuses and wishing them both good night returns to his room, determined to write up his diary and let his friends and family know the news of his unbelievable day.

CHAPTER 9

The Design Studio

"Hey, have you seen this email from Henry, Penny?" says Mark. "He has now got himself a job in a Design Studio, and there is also a woman somehow involved that he mentions perhaps more often than he should."

"Move over Mark and let me have a look," says Penny. The room is silent for a short while, only interspersed by the sound of Penny whistling through her teeth, before, "Well, would you believe it. The old dog. So this is what happens when you let him out of your sight. He certainly sounds pleased at the prospect, and I am very pleased for him. I was frightened that he would find it difficult to meet people and enjoy his travelling. I would imagine that there can be nothing worse than to visit places on your own and not make social contact with anyone. Good for him, I say.

"Well, if he is going to be working down there for a couple of weeks, I don't think there will be any need for us to visit him just yet. I will just reply and ask him if there is anything that he wants and to congratulate him on passing his interview, which I think he had before this David chap had even seen him."

"Hi Madge, sorry to trouble you at this hour of the morning, but if you have read my email, you will realise that I start work today in the studio that I mentioned, which means that I will need some more of my clothes to be sent down. Don't worry about those that I have with me, because there is a launderette in Dorchester that I can go to in my lunch hour."

Fortunately Henry has managed to catch Madge at home before either of them has left for work.

THE BUS PASS

Listing those items that he wants dispatched, he has a hurried conversation with her, relating a rough outline of his happenings and promises to ring again when he has more time.

As he replaces the phone, he hears the sound of David's car horn from outside the Mucky Duck that is beckoning him back to the land of work after so many years - an unreal feeling, to be sure.

Driving in to Dorchester, David apprises Henry of the work the studio is currently doing and the respective work each designer is handling. After he has spoken at length on these and various other work topics he says, "Look Henry, you are coming in with a fresh eye and a lot of experience. What I would like you to do is evaluate not only the type of work we are handling, but also how we are handling it to see if it could it be managed in other, better ways. If you see something that you think can be improved or done more efficiently, I would like you to tell me. Take your time and then perhaps in a couple of days we can sit down and discuss your findings. What do you say?"

Henry doesn't reply for a few seconds and then says, "That seems very reasonable to me. I think the first thing that I would like to do is be introduced to the designers and discuss individually the work they are doing and any problems they may have."

"Fair enough, that then is what we will do. Luckily I have time to do that today, but tomorrow I am out on the road visiting clients."

As they arrive at the studio Henry takes note of the entrance and car parking spaces at the front of the building. The board over the entrance reads 'Design Solutions Limited' in faded colours of pale and dark blue. Although there is parking, there are no allocations for parking spaces.

Making their way inside they come to a small reception area, in which there are two small cane-back chairs and a coffee table. In one corner is a vending machine for tea and coffee. The lighting consists of two six-foot florescent lights. Because there are is no receptionist, the only way to get attention is to ring the bell, which is placed just inside the entrance door. The door leading to the studio and offices is at the back wall of the reception area, which they pass through.

There are two offices at the front beyond the door which have seen better days, but passing these a further door leads into the studio area. After the dingy reception and office areas, Henry is agreeably surprised to see the studio which is painted in pale pastel colours; together with large windows in walls and in the roof make the area look light and airy. There are six computer stations of which only three are occupied. The computers seem to be various Apple Macs, two or three of which appear to be several years old.

Calling the three designers, David introduces each in turn to Henry, explaining his background and experience and why he has taken him on in the role of temporary studio manager, with the further objective to make constructive recommendations of any changes that he deems necessary to improve performance and quicker turn round of projects.

"Henry is not coming here to put your jobs in jeopardy, not at all. As you know we are up to our gunnels in work and it will do us good, I am sure, for a fresh pair of eyes to look at the way we operate and tell us, if necessary, where we are going wrong. So I will leave you now in Henry's capable hands. Please co-operate with him as much as you can, because doing so is all in our own best interests." As he finishes David turns and leaves, saying over his shoulder, "I have to go to the printers in town this morning and I will see you all again this afternoon."

Henry, left to his own devices, says, "Right, I will come and see you each in turn and we will take it from there." Turning to the woman, he says, "Can we start with you first Adrianne?"

Henry spends the whole morning examining each or their work, finding out how much work in hand there is. From what he can judge, Adrianne's work is competent and with just a few simple suggestions from Henry, it improves significantly. She can obviously see that the improvements give the designs the extra wow factor that clients are looking for, and by the time he has finished with her, any reservations regarding his competence have vanished like mist on a summer's day.

Moving on, Henry next tackles the trainee, John Abbott, whose work and potential impress him. However, never having had anyone to supervise his output, some of John's ideas are extreme, and it is obvious that instructions which have been given to him are not tight enough.

Seeing this determines Henry to sit them all down as soon as possible when looking at all future work, so that they can have brain storming sessions to get the briefs right before work is commenced. He knows from experience that much design time can be wasted and costs incurred by not addressing the brief properly.

Finally Henry meets Malcolm Manners, the older designer, who has seemingly been left behind by the technological revolution of computers. He still does some designs using the old method of drawing them onto graphic boards, which is slow, painstaking and expensive. However, the one big advantage of this as Henry discovers is that he is an excellent designer who has the experience to address the brief correctly, so although he takes more time than the others, his work is usually very accurate and needs no further adjustments.

Henry is drawn to Malcolm; he has a very dry sense of humour, not unlike Henry's own, and he finds him to be very supportive of the company, which is not surprising considering the length of time that he has worked here.

Currently he is designing some notices and banners for the summer fair at Goderston, which he tells Henry is a 'freebie' for Kath, and an annual chore.

Henry spends some time with Malcolm. His biggest concern is why he has never been taught or shown any of the computer packages. When asked, Malcolm assures Henry that he would be prepared for someone to show him, but that it has never been possible because of the volume of work going through the studio.

The morning spent, Henry has a number of things that he feels able to bring to David's attention.

As lunch time approaches, Henry thinks that it would be a good idea to treat them all to a pub lunch, a suggestion that is accepted with alacrity. Their reserves and nervousness thaw as lunch progresses and Henry finds them to be very genuine open people. They all live locally and idolise David who obviously treats them very fairly. When they return to work, David is already in the studio working, and Henry finds himself a station and commences some designs that John is struggling with.

So the afternoon progresses with Henry designing, but also checking on the others work and offering advice where necessary. This continues way after their contracted hours, which Henry learns later from David is their way of acknowledging their debt to him.

After the others have left and before the two of them leave for home, Henry asks David if he can spare a few minutes to discuss his observations for the day. After getting coffees from the vending machine, David says, "OK, what do you think so far Henry?"

"Well there are a number of areas that I think should be looked at in the short term and some others that can be addressed sometime in the near future. Taking things in no particular order, which have occurred I am sure because you have been between a rock and a hard place, I think that we need to go back to basics.

"The first thing to be addressed is that when you have won a brief, that it is brought into the studio and discussed by - for now - myself and the designer who is intended to do the work. By doing this we will ensure that the brief is tighter, and we can then allocate the necessary hours to give us the profit element that we think is appropriate. Doing this will necessitate time sheets being kept by the designers, which for now I can enter onto a spreadsheet to compare budgeted hours.

"Secondly, all of your designers are very competent, but some of your computers are several years old now and the software packages are also pretty ancient. I realise that this would involve some capital expenditure, but it would not be necessary to replace them all straight away, and the cost could be spread by leasing over, say, three years, perhaps on a rolling basis.

"The third element that I think needs to be addressed very soon is Malcolm and the fact that he cannot for one reason or another use computers. Quite frankly David, he is a designer of exceptional ability and it seems crazy to me that his skills are not being utilised. I propose that I investigate the colleges locally to ascertain if there are any short term courses to enable him to learn how they work. In the meantime I have already told him that I will spend time doing just that from tomorrow. I have every confidence that if he can be taught to use the computer that he will be able to take the position of studio manager that you are looking for.

"Also, I think it would be a good idea if you and I can find time to look at the work that has not yet been started, so that it can be scheduled in to the studio. From the little I have seen, I am aware that some are due to be presented to clients very shortly.

"On a different tack, I think that later, once all that I have mentioned has been tackled, that the reception area in particular needs a refurb. You do not have a receptionist and at this stage I don't think that you need or can afford one, but there are a number of things that could improve the company image which need not cost the earth. In particular I think that a dropped illuminated ceiling would get rid of the unsightly neon light tubes, and a one way mirror could be installed onto the wall behind the reception desk. This would have the advantage that anyone entering reception could be seen by the person sitting in the room behind, which at the moment is occupied by Kate. The buzzer could be left, so that if she or someone else is not in that office, then attention would be drawn to whoever requires it in reception. Next, a welcome board could be put, perhaps on the desk.

"Looking to the future, this could be a very useful tool, because it would be very advantageous if the company could get to the stage in which it could invite clients to your offices. This would have several advantages, the biggest one being that any design problems could be addressed on site if necessary, but it would almost be a form of empowerment. By that I mean that if your client comes to you, then you are more in control of things, than if the process is the other way round. If handled correctly it has more chance of leading to a continuous stream of work, and lastly, it would obviate the need for you to visit the client, saving you valuable time.

"Finally, if all this is done, there will be a need for another office stroke boardroom stroke meeting room, where clients can be brought to show presentations of their work, either by PowerPoint, or overhead display or any other media - or even where staff meetings could be held. Neither of the two existing offices is large enough for this purpose, but adequate space could be taken from the studio area, without a detrimental effect.

"I think that's enough to be going on with for now, but once we have got the studio running efficiently, I think we should turn our attention to how the company image presents to the outside world. I am sure that there are times when you have clients visit the studio, but the general appearance of the building and some of the interior areas leave something to be desired. I hope that I have not offended you David, but that is how I see it."

David, who has listened to Henry intensely without saying a word, says thoughtfully, "Henry, I suppose that I am aware of all the things that you have correctly identified, at the back of my mind, but it needed someone to confirm them. I thank you from the bottom of my heart for your constructive recommendations and as far as I am concerned you have carte blanche to introduce them as and when you are able. Obviously let me know any expenditure costs that we need to incur, such as leasing agreements etc. But other than that feel free.

Confidentially Henry, because of the problems that you have so accurately identified, I have to tell you that although I have continued to bring business in to the studio, it has been difficult to make a profit these last few years."

Henry says, "I can well understand that David. The trick is to get the work into the studio a.s.a.p. And then identify the quickest and most effective way to address the brief, to achieve the client's objective. Although I have only been here today, I can see that you are winning loads of work, but are then unable to process it quickly enough through the studio, which reduces your expected profit levels. One other point that I would make is that some of the work that you are taking on is never going to make money, because you are unable to charge the client adequately for the amount of time that it will require to complete the work. Now I am fully aware that this can happen, for example, if a client has supplied you with a considerable amount of work previously, and you knowingly then accept some other work on the basis that it is, if you like, for want of a better description a 'loss leader'. This happens throughout the industry and is an acknowledged fact.

"There are other times however, where work is given as a carrot or incentive, usually by a new client for the first time, with the promise that if they are satisfied with the product, further work will follow. This type of work, in my experience, should be avoided at all costs, because generally the client wants the work done on the cheap and if there is any future work given later, they will expect it to be done at the same discounted rate. Unfortunately David, I think that you have some of this type of work in the studio. Not much, just a handful of jobs, which you will be making a loss on. Better to either not accept the work at all, or insist on the correct price for the job and be prepared to lose the client. Genuine, real clients will pay the price for work well done which will improve their product or image."

David mulls Henry's comments over for a few minutes, before eventually saying, "I can't tell you how excited all this makes me Henry and I'm so glad to have you on board, even if only for a little while. Come on, let's make tracks for home, and I'll buy you a pint in the Mucky Duck. Blimey you have even got me calling it that now."

As they drive back to Goderston, David asks Henry more details of his proposed changes and after he has exhausted himself of any further questions, tells him that he will not be in to work the next day, but his mother will be going there in the morning, so he will arrange for her to pick Henry up, although he will have to find his way back in the evening because Kate only usually works until lunchtime.

After they have drunk their pint in the bar of the Mucky Duck, and as David leaves, he suddenly says, "By the way Henry, thanks for taking them all out to lunch today. An excellent piece of team building," to which Henry nods his acknowledgement.

When he has left Henry has some cheese sandwiches and quietly returns to his room, feeling absolutely exhausted, but with on overwhelming feeling of accomplishment. Finding just enough time to write his diary and email it, he turns out the light, and falls asleep dreaming of Kate, who he suddenly realises he has missed seeing all day.

CHAPTER 10

Malcolm's Mannerisms

"Rob, did you see the email from Henry? I wonder what's going on. I wonder who this Kate is. They certainly seem to be getting on like a house on fire."

Madge had parcelled up the things Henry had asked her for and sent them, but her curiosity was killing her. "Perhaps we could go down in a couple of weeks, just for the weekend and suss it out."

"You are going to lose your nose one of these days, if you continue to keep getting it caught in other people's business," laughs Rob. "Why don't you ask him and if he is OK with it, we can stay at the Mucky Duck."

"Well I think that I'll leave it for now, perhaps it is just a bit premature, but I might ring Penny to see if she is aware of the situation, and if she is, how she feels about it. But I won't mention it if she doesn't."

"Well she obviously does know, because all Henry's emails are addressed to all of us. Perhaps I will reply to this email," says Rob. "I think he may accept the fact that I am asking him details, rather than you."

"Hi Penny, it's Madge. How is everything with you? I just thought that I would ring and have a chat about your dad. He certainly seems to be having a whale of a time. In fact I don't think that I have known him to be so excited for a long time."

"Yes its great isn't it? That's how Mark and I read it. I am so pleased for him. I don't know if the woman - what's her name? Kate is it? - is relevant, or the fact that he feels that he is being useful in a difficult time for David. Mark and I were thinking of going down sometime, but I think that just now is a bit too soon."

"Yes both Rob and I thought that too, perhaps you and I should co-ordinate any future visits so that we don't all turn up at the same time."

"Good idea Madge. I just can't wait to get tonight's epistle. I will speak to you soon."

Henry wakes with a start, and quickly looking at his watch, sees that it is already seven forty-five. After hurriedly washing and dressing he grabs his back pack, filling it with dirty washing, and heads downstairs for breakfast. He just has time for coffee before Kate is at the door, so he rushes out, making a mental note to arrange for an early morning call in future.

Kate greets him with a smile saying, "Wake up slow coach, it's easy to see that you've got out of the daily work routine."

"Too right I have," says Henry. "I really enjoyed yesterday, but I was wacked when I got home last night."

"I have been thinking Henry, if you have no plans for tomorrow, perhaps the two of us could drive into Bridport. Its market day on Saturdays and we could have a browse and maybe get lunch. I was thinking of going anyway." Then with a mischievous glint in her eye she continues, "Or if you prefer, you could use your bus pass and I could meet you there. "

"I will ignore that last bit, but your suggestion sounds really good. Are you sure you don't mind me tagging along?"

"Of course not, I told you the other night that I enjoy your company, so I will take that as a yes. David rang last night and told me all about your suggestions; he was very excited. It seems to have given him a huge boost just to know there is some other person that can take some of the weight off of his shoulders. So I thank you for that Henry, because anyone who can help David is also helping me. It was a joy to hear the enthusiasm in his voice."

"Well, I did very little really, but if it makes you both feel better about things, then I am really pleased, because making you feel better makes me feel better. I only hope that I can live up to something like your expectations."

There is silence for a few minutes until Kate says quite suddenly, "Have you heard Malcolm on the phone yet Henry? He is hilarious. When talking he seems to think of common sayings, but gets them all mixed up. It only seems to happen when he is on the phone, but when it does you have to be there to believe it.

"For example, just the last time I was in, I heard him say to someone, 'Now just hold on two seconds for a minute.' If I didn't know him, I would say that it was some form of dyslexia, but as I say, it only happens during telephone conversations.

"The others are so used to it, that they have started to compile a list, which we have labelled 'Malcolm Mannerisms'. Even the clients have noticed and sometimes when speaking to David or one of the other staff, will tell them so that it can be added to the list. Ask them to show you."

"I will, it sounds hilarious."

On reaching the offices, Henry goes into the studio, where the other three have already started work, while Kate gets them all coffees before returning to her own office.

Before commencing his own design work Henry takes Malcolm to one side and tells him of the discussion that he has had with David about Malcolm learning to use the computer. Malcolm is thrilled at the prospect and tells Henry of a couple of training centres that teach computer skills for the sort of applications that he will need to learn, that could be done either in the evenings or over three days. He says that he has made investigations about doing it on his own behalf, but thinks that because the studio is so busy, David will not be able to let him have the time to release him for a few days.

Henry tells him to find out the cost and if it is not too expensive, he can arrange to do it as soon as possible, and ends up saying, "As far as I am concerned, training of any kind is absolutely imperative if the company and its staff is to develop."

Deciding to strike while the iron is hot, Henry, using David's unused office, begins to trawl through the internet to look for the latest computers.

After his retirement Henry continued to keep up to date with technological developments. He knows from his own experience that Apple Mac computers have the best operating systems and software design packages in the market. Looking at the Apple Mac site he can see that the nearest store to Dorchester is in Bristol. Googling the web he looks to find a training company that support Apple Mac installations, and then prints off the relevant information. The training company runs courses which are mostly based in London or surrounding areas. By taking one of these courses, certificates can be attained, qualifying the trainee for various levels of competence.

However the factor which Henry finds most attractive is that in-house training is another option which could be a better, particularly if a new system is to be installed, because if that is to be the case it is not only Malcolm who will require training, but also all the other designers.

Wondering what steps he should take next, he looks for Kate in her office and explains to her what he has been doing and the information he has found. After some discussion they both realise that if they are to move forward then David and Henry will have to go to Bristol to the Apple Mac store where they can not only see the equipment but discuss how installation and training can be achieved.

It is agreed that Kate will contact David and explain the situation and ask him when he would be available to go to Bristol to evaluate the equipment. Obviously, if Henry is to continue his bus journey in two or three weeks then time is of the essence.

Not being able to do any more at this stage Henry leaves it there and returns to the studio to see Malcolm and tells him to hold fire from looking locally for training and explains why. Kate hurries in to see him close to dinner time and tells him that David can be available on the following Monday if that is OK with Henry, and if so he will pick him up at eight in the morning so they can go directly to Bristol.

Feeling that something significant has been accomplished, Henry is slightly disappointed as Kate explains that she is finished for the day because she is going to meet Gina, David's wife, for some retail therapy. However, as she is leaving she reminds him of their proposed expedition the next morning to Bridport, and his mood lifts again.

He spends the afternoon mostly sitting with Malcolm at a computer terminal showing him the more basic instructions on how to use the software, while in between times he spends time checking the others' work or defining the client's brief for them.

On returning to his office around five o'clock he finds an envelope on his desk in Kate's handwriting. Upon opening it there is a short note from her which reads, 'enclosed is another of Malcolm's Mannerisms. This should brighten your day, love Kate.' He likes the sound of the 'love, Kate', then looks at the entry she has made and can't help laughing. So much so in fact that he has to quickly close the door and hold a handkerchief over his mouth to muffle the sound, because he does not want Malcolm to hear and offend him in any way.

"THAT'S THE BEST I CAN DO AT THIS JUNCTION."

As he reads it again he can just picture the confused look on the client's face at the other end of the telephone, who once he has recovered, will probably add it to his list of Malcolm's Mannerisms.

Seeing this makes Henry determined to earwig on Malcolm's telephone conversations whenever possible and he finds himself for some unknown reason strangely liking Malcolm even more.

Eventually the working day draws to a close, and as they all leave for home, wishing each other best wishes for the coming weekend, Henry reflects that it has been a reasonable start, but there is so much more that is needed before the studio can be considered to be an efficient and financially viable operation. He also recognises that the time scale of three weeks maximum to get all the things done to achieve both David's objectives is unrealistic. Surprisingly this revelation Henry finds comforting as he analyses his emotions and realises that Kate is the reason.

Since Isabel died he has never considered, or felt the need for anyone else to take her place in his life. Until now! As he confronts the way he feels about Kate for the first time, he is forced to face that which he has so far chosen to keep buried deep in his psyche.

All these thoughts and emotions are whirling round and round in his head as he catches the bus back to Goderston, arriving at the pub at half past six, leaving him just enough time to have a change of clothes before going downstairs to get a meal and prepare for the coming skittles match.

As he is eating his meal, Toby comes over and says, "By the way, a parcel arrived for you to day. I have put it in your room."

"That's great, thanks a lot, those will be more of my clothes from Madge. By the way, remind me what time the skittles match starts."

"Just after eight, so you had best be here on time if you want a ringside seat."

Returning to his room, he writes up his diary so far for the day, thinking that he will complete it and send emails at the end of the evening after the match. He finds himself looking forward to the skittles match as he goes to the bar and orders a pint. Suddenly from behind him he hears a voice say, "You'm best make that three pints Henry," and spinning round he is delighted to see Bill, Joe and Fred 'King' Cole from the Jack The Lad.

"Hello boys, it's good to see you. Three pints please Toby. Where are the others?"

"Well, Sparky, Tosser and Derek are coming in another car, but I am not sure if they will all make it. Derek was complaining of a sore back last night. Still we will see how we go."

As Bill finishes, Toby comes over and much friendly ribaldry ensues. Henry is introduced to the Mucky Duck team, some of whom he has already met during the week. He feels happy and comforted to be among them all, most of whom he has only known for just a few days, and when he contemplates why, the answer comes back, because they include him and make him feel valued.

Suddenly thinking of Malcolm's list of mannerisms, he relates those which he can remember to the gathered throng which causes gales of laughter, although he is careful to mention that they had occurred while he was working several years previously. He would be mortified if somehow it had got back to Malcolm that he was the source of his betrayal.

One of the members of the Mucky Duck team, Graham Way, known more commonly as Milky, then relates a happening that he witnessed that week. He works in Dorchester in a fairly large engineering shop and the men take it in turns in the morning break to go to the local shops for any food and refreshments that any of them might need. On this particular morning one of the men asked the person whose turn it was to get supplies if he would get him twenty Benson and Hedges cigarettes.

"OK," he replies. And then as an afterthought, "What if they haven't got any?"

"Then just get me anything."

"So what happened?" asks Joe, leaving Graham the perfect opportunity for the punchline.

"He brought him back a pork pie."

Just then Sparky and Tosser arrive, apologising for Derek's absence.

The skittles match starts without further ado, the alley being in a long building at the back of the pub, which has a bar, so that it is not necessary for any of the players to leave.

Henry takes up his place as an observer, but is quickly co-opted to put the wooden pins up as they are knocked down. He thinks that this is the least that he can do, because there has been talk of him playing for one or other of the teams, but he would have felt torn if that happened, being seen to support one side while being detrimental to the second. Anyway his ability at skittles is non-existent and suggested that by playing for one side he would in fact be assisting the second.

In fact putting up the skittles is hard work, as both sides know full well, and Henry is soon sweating and drinking profusely, to stop dehydrating. Or at least that is his excuse.

At half time Toby and Vera bring out an array of sandwiches, dips and crisps for both teams, which are consumed ravenously. It is pretty obvious to Henry that playing is just as exhausting as picking up skittles.

The game ends with the Mucky Duck victorious, evidently reversing the previous time that the two teams have played. After consuming more beer and much back slapping all around, the evening draws to a close. Promising that he will look them up again in the not too distant future, Henry says farewell to Bill and the boys from the Jack the Lad, before making his way a little unsteadily to his room.

Realising that he will not have time in the morning before Kate picks him up, he finishes his diary for the day before falling rapidly into a deep sleep.

CHAPTER 11

Bridport and Eggardon Hill

Waking surprisingly early, Henry rises and looks out of his window where he sees to his amazement a vixen and four cubs cavorting at the edge of the pond. The vixen appears to be in excellent condition with a superb glossy red coat that shows no evidence of mange, suggesting that she is probably no more than two years old.

Henry sits entranced watching them and loses all sense of time, before suddenly coming out of his reverie. By this time he is running late, so then with a rush he showers, shaves and dresses hurriedly before going down to breakfast.

To his chagrin, Kate is already here, and greets him with, "Come on lazy bones, I am just ordering my breakfast. Tell me what you want and we can eat together." Doing as he is told, they then sit down and while consuming eggs, bacon, sausage and beans Henry relates his experiences of the previous night to her, which makes her laugh uproariously.

Henry loves to make her laugh. He loves to see how her eyes crinkle and the pupils suddenly darken to a midnight blue, almost black even, hypnotic in their intensity. Her lovely mouth forms a large 'O' as she collapses with laughter, and tries to catch her breath, begging, "No more Henry or I will choke on my meal in a minute." Here is a woman who was born to laugh thinks Henry, but who, as he knows from her own account, has not had the opportunity to do so for a long time.

On cue they set off for Bridport in Kate's car at nine o'clock, and to Henry's delight, just before reaching Dorchester she turns right onto the A37 for a short distance before turning left onto the A356. Passing through Maiden Newton, a long straggling village which appears hardly to have changed for many hundreds of years, they continue for another two miles or so, until much to Henry's amazement, Kath turns left onto a small B-road signposted to Toller Porcorum.

He can contain himself no longer, and says, "Do you always come this way? I only ask because this is the route that we used to come when we were on our way to Toller Porcorum for our 'fishing trips'."

"No, I would normally go by the A35 along the coast road, but after you told me about the times you stayed at Toller the other night, I thought that perhaps you could show me some of the places you visited."

By now they are travelling down a small lane which is only wide enough for one vehicle with passing places every two hundred yards or so. To make driving conditions more difficult there are hedges both sides which are considerably higher than the car, so visibility is only possible as far as the next bend, which is never far away.

But Henry doesn't mind. He is back in his old stomping ground. He loves Dorset, particularly west Dorset, with a passion. He loves its ever changing scenery, its hidden little villages, the grandeur of its hills and valleys, its sheer beauty, something that he has not found in quite the same way anywhere else. In fact once the main roads are left behind, the countryside seems to become almost mystical. This, to Henry, is a magical, hidden land which is missed by so many people travelling through on their way to holidays in Devon and Cornwall. Indeed, Henry thinks of it in terms of Brigadoon, the mythical village in Scotland that only appears once every hundred years.

He feels he could live here in this beautiful county in complete isolation away from the trials and tribulations of the outside world.

Eventually they reach Toller Porcorum and Henry points out the self-catering accommodation, a converted school that the four fishermen had used for so many years as a base to go for walks, or from which they could visit other local areas of interest.

There are innumerable walks that they did over the years. Among those which Henry remembered with most affection is the old railway line that runs from Bridport to Maiden Newton which had been closed sometime in the nineteen sixties, a casualty of

Beeching's Axe era. The line runs through idyllic countryside, one minute passing through green verdant valleys, the next high on hill ridges overlooking the patchwork quilt of fields laid out either side. When walking here, Henry always wished that he could have been born in an earlier era so that he could have travelled along it, and have seen it at the time when it was functional.

Another walk was from the top of Eggardon Hill following it down through a narrow country lane which has steep banks either side, until eventually a wooded area was reached and the lane became covered for the most part by a green canopy of trees, with the sun filtering through the dappled leaves, always leaving Henry intoxicated by his surroundings. The lane then climbed steeply for another mile or so, until suddenly rounding a bend, the walkers were rewarded with the sight of The Three Horseshoes pub at Powerstock, a place whose reputation for its cuisine and ale was renowned for miles around.

The area was a haven for animals of all descriptions, and they would regularly see deer, badgers and foxes. Additionally, the locals assured them there were wild boar to be found if you knew where to look, which were hunted for their meat occasionally. Not only that but they could direct those who were considered to be able to keep a secret, to where the meat could be bought surreptitiously.

Often as an alternative to walking, the four of them would make excursions to places like Bridport, West Bay or Lyme Regis, where they would meander, taking in the local hostelries or cafes. Food and drink constituted very necessary ingredients on the fishing trips.

If the weather was inclement making walking difficult or impossible they would buy provisions and stay indoors, amusing themselves playing cards or doing crosswords. Food and drink would usually consist of suitable dietary items, the purpose of which was cancelled out by other totally catastrophic dietary items which would consist of things like corned beef, pork pie, sausages and cheese, all accompanied by flagons of the local ale. Over the years they had discovered a small local bakery which made the most fantastic lardy cakes which they invariably visited and got to know the owners very well, who welcomed them every year to such an extent that they were able to discuss their families with them, and although neither the bakers nor the fishermen got to meet any of them, nevertheless, they could each relate the progress of their children and wives. This continued for a number of years, commencing when most of their children were very young, through to secondary school, grammar, and in a couple of instances, university. Henry often reflected on the fact that the bakers and the fishermen all got to know about each other's families, without ever having met them.

At other times they would play cards for money, although invariably at the end of each trip the difference between winning and losing was no more than several pounds.

Sometimes they would go out for a meal in the evening, but this meant travelling several miles, because the local pub in the village had been closed for many years. This meant that Alan, whose car they had travelled down in, was always the driver and so was unable to have alcohol, so they preferred not to go, although they did arrange for a taxi on some occasions.

Henry relates all this as to Kate as they continue their pilgrimage, leaving her with a broad smile on her face as she realises how much the trips must have meant to him, and intersperses his conversation with questions of her own asking for more details.

Passing through Toller they travel on, until they reach the top of Eggardon Hill and Henry says excitedly, "Pull over there to that stopping place." Here there are a few spaces just off the road to allow travellers to get out of their cars to look at one of the most stunning views, anywhere in the world as far as Henry is concerned.

As they both get out of the car, Kate laughingly says, "I thought that you might like to do this Henry. It was partly the reason that I decided to come this way. I can see that it has the same effect on you as it does me." For several minutes they stand taking in the wonderful vista laid out before them, while Kate questions quietly to herself how much both she and Henry love this wonderful area and why it is that they have never bumped into each other before, because she has always used the Mucky Duck as has Henry fairly regularly on his 'fishing trips' although not for long periods.

By now the sun has burned off most of the early morning mist away, leaving a transparent, mistral fog shimmering across the valley below Eggardon Hill. This falls steeply away immediately in front of them. At the bottom and on the steep hillsides sheep graze all around them and several small farmsteads can be seen lying snugly in the valley. Deer can be seen roaming in the fields below them, and in the far distance the hills can be seen covered in turquoise covered mantles. Panning left the sea can be seen in the distance somewhere between Bridport and Lyme Regis.

Henry has stood at this very spot many times over the years, a place that he loves not only for its sheer beauty, but also for the memories it evokes in him.

He can feel the emotion welling up inside him now, almost choking him, and Kate looks at him and sees at a glance the turmoil he is going through. Gently putting her arm around his waist she says, "It's so beautiful Henry. I can see just how much this place means to you. It has the same effect on me too. Come on let's get going before we become all melancholy."

Henry is brought back to the present with a jolt as he feels the pressure of her arm around him which he finds comforting. Looking down he sees her head tilted up at him, and bending, he takes her face in his hands and kisses her slowly and luxuriously. Kate responds instantly, her lips slightly parted, and to his own amazement, Henry finds his body telling him things that he thought it had forgotten. Realising that there are a number of other people also enjoying the scenery to which they have both become oblivious, they part and return to the car. It seems to Henry like the most natural thing for him to do. Like breathing, or like a child taking its first step... inevitable.

There is silence between them as they continue to follow the course of Eggardon Hill downwards until they meander through the village of Uploders before joining the A35 from where they continued for two miles into Bridport.

It is now nearly ten o clock, and as it is market day the little town is buzzing with activity. They park in the municipal car park in South Street then make their way back again on foot back up the street looking at the many stalls with their vast array and variety of wares.

Henry finds a stall selling watercolour paints, and paper and accessories which he buys, intending to spend time as he travels to sketch local sceneries. As they pass another stall selling second hand items, Kate notices a watercolour landscape of Bridport which she takes a fancy to, saying to Henry, "I like that, the colours would go just right in my lounge." Without further ado, Henry buys it and gives it to her, brushing aside her protests by saying, "But I want to buy it for you, just look on it as a small gift from me in gratitude for your company, which means so very much to me."

So they progress down the market with Henry buying some clothes to augment the few he already has at the Mucky Duck.

Entering West Street they reach the Bull Hotel at eleven o'clock and decide to have coffees and cream cakes, all the while talking ten to the dozen, as if everything they want to tell each other needs to be told at this very moment. They talk animatedly of their families and friends, seeming to want to fill the voids in their lives that have been empty for so long. Kate is so alive and her happiness so infectious that Henry inevitably catches her mood, and he is hardly able to believe his luck that he is in this beautiful woman's company.

Feeling more relaxed with each other, they continue to peruse the market stalls, before they decide that they need to find somewhere to have lunch. Having done all they want to do in Bridport, Henry suggests that they go either to The Three Horseshoes at Powerstock or The Crown at Uploders. Kate counters and suggests The Acorn at Evershot, which Henry quickly agrees to. It is miles from their route home, but time is of no consequence to them because they are enjoying each other's company, so their consensus is, "What the hell."

The food is wonderful as they are both very well aware. Henry stayed here with Isabel, Rob and Madge several years before, something that he thinks it will be indelicate to mention at this stage.

Suddenly, during a rare lull in conversation Kate says to Henry, "I have been feeling very guilty that you are working for David (due mostly to my interfering with your plans) and that it is costing you good money to stay at the pub. I have given the matter a lot of thought and come to the conclusion which is very simple. You can stay with me. I have plenty of room, a four-bedroom house which I rattle around in on my own. You can always contribute to the cost of food if you feel that you want to, but if not it, is of no matter. What do you say?"

Henry is taken slightly aback and is thoughtful for a few seconds before replying. "Well, the first thing that occurs to me is what your friends and acquaintances locally will think, seeing a man suddenly moving in, and assuming all sorts of things to your detriment. I would never forgive myself were that to happen."

"Oh good heavens Henry, this is the twenty-first century, they won't see me as a scarlet woman, neither will they condemn. You have only got to look at the youngsters today to see how they choose to live, and nobody bats an eye. Anyway, it would all be in their minds. I am not suggesting anything immoral - although if it happens, I would certainly not be sorry. I also realise that your memories of Isabel are still fresh in your mind and that you are, in addition, trying to come to terms with the thought of moving to Australia.

"However, that said, I think that it would be good for both of us. We both enjoy each other's company. When I think how well we have got on today I realise just how much. I really like you Henry, and I think that it will solve some of your problems for now. When you are ready to move on we can part as good friends who have shown a little solace to one another."

Although Henry is delighted at the thought of moving in with Kate, he is still very concerned with her image in the community, and realises that if there were to be any vitriol shown towards them, it will fall mostly on to Kate after he moves on. He explains this to her, but she is adamant that the people around her and who care for her will be glad for her, so after much head shaking and thought, Henry agrees, but suggests that he does not do so until the next Monday, which is the day that he has told Toby he would staying until at the Mucky Duck.

Having finished lunch, and rather than stay and have coffee, Kate suggests that in that case they return to her house at Goderston where she can make them tea and show Henry the accommodation.

After strolling arm in arm through picturesque Evershot, which Henry finds both the most natural thing in the world, while at the same time slightly disconcerting, they return to the car and quickly join the A37 back towards Dorchester and home.

Letting them in, Kate shows Henry round her house, which is cottage style and deceptively large. Downstairs there is a small hall, leading to a reasonably good size lounge, with walls covered in pastel green. The floor is of polished solid wood oak floor boards, on which Kate has put a large plain deep pile Axminster rug in a beautiful light green colour which accentuates the burnished gold reflection of the floor boards, and complements the wall colour. The carpet covers the central area of the floor, around which there are two, cottage style sofas, which Henry recognises as Ercol, a company that was based in High Wycombe when he was growing up. The ceiling is quite low, but extra light is obtained from up-lighters being placed strategically around the walls with reading lamps at each end of the sofas. The lounge is at the front of the house, in which there is a small bay window. Around the inside of the bay window there is a continuous window seat. On the other outside wall there are patio doors, leading through to a conservatory which is on the side of the cottage, perfectly placed, facing north-south, to get all available sun, particularly after midday.

Kate has used her very considerable design skills to furnish the conservatory with two bamboo sofas, for which she has bought soft furnishing fillings and then made covers herself in lovely, hard wearing, pale cream material. There are two small matching bamboo glass topped coffee tables, while the floor is covered with large granite floor slabs which she has obtained from a public house in the next village when it closed. In the middle of the floor Kate has put a beautiful afghan-style rug, which is composed of mainly a warm background – cream - with various motifs of soft blues and red running through it. All along the longest wall is a bookcase from wall to ceiling which is filled with books of every description, which Kate explains she has built up over the years, from which she can select any to suit any particular mood she is in. Finally there are a number of table and reading lamps strategically placed for those occasions when Kate is seeking quiet solace or contemplation. Henry says that he thinks that the room is magical, and can see that this is a room that he too can find both soothing and relaxing.

Next to the lounge is a dining room, with a mahogany table and chairs, set for four place settings, which Kate explains can be extended to eight places. The room is painted in a dark dramatic red, which enhances the rich coloured mahogany furniture. Moving on, the next room is a small study cum computer room, which Kate explains she uses if she has to bring work home from the studio.

At the back of the dining room is a large spacious kitchen, which is furnished, again cottage style, with a large wooden dresser along one wall, chintz curtains and pine cupboards, and a butler sink, all of which gave the space a feeling of age. In the middle of the room is a large pine table and chairs, which Kate says she uses for breakfast, elevenses and lunch times when she is on her own, or when friends drop round unexpectedly.

However the equipment allows no such allegiance to age. There is a large Aga double oven which looks as if it is powered by oil, and a dishwasher, which Henry finds reassuring.

The kitchen is obviously the result of a more recent extension, which covers most of the back of the house, the remaining space being taken up by a utility room and a toilet and shower room.

Upstairs there are four bedrooms, the first of which is the master en-suite bedroom which has windows on two sides, making it light and spacious. Kate uses this as her bedroom and Henry can see exactly why.

There are three other good size bedrooms, two of which are doubles. Finally there is a communal separate shower and toilet.

The whole house had been decorated in pastel colours. This has the benefit of making the areas appear light and spacious. The master bedroom and the kitchen, which are both formed from the extension area, face south, which means that they receive more sun than any other part of the house.

The back garden is huge and climbs up the hill. Kate has turned a large part of it to lawn, with a children's swing and slide and other toys. Further back past the lawn area, Kate keeps a vegetable garden, in which Henry can see cabbages, runner bean sticks and rows of potatoes.

It is all kept in apple pie order, and Henry wonders idly how Kate manages to cope with it, because he knows from experience that gardening is a hard taskmaster and a time consuming one too.

Kate sees his look of surprise, and laughs, saying, "No, I don't do it all Henry, sometimes David gives me a hand and sometimes old Matt Higgins does some of the hard digging jobs, if I ask him nicely - and pay him, of course."

THE BUS PASS

Everywhere Henry looks both in the house and garden he can recognise Kate's influential touch.

By now the afternoon has moved on, and looking at the clock Kate says with a start "Look at the time, its half past five already. Just give me a couple of minutes and I will make some tea and sandwiches."

Henry though insists in helping, saying, "If I am going to be living here, then its best if I find out where everything is kept."

As they consume their tea Kate expands on the bedroom Henry might find the most suitable and encourages him to make use of the study where he can use his laptop, or to do any watercolour painting that he might want.

"I hope that you and I can be together some evenings. We can either watch TV or play cards, or best of all, just sit and talk."

"That sounds like heaven to me."

And so the evening progresses until Henry says, "Why don't we go for a walk? It's still a lovely evening, and you can show me your village." Kate is more than happy to do this, so they go out and meander through the confines of the village, ending up at the woods that run behind the pub. It is a magical time of day. The sun is starting to go down, a large fiery ball, the light from it filtering its way through the leaves on the trees making them look as if they are on fire.

As the light starts to fade they are held spellbound as the nocturnal creatures start to make their appearance. First a beautiful barn owl looking for field mice to feed its ever hungry young. As it spreads its huge wings the wonderful colours of gold, brown and white on its plumage is shown at its most advantageous, although Henry still finds it difficult to reconcile this beautiful bird with the predatory killer of small mammals that he knows it to be. But then he reflects that this is a silly stance to take, because it is nature in its basic form.

Dusk is now beginning to make their progress almost impossible, but just as they turn to retrace their steps Henry sees a movement out of the corner of his eye, and signalling to Kate for silence he pulls her to him so that she too can see the badger family, the young of which are gambolling with each other, while the parents snuffle around the tree roots looking for edible insects and roots. They stand watching, totally transfixed and absorbed, until Henry suddenly sneezes and almost immediately they are alone again.

Hastily they return to the common and Henry walks Kate back to her house for a nightcap. As they sit together on the sofa, Kate asks him whether he will be going to watch the tug of war and the cricket match on the common the next day, because she and some of the other women will be preparing the afternoon teas.

"I certainly am. I wouldn't miss it for the world," replies Henry, to which Kate, looking mischievously mysterious, responds, "Well, Goderston will definitely win the tug of war." to which Henry replies, "Now how do you know that?"

Kate rubs the side of her nose in a conspiratorial manner, before saying, "You just wait and see if I am not right my lad, they have won it for the last few years."

Despite asking why, Henry can get no further information from her, leaving him determined to find out, because from what she has just said, he gathers that there is something about the tug of war that is not strictly above board.

Just as Henry is thinking of leaving, Kate asks him if he would like to tell her about Isabel, hoping in some small way that if he tells her it might begin to cauterise his mental wounds. But she also emphasises at the same time that if he does not yet feel ready to speak about it, then that is OK too.

Although Henry feels able to tell her of Isabel's suffering now, he is at a loss to know just where to start, and so for a few minutes he gathers his thoughts together, before he begins…

CHAPTER 12
Isabel

Isabel was first diagnosed with breast cancer in her left breast in March 2002, as a result of her normal three year check-up. Prior to this she had not had any symptoms that she recognised. There were no lumps or changes in her breast or her nipples or swellings or lumps in her armpit. Neither had she felt any pain in her breast.

To say then that it was a shock would be an understatement of unimaginable proportions, although when she received the letter from the clinic asking her to return for another mammogram she did not feel too worried, because as it explained, of those women who had to return for further investigation, some ninety-five per cent were given the all clear.

However, this was not to be the case for Isabel. As her specialist explained, some women were called back because their mammograms or ultrasound showed evidence of lumps which proved to be merely cysts after further examination.

Unfortunately in Isabel's case the lump did not fit into this category and so the specialist decided that investigative surgery would be necessary to establish if the lump was benign rather than a cancerous tumour.

This then was the period that both Isabel and Henry's concerns became more focussed, although they both tried to hide their fears from each other, which was made worse because of all the various tests necessary to establish if the lump was cancerous, a fact that was established eventually by a biopsy.

It was then necessary to establish the type and stage of the tumour before any decision could be taken in respect of appropriate treatment.

This all took two months or so, before it was established that Isabel had a Stage 2A tumour and the decision was made after lengthy discussions with the specialist that Isabel should have surgery for a tumour excision followed by a course of drugs.

To both of their relief, the surgery was carried out within two weeks of the decision being taken.

After several weeks and further tests the specialist told them that there was no indication of any further signs of cancer and that Isabel would need to have further three month check-ups just to keep a watching brief.

The anti-climax to all the stress that they had endured came in the form of a complete state of exhaustion once they relaxed, followed quickly by a need to enjoy Isabel's escape from a potential death sentence. This took the form of a holiday to Australia to see Richard and Janet, who were delighted to see them.

A visit to Cairns along the Coastal Highway, then a boat trip to The Great Barrier Reef, followed by flights to Alice Springs and Ayres Rock, as well as more local events, like the climb to the top of the Sydney Harbour Bridge, a visit to the Sydney Opera House and eating out at some of the wonderful fish restaurants, were all enjoyed with a voracious appetite, as if to compensate for time lost (or even, as it eventually transpired, time won).

They returned to England buoyed up from their visit to see their son and grandchildren, but after some months, the euphoria dissipated, and much worse, on her second three monthly check-up, Isabel was distraught to find that she had come out of remission as the cancer reappeared. This time it was necessary to carry out more invasive surgery as her specialist recommended that a radical mastectomy be carried out as soon as possible, but that the decision must be Isabel's.

They returned home that night and wrestled with this huge decision. They both knew there was no guarantee that if she had the operation Isabel would be cured. All they knew for certain was that statistics told them that there was a better survival rate if she had the operation, as opposed to doing nothing.

For the first time in their married lives, Isabel's resolve was tested as she broke down in tears.

THE BUS PASS

Although Henry felt the same way, he tried to be constructive, pointing out the positives from having surgery, the success rates and the possibility of breast reconstruction, to encourage and motivate her, because he knew that to fight this dreaded disease, Isabel would need all the resolve and will power that she could muster. Isabel, being Isabel, responded magnificently to Henry's urgings, although he knew that she would have reached this conclusion on her own eventually. She was no quitter as she had demonstrated all their married lives.

In fact this was the watershed. Although the remainder of her life was to be spent in increasing pain and medical degradation, she would never again dissolve into tears caused by fear. She overcame fear, not pain and suffering which were twin unavoidable evils, but she seemed to reconcile the need to fight the tangible symptoms of the disease and ignore the nagging doubts at the back of her mind.

After the operation Henry found that it was not possible for him to continue working, neither indeed did he want to, preferring to be with Isabel at home acting as her carer.

With medication combined with surgery, Isabel's condition improved for a while, and Henry found this period to be among the best of times of their marriage. They talked endlessly, as if trying to tell each other of things that they needed each other to know, if…

It was also a time of doing things together. They went to London to museums, to Covent Garden, to Shakespeare's Globe Theatre. To Dorset and Devon for long weekends. Things that they had talked about, but had never found the time for. They enjoyed life and each other while they could, with words left unspoken that it might not always be this way. Adversity brought out the best of them as a couple. In some strange way they seemed to discover or find each other for the first time, as if all that had gone previously had been somehow inadequate or incomplete, a mere forerunner that had been necessary to have had to enable them to face their today.

Both children were concerned for Isabel. Penny visited often, sometimes staying for weekends with her family to give Henry some respite, which she continued to do until Isabel lost her battle. Richard telephoned several times a week, feeling helpless on the other side of the world, but Isabel soothed him with words of love and placated him as she always had done from the time when he had been a little boy.

But her condition worsened after a few months until the day that she was told that it had become terminal and that her life expectancy was about six months. By this time, it had become apparent to both of them. She was tired nearly all the time, and this combined with her weight loss meant that she was unable and unwilling to walk anywhere, or indeed go anywhere in a car.

A course of chemotherapy seemed only to add to her discomfort, resulting in the loss of her once precious shoulder length hair.

The death sentence, once issued, was enacted over a few short months, right in front of Henry's eyes as he watched her deteriorate. Diaphine was the only palliative that relieved her pain, but sometimes she chose not to use it, to enable her to stay alert and able to talk, mostly to comfort Henry. Her willpower was amazing and Henry drew strength from her resolve to fight this awful, all-consuming disease.

A few short months before her death, Isabel became unable to raise herself from her bed, so Henry would sit with her and hold her hand, whether she was awake or asleep, and all the time quietly talking and telling her of his love for her. He would only leave her to make meals. Madge called in daily to see them, to clean and tidy the house and bring any groceries that they needed. Seeing her gave Isabel great pleasure.

To give Henry some relief, hospice care was arranged for two days a week. Isabel gained great solace from these visits. Although she was not very religious, the quiet surroundings and wonderful staff left her with an inner peace.

There was no such relief for Henry who, although physically and mentally exhausted, missed her dreadfully when she was not at home.

The end, when it came was sudden and seemed to take everybody by surprise, both medical professionals and family alike.

It was during one of her Hospice periods, on a Tuesday evening. Penny, Mark and Henry were at her bedside. She had stopped taking pain relief for several hours because she knew they were coming to see her, and she wanted to be coherent.

After conversing for a while, during which they all tried to make her laugh, she suddenly said, "You have been my life and I want you to know that I love you all more than you will ever realise," and later, just as they were leaving, she whispered to Henry, "I have had enough now Henry, I don't want to go on anymore," and slumped back onto her pillow. She never regained consciousness from that moment. Henry received a call from the hospice during the night informing him that she had lost her last fight in the battle against her virulent adversary.

Henry was distraught with grief, torn between conflicting feelings of thankfulness, blind anger and helplessness, with not a little guilt thrown in for good measure.

Thankful, because he was relieved for Isabel that her suffering had come to an end, but guilt also because part of him didn't want her to leave him, and the thought of his selfishness made his feeling of guilt even worse. On one hand he said a silent prayer to her maker for ending her suffering, while at the same time he railed against an intransigent God who had taken her from him.

Both the children were bulwarks in Henry's hour of need. As soon as Richard heard he arranged a flight and was with them within twenty-four hours. Penny in her usual unflappable manner took control of the immediate funeral arrangements.

While she had been alive, the reality of Isabel dying never really impacted on Henry. Up until then she was still there after incredible suffering, and a small part of him thought – no, hoped - that some kind of miracle might happen. Perhaps a wonder drug would be found, or Isabel would go into remission for some unknown reason. Henry clung to these false idols until the end, which made her death even harder to bear.

To all intents and purposes Henry's grieving was borne with little sign of the suffering that he felt to the outside world. This he managed to do mainly for the children's sake, while inside he was distraught with grief.

The funeral and cremation came and went with Henry on automatic pilot. It seemed, to him at least, that he was not in his own body, but rather standing back looking at events that were happening to someone else entirely.

This feeling changed when everybody returned to the house for the traditional funeral wake. Here, Henry was amazed to discover how many friends and colleagues Isabel had. There were several women who had gone to school with her and had kept in touch, as well as a number of people that she had worked with over the years and who wanted to offer their condolences, some of whom Henry was only vaguely aware of.

Several days after the funeral, once Penny and Richard had left (not before the latter had insisted on him visiting him in Australia soon) Henry's resistance crumbled. He no longer had a reason to fight his feelings of loss and loneliness and he became gripped by a depression of overwhelming proportions, which eventually Rob and Madge recognised and made him see his doctor who gave him medication.

It was this, combined with Rob and Madge's and his children's staunch support, that, without even realising it, brought Henry reluctantly back from the abyss. For he had lost the will to live, wanting just to be together with his beloved Isabel once more.

Thus Henry slowly recovered, but such terminology is relative. It would be more appropriate to say that part of Henry recovered, but a large part of him had shrivelled up and was already with Isabel in her other sanctuary.

All this Henry related to Kate, who could see from his expression and the tears that he was unable to hide as he spoke, that his loss and pain were just as real now as they were on the day Isabel had died. Wishing to relieve his distress, Kate gathered him in her arms and soothed him silently. Knowing nothing she could say could ease his suffering.

They stood for several minutes in deep contemplation, like statues, until Henry, recovering his composure, pulled away, saying, "I am so sorry that you saw me like that. I thought when you asked about Isabel that I would be able to handle it, but obviously I couldn't."

Kate, putting her fingers to his lips, says, "You don't have to apologise to me Henry. Don't forget that I have had my own share of suffering. Anyway, I am not at all surprised that your memories of Isabel are as clear today as they were at the time. I think that I would have thought less of you if they weren't."

"It's the pain and suffering that still awakens the feelings in me. The happy times I can remember with gratitude and thanks, but her suffering will haunt me until the day that I die. I would not wish to see any other person having to go through that ordeal."

"Well, thank you for telling me Henry. We will not talk about it again, unless you want to. It helps me to understand you a little more." *And like and respect you even more*, thinks Kate.

CHAPTER 13

Netherton Rivalry

"How are you doing Henry, me old mate, or to be more accurate, you seem to be doing very well according to your daily missives. What's going on?" asks Rob on the phone the following Sunday morning.

"Well, nothing like you are imagining," laughs Henry, delighted to be speaking to his old friend once more. "Kate is just a very good friend whose company I am enjoying very much." he says, understating his emotions just a tad.

"Listen mate, Madge and I have been talking about you, and the upshot is that we would like to come and see you next weekend, if that's OK with you. Goderston seems to have evolved into Shangri La as far as you are concerned, and in any case Madge has never been there, so I think we could kill two birds with one stone, so to speak, and perhaps you could introduce us to Kate. Or better still, what if we travelled down on Friday afternoon and we could all get together in the evening at the Mucky Duck."

"That would be fantastic. I will book a table for the four of us for dinner. Tell Madge not to worry about bringing any of my clothes, because I can get them done in Dorchester. I am pretty sure that the weekend will be OK with Kate, but if not the three of us can still get together and chew the fat. It will be really great to see you. I am looking forward to it already."

Hanging up, Henry suddenly realises how busy his life has recently become, and the thought pleases him beyond measure.

He had spoken with Toby and Avril when he got back the previous evening, and explained the situation about moving in with Kate, which, to his silent amazement, they accepted without a murmur, making no criticisms whatsoever. Toby merely observed, smiling, in a hushed voice, so that no one else could hear, "Well good luck to you both. I have never seen a couple more suited than you and Kate."

After a lazy breakfast, he turns his mind to thoughts of the day's coming activities. According to Kate, the tug of war usually took place at noon, the purpose of which was so that afterwards the two teams could have a light lunch together in the pub, to be ready to start the cricket match at three o'clock sharp.

Returning to his room, he catches up with his diary, before despatching emails. Then, realising that he still has a couple of hours to kill, he considers calling on Kate, but then rejects the idea, not wanting to stop her preparations for the afternoon. But the thought that has come so quickly and easily into his mind brings him up with a start, making him question not only his motives, but also his assumptions. Yes, of course he would like to see her, but why should he assume that she would want to see him, just because they both get on well together, and because she has offered him accommodation? Based on these two facts, it doesn't necessarily follow that she wants a more meaningful relationship.

No, he must not jump to any conclusions in his relationship with Kate, a fact that he realises he has so quickly come to take for granted, and he resolves that he will take things a little more slowly, rather than jeopardise it, and risk losing all.

As an alternative, he decides to go for a walk to explore the village some more, and perhaps get a coffee, if there is a shop available. Once outside, Henry is struck once again with the sheer beauty of this magical little village. It is a warm bright summer's day, although the media has ominously forecast showers for the area later in the day.

Strolling round the common, Henry goes into the post office and store which not only sells newspapers, but also has several tables with umbrellas outside, where cakes, coffee and tea can be served. Seizing the opportunity, he buys a Sunday paper and a latte and sits outside intermittently reading while watching the world go by.

About half past eleven there is a sudden flurry of activity as a number of cars pull up outside the pub, with people, mostly men, spilling out, talking loudly and animatedly. From their appearance

Henry assumes that these are the combatants for the tug of war/cricket match from Netherton. Most of them move off to the village hall, presumably to dump their equipment and change into attire appropriate for the first of the day's challenges.

Almost simultaneously a number of the Goderston team seem to appear, as if from nowhere, some of whom Henry recognises from the quiz and skittles nights.

Within a very short space of time both teams gather outside the Mucky Duck for the purpose Henry supposes of contesting the tug of war. But, to Henry's amazement, Toby suddenly flings open the door of the bar, which makes everyone who knows the procedure rush forward to quench their thirsts on Toby's Dorset ales. Quickly realising his mistake, Henry closes his paper and hurries round, not to miss such an opportunity.

He finally reaches the bar after fighting his way through the assembled throng, who all seem to be nine feet tall and weigh eighteen stone of solid muscle. Not only that but they bear the appearance of men with clear blue eyes, and complexions that say that they probably work the land for a living.

These then are the Netherton contingent, and Henry finds them to be both very affable and full of fun. There is much talk of Netherton winning the tug of war this time, but Henry hears by listening to the conversation, that Goderston has won for the last few years, which he finds hard to believe when he compares the physical attributes of the two sides. Not that Goderston are seven stone weaklings, but they do not obviously appear as fit, or indeed as young as the Netherton team. There are a few paunches among the home team and Henry knows from conversations with a number of them during the week that most of them have sedentary jobs in Dorchester, so he thinks it most unlikely that Goderston will win again this year.

After half an hour of dedicated drinking, the two teams feel that they have loosened up sufficiently to contest the match. It is to be the best of three pulls, with one team standing on the pub side of the pond, while the other stood opposite them across the pond on the common.

Goderston, being the winners from the previous year has the choice of where to pull from, and they choose the side which is on the road outside the pub, leaving Netherton on the opposite side just on the common, with the rope being extended across the pond. Even this Henry finds a little strange, because it appears to give the Netherton team a slight edge, as they should be able to get a better grip with their feet on the soft grass of the green. Then both teams take the strain for the first pull and the contest is on.

For several minutes nothing seems to happen, the rope hardly moving one way or the other. Surprisingly the Netherton team seem to be expending more energy with sinews taught and breathing more heavily as the contest goes on. Goderston by comparison seem relatively fresh and appear to have contained Netherton's initial aggression, something that is confirmed after some fifteen minutes when Toby, who is team captain of Goderston, suddenly gives the order to pull.

The result is astounding, as Netherton are pulled slowly but surely, and then with gathering speed into the pond. Although he has witnessed it, Henry can hardly credit what he has seen, and is convinced that it is a fluke.

After both teams have taken a break before the second pull, they resume on opposite sides of the pond, but this time Goderston are on the common side. Given the result of the previous pull, Henry thinks that this side will favour Goderston even more, but to his astonishment, Netherton pull their opponent effortlessly into the pond within a couple of minutes. Henry thinks that the first successful pull must have taken more out of the Goderston team than their opponents, and he fears for his Goderston comrades, as both teams once again take up their positions, this time reverting to those of the first pull.

Once again Henry has a feeling of déjà vu, as he watches Netherton pull with all their might and muscle, while Goderston seem once again to relax and hold their opponents in a statutory position for some twenty minutes.

As he watches Henry suddenly catches sight of Kate out of the corner of his eye, and she appears to be laughing uncontrollably. She is standing on the path in front of the Mucky Duck, quite near the place where Goderston are pulling from, and as she sees him she beckons him over. As he reaches her, being mystified by the cause of her laughter, he asks her the reason for her merriment.

Still being unable to speak for laughing she draws her to him and points her arm discreetly at the Goderston anchor-man so that no one else can see.

Looking at the place indicated by her arm, everything is suddenly crystallised in Henry's mind. The reason why an apparently inferior body of men can beat a much younger and fitter team year after year is revealed as he looks at the rope at the rear of the last man, which is wrapped around the lamppost opposite the pub, meaning that no matter how hard they pull, Netherton are never going to win, unless they pull the lamppost into the pond as well as the Goderston team.

He remembers with clarity Kate's comments that Goderston will win and understands why she was so sure.

As Henry and Kate stand together, Toby, giving the appearance of an elephant who has been tickled by a bee, suddenly gives the order to pull once more. Netherton, who are unequal to the task of pulling the Goderston team *and* the lamppost into the pond, succumb like lava flowing down a mountain, and are unceremoniously pulled into the pond once again, much to the onlookers' joy.

Taking Kate to one side Henry asks her laughingly how long Goderston have won the tug of war, to which she replies, "Oh, about eight years, ever since they put up the lamppost. It's funny, but before that, they never won at all."

After they have all recovered, everyone retires once again to the pub, where Toby has laid on free booze for a limited period. This gesture is quickly rewarded as most people take the opportunity to order one of Toby's Sunday roast lunches, Kate and Henry among them. As they eat Henry relates the discussion he had with Rob and Madge on the telephone earlier. He has already told Kate about them the previous day and just what they all mean to him.

Although he has only known her for a short while, Henry thinks that Kate, being a very sociable person, will like to meet his very good friends, and is not in the least surprised when she suddenly claps her hands with delight and says, "Oh how wonderful, of course I would love to meet them. Perhaps we could all go out together over the weekend, or they could come to mine for a meal either Saturday or Sunday - you will already be there by then anyway. It sounds fantastic."

Henry is relieved and happy by her obvious enthusiasm and they spend the next half hour trying to decide what to do and where to go the next weekend.

At half past one, Kate tells him that she needs to go to the village hall to start preparing the teas and sandwiches ready for the cricket match. There will be a number of women, wives of players mostly, who take on this task. Kate has been doing it since her father, who died years before, had played, and she has somehow never got out of the habit.

Promising that he will join her later, Kate leaves and Henry quickly gets caught up in the camaraderie and banter between the Netherton and Goderston teams and their supporters. Although normally he would only drink one or two pints of beer at any one time, Henry has by now had three or four, which is only a fraction that some of the players have 'put down their necks' and he is at a loss to know how they will be able to see the ball, let alone hit it.

The beer has a soporific effect on Henry, who thinks retreat the better part of valour, and goes back to his room for forty winks. Waking suitably refreshed, and hearing cheering and clapping outside his window, he looks at his watch which is now showing three o'clock. As he opens his window he sees that the team batting is Netherton and he hurries downstairs with a rug from his room to find space to sit on the boundary. The weather is still warm although dark clouds are beginning to appear in the distance and a breeze is blowing in small gusts across the ground.

Finding space under a large oak tree Henry lays himself down to watch the titanic contest taking place in front of him. The match is a limited fifty overs contest and Netherton's score is a respectable seventy five for one at this moment, the first wicket having fallen at eighteen, so the two incumbent batsmen have put on fifty seven runs and look totally in control, putting pressure on Goderston who need to do something urgently to break the partnership.

The Goderston captain, Toby, for it was he again who seemed to fulfil the role in whatever Goderston were taking part, suddenly puts himself on to bowl, taking off his two 'quickie' fast bowlers who by now are blowing like humpback whales rising from the deep. Toby is a bowler of guile and experience. He is not fast, neither indeed does he spin the ball, but rather bowls a good line and length, enough to subdue batsmen, until from frustration of not scoring they make a rash stroke and he then has them in his pocket.

This is the case now, as he bowls a nagging length to the Netherton number two batsman, the first four of which he can do nothing with, only to block or leave alone. The fifth ball however is a humdinger, a full toss that the batsman is too late to bring his bat down on and his castle is decimated, the bails flying back as far as the wicket keeper. Seventy five for two quickly became seventy five for three as Toby bowls another full toss to the batsman who has not had time to acclimatise himself and is bowled comprehensively.

The score creeps up to one hundred and sixteen for three, Toby subduing the batsman his end, but the medium pace bowlers not being able to produce either a good length or to swing the ball enough to cause the batsmen any difficulties at the other end.

The condition of the two teams is now there for all to see, and unlike the tug of war the match the Netherton team's superior fitness will not be denied. Not that they are necessarily better cricketers than Goderston, in fact one or two of their batsmen look positively cumbersome when wielding a bat. No, the truth of the matter is that when they manage to connect with the ball, it is almost inevitable that runs, usually a four or a six will be scored, by virtue of the fact that the members of the Goderston team can only make token gestures in chasing the ball. In fact chasing is too strong a word, because most of their efforts seem to be more of a gentle stroll.

If Goderston is to win this game, it is going to need a lot more guile. Toby is their one true player who has this gift in spades, but he can't do it on his own. Seeming to realise this fact at the same time, Toby suddenly calls up one of the local lads, who cannot be more than seventeen years of age. Sitting close to the scorekeeper, a lady of some fifty years, wearing a straw hat, sunglasses and a cherubic expression, Henry notes that the new bowler's name is Alfie Bradford.

There is a huddle between Toby, Alfie and the wicket keeper for several minutes to discuss new field placings, the result of which is to have three fielders in the slip position, who stand right back in a semicircle in line with the wicket keeper. The lad is obviously a fast bowler of limited experience, because if Toby was aware that Alfie is any good, he would have used him much earlier. So this is a gamble on Toby's part, to say the least.

There is a hush around the boundary from the teams' supporters as Alfie runs in to bowl off of a very long run. As he reaches the crease he leaps in the air, releasing the ball from a great height, which pitches half way down the wicket and rises at an astonishing speed hitting the edge of the batsman's bat, which he has only time to raise in defence to avoid his body getting hit. The ball takes a diversion from the bat, and still travelling at almost the speed of light reaches the boundary before any of the fielders have time to realise where it has gone.

Although Alfie's bowling has given runs away, Henry is quick to realise that the lad's bowling is of a high order, and that if he can keep bowling consistently, further wickets will inevitably fall.

Even as this thought goes through Henry's mind, Alfie comes thundering in once more, and this time he gets everything right. The ball leaves his hand in a blur, and this time the batsman never even moves until the sound of timber falling behind him brings him back to reality.

Three more balls follow from Alfie, none of which the next batsman sees, which either sail past his off stump or hits his bat, which he has left in front of the stumps as a token gesture.

The final ball of the over however is the coup de grace, finding its way under the bat and almost setting light to the grass before taking out middle stump.

One hundred and twenty for five was now much more respectable from Goderston's view point.

Netherton's scoring rate has now reduced quite considerably, from almost six runs an over to four.

In the very next over, by the use of very astute bowling, Toby manages to get the next wicket by cleverly flighting the ball, encouraging the batsman to come forward outside his crease and take an agricultural swing, which, manages only to hit fresh air, as the ball suddenly dips and runs through to the wicket keeper, who has no problem in whipping off the bails for a well-crafted stumping.

The next man in however, is the Netherton captain, and although only a relatively low order batsman, he is strong and has fast reflexes, and probably knows that he is not likely to last long, so he has obviously decided to make as many runs as he can as quickly as possible. Playing to his strengths he comes out boldly to Toby's slower bowling and manages to cart his next two deliveries for six. On the last ball of the over he manages to steal a run, making sure that he will face Alfie's' next over.

Alfie steams in again, but to his consternation, just as he reaches the last few strides of his run up, he notices the batsman advancing down the pitch to meet him. Unable to slow down, Alfie decides to shorten the length of his delivery, which hits the pitch about ten yards from the bowlers hand with such force that the ball rises steeply and continues on rising even higher, way above the batsman's outstretched bat. Amazingly the ball continues to soar, way over the stumps, until it reaches the wicket keeper, who makes a despairing lunge to reach it, but it is still travelling way over his head, only to bounce once before clattering the sight screen.

This then is the pattern for the remainder of the over. Alfie coming in at top speed, only to be met by the batsman moving forward, resulting in a short ball delivery with similar consequences to the first. The batsman is a wily old bird however, and although he moves forward to every delivery, sometimes, at the last moment he will step back into his crease. This confuses Alfie to such an extent that he cannot find the rhythm of his earlier over, which is what the batsman has hoped to achieve. Thirteen runs are leaked in this over and Toby has to consider whether Alfie should be replaced.

But fortunes finally change in Toby's next over as he manages to take a further two wickets, the first caught and bowled and the second by bowling the batsman who is trying to turn the ball to square leg missing the ball, which is a full toss hurled at devastating speed. On the last ball of the over the batsman manages to squeeze a single, meaning that he, rather than his captain, will be facing Alfie's next over.

Thinking that he will emulate his captain's methods in the previous over. The batsman advances down the wicket, but overdoes it to such an extent that Alfie, noticing it in plenty of time, delivers a much slower ball which flies over his head and hits the wicket right at the top of the bails.

One hundred and forty seven for nine after thirty three overs. Everything still to play for.

Toby's bowling is still tight, but the last two batsmen, by dint of good running of singles and doubles manage to scrape another six runs before the bowler comprehensively bowls the last man.

One hundred and fifty three all out. After thirty four overs, and a run rate of four and a half per over.

It is now a quarter past four and with rain clouds gathering overhead it is time for tea!

Remembering his promise to Kate, Henry hurries away to the village hall to find her, reaching it a few minutes before the players. To his utter dismay all the preparations for tea have already been made, the trestle tables set out with huge plates of sandwiches and salads of every description, with fruit cakes, made by old Mrs Bluett to follow.

Looking for Kate, Henry spots her talking to Megan, and on reaching them is met by the latter with a twinkle in her eye, who says, "You are in trouble. We were expecting you to help make the sandwiches," only for Kate to say laughingly, "Don't worry, you can help us do the teas and wipe up afterwards."

Henry apologises and touches his forelock, saying, "So sorry Ma'am, it won't happen again Ma'am."

This makes Kate laugh and Megan to say in what must have originally been her stern schoolmistress voice, "I want you to write five hundred times, I will not be late again - and let that be a lesson to you."

Before any more can be said, both teams come hurriedly clumping in, taking places at the tables as if it is musical chairs and that the last person to in will be left standing without a chair. There is a lot of backslapping and bonhomie between them, both sides telling the other what might have been, rather than what actually happened. They all know each other well. Some of them even work together in Dorchester and other local places. This is a regular fixture, which in more recent years has usually been won by

Netherton. The rivalry between the teams is competitive, but always fair and friendly (unlike the tug of war).

As they finish their tea and make their way back onto the pitch the gathering clouds threaten to bring an early finish to the proceedings. If this is to happen, the result will definitely favour the visiting team, because their run rate for the first fifteen overs of their innings was at the very respectable rate of six runs per over.

Goderston are not renowned for their batting, but will obviously have to push on at a fair rate in order to win the match. The danger of this strategy is that if they do, and they lose a few early wickets, then there is a distinct possibility that their innings might collapse completely.

Henry however is not around to see the worst of it as he is heavily involved in the village hall, drying dishes, dismantling tables and cleaning up generally. By the time he makes his way back to sit under the tree the rot has set in and Goderston's score is a measly forty two for six after twelve over's, or only some three and a half runs per over.

Pushing the score along has indeed proved fatal for Goderston, but Henry thinks to himself, in all fairness they had little choice given the very real possibility of imminent rain. Even as he thinks it, the heavens open, and rain starts to cascade down in great sheets of grey, driven by gusting winds. The players come off the field and back into the village hall, but it is apparent to everyone after another forty minutes that the rain has settled in for the evening.

The captains, having agreed the fact, leave Toby to declare Netherton the winners, because of their better run rate, so the status quo of the last few years is maintained. He then formally invites everyone back to the Mucky Duck, which is now open for business.

Megan, Charlie and Kate join Henry and they all enter the pub which is heaving by now. Pushing his way to the bar, Henry orders a round of drinks, congratulating the cricketers on his way, who look set for a long session.

As he returns to them, Megan says, "Charlie and I applaud your decision to stay with Kate from tomorrow Henry. It makes sense in terms both for company and financial reasons." And then with her schoolmistress face on again, "But I have to tell you, if you try to take advantage of my very best friend, you will have me to answer to."

Tugging his forelock once again he replies, "Oh no, not another five hundred lines Miss," at which they all laugh, with Kate having the temerity to blush.

After they have consumed another round of drinks brought by Charlie, Megan invites Kate and Henry back to finish the evening with them.

It is still raining heavily as they make their way as couples under two large golf umbrellas across the common, with Charlie doing an impersonation of Gene Kelly, by clicking his feet together while jumping in the air, and at the same time giving his rendition of 'Singing in the Rain' which Kate, not wishing to be outdone, quickly joins in with. Holding the umbrella out in front of her she begins singing, "What a glorious feeling, I'm happy again."

Unfortunately, Henry is not quite so happy, being left with no umbrella and getting drenched with every passing second, which makes Kate giggle uncontrollably. Seizing his chance Henry closes in and as she stands helpless with laughter, he tickles her mercilessly around the waist, causing her to drop the umbrella.

However, before he can pick it up, Megan swoops down and retrieves it, then runs off with Charlie, leaving Henry and Kate stranded in the rain.

As they stand together, their arms around each other, with rain cascading down their faces, Kate says unromantically, "Please no more tickling Henry or I will wee myself."

So they make their way, following Megan and Charlie still singing in the rain, until in what seems no time, Megan and Charlie's house is reached, which Henry realises is only three along from Kate's. Theirs is a similar property to Kate's, but is smaller, not having had the benefit of an extension, which Kate's so obviously has.

Both Kate and Henry are so wet by this time that Megan quickly finds some replacement clothes for them to change into.

Luckily Charlie's clothes fit Henry pretty well, both being of similar build, but Megan is both taller and of a larger frame than Kate, and despite trying on various items, even the smallest makes her look waiflike, which Henry finds most endearing, leaving him wanting to hold and comfort this vulnerable, childlike woman, with her appealing bright blue eyes and 'lost' appearance.

As the evening draws into night they all talk on, obviously enjoying each other's company. The three locals explain to Henry about some of the characters in the village, while he in turn tells them of his life in High Wycombe.

Suddenly the subject of parents is brought up, with Kate explaining how supportive her parents had been to her, to which Megan and Charlie add similar comments of their own parents.

Henry in turn tells them of his own parents' unconditional love for him, which he had grown up in the shadow of. As he finishes a smile then comes over his countenance and he goes on to say, "They were both really lovely to me and were everything a child growing in those days could want, but they both had their own little foibles, which made me love them even more. For example, my father seemed to be accident prone all his life. To give you an illustration I can remember one occasion when I was about ten years old.

"It was just a few days before Christmas this particular year and my father, who served in the St John's Ambulance brigade on a part time basis, was due to play Father Christmas at an old people's charity party. This was something that he had done previously for a number of years and which he enjoyed very much. However this year was to be different, because as he went between the tables passing out gifts he passed one particular old pensioner who was just lighting his pipe.

"If he had been in any other place or at any other time, Dad would have been OK. Unfortunately the match lighting the pipe caught light to his beard, which was made from cotton wool and before he realised that anything was wrong the fire had spread to the rest of his costume.

"Other St. John's members were quickly on hand and lay him on the floor, and rolled him over to extinguish the fire. It was all over in a couple of minutes, but Dad was burned quite badly on his neck, arms and hands. If I remember right, Dad was off work for several months after that.

THE BUS PASS

"The worst thing about it was that my mother and I were both at home, totally unaware of this until much later on that evening, when the back door suddenly flew open and my father stepped into the room swathed in bandages from head to waist. Christmas was a very subdued affair that year, I can assure you. Accident prone, you see."

"Oh, how awful," says Kate, and then goes on. "Did your father play Father Christmas again after that?"

"Oh yes he didn't let a little thing like that put him off, but I can also remember many years later, my mother and he had been into High Wycombe shopping and decided to travel by bus. The type of bus they caught was one of the old style double deckers with an open end at the rear of the bus for people to disembark. There was one solitary upright support which allowed people a way of getting on the bus, but it was also used as a means to get off, sometimes before the vehicle had come to a full stop.

"This was done by facing the way the bus was going, and as it slowed down it was possible to alight, although strictly speaking it was not allowed, and there were notices up to inform passengers of just this situation. However, it was a common method and reasonably safe, provided it was done in the manner I have described.

"Unfortunately, my father, God bless him, in his wisdom, decided it would be quicker to get off while holding the rail, but facing towards the back of the bus.

"This had an immediate and tragic consequence as he stepped off, his motion carrying him at the exact opposite to that of the bus, the result being that he fell heavily into the road, his face and shoulder taking most of the impact. Mum picked him up and dusted him down, but he bore the marks of his injuries for many weeks after - accident prone again."

Although they sympathised with Henry, they can also see the funny side of his father's brushes with the afterlife, and laughing, Megan asks if there were any more anecdotes that he can recall.

"Well, there was one other that I am aware of. It was on the occasion that we were visiting my favourite uncle, just up the road in Stokenchurch. This particular uncle was my father's brother and was very successful in his line of business, which was contract landscape gardening. By this I don't mean your average back garden, but rather contracts for borough councils for schools and playgrounds etc. Just to give you a better idea I can remember the time when he got the contract to re-turf the old Wembley stadium, and he also did the same thing for several first division football clubs.

"I only tell you this so that you can appreciate that he was a wealthy man and he had the trappings that went with this kudos. Anyway, back to the plot. On this particular lovely summer day there were about twenty people gathered at his mansion, mostly sat round the outdoor pool under parasols, drinking cocktails.

"My father, who preferred to be active, decided to take my uncle's dog for a walk. Big mistake! The dog in question, an Irish Wolfhound, was about three years old and stood nearly five feet tall, and unlike some breeds had the weight appropriate to it size. I kid you not, it was big enough to take a saddle and go for a ride. Having said all that, the dog was the most amiable and gentle of creatures under normal circumstances.

"Unknown to my father, the dog must not have wanted to go for a walk at this particular time (he hardly ever got taken for walks, but was left to wander the several acres that went with the property on his own).

"So accordingly, as soon as my father slipped the lead over his head, Max the Irish Wolfhound took off at a great gallop, his speed not lessened at all by my father trying to hold him back. Anyway, the dog was much heavier and strongly built than my father, who unfortunately had wrapped the lead round his hand several times to get a better grip.

"This did my father no good at all as the dog plunged forward at a great rate of knots pulling my erstwhile parent with him. The path that Max chose to go went between the edge of the pool and the changing rooms.

"In this area there were a number of people, some on sun beds and some sitting at tables, who were suddenly confronted by an apparition of a half dog, half horse rushing towards them towing what must have appeared to them to be a rag doll.

"In the blink of an eye, one of my elderly aunt and her teenaged daughter were swept inelegantly into the pool, before Max changed direction and veered towards the wall, behind which were the changing rooms. My father, having no other option, was dragged along the side of the wall, making contact at those points that coincided with the motion of the dog.

"Up until this point, Dad had managed to stay upright, but suddenly unable to maintain the same momentum as the dog, tripped, and was dragged bodily along the ground until Max went one way round a bench, while my father went the other, which brought the proceedings to a final halt, both of them facing one another over the seat.

"This incident again left my father with the scars of battle. His face and body all down his right side had abrasions from his contact with the wall, leaving him bleeding profusely.

"However, Max the dog remained entirely unscathed and unconcerned at all the fuss going on around him, while my elderly aunt was fished out of the pool, and while wringing out her clothes as best she could, she was heard muttering to anyone who would listen that she would probably catch pneumonia. Her daughter by contrast was fortunately wearing a swimming costume and to her credit saw the funny side of the incident.

"The funniest thing in a non-funny situation was that my father's glasses, although broken, remained on his face, but were twisted, making him look like Benny Hill."

Henry finishes his oration, saying, "I hope that I have now demonstrated conclusively that my father was accident prone, while my mother had traits of an entirely different nature."

Henry's audience by now are laughing openly until Charlie exclaims, "Don't stop now Henry, what the heck did your mother do that could by any stretch of the imagination be compared to your father's sorry tales?"

"Well, she was not so much accident prone as scatty, I suppose. The classic situation that always sticks in my mind was the time that they were travelling somewhere in their car in the late fifties. The car was a 1934 Morris Ten, which they had bought for the princely sum of some thirty pounds and was their pride and joy. So much so in fact that my mother made curtains for the back window and would sit in the back wrapped in a woollen travel rug, looking for all the world like a lady of distinction, which she was of course as far as I was concerned.

"This was before any motorways had been built, and roads generally were pretty much as they had been since the war. Suddenly my mother said to my father, 'Shall we stop at that village that was signposted just back there?' My father, who was unaware that they had passed a village, replied, 'Which village was that then?' only to hear her say, 'You know, that one back there, called Lay-By.'

"She was never allowed to forget this little episode until the day she died.

"Another other incident that springs to mind was when, again they were travelling in their car and my father, whose bladder was bursting, decided to stop on a road that had trees on either side for a natural break (toilet facilities at that time were not as profuse as they are today).

"Finding a suitable place to relieve himself he was no sooner there than he could hear my mother crying out desperately, 'Tom, Tom, come quickly.'

"Hastily adjusting his dress he ran back to the car, only to see it moving gently away from him, down the sloping road with my mother still inside. Only by running hard was he able to catch it, when he discovered to his chagrin that he had forgotten to apply the handbrake, leaving my mother cowering in the back of the car, a quivering jelly."

Henry is pleased to hear his audience laugh, feeling a distinct need for Kate in particular to approve, and, looking across at her, can see her smiling broadly at him, her face flushed and those beautiful clear blue eyes sparkling.

Before he can say any more, Charlie interrupts, saying, "My parents, or at least my mother in particular, used to do some funny things, mostly centred on the fact that by the time that she was in her late fifties she had to wear dentures. This was pretty much the case for a large proportion of the population at that time, dentistry not being as good as it is today.

"Now although she had to wear them for all practical purposes, for example she would never leave the house before fitting them, but while she was indoors, and if there were no visitors, she would take them out and put them in a glass of denture cleanser which she would place carefully on the mantel above the fire.

"She worked hard all her life and by the time evening came around she was only too happy to sit by the fire and watch television, which had a soporific effect on her and before she knew it she would be fast asleep, at which point the fun started.

"Quite often we would receive telephone calls, my father being in the fire brigade and very often on call in the event of an emergency. When this happened, my mother would sit up with a start, and being only half awake would stand and put her teeth in before making a rush to the front door, thinking in her muddled state that the doorbell had rung.

"She would quite often get there and open it before realising that the ringing still continued, even though there was no one at the door.

"Amazingly this situation could unfold in exactly the opposite way. The front door would ring, mother would sit up with a startled look on her face, then reach for her trusty dentures, before answering the phone.

"As onlookers we were never sure which way round it would occur. It wasn't even as if we waited for her to perform, because at the sound of either the phone or the doorbell she would spring to attention, and before any of us could react she would go into her little ritual. However, it was always very obvious to us onlookers that although she looked in control, she was in fact almost sleepwalking."

As Charlie finishes, the others laugh and nod, perhaps at memories of their own families, and vie with each other for the privilege of telling their own stories.

So the evening continues, until Henry suddenly remembers that he has a journey to Bristol the next day with David, so he makes his apologies and prepares to leave, whereupon Kate also rises saying, "You can see me to my door if you would please Henry, it's getting quite dark outside now."

"Why of course," replies her gallant escort, wanting time alone with her, if only for a few brief moments.

As they bid their farewells to Charlie and Megan, promising each other that they will all meet the next Tuesday for the pub quiz, Kate links her arm through Henry's for the short walk to her door.

"Well, I have had a lovely day Kate. I haven't watched a local cricket match for a long time. Many years ago I used to play weekend cricket which I enjoyed very much and seeing it again today brought the memories flooding back. Your friends Charlie and Megan are great company. I can see how and why you have remained friends for so many years. However, most of all I have enjoyed your company."

"Why thank you, kind sir," says Kate, whose head is by now nestling against Henry's arm as they walk. "I have had a wonderful time too."

For the first time for several years Henry feels a wonderful, warm sense of wellbeing, peace almost, flooding through him, and realises with a start that for the first time since she died, his thoughts of his beloved Isabel are becoming slightly blurred.

Reaching Kate's house they talk for a further few minutes about the logistics of Henry's move from the Mucky Duck. When he will bring his clothes the following day and other desultory things which at any other time Henry would have found boring, but which he finds strangely exciting tonight in Kate's company.

Eventually he draws her to him and kisses her goodnight to which she responds positively, which in turn leads to a passionate embrace, neither wanting it to end.

Once again Henry begins to experience a stirring of emotions which he has almost forgotten existed, and both fearing and hoping where it will lead at the same time, draws breathlessly away, saying, "I had best say goodnight Kate, I don't think that I will be able to trust myself if I stay any longer," to which she replies, "Whenever you feel ready, Henry, you must know by now that I am an open door as far as you are concerned. Anyway, I trust you even if you don't trust yourself."

"Thank you Kate, you must know that I feel the same way about you, let's continue this conversation after I move in. In the meantime I will say goodnight. I wouldn't want your son to go to the pub to pick me up in the morning only to find me here with his mother."

Laughing out loud, Kate replies, "Good point, I think that I ought to speak to him first. I will call him and explain as soon as I go indoors."

"Tomorrow then," replies Henry, giving her a quick hug.

CHAPTER 14
Monday, 26 May

"Morning Henry you old lothario," greets David as he arrives to pick Henry up for their trip to Bristol. "I trust your intentions towards my mother are strictly honourable." and then in a conspiratorial fashion, while holding Henry by his left arm, "I think that we need to discuss your future prospects to see if you can keep her in the manner to which she is accustomed," before finishing by saying, "No seriously, I think it's a great idea, I wish that I had thought of it first."

Henry is stunned by David's candour and not a little nonplussed as how to reply. But thinking quickly he says, "Well David, I just saw her as one of the perks of the job."

And David, laughing, replies, "Almost like a company car then," before adding, "I just can't wait to tell her of your reaction," leaving Henry to say, "I was only joking, you won't really tell her will you?" which only makes David laugh all the more.

As they continue on their way the conversation turns to the subject in hand with Henry explaining the benefits of new computer equipment and software.

David however has no need to be persuaded further because once Henry raised the subject the previous week he immediately recognised that which had been staring him in the face for some considerable time, but due to a combination of factors had been unable to quite bring into focus previously.

On reaching Bristol they quickly find the Apple Store and are introduced to an account Manager, Alec Bampton, who is expecting them. After David explains their operation and the equipment they are currently using, Alec, feigning horror at the age of it (a situation common to all sales personnel as a standard response) suggests several options that they can follow. After some discussion, it is agreed that the best option available is a modular one, where various computers can be added to as the business grows. So it is agreed to lease a power unit that is larger than is required for their current levels of work, which will serve five terminals initially, but to which further terminals could be added as work demands grow.

As Henry is already aware, current software for Apple computers is vastly superior to that which they are currently using and will not only giving them a faster operation, but also give other areas of expertise, including a costing system from which actual profits can be measured against forecast.

This is something that they do not have at present, but once implemented it could enable them to tell not only those jobs that are financially viable, but even more importantly those which are operating at a loss.

Alec then puts them in touch with a local company that arranges the installation of Apple systems and also staff training, after assuring them that their current workloads can be down loaded to the new system, so ensuring that no data will be lost.

David, anxious to get the new system up and running before Henry continues his bus travel odyssey, asks Alec how soon the IT can be installed and training commenced. To his delight Alec tells him that installation could probably be done at the beginning of the following week, providing the necessary finance lease agreements are accepted, but that it would have to be agreed along with staff training by the company who were franchised to them.

By now the time is getting on to midday, and Alec suggests that he take them to lunch while he arranges for the paper work to be prepared by an administrator. Before leaving, he arranges an appointment for them to visit the company who will be responsible for installation and training for later that afternoon. Henry and David are happy to accept, as it will save them a further journey to Bristol, but more importantly it will hurry the process along.

Leaving the Apple offices, Alec drives to the Bordeaux Quay restaurant which is on the Bristol Harbour side.

Henry can remember visiting Bristol many years before and cannot help but recognise the progress the city has made since then. It is now a cosmopolitan, bustling city which offers visitors so much more in terms of retail outlets and the selection of eating places, many offering haute cuisine menus. The place that Alec has brought them to is just such an establishment and while they all enjoy a sumptuous meal Henry cannot help reflecting the differences this city offers now to those times when Kath and Mike lived here.

During lunch, both Henry and David use their time discussing with Alec those queries they have in relation to their proposed purchase of new equipment. With all his experience, Alec has no trouble in assuaging any fears they may have, and is happy to explain the answers to all of their queries. At the same time he informs them that there may well be some problems when the installation occurs, but that it is almost inevitable, and happens with almost every new operation. But he tells them that they should not worry, because all problems can be overcome by either Apple or the company responsible for the installation.

"We wouldn't be in business for very long if we didn't offer you the complete package of installation, support and training," Alec finishes by saying, which makes both David and Henry feel comforted.

Wishing to see the company who will be responsible for the actual installation, they waste no time in finishing lunch, before Alec drives them back to the Apple Store where the paperwork has been prepared in their absence. They then make their way to the Clifton area of Bristol to meet with the Apple franchise outlet.

After explaining the background to their visit, the manager, Len Best, who has been made aware of most of it by the Apple administrator, talks them through the logistics of installation and staff training once the paperwork has been approved. David is concerned that the installation should be carried out as soon as possible, because of Henry's possible time scale, and pushes for an early date.

All Len can promise is that as soon as finance has been agreed he will make arrangements with them, which David realises that he has no option but to accept. Nevertheless, both Henry and David feel that they have achieved a great deal in the time available to them, and leave feeling both excited and apprehensive at the same time.

"Once this is all done Henry," David remarks on their journey home, "We should be able to compete with the bigger boys." Suddenly, changing tack he says, "Oh, by the way Henry, it's the Goderston Village Fete in two weeks' time and I usually design posters and get about fifty laminated copies printed as a goodwill gesture, which are then put up around the village and surrounding areas. As I shall be out of the office for a good part of this week, as a great favour, could you do the design this year? If you give Mum a copy once it is done she will arrange for printing and laminating. It is for a good cause, fifty percent of the profits go to the village hall improvements fund and the other fifty percent goes to the breast cancer research fund."

"I would be only too happy. Anything that helps to develop answers to the causes of breast cancer has my vote," says Henry.

The rest of the journey is spent enjoying the beautiful landscapes of Somerset and Dorset and they arrive back at the Mucky Duck in the early evening just after six. Refusing the offer of a drink, David leaves Henry, promising to pick him up in the morning from his mother's cottage.

Henry, who had gathered together his few belongings the previous night collects them, before thanking Toby for his hospitality and promises to attend the quiz the following evening.

"You know you are always welcome here, Henry. I hope things work out well for you, whatever you decide to do in the future. One thing I do know is that you could not wish to find a more considerate, selfless, caring person than Kate, so the remainder of your stay here is sure to be a happy experience."

So Henry wends his way across the common to be welcomed by Kate, who has been waiting for him at her front door.

"You're just in time the dinner is almost ready," then, ushering him in, "There is a selection of wines in the kitchen, choose which one you would prefer while I serve and we will celebrate the occasion, then you can tell me how things went today."

Filling their glasses, Henry watches Kate as she dishes up dinner and he cannot help but admire her easy, competent manner. Her fluidity and economy of movement makes him feel as if he has lived here for years, and that they know all they have to know about each other. He feels comfortable and strangely relaxed here.

"*Salut*! Here's to that elusive quality, happiness. Something that I have felt since I met you." Then looking at her properly for the first time that day he sees her diminutive figure dressed in what is described in today's terms as 'a little black number for the older woman' which makes her look both childlike and evocative at the same time. By contrast her wild silver hair spilling to her shoulders gives her an air of sophistication, which is dispelled as she laughs, the child in her again manifesting itself. The little black number however allows Henry to note her lithe, slim figure which up until now has been hidden beneath sweaters and jeans.

Seeing him look, Kate smiles and replies, "Here's to happiness," and as they clink glasses, "Now let's sit down and eat our meal. I hope you like lamb, because Toby had some lovely local meat which I couldn't resist. Now tell me all about your day."

"Before I do, I would like to tell you how fantastic you look. That dress suits you and does terrible things to my blood pressure, so if you know what's good for me, or you for that matter, I suggest that you don't wear it again."

Kath smiles enigmatically before saying, "Thank you Henry, but you will just have to get over it. At these prices I will be wearing it morning, noon and night."

As they eat Henry tells her of the day's events and the probable time scale that implementation of the computer system will take. Kate, who has a good grasp of the decisions that have been taken, questions Henry about the equipment and the advantages that it will have on the business, some of which he is unable to answer, the consequence of which make him realise that she will need to be involved in some of the training.

Finishing dinner Henry insists on clearing away and putting the dirty crockery in the dish washer, while Kate puts her feet up. Then while she watches a couple of soaps on TV, Henry takes himself off to the study to catch up on his diary and read the daily paper.

THE BUS PASS

Before he realises it, a look at his watch reveals that it is nine forty five, so he returns to the Kate in the living room, apologising profusely.

"Don't be silly, I want you to feel free to do those things that you want to when you want to. I am very happy knowing that you are around."

They sit and talk about the coming week, Kate tells him which days of the coming week she will be working and then goes on to describe the coming village fete and the posters that David wants. Henry asks her if she would like to accompany him one evening while he does some watercolour sketches, which she readily agrees to, saying, "I would love to and I could take a book to read while you do so."

Finally, after watching the TV news Henry says, "I think that I had better get to bed, I'm not used to working full days anymore, and I need to be up in the morning if David is to pick me up. Thank you for the lovely meal and your company. I will take my things up to the room. Please stay there, because I don't think that I would be able to trust myself if we both went up together."

Kate rises to her feet as Henry moves to pass her and standing in front of him says, "What's to trust Henry, we are both unattached, single mature adults who feel a need for each other… don't we? We are not cheating on our partners. If Isabel were still alive this situation would never happen, you would never have looked at me and I would never have let you. But she's not, and so you have no need to feel any guilt. Oh my love, don't let's waste what little time we may have."

For a brief moment Henry stands transfixed as he hears Isabel's mantra of 'life is for living and every moment is precious, so let's not waste any more time', being repeated by Kate, and for the very first time he recognises that although both women are not at all similar in looks or build - Isabel, tall and blonde, Kate, short, dark and petite - they both have the same appetite for and outlook on life. This leads him to consider whether this is something that he has subconsciously recognised in Kate, and the reason that he has become so attracted to her.

All this is going through his mind as he suddenly gathers her to him in a long warm embrace and his head swims with the intoxication of holding her. As he continues to hold her he begins to feel her warm body moving erotically beneath the silky fabric of her dress. Their lips meet, his tongue seeking her mouth.

Running his hands across her buttocks he pulls her to him until their bodies meet, and she can feel his hardness against her groin.

Moaning softly, Kate steps back and says in a whisper, "Come on, let's go upstairs," but Henry who is by now at fever pitch, responds hoarsely, "No, let's use the sofa."

For about thirty seconds there is a flurry of arms and legs as they peel off their clothes, Henry taking off his own, before deliberately, slowly stripping Kate. His sense of wonderment grows as he holds her away from him, examining her flawless porcelain body. Despite her age, her breasts, which are small, still firm and full, the nipples hard and erect, dusky red in colour, her stomach taut, still showing stretch marks from a previous life, then his eyes move further down to her slender hips and thighs.

"My God, you are beautiful," he whispers as he lowers her slim frame onto the sofa, his hands and mouth exploring every part of her, until he can wait no longer and quickly mounting her releases years of pent up sexual emotion that he had not even been aware of after his beloved Isabel's demise. If he has considered the matter at all, it was only to discard it with the thought that such things would never happen again for him, neither would he want it to.

But here is nature, he thinks, once again demonstrating how futile and weak our resolve and thoughts are when confronted by reality.

True, he had always loved his Bella, and that would always be the case, but knowing her as he did, he was also aware that she would be happy for him that he had found someone else to share his life with, something she had made abundantly clear in the last few months of her life when they discussed Henry's life without her.

He, by contrast, had tried to brush such thoughts away, only to be told by Isabel that she would have thought that their love for each other had been less than complete, a failure even, if the situation arose after her death for Henry to find someone else and were he not take the opportunity because of his thoughts of her.

Such a happening she told him would be a vindication that their love had been good enough for him to try again with someone else.

These thoughts rush through his mind as he lies with Kate on the sofa, in a post-coital, tranquil haze.

Realising that although the experience was wonderful, but that it was over much too soon for both of them, he says, "That was great; now let's go upstairs where we can take our time."

Not bothering with clothes they reach Kate's bed and, taking things more slowly, they enjoy each other more, discovering the things that please one another most. Kate sits astride him, her breasts swinging pendulously over him as she lowers herself onto him. Moving rhythmically, she takes long deep pelvic thrusts, which bring Henry to a state of unrestrained ecstasy, and he can contain his emotions no longer, accelerating with long powerful thrusts, to which Kate responds, leading to a frenzy of activity, both of them whispering hoarse endearments to each other, until the storm breaks and Kate subsides to Henry's side. Strangely, even though he is spent Henry experiences something that has never happened to him before, a need of Kate again, which is almost a feeling of unbelief that this can be happening to him and he lays her down and enters her again. Although exhausted, Kate recognises both his need and more importantly the reason for it and as she responds. This time they climax simultaneously, every muscle and sinew spent.

They lie, spooned together until dawn with only a sheet covering them.

Henry wakes staring down at Kate's serene countenance, looking so peaceful in sleep. Her hair is now a riot of dishevelment, which seems to add even more to her lustrous beauty. Feeling him move, she wakes sleepily, before remembering the happenings of the previous evening, which brings a quiet smile to her mouth.

Henry, who is about to go downstairs to get tea for them both, sees her smile and gently kisses her, before saying, "Are you all right, no regrets?" to which she replies, "No, of course not, how can I when I wanted it to happen? You are the one that had reservations, although I understand completely why you felt that way. So how about you?"

"I suppose that after Isabel died I never thought that there would ever be someone else, so when we met, although I wanted you like mad, I never dared envisage us being here together like this."

Pulling herself upright Kate embraces him, saying, "You are a silly old fool, couldn't you tell that I felt the same way about you? And when I say you, I mean only you. A number of men have made advances over the years since I was widowed, some of them who genuinely wanted a relationship with a view to marriage. Some also who wanted 'a bit on the side'. I have been out with several of the former, none of whom interested me for any length of time and purely on a platonic relationship basis, but I never let any of the latter get past the starting post. You would be amazed at the number of men who see a widow as gagging for sex and therefore an easy mark, which shows just how little they understand the female of the species."

As she sits up the sheet falls from her body and Henry has to make a conscious effort to try and ignore it, which Kate notes with a knowing smile, saying, "Go and get that cup of tea, I don't think we have any more time for that if we are to be up and about before David arrives. There's still tonight."

"Well, that's something to look forward to," calls Henry as he makes his way downstairs.

Kate lies back sinking into the pillow, whispering to herself, "Thank you God for Marks and Spencer's and their little black dress."

CHAPTER 15

Tuesday, 27 May

Tuesday 27 May dawns bright and sunny as David drives Henry into the office, Kate first having told them that she will be in sometime during the afternoon and so will be able to bring Henry back in the evening.

When they arrive, David assembles the staff and explains about the purchase of the new computer system and hopefully what it will mean to both the company and their development over the next few years. There are a few anxious looks, but after a question and answer session, which Henry finds he has to respond to, the uncertainty on their faces seems to lift and they begin to see the undoubted advantages to them personally, from a much faster and comprehensive piece of kit.

At this point David takes over where Henry leaves off and explains the other procedural changes that will be introduced over the coming days and weeks, i.e. he will bring the clients' briefs into the studio and then talk it through with Henry and with the designated artist to ensure that correct design is achieved quickly, and that time scales will be set by agreement of all of them. The budgeted time scale will then be measured by means of completing job time sheets. This will be done manually for the present, but eventually the new computer system will automatically handle it, once installed.

By the time he has finished, the staff are beginning to look more relaxed and even enthusiastic, realising that once everything is up and running they will have more skills, but also because it offers great new chances to improve their skills, and as the company grows they will be well placed for promotional advancement.

Leaving them, David and Henry then spend the rest of the morning looking at briefs that have not yet been placed into the studio workload, agreeing time allocations for each - when and how much time needed to be allocated. Also which jobs need to be started immediately, of which there are quite a number.

Feeling that he has an adequate grasp of the current situation, Henry returns to the studio and talks through the work which needs to be started with each of the designers, while retaining several jobs that David would normally do. These are more complex, so Henry decides that it is one way to release David and thus enable him to carry out his more important function, namely talking to and visiting current and prospective clients.

David leaves later that morning to visit clients in Yeovil while Henry spends the rest of the morning with the designers assisting in problem areas.

He also determines to quiz Kate when she comes in about the Goderston Summer Fete which is due to be held on Saturday 7 June, so that he can design the poster that David has asked for.

She duly arrives at twelve thirty looking positively radiant and before Henry can say anything she produces a hamper, saying, "I have brought some sandwiches, crisps and one or two other things which I thought we might take to the park at lunch time. What do you think?"

Henry cannot help reflect that their night of passion had obviously done wonders for her, but has left him feeling shattered, exhausted, gloriously happy and euphoric all at the same time, a heady concoction that he finds exhilarating but also extremely wearing. Each time he looks at her he wants to sweep her into his arms and hold her until both the pain and the pleasure subsides enough for him to act something like normal towards her.

She is wearing a blue, scooped neck T-shirt with dark blue jeans which accentuates the colour of her hair, making it look like burnished silver in the light of the sun, which is now pouring through the windows.

All Henry can think is that she is not only beautiful and good company, but also caring and thoughtful, an intoxicating mixture that leaves him feeling both lucky and inadequate at the same time.

What can she possibly see in him, a dinosaur left over from an earlier age, with no particular attributes, in looks or interests?

Looking at her surreptitiously, he feels both lucky and proud because she shows such an interest in him, but inadequate because he wonders just how long she will feel that way.

"What can I say, that sounds wonderful, we can go at one o'clock, but before we do I would just like to ask you a few things about the summer fete, because, as I explained last night, David wants me to produce a poster."

At this point Kate becomes very enthusiastic, saying, "O yes, I think you will like the fete, it's a regular annual event which has grown over the last few years. It has the usual sort of things like tombola and arts and craft stalls. There are activities for the children, like sack races and team games. There's a marquee for flower and vegetable growers' competitions, the prizes for which are considered as important as medals won at the Olympic Games.

"There is a large arena in the middle of the common in which a number of events take place. Several of the farmers do exhibitions like rounding sheep with their dogs, or pony racing. Not only that but they also exhibit some of their animals which are judged for best of breed in show. There will be a silver band and later on an exhibition by the local Morris dancers.

"The whole thing goes on into the evening when the arena is lit by fairy lights. We have a local rock and roll celebrity, Rick Dolan who lives locally, and although of a much more vintage era, he has offered his services with his band free and gratis for the last event of the day, at which time there is a firework display. Oh, and there's much more besides."

"Stop," laughs Henry. "I think I get the picture, let's go for lunch and you can tell me again, a little slower next time please."

They wander down to the park about three hundred yards away and find a bench where they open Kate's food hamper, from which she takes out a small cloth and spreads out between them. Henry thinks that he has never tasted food so good, which is due no doubt to the fact that Kate is sat next to him, but also because it is alfresco, something that is not often possible to do in England, with its varied unpredictable weather.

They sit under a willow tree growing on the edge of a small stream which meanders and gurgles its way through the park, and as they watch they see a kingfisher, its bright blue and green iridescent plumage flashing in the sunlight as it follows the course of the stream. They are both relaxed as they consume the food, and drink coffee which Kate has brought in a flask, while, all the while they discuss the coming fete, before Henry relates the discussions that David and he had with the rest of the employees earlier.

There is silence for a while before their conversation then becomes more personal as they probe each other's backgrounds trying to find those areas of commonality that they can build their relationship on, although this is a subconscious procedure that they are not even aware of.

"Tell me about Rob and Madge, how long have you been friends and what are they like, just so that I know what to expect when I meet them at the weekend."

"As a matter of fact they are my next door neighbours, living there before we were," declares Henry, adding, "And we moved there in 1971. We all got on like a house on fire from the very beginning and they are some of those friends that I have known the longest."

Henry then continues to describe them and by the time he finishes Kate realises that they are very special indeed to him. In fact she can relate Henry and Isabel's relationship with Rob and Madge, to that of her and Mike's with Megan and Charlie. She knows just how important the latter have been to her over the years and senses that Henry feels the same way about his friends.

As these thoughts occur to her she makes a mental note to include Megan and Charlie at some point in the proceedings during the coming weekend.

Suddenly Henry hears the church clock striking two in the distance, and quickly starts to gather the plates and cups together, saying, "Where did the time go? We had best get back. I would hate for the both of us to get the sack from David for being late," to which Kate, laughing, replies, "Well, I think that I would be OK, but I don't fancy your chances."

Linking arms they stroll back to the studio, only to hear Malcolm, who is on the phone express one of his classic mannerisms, as he summarises his to his customer, saying, "Well, on a score of one to ten, that must be a B."

Henry doesn't realise it at the time, but of all the many phrases that Malcolm has mangled in his telephone conversations, this one will stay with him forever. In the years to come, if he is feeling low, he will only have to recall it to feel better, the warm glow that it gives him will always scour away the ominous dark clouds of depression, but right at this moment both Kate and he look at one another, both trying to stifle suppressed hysterical laughter, failing entirely, much to Malcolm's utter astonishment and bewilderment.

The afternoon passes in a blur as Henry develops a number of designs for the forthcoming fete, until he finds one that he feels happy with in poster format, and a second that could be used for banners to stretch across gates or hedges. Then copying them to a hard disk, he asks Kate which printers the studios use so that he can get copies printed ready for distribution.

"Oh, they are on the trading estate just round the corner. Why don't I take you there and introduce you, then if you have to go again you will know."

"That would be very useful, if you don't mind. I would like to see their operation anyway," says Henry.

They inform Malcolm where they are going, and as time is getting late, they explain that they may not be back before the end of the day.

Sure enough, the printers are only a couple of minutes by car and Kate, who is obviously a frequent visitor, introduces Henry to the manager William Morris, who is also the owner. Henry, who is interested to see what equipment and capacity the plant has, is delighted when William offers to show him round, and is even more impressed when he sees the scale of the operation.

There has obviously been a considerable investment in printing machinery in the recent past which is technologically capable of large print runs, a fact that pleases Henry, because quite often clients ask the design studios to arrange printing of their approved designs. This can be quite lucrative for the studio, which can often mark up the print cost to their client, effectively another way of getting added value.

Thanking William, they leave, and as it is now nearly a quarter to six, they decide to call it a day and make their way home to Goderston. Not having to prepare an evening meal because they will be eating at the pub later at the quiz, Kate prepares them both gin and tonics which they carry out to the patio and consume under the canopy while she reads a book Henry catches up with the daily paper.

The late evening sun is still high in the heavens, but the shadows are starting to lengthen and only the quiet song of the birds and hushed murmur of bees busily pollinating interrupt their tranquillity. Without even realising it Henry is swept into a languorous sleep, only to be woken by Kate laughing.

"Come on sleepy head, Megan has just called to say that they will be round in twenty minutes to go to the pub."

"Why, what is the time, do they always come this early?" complains Henry, not yet properly awake.

"You must have nodded off longer than you thought, because it's nearly a quarter to eight. I am going upstairs to change and I suggest you do the same."

"Well. It's your entire fault, you wanton temptress. If you hadn't taken advantage of me last night, I wouldn't be in this state," smiles Henry, reliving it once again in his mind.

"As if," chortles Kate as she makes for the stairs. "Well if that's the case we had best not have a repeat tonight, because it's obviously not doing you any good."

"Oh, I think that if we get more practice, I may be able to build up an immunity to it," says Henry as he makes a lunge for her, adding, "But I have a feeling that it may take a very long time." At the same time as he catches and holds her to him; they embrace, her perfume and musky woman scent intoxicating him.

"One thing's for sure, we don't have time now," says Kate pulling back. "I would hate for them to have to wait for us. I will consider your petition later."

THE BUS PASS

They are only just ready when Megan and Charlie arrive, after which they all set off across the common to the pub in time to order food before the quiz commences. As they all sit chatting and talking together as if they had known each other for ever, Henry has to remind himself that it is only just over one incredibly short week since he has met them for the first time. Like all true friends they make him feel easy in their company, taking care to include him as much as each other.

It is Charlie's turn to take centre stage tonight as he regales them with some of his experiences during his working life with Her Majesty's Customs and Excise.

"You would just not believe the ingenuity and risks that people are prepared to take to either avoid paying duty, or to bring in drugs illegally. Some of their antics are almost beyond description."

He goes on in his usual laconic manner which makes the incidents seem hilarious, describing hiding places from car tyres, compartments in suitcases, children's toys, or any other crevice, including anatomical hiding places, of which there were quite a few, but he doesn't dwell too much on the latter.

Some of the arrests that he was involved with were the result of tip offs and information gleaned by intelligence sources, particularly from drug smuggling, which often led to chases by sea before the culprits could dump or hide them. Charlie has received his fair share of bumps and bruises while in pursuit in this way.

Eventually Toby commences the quiz amid much ribaldry, but tonight is not quite as successful as the previous week for The Three Musketeers Plus One, although they come second overall of the teams competing, so they feel they can hold their heads high. However the jackpot questions evade them because they are not selected from the draw.

By the time the quiz is finished and it is time to go, Henry, who has consumed several beers throughout the evening without even realising it, is starting to feel its effects. In fact the four of them, talking ninety to the dozen as they cross the common all seem to be slightly the worse for wear. The two women's faces are flushed and they are giggling like school girls, while the men's voices rise gradually the farther they walk, making an enormous cacophony of sound as they laugh at the most innocuous things. But the real giveaway is that they all seem to need each other for support to walk, each knowing that they cannot manage on their own.

The result is that they walk twice as far as necessary to reach their homes and the two men, who are on the extremities of the line crossing the small bridge are fortunate not to fall into the swift flowing water.

Saying their farewells, Kate and Henry leave Megan and Charlie and enter the cottage going straight upstairs to bed, where despite all Henry's intentions and to Kate's amazement, he falls instantly to sleep.

With a smile hovering on her face Kate reaches across and kisses him gently on his lips, murmuring, "On a scale of one to ten that will be a B then," before snuggling into his back and falling instantly to sleep herself.

They both wake late the following morning, Henry having to get ready hurriedly before David picks him up.

Kate has prepared Henry sandwiches for him to take to work, before leaving, saying, "I have to go shopping in Dorchester this morning, so I won't be coming into the studio today, but I will have a meal ready for us when you return this evening, after which, if you would like, we can go for a walk and you can find somewhere to do your sketching."

Overwhelmed once again by her capacity of thought for others before herself, Henry thanks her and says, "That sounds lovely. Then perhaps we can have a quick drink afterwards. But only one mind. I have sussed your modus operandi and you aren't going to get me drunk again that easily."

Kate, not able to help herself, laughs, saying, "And there was me thinking that you were a lion, but you're only a pussy cat really, aren't you?"

CHAPTER 16
Getting To Know You

The rest of the week evaporates as they both explore the challenges before them.

During the day Henry develops and runs the studio, making sure that he involves everyone as he does so. The work levels and quality of product have started to improve. Imperceptibly at first, but with a gathering pace as the week continues, the outstanding work-in-progress reduces, meaning lead times can also be cut, and more work can be accepted into the studio.

David, seeing all this happen, is pleased, but also apprehensive, because he is the person responsible for maintaining work for the studio.

Henry assures him that there is no need to panic, but rather tries to point out to him that one way that he could improve input was to get more work from existing clients, because he has noticed that a considerable amount of the work was for one-off items.

"If the culture of selling to clients could be changed, so that existing clients can be developed further and work for more projects can be obtained, the need for a continuous supply of new clients can be reduced significantly, making your life so much easier. After all, you've done the hard bit, getting work from clients, usually at a smaller rate than you would prefer just to obtain the business, but I would also like to point out that if you can get further business from existing clients, it will be much simpler because presumably you will have built up good relationships with those clients and contacts and once they are happy with the studios performance, they will, in all probability give you the chance to quote for new work. When I worked in High Wycombe in my previous life it was generally agreed that an acceptable level of sales in this business should be eighty per cent from twenty percent of the clients," quoted Henry. "But I examined your turnover, and it would appear in your case to be something like eighty percent of your sales are coming from something like sixty percent of you clients.

"This means that you are getting more and more clients just to stand still, but if you can build on those you already have, it should be both considerably easier and more profitable for you."

In the evening, Henry and Kate stroll around the village, looking for somewhere suitable that he can sketch. The day has been quite hot and there is an eerie stillness in the air, as if all the wildlife and indeed people too, have decided that it is far too warm to expend any further effort and are conspicuous by their absence. The sun, however, has not yet had its final say for the day, as it slowly sinks in a molten ball of fire, seemingly into the woods at the far side of the village, silhouetting the trees starkly black with its intensity.

Eventually Henry stops on the common with a view to sketching the Mucky Duck with the pond in the foreground. Not possessing an easel, Kate lays out a blanket which they can both sit on, he sketching while she reads her book. Although conversation is sparse they both feel comfortable in each other's company. As Henry's sketch develops, Kate starts to admire his artistic skill and compliments him, saying, "Oh I like that Henry, before you go will you do one for me?"

Henry, who up until now is feeling totally relaxed, suddenly realises that his idyll is only temporary. That his purpose for being here is specific and forms only a small part of his journey, but as soon Kate mentions it, as a stark and simple fact, he wants to reject the whole idea, saying, "Of course I will, but I don't have any plans to go anywhere soon. Meeting you has changed my priorities." Not being able to gauge her reaction, Henry looks at her and asks, "That is of course providing that you feel the same way?"

A wistful smile crosses Kate's face as she replies. "You must know by now that nothing would, or could make me happier, but you must consider the reasons that you came on this journey, because staying here will not resolve them. Your family will still move to Australia and if you stay here with me for a while, you will not have been able to have the time to see all those other places you want to before you also emigrate."

"I understand what you are saying, but right at this moment I don't want to even think about it. I want to spend whatever time I have left before I go, with you."

"But don't you see Henry, by doing that you will be making it a hundred times worse for both of us by the time you do have to go. I just don't know if I will be able to stand you leaving in several months' time. The thought of it happening soon is quite unbearable enough."

"Please forgive me Kate, I'm not thinking straight. Look, we don't have to make any sort of decision just yet, let's enjoy what we have for now, and face decisions only when we have to."

Agreeing, the two of them pack up and make their way to the pub for a nightcap. They are both quiet and contemplative as they return to the cottage where Kate fusses around preparing food for both their lunches the next day, until Henry at last leads her up to the bedroom.

Kissing her tenderly, as if afraid she might shatter into a million pieces, he undresses her slowly, savouring each revealing glimpse of her, until at last she stands naked before him. But this night is more considered than the first. He looks for ways to please her, gradually building their needs until they can both wait no longer, climaxing in unison, totally and utterly spent.

As they lie holding each other, Henry whispers in her ear, "On a score of one to ten, I think that might even be an A."

Giggling madly, Kate retorts, "I must have a word with Toby about spiking your drinks in future if you are going to keep taking advantage of a poor widow woman."

They are woken early on Thursday with the sound of thunder rumbling above them, followed almost immediately by torrential rain. Pulling back the bedroom curtains, Henry looks down to see a number of mallard ducks scurrying around on the stream below, several females with their young herding them to the safety of the banks where they have nests, while the males ignore them and continue searching the bed of the stream for plants and small fish hiding in the gravel. With their heads underwater, leaving only their backsides and legs waving in the air, they remind him of a paddle steamer in its death throes sinking to the bottom of the Mississippi. He watches them fascinated for several minutes, marvelling once again at this beautiful part of England, reminding himself once again just how tenuous his stay here is.

Making his way downstairs, Henry makes tea for both of them and returns to find Kate just sitting up, her hair dishevelled, but her eyes sparkling, their blue intensity seeming to make everything else in the room fade into insignificance.

"Oh, now you are spoiling me Henry," she says as she drains her cup dry. "But I think that I could get used to it."

"Perhaps you will think the price too high when you realise the cost," replies Henry, as he pulls her to him.

But she doesn't.

CHAPTER 17
Rob And Madge

Thursday and Friday pass in a welter of activity, the days being spent honing the studio into a more effective operation, Henry ensuring that Malcolm in particular is involved with any changes that he makes, because he feels more and more that he can make a good manager. His use of computers has come on in leaps and bounds in the short period that Henry has taken him under his wing, and he can readily understand the reasons for the operational changes that Henry is introducing.

David also has taken to heart Henry's comments about getting more turnover from existing clients and although nothing has happened so far, two clients have already promised to give him the chance to pitch for future work as and when it arises, so he can see the benefit if he builds on relationships that he already got.

On Friday David receives a telephone call from Len Best at The Apple Store, with the fantastic news that finance has been approved for the computer system and, knowing that time is of the essence, by moving heaven and earth he can arrange to start the installation on the following Monday, if that is what David wants.

David confirms, telling him, "I would like that very much indeed Len, thank you for arranging things so quickly."

"That's OK David. The staff training will be run in tandem with the installation. So we can transfer all your current data from your existing setup to the new system as we go."

Replacing the receiver, David calls Henry to his office and tells him the good news.

Henry is delighted, saying, "Blimey, that was quick, I had best go and make sure that all the work is completed as far as possible, so that it can be easily transferred to the new system." Then he and David go out into the studio and tell all the designers.

Kate comes into the office in the afternoon, and on being updated about the computer installation, insists that she will be coming in for the whole of the next week to ensure that she understands the implications in respect of her input onto the new system.

So the afternoon passes in a hive of unexpected activity.

Leaving at the end of the day, Kate and Henry go to a local supermarket food shopping, so that they will have enough to feed Madge and Rob whenever they want to visit them over the coming weekend. Waving away her objections, Henry pays, saying, "Right, now all we need to get is some meat from Toby, and that should be the lot."

As they pull up to the Mucky Duck Henry notices Rob's car outside and both he and Kate hurry inside to meet his old friends. "Ah, there you are, you old reprobates, how long have you been here, I wonder? I hope we haven't kept you waiting too long. Oh, by the way, this is Kate Challis who I have told you so much about. Kate, these are my two very good friends, Madge and Rob. The only thing that I think it would be best to mention at this stage is, don't believe a word they tell you, particularly about me."

Sensing once again the affection that Henry holds for his two friends, Kate laughs and says, "Oh you don't have to worry about that, just wait until I tell you some of the things Henry has told me about you." Then turning to Rob, "Did you really climb Everest when you were only twenty-three?" and then to Madge, "And is it true that you were with Florence Nightingale in the Crimea?"

Rob laughs delightedly. "Well you got it almost right. I was twenty-four and it was only Snowdon. But you were spot on about Madge. She was in the Crimea with Florence Nightingale." Then turning to Henry, "I like her, she's a lot prettier and smarter than any of those other women from Age Concern that you've been going out with lately." For a brief moment Kate is totally disorientated, until she sees the twinkle in Rob's eye as he says, "Just kidding Kate, it's a real pleasure to meet you."

As they gather together, Toby comes into the bar, and recognising the notorious Rob, comes to meet them, calling Avril at the same time. "Rob, it's great to see you again after all these years," and being introduced to Madge, "Very pleased to meet you my dear, Rob has told me so much about you," to which she replies, "Well ignore the one about me and Florence Nightingale, Rob only tells that one because he wants everyone to think that he is my toy boy."

Toby looks disconcerted for a moment, but quickly realises that the others have drawn him into a world of their own, for which he does not have the tools to cope, and is brought back to the real world as Henry orders drinks for the six of them, before turning to Toby to explain that he would like to buy some meat for the weekend, hopefully to include some of Toby's special homemade burgers, because if the weather is right, it would be a good time to have a barbecue.

The next hour is spent catching up with all the local news with Rob relating more tales of the now defunct fishing trips, some of which Toby and Avril have heard before, but which are all new to Kate. Kate fits in easily because she knows a lot of the places and even some of the people that Rob and Henry are talking about.

But as time goes by it becomes more and more apparent that she not only has the same sort of humour as the others, but that she also has the indefinable ability to strike an instant rapport. This is particularly obvious with her relationship with Madge, the two of them talking in almost non-stop conspiratorial whispers, while Henry and Rob catch up on their own backlog of usual topics.

Eventually, Henry and Kate take their leave to go with Toby to buy meat for the weekend, promising to be back in an hour, in time for the dinner which Henry has booked.

As they return home Kate's conversation is full of Madge and Rob, and Henry can see that her enthusiasm is genuine, which gives him an enormous feeling of relief as he realises only now, just how important to him it is that they all like each other.

"Well I think she's a wonderful woman – any woman who can make Henry so happy in such a short time has my vote. Not only that, but we both have a lot in common. She enjoys retail therapy, hates politics and exercise, as well as enjoying the same sort of food."

"Oh, those are the criteria necessary for friendship," says Rob, laughing. Then, "But I agree with you, she and Henry look inseparable already. She is also a very good looking woman for her age."

"She was suggesting we all go to Lyme Regis or Bridport tomorrow for the street market, then in the evening that we go back to hers for a meal, which sounds lovely."

"Yes, I would like that too. But let's see how the evening goes first OK?"

Rob does not need to have any reservations as to how the evening will progress. The sound of their raucous laughter and incessant chatter gives the lie to any such fears. Their party grows as the evening progresses as first Toby and Avril join them, only to be followed shortly after by Megan and Charlie. As always, Rob, with his never ending stories, draws people to listen as if by a magnet, and he steals the show. Henry marvels once again as his friend relates stories and jokes from his never ending repertoire, some of which he has heard many times, but somehow in the manner of their telling, they always seem fresh and new.

Rob finishes by telling them all about the first time that the fishing trip had taken place.

"It was back in the early 1970s and came about when the four of us who were regulars at the Kings Head at Downley were persuaded mostly by Alan (who was a keen angler) to embark on a four-day fishing expedition to Christchurch in Hampshire.

"Of the other three, only I was vaguely interested in fishing, but they all came along for the craic and the promise of boozy evenings in the locals, which Alan assured us were numerous.

"On arrival, we were to say the least, surprised to find that our accommodation was on a caravan site which had on its southern boundary a tributary of the River Stour running through it. Luckily our caravan was on the last row before the river (which in effect was little more than a stream) so we didn't have far to go to fish.

"Unfortunately, the summer this particular year had been scorching hot, leaving water levels in the river at an all-time low. This resulted in there being few or no fish to be caught. In fact I was convinced that they all caught the same singular trout that was available, in rotation."

Henry's abiding memory of that trip was of Alan, who at times could be a little eccentric, going down to the river with his fishing rod, wearing only underpants and slippers.

"However although none of us enjoyed the fishing, we all found that we enjoyed each other's company. In the evenings we would go to the local hostelry, have a meal and a few beers, before returning to the caravan to play cards long into the night, while during the day we would yomp across the surrounding countryside, all the while arguing with each other about the correct route."

As the evening draws to a close, Kate, who is by this time feeling more than a little tired, repeats her offer for Rob and Madge to accompany Henry and herself to Lyme Regis or Bridport the following morning. She then continues on to invite all of them at the table to a barbeque at her house the following evening, both suggestions being accepted with alacrity by those concerned.

Arranging to pick up Rob and Madge the following morning, the cast of *Singing in the Rain* make their way home across the common considerably more subdued than the last time the four of them made this journey. It is a lovely balmy evening, after what has been a warm summer's day and their conversation is mostly of Rob and Madge, who have obviously made suitable impressions on all of them, much to Henry's delight.

Refusing a nightcap, but promising to see them at Kate's barbeque the next night, Megan and Charlie leave them, Charlie whispering conspiratorially to Henry that he is 'on a promise', before the moment is spoiled for him as Megan, who has overheard, laughingly says, "No chance."

Henry, whatever he had been hoping for, also experiences 'no chance' as they climb into bed, where Kate is asleep as soon as her head hits the pillow. As Henry looks down at her, he suddenly realises just how much meeting his friends have taken out of her, because of her need to be accepted by them as Henry's companion. Filled with an overwhelming feeling of both love and compassion, Henry gathers her into his arms where they lie locked as one until dawn breaks.

With Kate driving and the promise of another warm day from the TV weather forecast, the four of them set off for Lyme Regis, following much the same route that Henry and she had the previous week. First through Maiden Newton, then on to Toller Porcorum, where they stop so that Rob can show Madge for the first time, the accommodation that the members of the fishing trip had used for so many years.

Wanting to show Madge the inside of the apartments, Rob knocks on the owner's door, which is opened after several minutes by David Warnock, who recognises him immediately, and after Rob explains the reason for their visit, happily shows them around those places which are not currently occupied.

David and his wife Sheila then insist that they all have tea and cakes, while the men reminisce once again about the things they did and the number of times that they have stayed in this beautiful hidden valley, with its deafening silence, rolling green hills and soft meandering streams.

Bidding David and Sheila farewell, they continue on, reaching the top of Eggardon Hill, where Kate stops the car for them to step out and take in this, the most breath taking of views, which holds them mesmerised in its enthral for several minutes. Returning to the car they set off again, making their way down to the village of Uploders, then on to meet the A35, where they bypass Bridport, and continue on, passing through Chideock and Charmouth, eventually reaching Lyme Regis at midday.

Talk has been desultory since Eggardon, each of them individually continuing to be overwhelmed by the memory and enormity of its staggering beauty.

Parking, they walk along the esplanade, in front of the beach, the latter of which has recently had serious money spent on it. For months, dredgers have trawled the bay, shovelling up suitable stones off-shore, then returning them to dump on the beach, where they are distributed by a host of caterpillar tractors with huge buckets, which swarm like a host of angry ants as they go about their business.

Carrying on they walk on through an area of shops and restaurants, eventually reaching The Cobb, built several hundred years previously to defend the shore and land from the sudden ferocious winter storms that have always swept in through the bay. As they stand looking at the extreme end of The Cobb out to sea, Henry recalls from his school history lessons that it was here that the Duke of Monmouth landed in 1685 with eighty-two supporters from Holland before moving off into the West Country to gain support for his ill-fated rebellion, from which so many were to die or be transported as a result of Judge Jeffries Assizes held in Dorchester later that year.

By comparison, Kate remembers Meryl Streep, the actress, standing on this very spot, wearing a cloak with a hood, looking ethereal and mystical for her part in the film *The French Lieutenant's Woman* against a backdrop of an almost black thunderous cloudy sky, which was lit almost continuously by flashes of lightning, revealing the dark green sea below, with its mountainous crested foam flecked waves crashing with a tremendous roar on the shore, throwing cascades of spume on to The Cobb.

Kate had loved this film, so much so in fact, that the thought of it now brings vivid memories streaming back into her consciousness, leaving her with a lump in her throat.

Filled with their own thoughts, the four of them make their way back to the Pilot Boat pub, where they have a light lunch of crab sandwiches, before climbing Broad Street to examine the wealth of craft and gift shops. After a while, the party splits, and the two women go into an automatic ritual that retail therapy seems to induce in most females of whatever age, while the men continue behind them at a more leisurely pace.

Kate and Madge are darting from clothes shops to shoe shops at a furious pace, leaving Henry and Rob to catch up on gossip while visiting book shops, looking for motor car magazines for Rob and thrillers for Henry.

Rob starts by breaking the silence. "Well, come on Henry, you old dog, what is going on? You and Kate look like more than just friends to me," observes Rob.

Henry, not wishing to embroil Kate into an embarrassing situation, without discussing it first with her, replies, "Look Rob, Kate is very special to me, but we are just enjoying each other's company for now. If it becomes any more than that, then you will be the first to know. The problem for both of us is that I am only here because of my pilgrimage. It would not be fair or possible for either of us to make any sort of commitment now," he finishes, lying through his teeth, which makes him realise with a start, that he is already hopelessly committed. Lost in fact.

"If you say so," smiles Rob, making Henry realise that he is fooling nobody, including himself. "But Kate told Madge a different story yesterday, so I just wanted to hear your version."

"Oh Rob, I am so sorry, I just didn't want to compromise Kate in any way, but even so my concerns are still valid. What am I supposed to do? I can't possibly stay here forever. All my family will be in Australia within the next few months and I will still need to see them. I owe them that at the very least. Anyway, what would they think about their father, if he were to have a relationship at his age, with a woman they have never met, who, it would appear to them, has stopped him emigrating to Australia to be with them."

"Henry, my old mate, with the best will in the world, I have to tell you that you are talking out of the wrong orifice. Of course, they would like you to move to Oz, to be with them, but their overriding concerns have always been for your happiness, and they would understand perfectly if you did find another woman to spend your remaining years with. They love you and want what is best for your happiness, and even I can see that Kate and you both feel the same way about each other. Your children will never ever forget their mother, but they love you too, and nothing can bring Isabel back. Anyway, she would want you to be happy."

Henry does not reply, but Rob having said his piece, changes the subject, saying, "I think the girls have finished their blitzkrieg for now, Madge is signalling that she wants coffee."

Eventually they find a wonderful café at the bottom of Broad Street (the main road that runs up through the town), which is the complete epitome of that of which a typical English tearoom should be, with its rich chintz tapestry curtains and matching table and chair covers, soft wall lights and burnished gold floorboards.

Even the waitresses wear suitable costumes of white hats and black dress uniforms giving the whole place an aura of times past.

Once seated Madge and Kate seize the opportunity to order cream teas, despite Rob's gentle protestations that by doing so, they would not be able to do justice to the barbeque later on that evening. For his pains he is told in no uncertain terms by both females that in order of their priorities, cream teas are right at the top of the agenda.

They are all by now totally relaxed in each other's company, with Rob ensuring their laughter by dipping into his never ending repertoire of jokes and situations in which he has found himself over the years. Even Henry is just as entranced as he always is when Rob is in full flow.

After a while, Rob relates an occasion that he experienced many years before when he was an apprentice aircraft engineer at Heathrow.

"A captain of one of the fleet had complained that there was a malfunction with the height indicator of the aircraft, which was represented by a red light display in the cockpit, and that he had no intention of taking off until the fault was rectified. Rob was despatched with a senior engineer to correct the fault, who had strict instructions to solve it a.s.a.p., because by this time the aircraft was fully loaded with passengers together with their luggage.

"Well, the two of us tried for ages to correct the fault with no luck, until suddenly my senior asked me to go to another part of the aircraft to check some wiring which may have been the cause of the problem. However within a few minutes I was called back by my boss who told me that he had found the cause of the fault and rectified it. I was very relieved, because the cost of an aircraft missing its time slot was prohibitive which the captain continually pointed out to us.

"After all the checks that we had made, I was more than a little surprised that my boss had found and mended the fault in the short period that I had been gone, so as we went down the steps of the plane, I asked him the cause of the fault and how he had discovered it so quickly."

"'Well,' said my boss, not looking at me, but straight ahead and in a deadpan voice, 'I tried everything that I knew, with no luck, so I took the bulb out. Problem solved.'"

The punchline made them laugh uproariously for several seconds, until that is the enormity of the possible consequences cut in, at which point their jaws dropped alarmingly and moans of protest were made.

"Oh, that is funny when you tell it, but so horrible when you think of the plight of those poor passengers," says Kate, while Madge complains, "How could you not say something to stop the aircraft taking off?"

This went on for a while, until suddenly looking at Rob, who was grinning like a Cheshire cat, they realise that they had been had.

Returning to Goderston once again, after taking in more views from Eggardon Hill, they arrive back both relaxed and tired.

The sun has played its part too, having a soporific effect on them, and Henry is left wondering meditatively to himself how he will manage to keep going into the evening without falling asleep.

Leaving Rob and Madge at the Mucky Duck to change, Henry and Kate return to the cottage to prepare the barbeque in time for the evening.

Despite Henry's reservations, the evening is all that he could have dreamed or hoped for. Toby and Avril have managed to get away from the Mucky Duck, bringing a small flagon of ale and some more sausages, in spite of Kate and Henry's protests. Henry takes responsibility for the barbecue, donning an apron and a chef's hat, made hurriedly for him by Kate, using an old tea cloth.

Megan and Charlie, who only live just a few doors away have arrived first, followed shortly afterwards by Rob and Madge.

Sitting outside at the table, as the last rays of the dying sun begin to fade, drinks continue to flow, while Henry barbeques, the products of which are being hungrily consumed as they come off the fire. In the meantime the conversation flows like an effortless meandering river, everyone contributing in a totally relaxed manner.

THE BUS PASS

For him to see both his old and new friends acting and talking as if they had known each other for ever, gives Henry the most wonderful feeling of happiness. Almost as if she senses it, Kate catches Henry's eye, giving him a radiant smile, acknowledging the way they are both feeling.

Rob addresses Toby, and asks him for some of his experiences in his role as landlord, to which he replies, "Well, by definition, it is inevitable in my job that I get to see both the best and the worst in people under the influence of drink. Generally, most people drink within their capabilities, but there are a small minority who never seem to recognise the difference between a good night out, and hell."

Looking across at Charlie, Megan and Kate, he continues. "Do you recall that chap called Dido something or other?" and as they all nod their heads he continues. "If I remember correctly we all used to call him Fido Dido for some obscure reason that I can no longer recall. He used to circulate the local village pubs and seemed to know everyone, but I would hasten to add he never drank to excess or gave any cause for concern anywhere he went. He was in fact a most charming and affable man, always smartly dressed, who had from his conversation and demeanour spent most of his life in the armed forces, and at a high level too.

"Well, Dido had a daughter who was unfortunately not quite the ticket, or rather by today's standards would probably have been categorised as dyslexic or autistic or some such label.

"To cut a long story short, Dido's daughter, I forget her name, appeared at the bar one evening, and when asked for her order she replied, 'A pint of crème de menthe, please.' As you can imagine the barmaid was quite taken aback at this, but although she queried it several times and pointed out that a pint of spirits was both unusual, expensive and a danger to health, she still insisted that was what she wanted. In the absence of her father, Fido, my barmaid felt that she had no option than to serve her request, the cost of which was quite prohibitive.

"Fortunately, after she had drunk about half a pint Dido appeared as if from nowhere and summing up the situation, immediately, snatched the remainder from her grasp and, taking her to one side, talked to her quietly, explaining the rights and wrongs of her actions. This brief scenario, illustrated why and how Dido had risen to the top in his profession. He was both assertive and, compassionate and his stock went up in the bar from those who witnessed it.

"I think that most of the people in the bar at that time felt desperately sorry for Dido, recognising that even the most intelligent and erudite among us are not immune from the vagaries of genetics.

"However, none of that stopped the bar breaking out into uncontrolled laughter once Dido and his daughter had left, just because the sight of her sitting at the bar drinking crème de menthe from a pint glass was so mind-numbingly funny.

"There have been also many other occasions when I have found it necessary to bar people from the pub, usually young men or youths (but not always) who can't hold their drink, or drink too much, but that has always been the case I suppose.

"I did get scammed many years ago when the breweries used to give three pence (old money) back on any of their bottles that were returned to them. So, empty bottles would be returned to the pub, and I would give money or deduct the cost from a full replacement which I would eventually claim back from the brewery.

"Children were very often those who returned bottles. They would probably have rooted around at home for empties for this very purpose, without even their parents' knowledge. The whole thing was simple really, and worked very well, saving the brewery from having to buy new bottles.

"However, the mistake that I made in my ignorance, and which took me some little time to twig, was that I would put the crates of empty bottles in the yard at the back of the pub, which was secure because nobody could get down the side. Additionally I had locked gates at the back, some six foot high.

"I only discovered that something was amiss one evening, when on having to go out to the back yard, I disturbed several young children, no older than ten or eleven, who were climbing the gates by standing on each other's backs and taking the empties from the crates, which they obviously would then claim money from me again at the most opportune moment. God knows how many times

I gave refunds to these young entrepreneurs for the same empty bottles."

As Toby finishes, Rob suddenly takes centre stage, saying, "Talking of characters, I was employed for many years at Heathrow as an air craft mechanic, and the workshop seemed to attract extroverts of every description that you could imagine.

"Without doubt a chap called Stan McCarthy was head and shoulders above the rest of them when it came to being the best source of entertainment. Stan was quite short, five feet three or four, bearded, of Irish extraction and spoke in its soft lilting southern brogue. However, the most obvious characteristic that made him stand out in a crowd was his spectacles, which due to his poor eye sight were at least an inch thick and looked for all the world like those 'bullseye' pieces of glass that people used to put in their front doors a hundred years ago. These would hang over his eyes, giving him an impression of a myopic worm.

"In the days that I am talking about we used to work shifts, four days of twelve hours on days, then four of nights followed by four days off. Over the years Stan had perfected the art of doing very little, mostly by not being noticed. This was achieved mainly by sickness absences, some of which were pure strokes of ingenuity. On one occasion his wife rang in to say that he was suffering from malaria, but I knew for a fact that he had never been anywhere exotic, other than Spain for his holidays.

"Other spurious sicknesses were almost equally mind blowing. The litany of sickness excuses was endless, but even when he did condescend to come in, he never did much work of any significance, mainly because his work colleagues were loath to give him any because of his poor vision. He would take so long to do even the most menial of tasks that he would be almost forgotten by the others (who were not used to seeing him very often anyway) because he held them back.

"This was not for any altruistic reasons on their behalf, but rather because very often they could arrange an early 'trap' to get away before their shifts had finished, providing all their work was completed. The type of delays that Stan caused could seriously affect the chances of this happening, which meant that he was not very often asked to do work of any description.

"However this was not company practice, but rather something that the shifts arranged amongst themselves.

"So Stan sailed through his tranquil sea of life, totally oblivious to events happening around him, but amazingly despite all this, his work mates bore him no grudges, and were even in awe of him in his effrontery to buck the system.

"Socially, Stan was in his element, particularly in his local, where he could be found most nights at the bar, giving forth the benefits of his wisdom on virtually any subject that was raised to anyone who would listen.

"Unfortunately on one such evening, upon driving to his home a short distance away Mr Plod flagged him down for some obscure motoring offence, and the moment Stan's window was wound down his fate was sealed. A five hundred pound fine and a year's driving ban for drunk driving. As you can imagine this was a devastating blow, and for a while Stan was depressed, but eventually like the maestro he was, his ingenuity came to the fore and he found a variety of methods to overcome this problem.

"The first was simply to up his sickness and absentee record even more. The second was to arrange with me to take him to work on those days that were possible. He would ride his bike the three miles to my house and we would go in by car from there.

"The third alternative which he employed, but was only when the first two failed, was to ride his bike to work. As this was some twenty-odd miles it was not something that Stan did without exploring all other avenues first. It was during this period when Stan was not allowed to drive that a couple of incidents happened that still bring a smile to my face when I recall them.

"The first occurred one evening when Madge and I went out for an evening meal to The Kings Head with Henry and Isabel. I was standing in the saloon bar ordering drinks when I suddenly spotted Stan with his wife and one or two other friends standing at the public bar opposite. The pub was very busy and although I tried several times to attract his attention I was unable to do so.

"I did not pursue the matter further, and in fact forgot all about it until I arrived home, where my mother had been babysitting the children. We were not late home, because I was due to start an early shift at six o'clock the following morning, leaving my house at five to do so, taking Stan with me.

"You can imagine my surprise, arriving home, when the first thing my mother told me was that Stan had rung shortly after we had left to go out, asking her to tell me that he was not very well and so would not be going in to work with me the next day. To this day, I find it hard to think how Stan knew that he was going to be unwell the next day, before he went to the pub with his friends.

"The second incident occurred one day when all other of Stan's methods of getting to work fell through. He simply drove his car. This method was used very sparingly, because obviously the risk of him being found out could have led to a further ban or even imprisonment.

"On one of these fateful days, being low on petrol, Stan stopped for a refill at a service station. Getting out of his car he moved round to get to the petrol lock and as he did so a tanker loaded with petrol was negotiating its position to refill the tanks on the forecourt.

"Unfortunately the tanker driver had not noticed Stan as he did so, and Stan suddenly found himself trapped between the service station office and the tanker which is still moving inexorably towards him. Drawing himself up against the wall as close as he could to avoid a collision, Stan then experienced the indignity of the petrol lorry running over his toes, leaving him in agony. A number of people who had witnessed the incident hurried to his aid, all telling him that it was the tanker driver's fault and that he should call the police.

"Stan (never one to miss an opportunity), for a few moments has visions of lottery money compensation payments in front of his eyes, before suddenly remembering that he is disqualified from driving, and so any such action is not be possible, in fact would go severely against him.

"Brushing away their good intentions, Stan has to pretend, even though he is in absolute agony, that he is OK. Not only that, but he has to continue driving into work where he spends the rest of the day in excruciating pain but is unable to let it show, because management has no idea that he has been banned from driving, and would take a dim view of it were they to find out. For a long time after this incident, Stan would rave to me about the fact that this was the one time in his life when he could legitimately have claimed substantial damages for injuries, only to be thwarted by his own stupid actions.

"But the incident that I will never forget, was the day that Stan was told to repair a faulty electrical unit that had been causing problems in flight.

"Stan duly placed the unit on the workshop bench and began to dismantle it, completely oblivious of the fact that some of the engineers were nudging and winking each other as they saw an opportunity to cause him grief. As Stan peered at the dismantled unit, holding each piece up to within a couple of inches of his eyes, two of the engineers made their way past him, the first one distracting him, while the second threw a rogue screw down on the bench without Stan noticing.

"Stan now had an extra screw, which of course remains when he has reassembled the unit after finding the fault. However, if he has reassembled it correctly, no screws should remain. Thinking that he had made a mistake, he hurriedly dismantled the unit again, which had all the engineers convulsed in fits of laughter, which they try desperately not to reveal to Stan.

"It is only when Stan had repeated the process for a second and third time that they were unable to contain themselves any longer, and the whole workshop, who are all of aware of the situation by now, bursts into uncontrolled laughter.

"If I remember right, Stan never did work of any description by himself after that."

So the evening passes. By now the sun's rays have almost disappeared, but lost natural light is replaced by solar lights spaced around the patio at the edges of Kate's flower beds, giving an eerie glow, and throwing long shadows across the lawn.

It is Kate's turn next, as she explains about Malcolm to them, he of the mangled sayings. She regales them with some that she can remember.

"Well, he had a cold a few months ago, and I heard him telling anyone who cared to listen, 'I have a cold and I'm as thick as anything with it,' or on another occasion I heard him saying about the junior at work to someone, 'He keeps his nose to the ground,' which I am sure was meant as a most wonderful compliment. Another time I overheard him talking to a client, who must have been most confused to hear Malcolm say, 'What I need to know is where I'm coming from.'"

"The funniest part is that most of our clients are so used to his odd sayings, which they all seem to love, so much so in fact that they often ring us and tell us, because they know that we keep a list for posterity. They have sometimes asked for copies. Even Malcolm is aware that he does it, but seems unable to stop. I suppose that it's a form of dyslexia, but whatever the reason it certainly brings a smile to all our faces when it happens."

Kate has everyone in fits by now, but Rob in particular is delighted with these little nuggets and asks Kate if she would let him have a copy of the list.

Eventually Toby and Avril stand up to take their leave, thanking Kate and Henry for a memorable evening, but to the others also, saying they haven't had such fun in a long time.

Rob takes the opportunity to join the landlord, saying with a smile, "We will come back with you in case you lock us out," and turning to the others, "But before we go we would like to invite you all to lunch at the pub tomorrow," to which Henry replies, "You just try and stop us, but do you fancy a tour of the village in the morning first, to work up an appetite?"

Rob accepts with alacrity, but Madge hesitates. Kate, noticing her reticence, exclaims, "If you would rather Madge, you are most welcome over here while the boys go off on their hike, and we can sit and natter and have a coffee and some of my Victoria sponge cake."

"No contest," replies Madge. "I will come over as soon as Henry arrives for Rob in the morning."

"Count me in on that as well," comes Megan's voice from the darkness. "Charlie can go with the boys."

On this note the evening ends with Kate shushing them as they reach the front gate, saying, "Keep the noise down, its nearly midnight and I wouldn't want to upset the neighbours," but both she and Henry can hear muffled laughter as the four make their way across the bridge and onto the common, while Megan and Charlie make a much more sedate exit turning right and following the path running parallel with the stream.

Looking at Kate, Henry realises just how tired she is and taking her in his arms says, "You go on up to bed while I just tidy this away and put the dishes in the dishwasher. We won't want to face it all in the morning," and then, "I just don't know how to thank you for all you have done today, they were all eating out of your hand by the time they left."

Kate, lifting her head from Henry's chest replies, "Oh no, they are all such lovely people, it gave me such a wonderful feeling of contentment to see them all getting on so well together. I have had a simply wonderful day, but I must admit that I am ready for bed now," and finishes by saying, "Thank you for your offer to tidy up, which I accept, but don't be too long before coming up," after which she leaves.

Henry finishes a beer slowly, taking in the total silence of the surrounding darkness, rerunning with relish in his mind the events of the day, before cleaning up and joining Kate who is already fast asleep in the bedroom.

Waking slowly the next morning, both feeling sluggish from the previous day's exertions, they have a leisurely cooked breakfast, which is a rare event for both of them, before retiring outside to sit on the patio and catch up with the Sunday papers, until they are interrupted by Charlie's arrival.

"You had best get off, the two of you if you don't want to keep Rob waiting. Anyway, until you reach him, Madge won't come over here," Kate points out.

So they leave to join Rob, who is already waiting for them, dressed in shorts, T-shirt and trainers, which Henry feels is a bit dicey, knowing the amount of stinging nettles that lie in wait for them in the woods. They spend the rest of the morning wandering around the village and the woods, looking for the entire world, like the cast from *Last of the Summer Wine*. As they progress Henry explains in broad outline his terms of reference at the design studio and his concerns for the coming week when the new computer system is due to be installed.

"I can remember only too well the last occasion when I was working full time that my studio had a new system installed. Things were chaotic for a period until the training kicked in. I have tried to explain all this to David who has been very understanding, but until it is experienced first-hand, understanding and practical reality are worlds apart. The only thing that I would say in my defence is that I am absolutely sure that it is necessary for the studio.

"The equipment they are using has long passed its sell by date and desperately needs replacing, to enable the studio to develop sufficiently to compete in the graphic design world, which is fiercely cutthroat. It is crucially important that this coming week the installation goes well, and in that regard, I am somewhat apprehensive."

Rob and Charlie sympathise with him, understanding just how much Henry has on his shoulders. Asking for more detail they offer vague suggestions, but not having the necessary experience, they feel unable to help, other than encourage and support him generally.

They stop for coffee and a chance to soak up the sun, which is a flaming yellow ball in a clear blue, cloudless sky. As they sit, bees make their unhurried but remorseless flight among the flowers around them, while swallows swoop like hordes of enemy aircraft just above the common, looking for insects to feed their hungry young.

Continuing on into the woods under Charlie's intrepid direction, Rob gets severely stung by stinging nettles, much as Henry suspected, and although they continue for a short while, Rob's heart is no longer in it, so they return to the Mucky Duck for a precursor before lunch, where they find that Kate, Madge and Megan have already arrived.

Realising that Rob and Madge will be leaving later in the afternoon, the level of noise increases as they each try to contribute to the conversation as a way to confirm how much they have enjoyed each other's company. Toby and Avril join them all in a toast and promises are made that they must repeat the experience soon.

The afternoon passes as they sit on the common outside the pub, until eventually Rob and Madge collect their cases and go, leaving Henry with a nostalgic lump in his throat.

Sensing Henry's loss, Kate says to the three of them, "Come on, let's go back to mine and have tea and cakes. We can sit outside and watch the world go by. What do you say?"

"We will take a rain check on that if you don't mind, we promised Charlie's sister that we would drop in sometime today," says Megan. "Although your offer is by far the more tempting."

CHAPTER 18
The New Computer System

Monday the second of June arrives all too soon for Henry, who is awoken early by interminable birdsong chatter. He can recognise the beautiful sounds of a wren, who produces the most melodic and powerful tune, belying its diminutive size. This is interspersed by the dominant sound of blackbirds calling each other, accompanied by the soft swish of pigeons softly warbling as they land on the windowsill.

The one thing that spoils Henry's enjoyment is the harsh, rapidly repeated 'Kaa-Kaa- Kaa' sound of magpies, which seems to be the signal for them to gather and place themselves logistically in positions where they know that other birds have nests and chicks. Although he tries not to, Henry hates these black and white angels of death, which cause so much damage and destruction to the rest of the bird population. He can accept the natural order of things. Sparrowhawks eat sparrows for example, just as other hawk family members kill pigeons. No, the thing that Henry finds most distressing is the organisation and orchestration of the magpies, who seem to work in co-operation with each other to first locate, and then distract the parents of their victims, enabling others of their clan to close in and steal their chicks.

The sheer numbers of magpies, which appear to grow enormously with every passing year, seem to confirm Henry's thoughts of their clinical efficiency.

Continuing this train of thought, he idly considers as he now lies wide awake, the most successful exponent of organised killing of all kinds of life. Man himself.

This seems to somehow reconcile Henry's thinking, because the next thing he experiences is the strident sound of the alarm waking him, after having fallen into a deep sleep.

The next week passes in a blur, in much the manner that Henry has anticipated. Len Best, good as his word, arrives on time and his team commence installing the new Apple system, which entails laying cable to replace that which already exists. Then new work stations are attached. This takes two days, during which time Henry and his team continue to use the existing system. On Wednesday data from the old system is transferred to the new, and staff training begins in earnest.

Long days follow for both Kate and Henry, early mornings and late nights which take their toll on both of them. Grabbing ready meals or eating at the Mucky Duck, they then go to bed totally exhausted, only to have to get up again as soon as (it seems to them) their heads hit the pillow.

As the training progresses and staff performances rise through the first week, so do all their spirits. David has also managed to stay at the studio for most of the time and begins to appreciate the benefits of the new system.

Kate's situation is slightly different, due to the fact she is the only person who will have to learn how to use the accounts and costing package on the system, although David also gets involved as much as possible.

It soon becomes apparent that the system is a far quicker vehicle than the old one, not only in terms of design application, but also in its sheer scope. The designers quickly discover that the new system will do so much more that the existing one. However if the increased levels of control are to be implemented, particularly in terms of time allocation to jobs, then more administrative time will be required.

From his own experience Henry is convinced that this is the way forward, to get the disciplines necessary for the studio to be effective, and suggests that David might consider a part time clerk who can oversee this part of the operation, but who can also help Kate with the accounts, pointing out that any such move would have to be sold to her carefully, because she might see it as a slight on her abilities.

THE BUS PASS

At the end of the week, before leaving, David invites Kate and Henry to his for Sunday lunch, which Kate accepts with alacrity, seeing it as an opportunity for her daughter-in-law and her grandchildren to get to know Henry.

Henry and Kate spend the Saturday relaxing and recharging their batteries before joining Megan and Charlie for the evening in the Mucky Duck.

The effort of the previous week has taken its toll, understandably, on their growing relationship, but, Henry thinks, it has also enhanced it in an almost imperceptible way, because it has shown them that they are compatible in their practical joint approach under pressure.

Sunday is a warm sunny day, but intermittent showers are promised by the meteorological office in their usual confident fashion, seeming to take great pleasure in conveying such matters to the mass of the Great British public.

Henry spends the morning catching up with his diary and email communications, while Kate does some cleaning, before they set off to David's family at Netherton.

They are both welcomed effusively by David, who introduces Henry to his wife Gina and his children Elise and Joseph, who are about seven and five respectively. David's wife is quite tall at about five feet nine inches, elegant and poised, with a bob cut hair style that suits her brunette glossy hair. Meeting her for the first time Henry can imagine her as a fashion model, a thought that is confirmed to be the case by David during the afternoon.

But much more than that, Henry is impressed by her down to earth attitude, which is exemplified by the manner in which she puts him at ease, saying, "Welcome Henry, I am so pleased to meet you at last, particularly for the wonderful tranquillising effect that you have had on David. The difference in him over the last few weeks since your arrival has been astonishing. He even manages to talk to me now and has started getting involved with the children again, taking them out for rambles and playing with them, something that he has not had time for in ages."

Henry is taken completely unawares by Gina's frank admission of just how much pressure David has been under for such a long time, which makes him suddenly realise just how much that he admires and respects this open young man who has achieved so much, in spite of, his father's early demise.

He tries to convey this to Gina, saying, "David is a joy to work for and if I have been able to take some pressure off him, he has more than repaid it by giving my life a sense of purpose and worth, something that I have not had for several years, so no thanks are necessary."

David is a very good host and as soon as lunch is finished they all retire to the patio where there is a small outside swimming pool in which the children frolic while the adults use sun-loungers to relax and chatter in a desultory fashion until David suddenly brings up the subject of the Goderston Village Fete, saying, "I like the poster designs, Henry. I will arrange to get them put up this week. I usually run a stall or side show, but I'm sure that we can all get together during the day and enjoy some of the exhibitions."

As Henry watches David's children playing and laughing together, he is suddenly emotionally overwhelmed, as he is reminded of his own grandchildren, which brings an immediate feeling of longing... loss almost, as he realizes that he has not seen Penny's children for several weeks.

Kate, perceptive as ever, notes the tears in his eyes and the catch in his throat as he continues to make light conversation, despite the way he is feeling. She puts her hand on his and squeezes it while giving him a wry smile, saying without words, "I understand what you are going through, let us sort it out once we have left."

The day continues and they eventually take their leave of David and Gina, and once in the car, Kate puts her unsaid words into reality, adding, "You are missing your grandchildren Henry, which is really not surprising. It would probably have hit you a lot earlier if you had not been so busy. Why don't we see if Penny, Mark and the children would like to come down and visit us next weekend? Then we could all go to the fete, if they would like to."

For a moment Henry is overcome once again by her intuitive skills and giving spirit, before replying, "Oh, that would be fantastic Kate, are you sure you don't mind?" to which she replies, "Of course not, I am just so sorry that I didn't think of it earlier. The only thing is that I am not sure if I have room for all of them, perhaps we could have the children and Penny and Mark could stay at the Mucky Duck, what do you think. Alternatively they could all stay with us, but that would mean that they would be taking up the other two bedrooms, leaving us in the third. I don't know if Penny, or you, is ready yet for that scenario."

"That situation had not occurred to me, I wouldn't want to upset or offend them. Why don't I explain it all to Penny and see how she feels, and then we can decide which way to play it… let me contact them when we get back, so that we give them as much time as possible to make their arrangements," replies Henry, experiencing a warm glow at the prospect of seeing them all again.

"Hi Penny, love. I thought that it was time to speak to, rather than just email you to let you know what I have been doing. A couple of things suddenly occurred to me, first, that I am not getting any feedback on how you are all doing and secondly how much I miss seeing you all and hearing the sounds of your voices and how you are all getting along."

"Don't be daft Dad, of course we miss you too, but you let us know regularly what is happening in your life, and anyway, we talk to Rob and Madge all the time and they fill us in with any missing bits."

I bet they do, thinks Henry, wondering just how much his friends had said to Penny, before replying, "No doubt they have told you the current situation in respect of Kate and myself and how well we are getting along. I hope you understand, Penny love, that if your mother was still alive, nobody, but nobody would take her place, but in Kate I have found someone who is good for me. I would like to think that I am good for her too. I don't know how long it will last, because I still need to continue my journey to visit all those places on my list, if I am to follow you all to Australia."

There is a catch in Penny's voice as she says, "Oh Dad, I am so sorry, what have we done to you, to put you in this Catch 22 situation. Anyway with regard to your relationship with Kate, I can tell you that we are all delighted for you, including Richard, who bombards me almost daily for the latest up dates. We both know just how much Mum meant to you, but more than that, we know that she would be delighted that you have found someone because it is a tribute to the strength of your relationship together, that you are ready to start living again. Mum's early death reminded me of that which she was always saying, that life is for living and every moment is precious, so don't waste it."

Unable to speak for several minutes, Henry eventually replies, "My thanks to you both my wonderful children, neither Kate nor I can see very far in the future, but for now we are grateful for what we have. Anyway, the reason I am ringing is because we would both like to invite you down next weekend, if that is suitable for you.

Saturday is the day of the village fete, where I am assured by everyone who has any knowledge of the subject, that it will be 'a blast', whatever that is. There will be lots of things going on for both children and adults, and best of all it will be lovely seeing you all again. Kate has kindly offered to put you all up. She has three bedrooms, so space is not a problem and to save any embarrassment, I can stay at the Mucky Duck."

"No, you will certainly not," comes Penny's unequivocal reply. "I have just explained that we are all happy that you are together, which is due in no uncertain measure, I have not the slightest doubt, to Kate." We would love to come down, say after work on Friday and stay until Sunday afternoon, does that sound all right?"

"That would be wonderful, love," replies Henry with a tremor in his voice, before adding, "Now let me speak to those two rascal grandchildren of mine."

After several minutes catching up with their latest information on how they are doing at school, play station games and other electronic gadgets, which are completely over his head, Henry explains to them about the fete the following weekend before ending their conversation.

In terms of work, the following week is a continuation of the previous one for Henry and Kate. Training on the computer system continues by Len and one other member of his team until Wednesday, when he is satisfied that Henry and his team are sufficiently capable to continue on their own, but at the same time assuring them that if any problems arise they can phone him and if necessary he can return.

"But in any event, most problems can be resolved over the telephone or by email."

The studio team have responded well to the new system, beginning to appreciate more and more the scope and speed now available, while it has become increasingly apparent that if accurate information of time costs are to be inputted, time sheets will have to be entered onto the system against jobs, which can then be compared against budgeted hours and thus establish if margins have been maintained.

This is an additional area for Kate's expertise, but one that will take more of her time, which she is prepared to do for a short period until such time that a part time accounts person can be employed to assist her. David has no hesitation in agreeing to her request and tells her to contact local employment agencies when she is ready to start the ball rolling.

As Kate and Henry return home on Wednesday she suddenly remembers that she has an appointment at the mobile breast scanning clinic at the library car park in Dorchester the following day for her three year check up at the mammary clinic.

"So I'll drop you off at work in the morning, and either come to work later, or pick you up at the end of the day, because I would like to do some shopping and I am not sure how long it will take. I will probably take Gina as well, she enjoys retail therapy even more than I do."

Laughing, Henry rejoins, "In that case, I think I'll buy some Marks and Spencer's shares."

So accordingly Henry gets dropped off at the studio, while Kate and Gina leave, returning to collect him in time to return home. The reason for Kate's shopping expedition becomes apparent when she reveals her purchases, nearly all of which are food related, explaining that she wants something special for Penny and her family's visit the following day.

Henry's emotions fluctuate between just how thoughtful and generous Kate is, saying only lamely, "Thank you my love, what a wonderful, thoughtful, thing to do. Knowing Penny, she will appreciate your efforts, but will be happy just to be here."

"I just want it to be such a special weekend for you all… and me." replies Kate, and laughing, "Perhaps she will not see me quite as much as a scarlet women, rather as someone who has your best interests at heart."

"She doesn't, and never will see you in that way," says Henry, alarmed that she could even think it. "You come highly recommended. Penny's attitude is that if you are good enough for me, then you are good enough for her."

On that note their conversation drifts into the arrangements for the following day, Friday, the day that Penny arrives. It is agreed that if possible they will try to leave work midafternoon, to give them enough time to get any further supplies, before she arrives.

Henry awakes the next morning to the sun's golden rays filtering through the curtains. As he opens them the light becomes a golden ball, flooding the bedroom hungrily, seeking to impose its presence into every nook and cranny. It is going to be a glorious day, reflects Henry to himself, before waking Kate from her slumbers. He has not slept very well, with thoughts of Penny and her family arriving later on making him anxious that they will like Kate and vice- versa.

As they drive to the studio Kate says that if he thinks that it would be a good idea she could invite David, Gina and the children sometime over the weekend. After some thought Henry agrees, thinking not only that more people might mean less potentially embarrassing silences, but also because he is sure that he and Kate's children and grandchildren will get on famously. Kate, once again recognizing Henry's anxiety, reassures him, squeezing his arm, no words being necessary between them.

CHAPTER 19
Penny And Mark

It is seven o'clock before Penny and her family arrives, by which time Henry is beside himself with all the apprehension that their visit potentially entails. But all such worries disappear instantly as he embraces her.

"Oh it's so good to see you all, I have missed you so much," he tells her, before welcoming Mark and saying, "You wait until you see the selection of beers in the Mucky Duck, Mark. You and I have some serious beer tasting to do, my lad," then turning to his grandchildren, "Hello boys, come and give your grandfather a hug, then tomorrow we will all go to the fete where you can have a ride on the ponies and have sack races and play lots of other games."

As they get luggage from their car, Kate comes out to join Henry, who introduces her to each of them in turn.

"Come on in. Don't let's stand out here," she says. "I have prepared a meal, I hope you all like fish. Toby had some lovely sea bream which I just couldn't refuse." It may have seemed an innocuous statement, but Kate's choice of food was in fact the result of much consultation with Henry, who assured her that all Penny's family like fish.

Henry shows Mark his and Penny's room, and then the boys' room, while his daughter remains downstairs helping Kate in the kitchen. He is delighted to hear them not only discussing the meal, but also laughing and joking as if they have known each other for ever. In between time the boys are busily exploring, beginning with their room, before moving out to the garden, where Henry and Mark go out to join them to play football on the lawn.

Henry's memories are transported back some forty years to the time that he was doing exactly the same thing with his children, only this time Oliver plays centre-forward for England, while Joshua is content to kick the ball just anywhere, quite often into his own net, laughing deliriously every time he makes any sort of contact.

Forty years have taken their toll on Henry, who is reduced to playing in goal (although he is now the England goal keeper, Joe Hart, having been nominated so by Oliver). Somehow Mark and Joshua manage to win by a score of twenty to Henry and Oliver's eighteen goals.

Kate's efforts have been worth all the thought that has gone into her cooking. The meal is an unqualified success, sea bream in a beautiful parsley sauce, with new potatoes, runner beans and sweetcorn, a specialty of hers, followed by apple and blackcurrant crumble with custard (Henry and the boys' favourite).

As their hunger is sated, talk returns between them, Henry catching up with Mark and the boys, while Kate and Penny discover more about each other, and discuss arrangements for the fete the following day.

They are so relaxed in each other's company, that no one recognizes how late it is, until suddenly Kate says, "Look at the time, its nearly nine thirty. If you want to take Penny and Mark to the Mucky Duck, you'd best make a move," at which Penny interjects.

"Oh no, that's OK. I'll stay here and help you clear up, and then I can put the boys to bed."

So it is agreed. Henry and Mark make their way across the common, where various areas have been marked out in readiness for the fete the following day.

The evening is still, the end of a perfect day in fact, Henry reflects. The sky is slashed a vivid red with the sun dying on the horizon.

Reaching the Mucky Duck, Henry initiates his son-in-law into the various local beers that Henry has mentioned previously. As they sit quaffing their drinks, Henry is greeted by a number of regulars who he has got to know and whose company he enjoys. Accordingly, his little party grows as Henry introduces them to Mark. Like those in the Jack the Lad, the regulars of the Mucky Duck also have a penchant to giving each other pet names which over a period of time became their definitive titles that they are recognized by. Thus those that are introduced are as follows:

Graham Way, also known as 'Milky'. Roger Friar is 'Abbott', James Richard has become 'Cliff'. Then there's Donald Lumb also solemnly referred to as 'Red Rum' for two reasons - the first because it rhymes but also because of his interest in horse racing, and last but not least is Fred Hovell, known affectionately as 'Scruffy'. One other is Adam Collins who is known as 'Bunter'. His nickname is a little more obscure, but it started when he was very young and had been very chubby, thus Billy Bunter, but the connection is more difficult to reconcile nowadays with the tall lean man that he has become.

Much leg-pulling ensues, while the beer flows freely, with Mark finding that he is being treated as a regular, and his contribution to the conversation is sought equally to that of the others. Eventually Henry and Mark take their leave after first giving their assurances that they will see the others at the fete the next day.

Although it is now eleven o'clock, as they return to the house they are surprised to hear Kate and Penny's murmured voices coming from the patio. The evening is still and warm and Henry and Mark make their way to join their women who are sat round the patio table drinking Chablis from a bottle that is nearly empty (which Henry subconsciously notes almost as a reflex). But much more than that, they are chatting and laughing together as if they have known each other all their lives.

Looking up, Kate says, "Come and join us. It's such a lovely night that we decided to spend some time out here to catch up on some girly talk, while we waited for you to return."

The men do that but with neither of them wishing for any more to drink. Once seated, the effects of Henry's alcohol consumption at the pub leaves him struggling to stay awake, but as he looks across at Penny, whose profile is lit up by the lantern lights which surround the patio, he sees, for the very first time, how her features are so very much like Isabel's, which makes him wonder to himself why he has not noticed it before. The revelation is so strong that he almost chokes with emotion, and indeed, pleasure, realizing that part of his beloved late wife lives on in Penny.

Now that recognition has been made Henry starts to notice other characteristics that have emanated from Isabel. Penny's mannerisms, the way she uses her hands when making a point, the way she throws her head back to shake her long fair hair back into place, the way she laughs, her mouth pulling into a wry grin when telling a joke and delivering the punch line.

Henry is saved any thoughts of embarrassment regarding sleeping arrangements as Penny rises, saying, "Well, I don't know about the rest of you, but bed is calling me. In fact I think only adrenaline has got me this far. I have had a lovely evening, so thanks, Kate and Dad, but if I don't get some sleep soon, I will be one grumpy bunny in the morning."

Henry is suddenly made aware of just how long a day it has been, not only for Penny and Mark, but also for Kate and himself, and replies, "Good idea, we all have another long day in front of us tomorrow," and then finishing, "Sleep well, see you in the morning."

Saturday 14 June arrives spectacularly with the sun a golden blaze in the heavens. By nine o'clock the temperature is already twenty degrees, with a promise of more to come. They breakfast slowly, again out on the patio, with sounds being carried from across the common of tents and other paraphernalia being erected. Somewhat to Henry's surprise and pleasure, David, Gina and their children arrive at eleven o'clock, the reason for which becomes apparent as Kate welcomes them, before turning to Henry, saying, "I know we were all going to meet up at the fete this afternoon, but I thought that it would be nice if they could come earlier then David could tell Penny and Mark how much you have contributed to the business and just how grateful he is."

As they are introduced, David proceeds to do just that (much to Henry's chagrin) and finishes, saying, "So you see we just could not have managed without him. Until he came onto our radar I was struggling to hold onto the business, let alone develop it, but thanks to your father's efforts, we are in a much better place. However long he stays or whatever he does in the future, my family and I will be forever grateful to him."

Before anyone else can respond, Penny replies, "Well thank you for all the lovely things that you have said about my dad, which only confirm all the things that I know about him. He has always been a rock, a star in our firmament if you like for both of us, his children, but also for my mum always, but particularly once she became ill. Finally, I hope that I am not talking out of place, but I am so pleased to see him looking happy and content again, which I can only ascribe to your mother's administrations, so let's drink a toast to the two of them."

The rest of the morning disappears in a flash, Penny and Mark catch up with David and Gina as to how Henry was 'discovered' by Kate and then how they discovered each other, while all the children play games on the lawn, Oliver and Joshua treating David's younger children with due reverence.

At one o'clock they all make their way onto the common where people are already gathering, to hear the local celebrity, Rick Dolan (a rock musician of the sixties and seventies era), declare the fete open. With so many stalls and events to see, Henry turns to David and Kate for their advice on where to start.

"Well, we usually go round the stalls and fun fare rides first, and then spend most of the rest of the day at the arena where there are lots of things for both the adults and the children to enjoy," explains Kate.

So it is decided, and they make their way around the stalls, playing tombola and crazy golf (which the children love), then skittles followed by guess the number of sweets in the jar. They are all happily spending, knowing that the proceeds are going to very good causes. They take the children to try various rides, and afterwards they visit some of the arts and craft stalls, where Henry buys Kate a beautiful bracelet and matching earrings in blue cloisonné enamel, the colour of which matches Kate's eyes.

Catching up with Penny, David and their families, they are just in time to see the children go on to the helter-skelter, and to hear their excited laughter as they whizz down it from top to bottom. Then once down requesting, "Again, again!" in very excited voices, which of course they do. So the afternoon passes at a leisurely pace as they find places around the arena in which a number of events are occurring, from pony rides to dog, cattle and sheep shows. These are followed by egg and spoon, sack, and three-legged races for both children and adults. These are a source of endless enjoyment as Kate comes last in the sack race after falling over after only a few yards while Henry does little better in the egg and spoon race.

Penny, deciding she needs to do something to restore the family honour, enters the three legged race together with Mark, but fares no better after getting confused between them as to which leg to use first and ending up to everyone's amusement by going round and round in circles rather than in a straight line. Family honour is eventually restored by the respective children, much to their parents delight as Oliver and Joshua win three-legged race, followed soon after by David's children winning the sixty yards dash for both their age and boys and girls groups.

So the afternoon passes and they now turn their attention to the arena which is a large area that has been cordoned off by rope. Here there are a number of various shows which they all watch as the afternoon continues in much the same manner as that has gone on before, with beautiful cloudless blue skies, the colour of which is intensified by the golden glow of the sun blazing down upon them. Occasionally, Henry or David or Mark will make forays to get supplies of hot dogs or burgers from the assorted snack vans, or ice creams and soft drinks for the children.

Several local farmers have arranged sheep dog trials which captivate the children, particularly Henry's grandchildren, who he suddenly realizes have probably not seen sheep before.

Once all the various displays are finished in the arena, the rope cordon is taken down and people move forward to the far side where a covered stand has been erected for Rick Dolan to perform. By this time a languor has settled over them all, and as the sun starts to descend, they wait in anticipation for the arrival of Rick Dolan and his group.

Suddenly he and his group are on stage and he begins by making an announcement thanking everyone for attending and contributing to such worthy causes. He then commences his performance by announcing that he will begin by playing one of his older hits called 'Perfect Love' and continues by saying that it has been requested by Kate Challis, which she would like to dedicate to Henry Long. As his mouth drops in amazement, Henry is left speechless until Kate reaches up and brushes her lips to his

THE BUS PASS

before whispering conspiratorially and laughing, "I think that you will find that on a range of one to ten I have scored a B."

"Oh you have indeed my love?" he whispers in return, adding, "How did you manage that you clever little minx?" only to hear her chuckle and say, "Well, it was easy really, because you see I grew up with Rick Dolan, so I have known him all my life. Only his birth name is Richard Dangerfield, so you can see why he changed it when he began making records." The two of them stand together and as Rick begins to play, the rest of the group gather round and congratulate Kate on springing her surprise, with Penny laughing uncontrollably, saying, "You should have seen the look on your face, Dad. It was a picture." Taking Kate in his arms Henry begins a slow dance in time to the song, followed by David and Gina, who are quickly joined by Penny and Mark.

Henry can't remember a time since Isabel died that he has felt better...

Much later as Rick ends his performance with his most famous song, 'Never Let Me Go'. Fireworks are lit and the trails from the rockets weave a tracery, in a myriad of colours across the darkened sky.

Children and adults alike are transfixed by the pure beauty of the display which continues seamlessly from one scenario to the next. But eventually the show comes to its inevitable conclusion and they are all left with a feeling of anti-climax.

Saying their farewells to David, Gina, Elise and Joseph, they wend their way back across the common to Kate's, where Henry puts his grandchildren to bed. This is a rare treat for him, reminding him of those times years before, when he and Isabel, having babysat the two of them, would take it in turns to read to them before they went to sleep.

Although extremely tired, both Joshua and Oliver talk excitedly about the day's events, which Henry is only too keen to encourage, and asks them, "Well, what things did you like most?" to which Oliver, being the eldest, replies, "I loved seeing all the animals and riding the pony."

While he is talking, Joshua, not to be outdone, is saying loudly, "Well you know what Granddad I liked the races and the sheep and the fireworks." Henry kisses the boys goodnight and returns downstairs, hoping to be able to talk to Penny and Mark with Kate, but is met by the sight of Penny lying across Marks leg's, both of them fast asleep on the sofa.

"I didn't have the heart to wake them up," says Kate, to which Henry replies, "No, I don't think that I can either. Let's leave them and go up ourselves. They will be up fast enough when they wake." So the day ends, leaving everyone exhausted but happy, with memories that they will dip into for many years to come.

Waking next morning, Henry is unsurprised to find that it is already nine o'clock and that he is the first to wake, apart from the boys, who he can hear playing together in the next room. Kate lies next to him semi-comatose, her hair splayed out across the pillow like a silver filigree. Not wanting to wake her, he decides to take the boys downstairs and give them breakfast.

"Hello Granddad," they both exclaim as he goes in to their room. "Do you want to play some games with us?"

"Well boys, I thought that I would get you some breakfast first, and then we can do that, or perhaps we could have a walk round the village, or play football in the garden. What do you think?"

"Football, football, football!" they both cry out excitedly. So the decision is made.

The rest of the house slowly comes alive, Penny, Mark and Kate finding their way to the kitchen by ten o'clock, although still only half awake, by which time Henry is shattered after playing football with the boys in the garden. It is another beautiful sunny day and after discussing what they would all like to do, it becomes apparent that they would like to do a lot of nothing, at which point Henry says, "Why don't we all stay here this morning? I will go and get some Sunday papers and we can sit out here until lunch time, and then we can all go to lunch at the Mucky Duck," to which Penny replies, "That sounds great Dad and it will suit us because we don't want to leave it late before we go home, because of work in the morning," to which they all agree.

The morning passes in a relaxed, lazy fashion with Henry and Kate reading, while Penny goes inside to make teas and coffee for them.

THE BUS PASS

As she returns Henry can see a smile on her face, and asks, "A penny for them?" to which she answers, "I'm sorry, but I was just thinking of one day last week, when I was preparing Oliver's lunch box for school. I had opened his box ready to put sandwiches, crisps, some soft drink and a bar of chocolate in it ready for the next day when I suddenly noticed that there was some chocolate left in it from that day, so I said to him, 'Why haven't you eaten the chocolate that I put in your box today?' to which he replied, "Cos I don't like chocolate.' I said, 'Then why didn't you tell me, because I have been putting it in for the last two weeks?' only to hear him say, 'I know, and I am fed up hiding it.'

As their laughter subsides, Kate suddenly says, "Hey Henry, did you tell Penny and Mark about Malcolm's mannerisms?" to which he says, "No, but I think that I ought to, after hearing that." So he goes on to tell them of the wacky things that Malcolm is prone to say, which only seem to occur when he is on the phone.

He has them all in stitches until Kate says suddenly, "Oh! I found another one the other day in my desk. Shall I read it out?" As they all acquiesce, she reads out Malcolm's latest little gem, saying, "Well I heard him on the phone the other day tell a client, 'I got new glasses at the weekend and I can't hear a thing.'"

As she finishes Penny and Mark are in floods of laughter, with Henry grinning from ear to ear, while saying, "I told you so, he's priceless."

Once the merriment subsides, Henry turns to Penny and asks, "Well my love have you heard any more about going to Australia? I guess things are moving forward now," to which she replies, "Well I'm not sure you're right about that Dad, the company is still negotiating various things in Oz, which seem to be taking forever, but I get the feeling that the recession in the industry has affected us just like everyone else so it's a case of watch this space. Mark and I have not pursued selling the house, or, in his case, not looked any further for employment in Oz. There is just no point at this stage."

Henry tries not to show his pleasure at this, not wanting to appear in any way selfish, because he also realizes that a move to Australia would be advancement for Penny, Mark and the children.

"Never mind Pen," he says. "Sometimes these things are not meant to be, or sometimes it can lead to even better situations. Perhaps if you have to wait a little longer the eventual result will be even better than you hoped."

Kate rises to her feet. "Well, I think that we had better be moving. It's a quarter to one and I told Toby we would be there just after one." There is a mad dash as each of them rushes to change and brush up before assembling in the hall at one o'clock. From here they stroll leisurely across the common to the Mucky Duck, with the exception of Henry, Joshua and Oliver, because the boys have smuggled a football out and insist that Henry play with them as they make their way.

Toby and Avril greet them warmly as they enter, before taking their order, which makes Henry reflect just how much he likes and enjoys their company. Toby is in ebullient mood and regales Penny and Mark with stories of Henry's fishing trips, which they have not heard before, or if they have, only expurgated versions.

All too soon comes the time which Henry has been dreading - the time for Penny, Mark and the children to leave. So they all wend their way back to Kate's, mostly in silence, each in solitary contemplation, with Henry thinking of the coming days, realizing just how much he will miss his daughter who reminds him so much of Isabel.

After packing, they are ready to depart and Henry hugs Penny, saying, "It's been wonderful to see you love, let us know when you get home," before turning to Mark, adding, "Look after her, son, and those two cheeky monkeys."

Penny embraces Kate while whispering in her ear, "Thank you for a wonderful weekend, and for all the things that you are doing for my father," only to hear her reply, "No thanks are necessary my dear, it's simple really, you see, I love him."

Soon they are gone and Kate, realizing that Henry is at a loss, says, "Why don't we invite Meg and Charlie round for afternoon tea or something? Come on, I'll go and fetch them, I'm sure they're not doing anything this afternoon." Before he has time to reply, Kate does just that, and within a short while Megan and Charlie are round having the proposed tea, or in this case the 'something' being wine for the ladies and chilled lager for the men, perfect for a hot day like today.

This proves to be the perfect antidote for Henry's earlier low mood, and Henry finds Meg and Charlie's quiet humour and warm company very comforting. It takes a little longer for him to realise how astute Kate has been to identify his mood and recognize the cause of his anguish. Not only that, but she has also found an answer and he marvels yet again at her ingenuity and his sense of gratitude becomes almost overwhelming. So the afternoon and evening pass in their magic company until it is time for them to say goodnight.

Once they have left, Henry and Kate look at each other, as lovers do, and no words being necessary, they make their way to bed. They both slowly undress one another, until Henry bends to kiss her hungrily, his tongue lightly flickering between her parted lips. Kate responds, pushing her hips against his hardness, until Henry can withstand the inevitable no longer. Picking her up in one smooth movement he lays her gently down on the bed where they both explore each other, until suddenly a shudder of ecstasy goes through Kate, and she murmurs, "Oh! Henry, I feel as if I am being invaded," to which he replies hoarsely, "Oh, my dear, you are."

They continue to seek to find ways to satisfy each other, until Kate, unable to wait any longer, whispers, "Come on Henry, I am ready." His response is immediate, having held back, wanting them both to climax together, because he is only too aware that his control all too often is premature.

But this time it is perfect and afterwards they both lie exhausted in each other's arms, a quiet feeling of completeness spreading over them. After a few minutes Henry, to his utter surprise, begins to feel his body responding again to the need of her, and says, "That was fantastic my love. In fact it was so good that I want some more."

Kate's reply is instantaneous as she rejoins, "Oh, Henry, me too."

This time, unlike previous times, this is emotional sex, not ferocious in its intensity, but deeply satisfying to both of them. When they are expended, Kate drapes her naked body over Henry's chest and he closes his arms around her as they fall into a deep sleep.

CHAPTER 20

Monday, 16 June

Monday 16 June and dawn breaks very like the previous day, warm and hazy, the only difference being that there is a slight zephyr of a breeze, sufficient to stop the atmosphere from being stifling.

After their busy weekend, Kate and Henry rise lethargically, both lost in their own thoughts of the previous few days. Suddenly, as he realises that Kate still has some clearing up to do after Penny's visit, Henry offers to go in to the studio on the bus, but she hates the thought of him having to do so, and telephones David to see if he can pick Henry up on his way. Fortunately, David does not have any client appointments and is only too happy to stop by on his way and to take the opportunity to speak to Henry on various outstanding matters in relation to the progress of the studio.

He duly arrives and picks Henry just as Kate hands him a lunch box, saying, "Take this, because I don't know what time I will make it in today, but I am definitely coming." With her words ringing in their ears they leave, and it is only after a minute or so that David turns to Henry and says, "Well that was a fantastic weekend, and it was so good to meet Penny, Mark and the children. Both Gina and I enjoyed their company and sense of humour," and finishes by saying, "I hope it's not too long before we see them again."

Thanking him, Henry replies, "I am sure that the feeling is mutual because they told me how much they enjoyed your family's company too."

There is a pause for a while before David broaches the subject of the progress of the studio. "I would like to discuss where we are, in respect of the objectives we want to achieve. The new system seems to be running very smoothly, apart from one or two minor cock-ups, which turned out inevitably to be operator error and were rectified almost immediately by the training team. I am asking you now Henry because I am all too aware that when you agreed to come and offer your experience and knowledge it was for a short period only, and it is already over three weeks since you began. We have achieved so much in such a short amount of time. So much so, I guess, that I am afraid that you will want to move on before I am ready, because I have begun to rely on your skills and experience so much that the thought of you going quite frankly, frightens me."

Henry is emotionally overwhelmed as he replies. "David, I am so very flattered that you feel this way, it has been a very uplifting experience for me too, but I can assure you that I have no intention of moving on in the near future. You must realize the strength of feelings that I hold for your mother, and my original plans have been put on hold for the moment, because I don't know what is happening to my children and their families. If they do eventually move to Oz I will be torn between moving myself and staying here. So you can see that I am even more confused now than the day I set out on my journey.

"With regards to where we are in the broad scheme of things, I think that the installation of the new computer and software has gone really well, apart from one or two minor issues which we have talked about and are being addressed. The backlog of work has also been eaten into and should be up to date within a few days. I think that all the staff have responded magnificently. In fact it seems to have given them a new sense of purpose. Malcolm in particular has grabbed the opportunity with both hands and I think that when I do decide to step back, that he has the ability to take over my role.

"This should then release you to do what you are best at, selling design concepts to clients. One area that now needs to be addressed is the filling in of time sheets, which can be done now through the use of the system as work is created. This, once you have established a studio cost, should enable you to tell if you are making money on jobs as they go along. I think that Kate will need to get involved in this, and she has the knowledge to establish a costing system for the studio. It may well be that she will need some help to establish an hourly studio cost, in which case I suggest that you arrange for your auditors to come in as a one- off, to explain how this figure can be achieved.

"The next thing that I think that you ought to look for is part time clerk, who, under Kate's guidance, can operate the costing system. In fairness, I don't think that your mother will have time to do all the work that the new costing system demands, but I do think that she can oversee it, if she gets the extra help that I am suggesting. There is no reason why you should not try to find someone for this clerical position as of now; your mother can, I am sure, contact local staff agencies, or advertise in the local paper, which should be cheaper I would imagine.

"When you quote clients prices for jobs, you will from your vast experience, be able to judge how many hours that the work should take. If you also know an hourly cost figure for the studio, you should then have a fairly accurate way to know how much to charge. It is then the studio manager's job to see that the work is completed to the customer's satisfaction within the allotted time.

"The next item to be addressed is the refurbishment of the offices and studio. I have taken the liberty of doing some draft plans along the lines that I discussed with you on my first day, which I will show you when we get to the office. I thought that we could have a look at them and make any changes that you want. Once that has been agreed I think we should proceed to get some quotes from local builders and then take it from there. I hope you don't think that I have presumed too much, but I too, like you, felt that time is of the essence."

As Henry stops speaking, there is a prolonged pause before David says, "Yet again Henry you have taken the initiative, for which I am so very grateful. You cannot possibly imagine how difficult it is and has been for me, for such a long time to have to make all the decisions to keep the ship afloat. Of course Mum helps as best she can, but she is not getting any younger, and she deserves a life of her own. I'm just saying that it is such a relief to have someone like you around, who is capable of making decisions. Let's have a look at your plans when we get to work and we can proceed from there."

The rest of their journey is travelled in silence, both wrapped within their own thoughts.

Upon arrival, Henry shows David the plans that he has drawn

up for the redesign of the office layout. After making one or two minor adjustments, David is happy with the resulting final draught and, leaving Henry, returns to his office to get in touch with some local builders that he trusts and has used before on some of his own projects; in this way he is able to arrange for two builders to visit and quote for the work within the next two days.

This he then relates to Henry, before saying, "I have to go to Swindon to see a client now and I doubt that I shall be back in the office today, or if I do, it will be very late, so can I leave it to you to explain to Mum the situation regarding the new costing system and the extra staff that she will need to administrate it." And then as an afterthought, "If she has time she can contact the local recruitment agencies to get the ball rolling."

Henry notes the gleam in David's eye and the new lightness in his step and realizes that the world has become a much better place for this attractive and honest young man, and is pleased for him.

Henry returns to the studio just in time to hear Malcolm, who is on the telephone talking to a client, say, "From a great height I think that is what happened." Almost doubled up with laughter, Henry hurriedly writes down Malcolm's mannerism while he can remember it, so that he can add it to his list.

The rest of the day he spends continuing to help the designers as well as taking on some projects of his own. Good progress continues to be made by the designers, and Henry is pleased to note that if they are not sure about certain aspects of their brief, that they will come not only to him for clarity and instruction, but also to Malcolm, who they seem to recognize almost sub consciously as someone with both the experience and ability to help them.

Kate arrives just before lunch and Henry relates his earlier discussion that he had with David. She can see immediately the need for an accurate costing system. Not only that, but she can also see that she will need help to operate and record time sheets, and begins immediately to contact local staff agencies.

Showing her his plans for the office and studio renovation she is totally captivated and makes one or two of her own suggestions. This pleases Henry enormously, as he realizes that she is on board with the ideas and the need for change. Kate then goes on to point out to him that she has always, over the years, been involved with changes, and recognizes that nothing stays static, rather that evolution in methods and operations are continuous.

On the way home that afternoon Kate says, "Oh Henry, by the way, I spoke to Sarah, Geoffrey's wife, this morning and during our conversation I said that I would go and see her tomorrow at Beaminster. It's been such a long time since I saw them all. So much so that I have been feeling guilty for neglecting them. I will go in the morning, but I don't know what time I will get back. Would you mind?"

"Of course not my love, why on earth should I?" replies Henry, "I'm only surprised that you haven't been to see them before now."

"Well I would have gone earlier, but it has been difficult while David has been struggling so much with the company, so I just put it off, but really it's not very fair to Geoffrey and his family."

As Henry contemplates Kate's remarks a number of questions come to mind, the first one being that although he knows a lot about David and his family, for some reason, Kate has said very little about her younger son, and he wonders how this has happened. Did Kate forget about him while she was getting involved with Henry? He thinks he knows her by now and is aware that this is not the case.

Not being able to think of a suitable reason, Henry asks "Tell me about Geoffrey and his family. It has been very remiss of me not to inquire before now. We should have invited him last weekend and he could have met Penny, Mark and the children, as well as David, Gina. I feel dreadful now that I overlooked them. Please forgive me, I was so wrapped up in my own little world that I ignored yours completely."

"Don't be so daft," replies Kate. "I haven't invited them before for one very good reason which Geoffrey understands perfectly well. You see he and Sarah managed to develop a barn for self-catering holidaymakers where they live near Beaminster a couple of years ago, which means they have very little time for socializing. They spent several months doing it up and opened for business last summer. Geoffrey also has a feel for the arts, being a very competent artist in his own right, but there the likeness to his big brother stops. He is completely different to David. I think the death of his father affected him considerably. Although he was twenty-one when Mike died, he was totally devastated. Big brother David had always looked out for him and shielded him from the nasty realities of life, but although David tried, he was unable to console him or reconcile him from the death of his father. Up until then Geoffrey had been a normal, home-loving boy who looked up in awe of his big brother, but after Mike died Geoffrey seemed to turn both against David and me, but also in some strange way also against himself.

"For a few years Geoffrey fell apart. Drink and I think sometimes drugs were his only defence, against a world riddled with iniquities. This behaviour continued for several years, by which time both David and I were at the end of our tether."

"What happened to change him?" asked Henry. "I gather from what you have told me so far that things did change, so it must have been something very drastic to overcome his adversity."

"It was luck really... and Sarah of course," replies Kate. "The family had always known her. She grew up in the village and went to school here as well. She was a couple of years younger than Geoffrey but was always included in the gang of children that got involved in the evenings and at weekends, playing games on the common, taking part in amateur dramatics in the hall and all other myriad activities that they do at that age. She and Geoffrey had always got on in a platonic way, but I think that she always had a soft spot for him, looking upon him as someone to be admired, but as well to always be disappointed by. He, on the other hand almost ignored her on a personal level and acted almost as if she did not exist."

"What changed to make him see her differently?" asked Henry, who was now intrigued by Geoffrey and his problems.

"Well, Sarah eventually passed her A Levels and got entry to the University of Southampton on a business course and was more or less away for three years. When she eventually returned she got a very good job in Dorchester and so continued to live back in the village. Of course, as so often in life, the rather plain young girl who left to get a good education, returned a sophisticated woman of breath-taking beauty. Geoffrey had during all this time been going through his own vortex of horrors, drinking to excess and moving from one job to the next, knowing that he was dreadfully unhappy but not knowing why. Then Sarah happened again! The group of children that they all grew up with - most of them, anyway - still kept in touch, although some had married and one or two had moved away. Anyway, to cut a long story short, there was a reunion soon after Sarah had returned to the village. A party in the Mucky Duck in fact. It was here that Geoffrey had his epiphany. He saw Sarah. No, I will rephrase that, he saw a beautiful woman that blew him away. He didn't even know it was Sarah until she spoke. It could have been game over for Geoffrey at this stage, because seeing her made him realize just how far he had deteriorated as a person, both physically and mentally. He felt a deep sense of shame that Sarah should see him like this, she who had looked up to him. He wanted to escape, crawl away, anything to avoid this ravishing woman who had transformed from an ugly duckling into a beautiful swan.

"Sarah however had other ideas. She could remember the young man who made her laugh. Who was sensitive and handsome in a rugged sort of way, and as the recollections came flooding back to her, she found much to her own surprise, that the feelings that she had for him all those years ago, still remained. She also realized that, because of his circumstances and history, Geoffrey had withdrawn into his own little world, the reason for which being, she surmised correctly, that in that place he could hide from the world and not be hurt. But here among his old friends he was exposed and vulnerable to her, something that Sarah was able fortunately to recognise. But how was she to get him to overcome his feelings of inadequacy so that he could regain his confidence and respect?

"The first thing she thought would be to talk to him, perhaps by telling him of her experiences since she had left to go to University, and then to lead on to finding out what he had been doing. Under normal circumstances it would seem a logical approach to break down his invisible but, to him, very real barriers. Unfortunately Sarah just didn't realize how far Geoffrey had sunk into his private place. Not only that, but she also had no idea the effect that she was having on him either.

"He had managed to deliberately avoid her up until this point, talking to one or two of his other friends, with whom he felt comfortable, although in a monosyllabic way, giving one or two word answers to any questions posed.

"Working her way around her various friends, Sarah eventually came face to face with Geoffrey, a situation of which he was unaware until he was suddenly confronted with this gorgeous, tall, willowy blonde of flawless complexion and pale green eyes, which seemed to engulf him as she said, 'Hi Geoffrey, isn't this a good idea to get us all together again, it's been such a long time. I did look out for you on a number of occasions when I returned from uni, but you never seemed to be around. I am back here more or less permanently now, so perhaps we can catch up and get together sometimes with some of the others. What do you think?'

"Sarah can see as she is speaking to him that Geoffrey is desperately looking around, trying to see if there is anyone or thing that he can bring into the conversation, to help take away some of the need for him to be the centre of her attention. He feels overwhelmed by her luminescent beauty while at the same time experiencing an indefinable need for her, which frightens him even more, because he cannot imagine anyway that he can find to bridge what he sees as the huge gap between them.

"Unable to avoid the situation any longer he manages to say, 'Hello Sarah, you're right, it has been a very long time since we all used to go around together,' and slowly gathering confidence, 'So long in fact that I hardly recognized you at first. I hear that you did very well at uni and am now working in Dorchester.'

"Smiling because she has managed to get at least a measured answer from him, she replies, 'I think that I was very lucky in the jobs stakes, because I was recommended for the post by one of the tutors at the uni.'"

Interrupting Kate, Henry says, "So that was how they got together? Sarah must be some woman, to be able to reach out and get him to overcome all his problems."

Taking her time, Kate replies, "Well she certainly is the most understanding, intuitive person, but this evening was only just the beginning of a long hard road for the two of them. But being the astute person that she is, Sarah took Geoffrey's rehabilitation one step at a time, realizing that if she rushed him too quickly, she could lose him to his demons.

"The first stage in her strategy was to arrange several innocuous meetings with some of their other friends, so that they were not on their own together, because she realized that Geoffrey needed to be brought back into the world and that a group of people was the best means to make that happen. This then went on for several months, during which time the group would meet for amateur dramatics in the hall, something that Sarah, bless her, had managed to resurrect. Quite often after the sessions had finished they would all drift to the pub. This was a stroke of pure genius on Sarah's part, because appearing on stage in public and having to speak his lines had the most dramatic effect on Geoffrey. He became more confident in company, garrulous even, mainly because he enjoyed the whole experience.

"However, it did not escape Geoffrey's notice that Sarah was the real reason for his transformation, and by this time his feelings for her had escalated from awe to love and respect. Nothing had happened between them up to this point, but Sarah was patient and prepared to wait, as he emerged slowly from his chrysalis.

"After several months Sarah put her next stage of 'Operation: Geoffrey' into play. It happened one day when they were on their own for a few minutes that she mentioned that there was a musical production that she particularly wanted to see in Bournemouth. She knew not to pursue it any further, but left it hanging in the air, hoping that Geoffrey would eventually pick up on it and take the matter further. Geoffrey had by this time began to come out of his shell, but for the ruse to work, Sarah's timing needed to be spot on. As has been proved so many times before and since, Sarah's intuitive feelings were right again, when two days later Geoffrey asked her if she would like to go to see the musical with him.

"Sarah was delighted, but also realized just how much courage it had taken for Geoffrey to ask her. This seemed to be the turning point and things moved on at a fair pace after this and their relationship blossomed, but the main obstacle between it developing further was still the feelings of inadequacy that Geoffrey felt about himself. He still saw himself as a failure, unable to offer Sarah a future. Eventually Sarah managed to sit him down and talk about his feelings and it soon became apparent what the problem was.

"Being Sarah, she soon came up with a plan, which she

explained to him along the following lines. 'Look Geoff, I know that you're not happy with the job you're doing and that you think that you have wasted your working life so far, but it doesn't have to be this way. Why don't you take a study in further education, even perhaps go to university and take a course which would eventually give you qualifications to do something satisfying with your life?'

"Geoffrey was slightly taken aback at first when the idea was put to him, but after lots of discussions with Sarah he was surprised by his own positive reaction the longer they discussed it. He had not shown the same interest as David in the company business, although he also had a flair for art which he only pursued for his own satisfaction, but Sarah realized that if he could channel that skill into something that he could use in a commercial working environment, he could hopefully become fulfilled for the first time in his life. Sarah could see immediately that once the seed of further education had been planted into Geoffrey's psyche, it began to grow at an alarming rate and he began to look for courses that would help him develop his burgeoning aspirations.

"They were by now becoming recognized locally as a pair, although their relationship was still only platonic. The main problem was that Sarah still lived in the village with her parents, while Geoffrey still lived with me. Not an ideal situation as you can imagine.

"Sarah had experienced several relationships during her time at university, which she had viewed as part of life's learning curve. These were as nothing compared to the emotions and feelings that Geoffrey stirred within her.

"Amazingly it was he who managed to overcome this difficult hurdle, which was accomplished eventually in the most simple of ways. Again it was their love of theatre that provided the answer. Geoffrey knew that Sarah had always wanted to see *The Phantom of the Opera* which was still on in London after a number of years. As a surprise he arranged to take her to see it, but taking his life in his hands he also booked a hotel double room overnight after the show.

"Nervously broaching the subject with her, Geoffrey was delighted when she hugged him to her, showering him with kisses to let him know that she felt the same way too.

"So they duly went to the show, after which they went out for a slap-up meal, before returning to the hotel for the night. Now I can't tell you just how that went Henry," said Kate. "But I think that it is pretty fair to assume that it was successful, because immediately upon their return they started to look for a flat in Dorchester."

"So, how did you feel about that?" inquired Henry. "I expect you were a little concerned knowing how fragile Geoffrey was."

"Well I was to tell you the truth," explained Kate. "But as it turned out I had no need to worry, because with Sarah to guide him he was, by now, a different, more confident person. They managed to find a small flat in Dorchester within a short space of time and he has never looked back since.

"However, the next and final part of Sarah's rehabilitation plan for Geoffrey was to follow up on his further educational needs. They had discussed the many various options open to Geoffrey which covered a huge spectrum of opportunities, but it was only when Sarah began to try and filter out some of them by asking him what he would like to do to develop his skills that a pattern began to take shape. After going round in verbal circles, the picture emerged that what Geoffrey would like to do was to use his artistic skills to create crafts of some kind. He had always taken an interest in things like fashion and textile design, pottery, jewellery design and glass etching. Things that he could mould, feel and touch, and watch them grow under his skilled fingers.

"Carefully, both he and she explored the web for suitable courses that Geoffrey might find interesting and eventually found a one year course in art and design - foundation studies, which was held at the Arts University Bournemouth. By this time he was working in the kitchen of a hotel in Dorchester as an assistant chef, a job which he enjoyed as a short term measure, but it was hard work with unsociable hours. He applied to the university and was accepted. The not inconsiderable downside to this was of course that it meant that Sarah would have to continue to be the main source of income during all this time, but for her it was of little moment, if at the end of it Geoffrey could find something that he would fulfil him.

"One major factor was that Geoffrey did not want to live on campus. Having just found Sarah he could not face the thought of only seeing her at weekends, so the only alternative was to travel daily. This too, was a problem because he had no independent means of transport, but Sarah encouraged him to buy a second hand motorbike to overcome this problem.

"All the time that Sarah and he spent looking for a suitable course proved to be invaluable, as he took to it like a duck to water. From the very first he absolutely loved it, which was reflected in his work. He felt that was as if this was the thing that he had been born to do. The first stage of the course explored broad concepts and assignments which allowed the students to diagnose which methodology - art, design, or media - that they felt most comfortable with. The second stage gave an insight into what it would be like to study within a specialist art program.

"It was at this point that Geoffrey had his next epiphany when he started to look at textile design and discovered Batik printing and art. Geoffrey could see at once this was the medium which fascinated and inspired him. Put simply, Batik is a process for making designs using wax on fabric to prevent dye from entering the cloth. It can be done with many types of dye of fabric paints and waxes on cottons, silks, leather and other natural fabrics. Now the examples the class were shown were all small and pretty basic, using paper and wax, but even at that stage, Geoffrey could see beyond them, to large beautiful creations made of silk which could be used as wall hangings in corporate offices, or public buildings, or for church and ecclesiastical use.

"His vision hit him like a steam hammer, and the possibilities even more so. The other area which interested him was glass etching and the sheer beauty that could be attained from this medium.

"At the end of the course, Geoffrey had worked up an impressive portfolio and the tutors were singing his praises, which did his confidence no end of good. But where to go from there was his next problem. He had done his homework and knew where to source the products he needed, but his main problem was that he needed suitable light space in which he could develop his skills to produce items that would make him recognized in this field.

"Batik is a skill originally from Asia and India, and has been around for almost two millennia, so to get established, Geoffrey needed to be able to produce something special or different from the rest of the herd. As an interim step Geoffrey asked David for some space in his studio for a short period only, and David, bless him, agreed immediately. So this was how he got started. But Geoffrey also realized that he now needed to design a number of products that he could market. His dream was to design large silk works that would express his artistic skills, but to do this he would need to find clients who could afford such projects. So he took the decision to also design and make smaller items like decorated cotton shopping bags and smaller pictures which were relatively inexpensive, but from which he could print high quality giclee versions in various laminated card sizes, thus maximizing their initial concept.

"Sarah, of course, with her business and marketing background, was a tower of strength in these areas, sitting him down to decide which designs to develop to achieve the most impact. Together they designed an internet site which show-pieced his products, after which Sarah contacted the Batik Guild and registered with it. This gave them access to what was happening in the Batik industry, but more than that, it informed them where materials could be obtained and where exhibitions were being held. Geoffrey found this extremely useful, and Sarah and he then looked at suitable places where he could exhibit his portfolio.

"One other approach that Sarah made was to contact art galleries within a fifty mile radius to try to get them to exhibit some of his work. Even while all of this was happening, Geoffrey was developing his skills doing glass etchings. In layman's terms these were done by first applying two layers of vinyl, upon which Geoffrey drew his design before starting the long and demandingly accurate task of cutting out the design by hand, to make the mask. Once sandblasted, the existing vinyl was carefully peeled off revealing the clear glass. This was then cleaned and the sandblasting protected by a spray.

"Geoffrey made several panels, getting accustomed to the new medium and building up a portfolio that he could use to show potential clients.

Now that he and Sarah of course, had reached this stage, his work started to become recognized and respected, but his major breakthrough came when he was asked to produce several Batik panels on silk for a local church depicting various stages of Christ's life and crucifixion. The panels were some eight feet tall by six feet wide and they were hung high on the pillars of the central aisle of the church so that parishioners and tourists would have to pass under them as they walked down the aisle. They were suspended by the use of poles top and bottom of the panels. Because they were silk, the material moved gently with every slight breeze in the church, giving them a feeling of movement, making them appear almost alive. The results were stunning, exceeding even Geoffrey's expectations, and the church commissioners were delighted.

"All this took some eighteen months before Geoffrey had reached this stage and although he had some revenue from the results of all his efforts, they were not sufficient yet to cover his costs, so Sarah continued to fund all their living costs while helping him at the same time. But there was now a chink of light at the end of their long tunnel as commissions from other churches, public corporations and major retail outlets became reality.

"Geoffrey's final need was a studio of his own where he could develop his range of items which could also be used as a shop, where people could visit or buy online. David had been very supportive, never making any demand of his younger brother, but Geoffrey now wanted his independence, if you like. So once again he and Sarah sat down to discuss the next stage of his development, or rehabilitation, as she saw it. Their ideal needs they felt could be attained by moving from their flat to a house which was either large enough, so that Geoffrey could use a room for his studio. Or ideally a house with an annexe or Holiday let or large building in the garden, be it a barn or a workshop of some description.

"There were other criteria which they couldn't ignore, which were that they would still need to be in travelling distance of Dorchester, because of Sarah's work commitments. After much searching they eventually found the place of their dreams just outside Beaminster, near Netherbury. It was a small three bed cottage, which lay in glorious isolation at the end of a lane some hundred yards off the centre of the village.

"The setting was perfect, set high and surrounded by fields that dropped away at the back of the house. It was in dire need of some tender loving care but it was for this reason that it fell into their budget. The thing that clinched it for both of them was the huge workshop at one end of the garden overlooking the fields that spread before it into the distance. Some previous owner had obviously used it as a workshop for motor repairs. However, it was solidly built of brick up to five feet from ground level, which was then continued above to roof level using hardwood planking which was attached to a timber frame, all set on a good concrete base surface.

"Because of its previous use, extensive work needed to be carried out before Geoffrey could use it as a studio, but it already had an electricity and water supply laid on and he could see the immense potential that it offered.

"Additionally, also in the half acre site, there was an old barn, suggesting that at some time many years previously, the cottage had perhaps been a farm, but had subsequently somewhere along the line had to sell the land surrounding it. The barn was pretty derelict, its recent use from all appearance being merely that of a dumping ground for unwanted items. But the roof looked to be in fairly good order, although neither Sarah nor Geoffrey gave it much thought other than to recognize its existence.

"Their offer, which was several thousand pounds under the asking price for the cottage, was accepted and after moving in, the first thing that they did was to convert the work repair shop into a studio. To do this it was necessary to take out most of the back of the building, which faced south. This was then replaced with two large patio doors, through which the natural light flooded in. However, not just satisfied with this, Geoffrey had two large windows installed into the roof, which gave the interior masses of light, even on an overcast winter's day.

"The effect was inspirational, because people's attention on entering the studio was drawn to looking out of the patio doors to the vista beyond. This was of green rolling Dorset hills that stretched away into the distance. It was here then that Geoffrey continued his work, creating Batiks and etching glass. They had not had the time or money to make any changes to the cottage, but Sarah had managed to freshen up the main rooms downstairs, while they promised each other that as soon as money and time became more available they would tackle it properly.

"They both worked like maniacs for the next year," says Kate. "In fact watching them both reminded me of Mike and myself many years earlier, which gave me goose bumps whenever it occurred. Anyway, where was I? Oh yes, well by scrimping and saving they then did the necessary changes to the cottage, which was, as I say, more than slightly dilapidated, turning it into a beautiful house with character in bucket-loads. The house was some two hundred years old but they carefully kept and enhanced the older features, while making the rest modern, like the kitchen, and installed a shower room and an en-suite bathroom and toilet.

"They had by now been together as a couple for several years, and although neither of them had mentioned the 'M' word, they had both discussed the fact that they would like to have a child or children together. By this time Geoffrey was in his late twenties, with Sarah a couple of years younger. But additionally Sarah's biological clock had started to kick in, and Geoffrey, being slightly old fashioned and realizing the situation, decided to act.

"By now things were going very well for him, his portfolio had grown and he could point potential clients to a number of his works that hung in public buildings and corporate offices. These were mostly large Batik panels which were usually hung in prominent positions, reception areas or board rooms. They were sometimes on silk or cotton and they depicted scenes relevant to the recipient's activities. Thus, the scene in a council office might show historical events or people that achieved much for the town, of which it was duly proud. In the case of corporations, the scenes would depict its products and history.

"Also, Geoffrey had continued glass etching, where he found an insatiable demand from churches for its use in screens and windows. There was also a demand for small screens for domestic use in doors and borrowed lights over doors. As this wasn't enough, he had also started to give lessons in both mediums. These were usually for one day, and arranged online. These would be held in his studio, where he would take up to five people at a time. This was quite a lucrative business, which he would do perhaps once a month, workloads permitting.

"There was never any question in Geoffrey's mind that he loved Sarah, even if she hadn't been beautiful, smart and capable. He had fallen for all those things, but much more than that, he loved her thoughtfulness, her smile, her dimples when she laughed (which was often), her tenderness when he was down, and most of all, the confidence which she exuded, which she managed to instil in him, making him believe that he could achieve anything he set his mind to.

"Deciding to surprise Sarah, Geoffrey arranged for a weekend break in Paris. While her mind was still in a whirl, he managed to get her to the top of the Eiffel Tower, where to all the tourists' amazement, including Sarah's, he dropped to his knees and, taking her hand, asked her to marry him. The sudden shock and surprise were too much for Sarah as she broke into tears of happiness, before saying, 'Oh, Yes, yes, yes,' at which moment people began clapping and congratulating them both. They were married in Goderston church two months later among their many friends and families. David was best man, while Sarah's younger sister was bridesmaid.

"Their world was complete a couple of years later when Chloe, their daughter, was born. She is now three years old and a joy to behold. Geoffrey is completely captivated by her, and cannot believe just how lucky he is to have two such fantastic women in his life."

As Kate finishes speaking, they draw up to her house and all conversation is temporarily on hold until they get inside.

As the dinner is being prepared, Henry says, "So Geoffrey managed to turn his life around, with Sarah's considerable help. You must be very proud of him."

"Oh, of course I am, but just to see him happy, confident and content is more than I could have possibly hoped for," says Kate. "But I haven't told you everything, in fact the main reason that I haven't seen them recently. You see after they finished renovating the house and knowing that their child was on its way, they looked for other ways that they could develop Geoffrey's artistic skills. What they both wanted was that once the baby had been born, that Sarah could give up her work in Dorchester, so that she could be a full time mother. Geoffrey in particular wanted if possible for his family to be 'on site', so to speak, so that they could all grow together as a family.

"They thought long and hard of other ways they could develop Geoffrey's business, or for other things that Sarah could do so that she didn't have to leave the home. After many discussions they had a brainstorming session, out of which came two possibilities.

THE BUS PASS

"Geoffrey was first when he said, 'Why don't we start a play school for young children? There must be a huge demand for something like that, where harassed mothers can bring their kids for several hours a day, to enable them to get some respite.' Sarah liked the idea, but once they started to discuss it in detail, problems of how it would work appeared to be insurmountable. What qualifications were needed for such an enterprise, together where such an operation could be run from was paramount, but it was the latter that gave Sarah her big idea. It was while they were discussing where a play group could be placed that Sarah suddenly thought of the old derelict barn. The play group idea was eventually rejected by both of them, but then suddenly Sarah suggested that perhaps they could renovate the barn and turn it into self-catering summer lets.

"Geoffrey thought that this was a distinct possibility, but didn't know how or where to start to find out how to begin such an enterprise, but Sarah with her business skills did. She spent the next few months applying for change of business use for the barn, while at the same time employing a local architect to draw up plans to convert the property into three accommodations, all with two bedrooms and self-catering facilities. Once this had been done, she sourced several reliable local builders to give her quotes for the work to be carried out. Once planning permission had been obtained, the next problem was to get funding. This was where Sarah was at her best. Using connections that she had made in her job, she managed to get the funding needed for the project, which was of the order of one hundred thousand pounds at a very favourable interest rate.

"So the work commenced while Sarah was still working, even though by this time she was pregnant with Chloe. They both knew that financially they could manage while Sarah continued to work, and even after this time, until she had to return to work (which they had both agreed would not happen). Meanwhile, Geoffrey continued to grow his business, thus closing the gap between what he earned and what they needed once Sarah stopped work. But hopefully the apartments, which were now taking shape, would fill the short fall. To cut a very long story short, Henry," continues Kate, "The work was completed some two years ago, and they started taking bookings in time for last summer, which was quite successful, considering that it was their first year. This year however, after a lot of marketing by Sarah, they are more or less fully booked for the summer season. Not only that, but they have extended the season, because any number of people now are looking for accommodation, more or less throughout the year, for weekend or short breaks.

"That more or less brings me up to date with Geoffrey, Sarah and Chloe and I hope explains why I have not visited them since you and I first met. They are so busy, with Geoffrey exhibiting, giving classes and having to visit on site for potential clients, while Sarah is managing the apartments and looking after Chloe, so time for them is at a premium. But they both love their lifestyle, which I think is the most important thing.

"So now you can see why I have not visited them recently, but I was talking on the phone to them the other day when you were at work and finally managed to arrange to see them tomorrow."

Henry, who has been listening avidly to Kate explaining her youngest son's background, is entranced by her description of Geoffrey's work, and says excitedly, "I can tell by your tone that you are as proud of Geoffrey every bit as much as you are of David. I can't wait to meet them all and see his studio. In fact I feel a little envious, because in a different life it is something that I would have liked to have done, but never had the courage. So bully for him."

"I will make sure that I arrange a suitable time so that we can both go together the next time. I have told them all about you and the way that you have helped David, and they want to meet you too. Now let's have dinner and then see if Megan and Charlie want to go to the pub for the evening," replies Kate.

So the week continues. Kate goes to see Geoffrey and his family the next day, while Henry continues going into the studio to help David, both feeling content with life and each other. Neither of them realising that events are already in hand that will topple their fledgling relationship.

PART TWO

CHAPTER 21

Totnes

The blow when it falls is of seismic, mind-numbing proportions, and is to shatter Henry's hopes and dreams forever.

It is now Monday 23 June, and Henry on waking, finds that Kate has already gone downstairs. After showering and getting dressed for work, Henry makes his way to the kitchen where, somewhat to his surprise, he finds Kate standing motionless with her back to him at the sink.

In order not to frighten her, he says gently, "Well, you're an early bird this morning, couldn't you sleep?"

She makes no reply, for what to him, seems like an eternity, before she states shakily, "I have something to tell you Henry, and however I dress it up, the result is just the same and you will be hurt. I am sorry my dear but I think it's for the best if you move on and forget about me. If you remember I did say that at some stage you would need to carry on with your journey to see the places that you wanted to see before you had to move to Australia. Well I think that time has arrived." Seeing Henry about to object, she rushes on. "Oh I know you are going to say that we have a good relationship going, but I would hate it if at some time in the future you would come to resent me for having sacrificed your future to be with your children. But it's not only just that. As you know I have lived alone now for many years and I suppose I have got used to it. Believe me I think it's for the best for both of us."

During the time Kate has been talking, all the colour has drained from Henry's face and he can feel his whole body begin to shake. It is as if someone has taken a hammer and struck him.

He feels hurt and betrayed and doesn't have a reply, but knowing he has to say something he says, "Look my love (because this is now as he sees her), the situation in regard to me moving to Australia is no longer an issue, as far as I am concerned. You must know that my feelings for you transcend that scenario. If both my children end up in Oz, then I am quite happy to see them whenever possible, but to lose you is unthinkable."

But this is a Kate that he has not seen before, obdurate and determined, and as the conversation continues with Henry imploring her, using every verbal lever that he can think of, he finds at every turn that she is implacable and immovable.

As the conversation continues, Henry finds his resolve weakening. He is appalled at the thought of life without her and suddenly he finds that despite himself he is crying uncontrollably, unable to change Kate's mind.

Noticing this, Kate seems to gather herself together, saying in a sudden steely tone, "It's no good Henry, I am not going to change my mind, so rather than drag the situation out any longer I think that it would be the best for both of us if you left today."

"Today!" cries Henry abjectly. "Why today? I still have some work to finish with David, have you thought of that?"

"Don't worry about David, I will speak to him and explain, and I am sure that he will understand. You have done a remarkable job for him and I am so grateful to you for that. Now I think it best if you could go and pack the things that you will need for the next few days and email me when you have found somewhere that you are likely to stay for a while and I will then send the rest of your things on to you."

What Henry at first thought was an emotional wave has now emerged at full pelt as a tsunami of frightening proportions that is threatening to drown him. He continues to try to get Kate to change her mind, saying, "I thought that you felt the same way about me as I do about you my love and although I have never said so in so many words I thought that maybe one day we would marry. But we don't have to, if you would rather that we just lived together, that would be fine with me too."

"I am so sorry Henry if I led you into thinking that we had a

THE BUS PASS

long-term relationship, but I just didn't see it that way. Of course my feelings for you are very strong, and if it were ever going to happen to me that I would settle down permanently with anyone, that would be you. There is nobody else in my life and after you I don't think there will ever be. But I have to do this and I hope and trust that given time you will come to see that it is for the best if we part now."

Henry is by now bankrupt of all reasoned arguments and after several minutes of absolute silence between them, moves to the door, saying, "If that is what you wish, I will sort out my stuff and leave. Never in my wildest dreams did I imagine that things between us would finish like this. If you ever change your mind just call and I will come running. Just so that there is no misunderstanding about the way I feel for you I will say it one last time. I love you and always will. You gave me hope when I had none and I will never forget you. Goodbye my love, give my love and best wishes to everyone. I will pack and leave by the front door so that we don't have to see each other again, because for me that would just be a bridge too far."

With that Henry goes upstairs to pack, which takes a few minutes only and then lets himself out by the front door.

Kate stands motionless by the sink, not having moved since Henry first came downstairs, but as the front door closes behind him she give a huge shuddering gasp, before breaking down into uncontrollable floods of tears. Her resolve, which she has kept in check up until this moment, is released and she is utterly at the mercy of her emotions for the first time.

As she continues to be wracked by tears, the letter that she has just received from the mammary clinic flutters from her nerveless fingers to the floor.

Once outside the door Henry walks towards the bus stop that leads to Dorchester.

His mind is a turmoil of mixed emotions, none of them happy. He cannot reconcile himself to the fact that Kate is no longer part of his world and he is still reeling at the sheer speed at which it has occurred. However, he also recognises that the way he feels at the moment, he cannot possibly face meeting anyone from the village and have to explain what has happened. He feels in some way that he has failed not only himself but also Kate.

No, far better that he leave without having to explain to any of the lovely people that he has come to know and respect.

His options he considers as either, to return home and lick his mental wounds, or to move forward with his original itinerary by bus. The latter is by far the more appealing, because to return home would signal yet another failure on his part. Having made this decision he catches the next bus into Dorchester. The journey passes in complete silence, or rather Henry is so wrapped up in his own contemplation that he fails to hear the sounds of the young children's laughter and their mothers' banter with each other.

On reaching Dorchester he decides after consulting his original itinerary that he will make his way to Totnes in Devon, a town that both he and Isabel had enjoyed many times over the years. Henry is brought to a sudden jolt as he thinks of Isabel in this way, something that he has not done for several weeks, and feels almost guilty that he has been so remiss. This only adds to his misery as he finds himself mentally asking for her forgiveness. But there is no reply, leaving him to feel even more bereft.

Trying to pull himself together, Henry decides as a first step to make for Bridport, and catches the next bus before he can change his wavering mind.

Bridport helps to lift his spirits marginally, because he has always loved this quaint market town with its hustle and bustle, and colourful characters, some of whom he has got to know during his many visits. Warm memories of staying at the Bull Hotel with Isabel, come flooding back - candlelit dinners and laughter, and walks along the coastal path. Then exploring the market stalls looking for bargains in West and South Streets. Isabel had been so good at finding little knick-knacks, which Henry very often thought of as rubbish at the time, but upon getting them home Isabel would put them in the space that she had them in mind for when she brought them, and her choice would immediately have been vindicated.

It was as if it, whatever it may have been, a vase or picture or a small coffee table would have always been intended for wherever Isabel put it. After a while Henry realised that she possessed this unique skill, and he didn't ever question her judgement when she wanted to buy any bric-a-brac, because he knew that it would look fantastic when they got it home and Isabel put it in the special place that she had imagined for it.

He has hoped for enough time to explore some of his favourite places further, but on checking the bus schedules he is suddenly aware that the Stagecoach X53 bus is due to leave West Street at nineteen minutes past ten, which will get him into Exeter at twelve thirty two.

Exeter will be a large step in his next chosen destination of Totnes, so he hurriedly makes his way to the bus stop just in time. As it transpires, this proves to be an excellent move, because almost as soon as he boards the bus Henry's emotional and physical exertions overcome him and he falls into a deep sleep and remains so until Exeter is reached and the kindly driver is shaking him awake. Smiling, he says, "Do you want to get off here mate or are you coming back with me to Bridport?"

Feeling dishevelled and dejected, Henry looks for toilet and wash facilities. When he looks in the mirror he is horrified to see the gaunt bedraggled figure staring back at him. His eyes are bloodshot and his skin a faded yellow, when once it had been tanned brown by the Dorset sun. He washes before going to find somewhere to eat, and after a sandwich and a coffee, which revive his flagging spirits somewhat, he feels more able to decide his next move.

Although he has visited Exeter several times, his stays have only been for short periods, so he has never taken in much of, what he can now see, is a beautiful city.

Recognising that he has some time to spare before his next bus leaves for Totnes, Henry decides that he would like to visit the cathedral, so he makes his way to the centre of the city. On entering this beautiful building, Henry discovers that it was founded in the early twelfth century and is surrounded by a green, beyond which is Cathedral Close with its wealth of shops from earlier centuries.

There is an arts exhibition on the green, with about fifty or so stalls exhibiting local products, which Henry explores. The cathedral sits right in the heart of the city, which Henry finds strangely comforting. Centuries have passed, many wars have been fought in and around this city, including being bombed in the

Second World War, but here it still stands, a glorious memorial to those people who built it so long ago.

Without realising it, Henry is now slightly less tense, entranced by the beautiful surroundings, until, looking at his watch, he is surprised to find that he has only a few minutes in which to find the bus station to get the bus to Totnes. The Stagecoach X64 leaves promptly at two forty with Henry on board after a hurried dash to the station.

Although his emotions continue to play havoc with him, the memories of this morning's events with Kate still very strong in his mind, Henry is more relaxed and is able to absorb the beautiful Devon countryside as it passes with every swish of the bus wheels. At this time of the year Devon's countryside is at its most breathtakingly beautiful, showing off its limitless array of colours. From the yellow-gold rape fields to its vibrant green pastures in which jersey cows with their light brown colours and soft brown eyes, which are surrounded by black markings, making them look for all the world like jesters from a bygone age.

Then there are a multitude of different greens from trees and hedgerows, but all these are eclipsed where the rich Devon earth has not yet been planted, showing off its dark red hues, making it look as if it is wounded and bleeding. But this is a total misconception, for the earth will yield a rich, heavy crop in due course, once it has been planted, and the Jersey cows will supply the milk, from which Devon cream will be made, which is among the best in the country.

Henry takes all this in as the bus travels on its winding route through the narrow Devon lanes, with its high hedges almost to eye level. By this time a number of children have boarded the bus, and Henry is brought out of his reverie by their laughter and excited chatter. As he does so he is brought back into the present with a bang as he remembers that he has not arranged for anywhere to stay once he reaches Totnes.

Pulling out his laptop he googles local pubs and small hotels in Totnes, and soon finds a public house, the Bay Horse Inn, located at the top of the town in Cistern Street. Using his mobile phone he quickly rings them and to his delight, is able to book a room for the next three nights at a reasonable rate.

THE BUS PASS

The sun is still high in a clear blue sky as Henry's bus arrives at Totnes in Coronation Road, opposite the tourist information centre, which he visits to get some local information.

Totnes is a historic market town, built on a steep hill. It is known to have been inhabited by the Anglo-Saxons for more than a millennia. Although relatively small, with only some seven thousand five hundred inhabitants, it is rich in traditions and history. Henry also knows that it a centre for the arts from the worlds of music, comedy, theatre and dance.

The time is now a quarter to four and Henry realises that the bus station in Coronation Road is at the bottom of Fore Street, just a few yards from the river Dart. This street is the central road that runs from the bottom of the town. It is with a heavy heart that he commences walking up to get to the Bay Horse Inn.

Most of the buildings are old, several hundred years in some cases, and there are tucked away side passages giving glimpses that strongly evoke the past.

Henry's spirits are lifted somewhat as he walks steadily up Fore Street until he passes through East Arch Gate into High Street and eventually reaches Cistern Street and his accommodation, the Bay Horse Inn. Checking in, he makes his way to his room and falls exhausted onto the bed, but his sleep is fitful, with thoughts and reminders of the earlier terrible situation with Kath constantly interrupting his efforts to vacate his mind completely.

Eventually he gives up trying to sleep and looking at his watch sees that it is now seven thirty. Turning on his laptop he notices a message from Penny asking how he is, and then keeping him up to date with news of his two grandsons.

Henry is suddenly mortified to realise that neither Penny, nor in fact anyone else, is aware of the situation between Kate and him. Although he does not know how to break the news to her, he also knows that she must be told immediately. It would be intolerable if Penny or any of his other friends were to contact Kate and find out from her what has occurred.

Not being able to bring himself to phone her, because he knows that any verbal explanation from him could be misconstrued, he resolves to email her.

Hi Penny love,

Thanks for your message. The boys seem to be getting on fine. Do they have any exams before the end of next term? How are things looking with you ref Australia?

I was just going to contact you funnily enough, because there has been a sudden change of plan my end. Kate and I both talked over our situation recently and we decided that it would be for the best if I carried on with my original objective of visiting places that I would like to see, prior to moving to Australia. So today I set off to my next port of call, Totnes, where I am now, at the Bay Horse Inn in Cistern Street, which is situated right at the top of the hill, off the High Street.

I had a lovely journey down, starting from Dorchester, to Bridport, then on to Exeter, before arriving here.

My thoughts at the moment are that I will stay here until perhaps Friday, because there are several places locally that I would like to see before moving on.

I will let you know my situation as it arises,

Love to you all,

Dad

Reading it before he presses the send button, Henry tries to think what Penny would think, if he were she.

Has he apportioned any blame to Kate? That is the last impression that he wants to create. No, blame, if any, is his for ignoring the signs that Kate had given once or twice over the last few weeks. He could not contemplate the thought of Penny contacting Kate to find out just what had happened. Far better this way that everyone thinks that it is by mutual agreement.

His next missive is to Kate, which he thinks long and hard about. How to strike the right note. Not too long so that she is angry with him, but just enough to let her know where he is and what he is doing, but also to give her an address where she can send the rest of his clothes.

So he starts....

THE BUS PASS

Hi Kate, my love,

I have arrived here in the wonderful picturesque town of Totnes and am staying at the Bay Horse Inn in Cistern Street, where I will be for at least three days. When you have time can you forward the rest of my things on to me at this address?

My remarks about how I feel for you remain and always will. I hope that at some-time in the future that you can feel the same about me. If you do, just say the word and I will come running.

I know that this is not very likely, but I will hang on to the thought, because without it I am lost.

Give my best wishes to David and family. I will not contact you again unless I have to, because it hurts too much. I am sure that you will understand.

Goodbye my love,

Henry.

Finally, he sends another email to Rob and Madge, giving them a potted version of the one he sent to Penny.

Still feeling utterly miserable, Henry goes downstairs to get a bar meal where his spirits are lifted when he finds that there is a group singing folk songs in the bar. After a wonderful meal of sea bass with new potatoes and spinach, followed by a banana split ice cream, he spends another hour or so listening to the folk group while consuming a couple of pints of Dartmoor Jail ale before ascending to his room for the night.

The meal, music and ale have worked their magic on him and he falls deeply asleep as soon as his head hits the pillow.

"Mark, have you seen this email from my dad? I cannot for the life of me make head or tail of it. He has started to travel again. I thought that he was settled in Goderston with Kate. They looked so happy together and there was no mention of him continuing his bus travel. Something is not quite right about this, I can smell it. What do you think?"

"Well Penny, I have to agree with you, when we last saw them they seemed blissfully happy. If you are not sure why don't you ring Kate and ask her if anything has happened to trigger the situation."

"Oh, I don't think that I can do, that. It would look as if I were blaming her somehow, when it all might have been Dad's idea, you know what he's like about possibly moving to Australia. He wants, no, it's more than that. He needs to see the places on his list, because they will be his abiding memories of England once he emigrates."

"I get that Penny, but if you are worried about it, why don't you ask him, or perhaps Rob Nugent has heard more. They have always been very close friends, so it's possible your dad has spoken to him about it."

"I may well do that, but I think that I will leave it for a day or so, to see if there are any further developments."

"Hey Madge, look at this email from Henry," demands Rob. "I can hardly believe it, he has left Kate and started on his journey of discovery again. I wonder what that's all about. They seemed inseparable when we last saw them, do you think that I should go down and join him in Totnes, or wherever?"

"Well, it's early days yet Rob, it could all change in the blink of an eye, and you would feel put out if you got down there only to find that the circumstances are not as we imagined them. Leave it just for now, but by all means reply to him. You may find out more information which might make the situation clearer."

"That sounds a good idea Madge. Let me give some thought to what I want to say."

Kate has spent most of the morning after Henry left moping dejectedly round the house, sobbing helplessly, not knowing what to do next. She cannot think coherently, already missing Henry, although she still thinks the reason for telling him to leave a valid one.

She knows that the one person that she owes an explanation to is David, but what will he think when she tells him? Steeling herself she phones him at work and when he answers she says, "Oh hello son, you are probably asking yourself where Henry is and I have to tell you that he won't be coming in anymore. But I owe it to you to explain, and to do that properly I will come into the office this afternoon. However, I am not prepared to tell you over the phone, so I think it is for the best if I call in."

David, who is completely mystified by this stage, says, "Well I was wondering where Henry had got to, but I felt sure that you or he would let me know in due course. I am so grateful to him for all that he has done that I would never dream of questioning any decision that he has made. So I look forward to seeing you this afternoon, and you can tell me what his problem is."

"Well Mum, come and sit down and tell me all about it," says David when Kate arrives after lunch. "It must be pretty serious if it's something that you can't tell me over the phone. You look as if you have been crying, so is it something he's done to upset you? If so I shall be very disappointed with him."

"Oh no David, it's not Henry's fault in any way. Quite the contrary in fact." and then, steeling herself, "The truth is that I asked him to go this morning, because I thought it would be best for him if he were to continue his bus itinerary, so that when he had to go to Australia he would have all the memories of those places that he held dear about England. I also told him that I had got used to being alone over the years and that I quite liked it, although that last bit is not true, because he has changed and enriched my life immeasurably over the past few weeks, and in fact I miss him so much already."

"So what's it all really about Mum?" asks David, with a puzzled look on his face. "Because from where I'm sitting it looks as if you have let Henry go for no valid reason. My perception of your relationship, right from the outset has been that of two people finding extreme happiness with each other relatively late in life."

Kate pauses, looking flustered, before saying, "I have a good reason for doing this David, but you will have to trust me on this one. I feel that I am doing this, if anything, for Henry's sake, because if I didn't, then he could be hurt a whole lot more. So please don't ask me anymore."

David is silent for several minutes, wondering why or what on earth could have happened to make his mother come to such a drastic decision. Eventually he seems to make a decision and says, "But where has he gone, Mum? I don't like the thought of him travelling on his own, all over the country. Oh! I am sure that he can manage perfectly well, but it can't be much fun sitting in hotel rooms alone, having no one to share experiences with and help to make decisions. I just don't like the thought of it, he is such a good man and I owe him so much."

After what is for David a long speech, he falls into a reverie again, until suddenly his face lights up and he says, "Well, if the mountain won't come to Mohammed, then Mohammed must go to the mountain."

Kate is totally thrown by this remark and questions clarification.

David replies, "Look Mum, let me know where he is staying as soon as you can and once we know that, then this is what we will do…"

As she hears his suggestion, Kate's face too, lights up.

Henry wakes the following morning feeling lethargic. This feeling is compounded with just the suggestion of a hangover, something that he has not experienced for many years. As he slowly gathers his thoughts, Kate is still prominent in his mind, making him feel what Winston Churchill, who also suffered from depression, called 'the black dog' and he wonders if he will ever experience happiness again.

Going down to breakfast he is somewhat surprised to note that he appears to be the only resident, which the waitress confirms when he enquires, saying, "We don't get too many guests at this time of year, but give it a few weeks and we will be buzzing."

Henry is disappointed to hear this, because he is by nature a gregarious person, although just at the moment the thought of having to make idle conversation with someone he doesn't know is an anathema to him.

Not having any specific places to see, he wanders down Fore Street and explores passageways which appear at frequent intervals, but nothing seems to lift his mood, so eventually he returns to his room where he alternates between lying on his bed and sleeping, and watching daytime television, something that he has never done before.

By now Henry is at his lowest ebb and seriously considers not proceeding any further with his quest, and to return home, where at least he knows both Rob and Madge and Penny and her family will welcome him. But still he procrastinates, being too depressed and completely unable to make a decision of any kind.

The next two days pass in a similar kind of stupor, with Henry hardly leaving his room, other than to go for meals in the dining-room, or to go to the nearest shop to get a paper, until the morning of Friday 27 June, when his life changes, temporarily at least, for the better.

CHAPTER 22

Gee

When he arrives for breakfast he finds to his great pleasure that there is one other person in the dining room, who presumably had arrived the previous evening.

The man, for it is so, passes the usual pleasantries of 'good morning' with Henry, before they sit at their separate tables while eating their meals, consuming coffees and reading their daily papers. As they continue their individual activities, Henry takes stock of his new companion, noting a fairly young man in perhaps his late twenties or early thirties with a complexion that suggests that he spends a lot of his time in the open air.

When he stands, Henry assesses his height to be somewhere between five foot ten inches and six feet. He is of slim build with a ready smile and vaguely familiar clear blue eyes. He is dressed in a casual short sleeved blue shirt with cream coloured chino trousers. His hair is very fair, close cropped, and he sports a short designer stubble type beard that many men seem to wear these days.

Eventually Henry, being pleased to see another person in the dining room, decides to try to strike up a conversation, and starts by saying, "I hope you don't mind me saying, but it's good to have a bit of company in here for once. I have been on my own for the last two or three days. My name is Henry, by the way, and I am on a pilgrimage to visit a few places in England before I emigrate to Australia to live with my two children and their families. When I started, the main objective was to get to various places using my bus pass, which generally I have managed to do so far."

Having got this far Henry is alarmed at his own impertinence, and wonders at the same time from where he has found the courage to say such things to a complete stranger. But at the same time he also knows that, in some strange way, this man who is vaguely familiar will understand how he feels, and he can see his interest as he is speaking, and for some unknown inexplicable reason that he can't even quantify, he knows for certain that he is being listened to both sympathetically and understandingly.

As Henry finishes speaking the young man replies, "Well that seems a fascinating thing to do, where did you start and where have you been so far? And of course where do you plan to go to from here? Oh, my friends call me Gee by the way."

Once this verbal watershed is broken, Henry finds it remarkably easy to converse with Gee, and within a few short minutes has given him a potted version of his adventures so far, ignoring his relationship with Kate, which he feels is both too personal and not appropriate to the current discussion.

There is a brief space in their conversation, with Gee looking thoughtful as if considering all that they have just discussed, until, after a few moments, he seems to come to a decision, and says, "Well Henry, it's strange really that we are having this conversation, because you see I am on a sabbatical from my home at the moment. My wife and our young daughter have just gone on a trip to Venice with my wife's sister, leaving me to fend for myself, and as I am interested in arts and crafts, and also knowing that this area is alive with all sorts of exhibitions and places to visit, I thought it would be too good an opportunity to miss. So here I am. Now I have met you I was wondering if we could combine our objectives and visit some of the places that we would both like to see. It would certainly be better, from my perspective anyway, if I had someone to accompany me. Please say no if you would rather continue on your own, but I have my car with me and we could get round some of the places so much quicker. Some of them of course are in the town which we could walk to. From what you have told me with your design and art background, I think that we have got a lot in common. What do you think?"

For a moment Henry is stunned as Gee looks at him questioningly with his intense blue eyes, but only for a moment, because Henry is so overwhelmed, and he knows almost before Gee has finished speaking that this is something that he would enjoy.

He feels his spirits lift as he enthuses, "That sounds great and I would be pleased to accept your kind offer. So where do we start?"

"Well Henry, from what you have told me already, I think that we first ought to look around Totnes, which has a number of art centres, exhibitions and activities. We could take our time, make a day of it if you like. Then perhaps tomorrow we could do the Round Robin excursion from the river Dart at the bottom of the town. Take a boat to Dartmouth, have a look around and then catch the steam train back. Dartington Glass and arts and crafts centre is only a mile or so out of town, and there is always something exciting going on there. After that there's Slapton Sands, Kingsbridge and the South Hams, some of the places that you would like to visit, and so would I, because I have not seen them before. How does that sound for starters?"

"It sounds like heaven to me Gee," says Henry who has found the conversation thus far to be completely surreal, but is happy with the result.

So it is decided and after going to their rooms, they meet together at the front of the Pub before setting off down High Street.

The rest of their morning is spent languidly walking round the town, stopping occasionally at cafés, of which there are many, for coffees and cakes. Henry finds Gee a very lively and witty companion, who has a wide repartee of many little stories, mostly concerning his daughter, which he finds very amusing.

Continuing down High Street they reach the church which is holding an exhibition of local arts and crafts, which draws their attention. As they enter, they are both amazed at the quality of the works on display. After spending an hour or so browsing, they both buy items. Henry, a silk scarf for Penny, and Gee a silver bracelet made by a local artist for his wife.

After having a break for lunch they pass under East Arch Gate into Fore Street and continue to the bottom, where they reach the River Dart and find the booking office for river cruises.

After some discussion they agree to book tickets for the following day, which will take them from Totnes by boat to Dartmouth where they can look around, before getting the ferry across the river to Kingswear. From here they can get a steam train

THE BUS PASS

to Paignton, before finally returning to Totnes by bus. All this is arranged as a package starting from ten o'clock the next morning and getting them back to Totnes by six o'clock in the evening.

Determined to explore as much as they can they visit the information centre at the Town Mill in which they find details of a number of walks around the town which include a number of places of local interest. Starting at The Mill, which is an old restored Victorian Water Mill, they see a small exhibition showing the development of the town, after which they then make their way leisurely round the featured walk. Stopping once more, obviously, for coffee and cakes they eventually arrive back at the top of High Street, almost at the place where they had started from.

By now the time is nearly five o'clock and, looking at each other, they decide almost simultaneously to call a halt to their exploring, Henry saying, "Well Gee, that was a very full day and I am fair done in. How about we go back to our rooms for a couple of hours, then meet back down here for dinner at say half past seven. I could do with a rest, and I also need to catch up with my emails," to which Gee replies, "That Is a great idea Henry. I need to try and get in touch with my wife if I can and I would also like to talk with my daughter."

As Henry returns to his room, the landlord, who is a bluff stout man of about fifty years of age, calls out to him that a parcel has arrived, which he has placed in his room.

The parcel is from Kate and upon opening it he finds the remainder of his clothes, together with a short, cryptic note.

Dear Henry,

Please find enclosed some more of your clothes. I didn't send all of them at once because I thought that you might not be able to carry them all with you as you moved around. So if you would like to send me your dirty washing as and when you can, I will wash and iron it and return it to you wherever you are. This way you will hopefully not have too much to carry around with you as you travel. I understand that you may not wish for me to do this, because it would mean that you would have to continue being in contact with me, which is something that you mentioned in your email that you find difficult to deal with.

Believe me, I do understand how you feel, because although I have caused you unhappiness, you must also realise that it was very difficult for me too, and that after our short wonderful time together, I am also hurting, even though at the end of the day, I still think that I made the right decision.

Anyway, please let me know if you want me to launder your clothes.

Take care of yourself Henry, you are such a good man who deserves only the best. I am just so sorry that I cannot be the person who makes it possible,

Love

Kate.

On reading Kate's note Henry is overwhelmed with emotion, her words reviving again the kaleidoscope of memories of their time together. He experiences the same pain of their parting, which today had to a small extent subsided, after his time spent with Gee.

Tears flow down his face in a torrent, as he moans softly, "Why oh why is this happening to me? I wish that I had never met you my love, because then I would not have to experience this awful pain." He remains like this for several minutes, before reaching for his laptop to see if he has any messages. To his surprise the first one, which he has not expected to receive is from David, as he reads:

Hi Henry,

I am so sorry to be writing to you under these circumstances. It is something that I never expected to happen. I can't begin to explain how or why my mother has made this decision, although I have tried to discuss it with her several times, only to be told mysteriously that she has her reasons, which I have to trust her on, but they are for your benefit. I can't honestly see how, and I don't for one minute suppose that you can either.

Everyone at the studio misses you, not only for your skills and common sense, but so much more in my own case. You have been my confidant, the person that I can trust and whose thoughts I respect. In many ways you have filled the role almost as a father to me and I thank you for that.

I hope that whatever feelings that you now have about my mother do not extend to me, because I am, and would continue to be distraught, if I thought that was the case. I want you to know that you are always welcome here, not

THE BUS PASS

only at the studio, but also at my home. Please contact me, or call in when your journey brings you round this way, or any time in fact.

Finally I have credited your bank account with your unpaid salary, plus a bonus of three thousand pounds, in recognition of your input and hard work. Even this amount does not appropriately reward your efforts, which were extraordinary within the time scale that they were completed.

I hope and pray that you will keep in touch and look forward hopefully to hearing from you in due course,

Regards and best wishes,

David.

Henry has to read David's communication sever times before he can assimilate all that it contains. When he did however, his spirits lifted slightly as he considered what a fine young man he was. The fact that he had bothered to contact him and that he looked on Henry almost as a substitute father figure was very consoling. He was also pleased that David had recognised his efforts with a bonus, but would have been more than content just to have his words of praise, which meant more to him than any payment could possibly do.

After mulling over both emails, Henry decides that although Kate's kind proposal of laundering his clothes on a continuing basis is tempting, the thought of having to correspond on a more permanent arrangement will just hurt him too much. To hear from her but not to be with her anymore is just a bridge too far. No, he will just have to bite the bullet and tell her accordingly.

He will also reply to David, but not for a day or so, until he has had time to compose a response.

Feeling not quite so emotional, Henry lies back on his bed to watch the evening news, but within a few minutes has fallen into a deep dreamless sleep, his day's exertions finally catching up with him. Waking to a gentle tapping on his door, he looks hurriedly at his watch, which shows the time to be half past seven. Upon answering the door he is met by Gee's smiling face.

He says, "I thought that I had better knock you up, because I tried your internal phone a couple of times and got no reply, so I guessed that you had fallen asleep. Do you still fancy dinner together?"

"You bet. I'm absolutely famished. Thanks for waking me up."

"Well, I thought that you would have probably dropped off, we did do a lot of sightseeing," replies Gee, as they make their way to the dining room.

Once they are seated and have ordered, Gee pulls out his iPad, saying, "I didn't manage to contact my wife, I guess they must be out, probably doing some retail therapy, but she has sent me several photos, taken during the day. Here have a look."

Henry takes the tablet from Gee and has to smile immediately as he sees a video clip, of a young child of about three years of age, standing up in a gondola singing in tune with the Gondolier, '*Oh Solo Mia*'. Her arms are extended heavenwards and her head is thrown back as she gives it her all, while a stunning looking woman, who Henry can only assume to be her mother, is creased up with laughter as she looks on at her protégée.

There is a second clip, taken at The Rialto Bridge, in which the child is saying excitedly "Hallo Daddy, we are having lots of fun, we have been on a boat and we are going to get some ice cream."

She would have obviously continued longer, but her mother interjects, saying, "Hi Gee, we are having a great time, you would love this place, it's so romantic. Perhaps we can come on our own sometime. I hope that you're OK. And that you are enjoying your sabbatical and that you have found some suitable places for exhibitions. Take care of yourself and we'll see you soon my love."

Henry cannot help noticing how beautiful Gees wife is. She has a long, pointed face which is framed with long blond hair. Her fair complexion accentuates her almost hypnotic green eyes, which seem to sparkle with laughter as she talks. Her mouth is sensual, which Henry can imagine has haunted many men over the years.

The little girl has much of her mother's features and colouring, with a couple of exceptions, her nose is short and stubbed, while her mother's is long, Romanesque almost. She also has freckles which makes her very vulnerable looking and endearing.

Before he can comment Gees says, "Claudette has me in stitches, she is so funny and full of life. I can't imagine what our life was without her now." He then goes on to relate stories about his daughter which have Henry smiling and laughing by degrees as he makes comparisons of his own children growing up.

"I owe so much to Sally, my wife," continues Gee "She pulled me back from a very bad place mentally. I don't know what I have done to deserve her, I just know that I am so grateful that she did and that I will spend the rest of my life trying to be worthy of her."

Henry is surprised at this frank admission, which only makes his opinion of this young man even more elevated.

They continue the evening discussing family life, before turning their conversation to the itinerary for the next day. By this time they have eaten and Henry suddenly looking at his watch realises how tired he is. Apologising to Gee, he tells him that if he is to get up in the morning in time to catch the boat, he needs to go to bed.

So the evening finishes in mutual agreement, with Gee staying behind to have a final whisky before he too retires to bed.

CHAPTER 23

Dartmouth

Saturday 29 June

The following morning dawns bright again, the sky blue and clear, as the two intrepid explorers make their way down to the harbour in time to catch their boat to Dartmouth.

Conversation has by now come easy between them and they are completely relaxed in each other's company. Henry has visited Dartmouth several times with Isabel and the children over the years, and they all enjoyed its mix of charm and sheer beauty. He has never, though, approached the town via the river and he finds this exciting and exhilarating, the boat moving down between ever increasing high sides of the gorge, until they finally arrive at Dartmouth quay, or more properly marina. The gorge in which they have been travelling has now widened out and on each side is covered with trees and bushes, giving it a lush green aspect. But on both sides, houses and cottages appear and cling to the climbing hills like limpets, each with verandas or balconies facing out across the estuary.

Dartmouth harbour is wide and deep and is a hive of activity with yachts, boats and ferries of every description scurrying around like worker ants from their nest.

Colours everywhere are intense and vivid, so much so that Henry and Gee have to hurriedly put sunglasses on to avoid the glare.

Knowing a little about the town Henry suggests to Gee that perhaps they should visit the Britannia Royal Naval College, because he knows that conducted tours can be arranged from the Tourist Information Office near the centre of the town. So, once they have disembarked they make their way there and book for the next tour which they are told takes a little over two hours to complete. The tour that they have booked commenced at eleven thirty and the tour includes a bus transfer to the college which is some three quarters of a mile away.

As it is now only a quarter to eleven, they find a café for the obligatory coffees and cakes - a Danish pastry for Henry and a scone for Gee.

Catching the bus at the appointed time they join the tour, which is conducted by Mike, a retired Naval History Professor at the academy. He begins by explaining that the Britannia Royal Naval College is now known more simply as Dartmouth, and is the initial officer training establishment of the British Royal Navy, which has taken place since here 1863. Mike continues to entertain them with stories of heroism and by giving them detailed accounts of past events. He then goes on to explain that the college has a long history with royalty over the years, including George V and of course our current Queen Elizabeth II, who, as Princess Elizabeth, met her husband to be, Prince Phillip, here. The college itself is beautiful, all red brick and set in acres of ground. Both Henry and Gee love the tour. Once it finishes, they are both transported back to the Tourist Information Office in town.

In an effort to find more activities and more about the town they collect several leaflets from The Tourist Information Office and discover that the town itself is very old, and being built on a hill the streets rise up from the quay. The earliest street to be recorded by name (in the thirteenth century) is Smith Street. Several houses on the street are originally late sixteenth century or early seventeenth century and probably rebuilt on the site of earlier medieval dwellings. The street name undoubtedly derives from the smiths and shipwrights who built and repaired ships here, when the tidal waters reached as far as this point.

So they idle their way among its narrow ancient streets, stopping only for more refreshments, until Henry suddenly remembers a trip that he had taken many years previously with Isabel and the children, to Dartmouth Castle. Thinking that this might be of interest to Gee he explains that it is possible to get a small boat from the quay which will take them further down the estuary toward the sea, to a place where they can embark, before climbing the hill to Dartmouth Castle.

Later on they will need to get a ferry across the harbour to Kingswear, where they will get the steam train that will take them on the next step of their journey to Paighnton.

Deciding that they have sufficient time, they hurry to the quay and get the boat that will take them to the place where they can get to Dartmouth Castle by foot. This had been built some six hundred years before to guard the narrow entrance to the Dart Estuary and the busy port of Dartmouth, which was the home of the Royal Navy from the time of Edward III.

Once at the castle the views are stunning, looking both across and down the estuary and then out to sea. It is obvious that strategically this was the best place with which to protect the harbour from attack by ships approaching from the sea. There is another similar building on the opposite side of the estuary at Kingswear Castle. During the Hundred Years War, Dartmouth harbour was twice surprised and sacked, after which the estuary was closed every night with a great chain.

They buy ice creams and sit together on a grassy bank before deciding that they had best return to the quay to get the ferry. It is now four o'clock and the train is due to leave at a quarter to five.

Taking the ferry across Dartmouth Bay, they duly arrive on the Kingswear shore, and make their way to get the steam train that will take them north up the river estuary, close to Galmpton, then Goodrington, at which point they will have Tor Bay on their right, an area referred to as the Cornish Riviera. They continue on for a few more minutes before arriving at Paignton, their final destination by train.

The whole party who had left Totnes in the morning now transfers to buses that have been laid on for them, and the return journey to their original point of departure gets them back at six o'clock.

By now they are both really weary, and stumble their way back up Fore Street to the High Street. Finally they reach their destination where they make their way immediately to the bar, Gee saying, "I can't go a step farther until I have quenched my raging thirst," which Henry acknowledges, replying, "You and me both Gee," and then more thoughtfully "Still, it's been a wonderful day, thank you for your company."

THE BUS PASS

After having a couple of bevies they leave for their rooms, hoping to rest and catch up with their correspondence before they get their evening meal. However, all Henry's good intentions are for nought as he lies back on his pillow and within minutes the exertions of the day take their toll and he is asleep.

Eventually his room phone rings, waking him. He answers Gees request of, "Are you ready to go down Henry? Because it's nearly eight o'clock," in a weary voice, saying, "Let's do it." Hurriedly changing, Henry joins him and they return to the dining room where, much to Henry's delight he finds local sea bass on the menu, while Gee orders steak and chips.

They are silent, each with their own thoughts for a while, until Gee says, "Right Henry, what's the plan for tomorrow? We did talk about visiting Slapton Sands, and I know you would like to see the South Hams.

"That being the case, I think it would be easier if we took my car. We will probably see a lot more that way. I know that you want to do your journey using your bus pass, but in this case I think it would be more practical by motor, what do you say?" He finishes by saying, "I would like to do as much as we reasonably can tomorrow Henry, because it will be my last day here. My family returns on Tuesday and there are a number of galleries and studios that I would like, no, I need to visit on Monday on my way home."

Henry replies, saying, "I think it's a no-brainer Gee, if you have no objection in using your car. Although my journey was put together on the bus pass basis, I always recognised that there would be some occasions when other means of transport would be more applicable, although I must say I have enjoyed your company enormously, something that I am very grateful to you for." So it is agreed.

Although they are both quite tired, their evening is livened up almost immediately as the pub welcomes another Folk Group who are obviously not only local, but also very good. The bar fills up very rapidly as, they begin to play. Gee is also interested in the music, as he turns to Henry and says, "Well this is a nice surprise, I have always liked this kind of music, and this group are very good."

This then seems to be the catalyst for a few more beers to flow, and the rest of the evening seems to Henry anyway, to pass in a blur, until eventually the music and the beer take their inevitable toll and just before closing time he announces that he is off to bed.

Gee, still enthralled with the music, says, "I don't get the chance to hear this sort of music, which is so redolent of my youth, so I will stay a little longer while I can and I will see you in the morning, at the crack of sparrow fart," to which Henry raises a hand in acknowledgement before making his way to the stairs.

Arriving at his room, Henry sends emails to those on his list, as he has continued to do every day. Feeling slightly elated with the success of the day, he describes both Gee and his activities, making it how clear just how much he has enjoyed his company. He continues on to explain how they met and tells them as much information that he knows about Gee, and of their plans for the next day. He then goes on to say how much he is going to miss him, because tomorrow is his last day.

Finally, Henry can keep his eyes open no longer, and falls asleep dreaming of the day's events, Kate for once not intruding.

Sunday morning finds Henry struggling to get up, mainly because he has a headache to beat all headaches, which he recognises reluctantly is due to over imbibing the previous night. He wonders idly how Gee is feeling, because he stayed on after Henry had left.

Quickly showering, Henry makes his way for breakfast, where he finds to his utter amazement that Gee is already there. Not only that, but he is also as bright as the proverbial button, as he says, "Come on Henry; I thought that you would be down by now," and then looking a little more closely, "Oh, don't tell me, let me guess. You have a hangover, quite a bad one if your face is anything to go by. Never mind, I have the perfect antidote for that." As he finishes speaking he goes out to the kitchen and has a loud conversation with the chef for several minutes, during which much laughter is heard. When he returns he is carrying a glass which is full with a red coloured liquid, which he gives to Henry saying, "Here you are, have some hair of the dog. You have to swallow it in one go, because it tastes pretty awful, but that should do the trick."

When Henry starts to ask what is in the dubious looking liquid, Gee brushes away all such questions, saying only, "It's an old family remedy which has been passed down over many generations, so I cannot possibly divulge its contents. If I told you I would have to kill you."

This is all said with a twinkle in Gee's eye, and he appears to be enjoying Henry's misfortune. Having, or so it appears to Henry, no option, he swiftly downs the foul smelling brew, only to hear Gee say, "The concoction is based on the premise that the taste is so bad that all thoughts of a hangover are as nought by comparison," after which he collapses slowly in riotous laughter, to which Henry indignantly replies, "Well thank you very much for your sympathy to an old man who is suffering," only to hear Gee say, "Oh, come on Henry, don't be a sore loser. Anyway, it worked didn't it? Go on, admit it, you feel much better now."

To Henry's amazement he has to admit Gee is right. Whatever psychological tosh that was all about, seems to have done the trick. He feels much better and says so reluctantly, before ordering and devouring a full English breakfast.

With both of them now chuckling at Henry's hangover experience, they begin their final day together. Driving down small country roads they reach the outskirts of Dartmouth, before branching south along the A379, which takes them south through Stoke Fleming, Blackpool beach, Strete and finally to Slapton Sands, the last of which holds so many memories of events during the Second World War.

The village of Slapton is approached on the A379 from Strete, with the road itself forming a causeway between the sea on the left and a large brackish lake on the right.

Henry is aware of the stories about events leading up to D Day that happened in this quiet unpretentious place, which he relates to Gee as they arrive.

He begins by explaining, "During the months leading up to the invasion of Europe in June 1944, this whole area of South Devon was occupied by some quarter of a million men, mostly American, who continued right through the period doing training for practice landings. This was because the beaches at Slapton Sands mimicked almost exactly the beaches in Northern France which they would have to land on and get ashore to enable them to free Europe of its terrible tyrant.

"Before they could even get troops into this local area of South Devon, most of the surrounding villages had to be cleared of their inhabitants. This caused a lot of hardship for the locals who survived largely from farming. Conditions were not ideal either for the men of the army, because they were camped in tents for the whole of the period up until D-Day. However, the most tragic event that occurred here was the huge loss of life, mostly American, but also some British. It happened just after midnight on the night of 28 April 1944, during a training exercise prior to D-Day.

"A few hours earlier assault forces of the U S fourth infantry division had gone ashore on Slapton Sands. The assault of Slapton Sands was known as Exercise Tiger. So vital was the exercise of accustoming troops to the combat conditions that they were soon to face, that commanders had ordered the use of live naval and artillery fire. Individual soldiers also had live ammunition for their rifles and machine guns.

A flotilla of eight LSTs (landing ship tanks) was ploughing through the water towards Slapton Sands for the assault, when, out of the darkness, nine swift German torpedo boats suddenly appeared. German torpedoes hit three of the LSTs. One lost its stern, but eventually limped into port. Another burst into flames, the fire fed by the gasoline from the vehicles aboard. A third keeled over and sank within six minutes.

When the waters of the English Channel at last ceased to wash bodies ashore, the toll of the dead and missing was something between 700 and 800, although in subsequent years figures were disputed as being on the low side."

As he finishes speaking, Henry can see Gee's expression as one of disbelief, which is confirmed as he says, "That is unbelievable Henry. I just can't reconcile events of that magnitude happening in this beautiful place. Why didn't anyone tell me before?"

"Well, I guess there is a lot that happens in times of war, but this particular catastrophe was to some extent hushed up, because it would have been a propaganda coup if it became known to the Germans about the purpose of the exercise, and the Allies had to hope that the Germans did not get to find out why the flotilla was where it was, and why," says Henry. "But there has been a lot of material written and documentaries on TV, so if you wanted to know more, I am sure that it won't be difficult to find."

Gee says, "I will definitely do that. Thank you so much Henry."

Henry is pleased with this and says, "Right, now let's explore these shops. The one thing I do remember is that among them is probably the best fish restaurant that I ever experienced when I brought my wife and children many years ago. It's too early for a meal, but I am sure there must be a café where we can get our necessary coffee fix. What do you say?"

A huge beaming smile is enough to tell Henry that he has said the right thing.

"Where to next," enquires Gee as they leave the café.

"Well, I think that we had best prioritise, because it is not possible to visit all the places we would like, in the time we have available. Why don't we make our way up through Kingsbridge and keep on to the A379, which follows the coast all the way into Plymouth. We don't need to go that far, because I would like to get to Bigbury and Ringmore, which I have wonderful happy memories of."

"Your wish is my command," replies Gee, doffing an invisible cap before they start wending their way through a host of tiny villages on their way to Kingsbridge, making him think to add, "It must have been a logistical nightmare to get such a huge number of men and materials down here through these tiny lanes. Can you imagine tank transporters. Troop lorries, fuel, ordinance, and all the rest of it manoeuvring these roads, with their tight bends and narrow roads. It must have been horrendous."

It only takes them half an hour to get to Bigbury, a journey which takes them down through narrow lanes that have high sided hedges and walls each side, with only a handful of passing places, making visibility impossible.

As they arrive they can see, lying some two hundred yards off Bigbury, the lovely Burgh Island, which is surrounded by the sea at full tide, but when it recedes, can be approached on foot. At low tide the whole area becomes a lovely sandy beach, which is ideal for children, provided that due care is taken when the tide starts to rise.

Henry loves it here, but the main reason for bringing Gee to this spot, and indeed his own, is because he wants to revisit Burgh

Island Hotel, which sits high up, and apart from a pub called the Pilchard Inn, is the only habitable building on the island.

It was here that Isabel brought Henry as a surprise fiftieth birthday present. They stayed two days at this wonderful hotel, which was built sometime in the early 1920s, and was one of the most sought after places for the wealthy of the day. The future King Edward VIII spent time here with his friends, as did Noel Coward, and Agatha Christie, the latter who wrote crime novels here. Her *Evil under the Sun* was not only written here, but the story was also based upon a fictional murder on the island.

Having been built in the twenties it is decorated throughout in the Art Deco style, a period which Henry loves. Much to his great pleasure and delight on visiting it, he found that the owners had retained all the existing features, both of furniture and decoration, which, for him, meant seventh heaven.

It is now nearly midday and as the tide is about an hour or so from its zenith, they are able to walk across to the Island where they explore its rocky outcrops, before returning down to the Pilchard Inn, the only other building on the Island. After perusing the menu, they decide to have crab sandwiches, washed down with Cornish beer.

Leaving the pub and by now wanting to return to Bigbury, they find that they are now cut off by the tide which has swept in from both sides of the island, cutting off Bigbury on the mainland, from the Island. However, their plight is not insurmountable, because, as Henry is aware, the hotel owns a tractor type vehicle, which has huge wheels that can carry passengers safely across the gap, even in quite bad weather condition. So this is the form of transport they choose to return to Bigbury.

Deciding to move on they drive back until they reach St. Anne's Chapel, where they turn left and follow the road down towards the sea, but stop at the sign marked Ringmore.

This is another of Henry's old haunts, and is indeed on his bucket list of places to see again. It is the most exquisite little village, all thatched cottages giving the village a chocolate box appearance. They stop just above the village where there is a convenient car park opposite the local medieval church, before they meander round and down the village, Henry explaining to

THE BUS PASS

Gee, various places that he knows, until they reach the village pub called Journey's End, which is several hundred years old. Here they have coffee while they enjoy the tranquil atmosphere and beautiful wood panelled walls. The pub has a large bar area, in which there is a large selection of beers, and this pleased both of them. At one end of this room there is a huge log fire, which Henry knows from previous visits, gives the room a most welcoming atmosphere on cold wintry days. There are also a number of smaller rooms which can be used if privacy is required.

Once they have finished their repast they set off once more.

Henry has stayed in the village on a number of occasions with Isabel, after the children had got older and did no longer want to accompany their parents. He now finds his way round the village, past a few scattered cottages, and follows a progressively steep and narrowing lane which has trees either side. To all appearances it looks as if no one ever uses this overgrown track, but they eventually pass a complex of farm buildings which have obviously been converted to accommodations for self-catering purposes. They continue on down into the valley until they reach a National Trust sign post indicating Ayrmer Cove. It is another half mile or so before they reach their destination, but when they get there they both agree their walk has been worth it.

The cove is completely isolated from any other beaches and apart from the remains of a barbeque, brought here no doubt by locals, there is no other evidence that anybody else has ever been here. It is an idyllic spot, and after their exertions of the day, they sit and look mesmerizingly out at to sea, an ogre, which can be angry and fierce, but today it has the appearance of a sleeping giant, both smooth and placid.

They sit for a time, each in their own quiet contemplation, until Henry's head starts drooping as he tries in vain to stay awake. Gee, noticing this, rises and goes to the water's edge, before taking off his shoes to have a paddle.

Eventually Henry wakes with a start and calls to Gee. "Hey, it's nearly half past four, shall we make a move?"

Gee nods his head in the affirmative, before saying, "OK, where to next?" After they discuss a number of possibilities, they both agree that if they retrace their footsteps back to the car park, they can then get to Salcombe in time for a cream tea.

Making their way back across the National Trust path which runs alongside pastures for sheep and cattle, they begin their climb up the narrow winding lane, which causes Gee to begin to understand why the cove is so isolated. He realises that unless you live here, there would be no way that you could find this beautiful spot. The locals also probably would keep it quiet, wanting to use it for themselves, particularly in the holiday season when parents and children descend on the West Country in their droves.

The climb saps their energy, and they are glad to reach the car park, and spend a few minutes resting before starting their journey to Salcombe, which they reach after half an hour.

Nearing their destination, Henry tells Gee as much as he knows about the town, saying, "Salcombe lies close to the mouth of the Kingsbridge estuary, and is a haven for yachts and boats of every description. Its position in the estuary ensures safety from the worst of the weather coming off the English Channel, and the water in the pool is deep enough for large yachts, which during the summer months visit here from Europe, Scandinavia and other far-flung places. It's built mostly on the steep west side of the estuary. It has an extensive waterfront, and the naturally sheltered harbour ensures its success as a boat, shipbuilding and sailing port. It has a crabbing industry, but also relies on its travel industry."

Parking, they make their way down, following narrow winding roads, or sometimes steep steps, until they reach the waterfront. Continuing on they reach the town, where to Gee's amazement, the roads are still just as narrow, with traffic directed on a one way system. The streets are alive with shops of every description, and Gee in particularly shows interest in a number of art galleries.

The town is awash with people of all ages, crowding the narrow streets making it almost impossible for private drivers to get through or for deliveries to be made. Their sheer numbers block entrances to shops, making it impossible for those inside to get out. Dressed in attire of every description, in a cacophony of colours, they spill out across the narrow streets, their excited chatter reverberating, the sound echoing, their voices rising to be heard above everyone else. A self- defeating exercise, only increasing the sense of mayhem.

THE BUS PASS

Walking a little further on to a point where the hordes of people begin to peter out, they find a café which, among other delicacies, serves cream teas, which they both order and devour as if it were the first meal they had eaten on this day. As they finish, Henry suddenly realises that his time with Gee is almost up, reviving the hopeless feelings of loss that he experienced earlier in the week.

Gee seems to notice what Henry is going through, and in an effort to jolly him along, says, "I guess that we are nearly at the end of our pilgrimage Henry, thank you for showing me all these wonderful places. I guess when I was growing up things were fairly tight, so we never went very far for holidays. It was mostly camping in Wales or the Peak District, both of which I loved, so I never had chance to see anything else. Before I leave can we swop mobile phone numbers, so that we can keep in touch. Or even better still, when you have finished your sojourns down here, why don't you stop off and see me and my family on your way back to your home, or wherever you intend getting too."

For a minute Henry is overcome by Gee's kind, thoughtful words, recognising in them that he can see how Henry is feeling.

"I would like that very much," says Henry, wondering not for the first time who Gee reminds him of. He can't quite put his finger on it, but it's something about his ready smile and the intense gaze of those clear blue eyes. Then he thinks that maybe he reminds him of a certain television presenter, but he is not sure.

"But I don't know where you live," Henry continues.

Gee looks slightly perturbed at this question, almost as if it is something that he didn't expect to be asked, but he quickly replies. "Sorry, how silly of me, I live just south of Crewkerne. But if you ring my number and let me know when you expect to arrive, I will make sure that I will be at home, and will give you instructions how to get to me."

They are both lost in their own thoughts for a few moments, until Gee says, "Well, I think that we had best find our way back to Totnes, unless there is somewhere else you would like to see."

"No, I am just about all in Gee, anyway by the time we get back I would like some time to rest before dinner. I expect you would like to do some packing ready for the morning."

"Oh! It won't take me long to throw my bits together. I didn't bring very much anyway," Gee says.

On returning to Totnes they retire to their rooms, arranging to meet at eight for dinner, which is surprisingly a sombre affair, unlike the rest of the time that they have spent together.

Truth to tell, Henry is feeling depressed at the thought of losing his new companion, which Gee recognises and tries desperately to get him to focus on the next few days by asking, "Tell me where you are going next Henry, then I will be able to know where you are at any given time, and will envy you accordingly."

So Henry explains, and as the evening continues, he becomes more animated which Gee notices and breathes a sigh of relief to see his new friend becoming more relaxed.

Finally Gee says, "Well Henry shall we have a last toast to what has been for me a wonderful few days. I shall have so much to tell my family when I get back. Thank you for your good company and best wishes on the rest of your journey. I probably won't see you in the morning, because I want to make an early start," then brandishing a piece of paper, "Here is my mobile phone number, so feel free to ring me any time."

Henry is slightly overcome by this, but manages to reply. "Thank you Gee, but I can assure you that the pleasure has been all mine. I was in a bad way until you arrived, and although I still don't feel a hundred per cent, your company has made a huge difference. Have a safe journey home, and you never know, I may see you again sometime," and, raising his glass, "Cheers."

CHAPTER 24
Rob

Monday 1 July

Kate wakes early, having slept fitfully all night, the thought of her appointment at the breast clinic in Weymouth weighing heavily on her mind. As if still unable to believe it, she reads the letter again for the zillionth time.

We are writing to inform you that your recent mammary examination, which was performed at the mobile breast clinic in Dorchester, has proved to be inconclusive and consequently we need to take more pictures from different angles to get clarification. This does not mean that you have been identified with any form of cancer. It is very often necessary to repeat this procedure, of which only a small percentage of people need further investigation. This is just a precautionary measure.

We have made you an appointment for Monday 1 July at ten thirty, here at Weymouth Hospital, where you can be seen by a radiologist. Would you please let us know if this is not convenient or if you would like to make an alternative.

Kate shudders, as she has done many times before on reading this missive. She wishes with all her being that Henry was here to sooth and comfort her, then steals her resolve, realising that this is the very reason that she broke off their relationship. She also realises that her reaction upon receiving the letter was of the knee jerk variety and that perhaps she should have waited to see the results of her prognosis. But even though she had responded on receiving the letter in a detrimental way to Henry, she still didn't see what other position she could have taken.

Here was this man, who she had come to love so deeply, being told that she didn't have the feeling for him that he so obviously had for her. But how could she tell him that the letter had frightened her? The thought of being diagnosed positive with breast cancer would raise terrible memories of his wife Isabel's suffering and death. If there was any possible chance that she too, would also have to go through this scenario, there is no way that she could put Henry through the situation for a second time. No, better this way, even though the separation has given them both a sense of unrequited loss, Henry will come to see that it is for the best eventually.

She doesn't know how she will feel if her condition is negative, meaning that she has sacrificed her love for Henry for nothing, but also recognises that if she had told him about the letter and her diagnosis was positive, everything would change. Knowing him as she does, if it was positive he would want to be with her, and suffer with for a second time the same slow debilitating disease that he had watched and endured Isabel experience. She could not bear the thought of this happening to him again, so felt that she had no other option than to take the course that she had.

It was a different situation when it came to her children who she had not told either at this stage. Unlike Henry, she decides that she can wait before telling them anything, because it might very well turn out to be a false alarm. She had avoided doing so when she told David about the break in the relationship between her and Henry, only telling him that her reason for doing so was personal and he needed to trust her and that it wasn't about Henry. If her diagnosis turns out to be bad news, then that will be the time to tell them.

Arriving at Weymouth Hospital at the appointed time, she is ushered in by a radiologist who is obviously experienced at dealing with women in Kate's situation. After a few minutes she is taken to have another series of pictures taken from a number of different angles this time, and then asked to return to reception while they are developed. Her sense of foreboding is confirmed after forty minutes, when the radiologist calls her to her office, where she explains that her results are not as they expect them to be, so the next process will be for her to have ultrasound treatment, which should hopefully clarify the situation.

By now, Kate is concerned and asks what is it that can be seen on her pictures, that are not seen on those of a normal procedure, to which the radiologist replies, "Well there are two what appear to be lumps in your pictures, which we need to establish as being benign or as being malignant, but don't worry, we see these all the time and almost always they prove to be benign cysts, for which no treatment is necessary."

Slightly consoled, Kate proceeds to have ultrasound treatment, only to be told that the results cannot be determined immediately, and is asked to return home and the clinic will contact her once the results have been determined, which should be in several days' time.

This is the worst of all possible scenarios that Kate has envisaged, and means that she will be in a state of even more emotional turmoil than previously. On arriving home she realises that she can no longer put off telling her children, and so it is with a heavy heart that she picks up the phone with a trembling hand to break the news to David, Geoffrey and their families.

Meanwhile, Henry wakes slowly after the exertions of the previous day, feeling lethargic and still tired. He has not slept very well, the thought of Gee leaving making him wonder where and how he is to proceed. He questions if he still has the resolve or indeed the desire to continue with his quest. As he gets to the dining room for breakfast, these feelings of inadequacy and lack of purpose are reinforced, because, not only is Gee no longer there, which Henry expected, but neither is anyone else. The room is deserted, which the landlord reassures Henry, is temporary, and that he is expecting a further eight or nine people later on that day.

Not having a specific plan, Henry spends the morning looking round Totnes, before returning to his room, thinking that he should contact a few people who may be worried that they have not heard from him for a couple of days. So thinking over what he should say to them individually or as a group, he commences by first emailing Kate. He chooses her first because he knows that hers will be the most difficult, and that just the effort thinking about her will bring his feelings of loss back again. So, he writes.

Hallo Kate, My love (for that is what you will always be),

Thank you for cleaning and forwarding my clothes, and for your very kind offer to continue to do so. I have thought about it a lot since, but although I am tempted, I feel that it would only prolong the misery that I am feeling without you in my life. Part of me says to continue, because if I did it would mean that I could still be in touch with you, but the other part says no, because being in contact but never being able to see you or hold you would be an absolute living hell for me. I hope you will understand, but for this reason alone I have to so no.

You know that I will always be therefore you, should you ever need me,

Love always,

Henry.

As he finishes and presses the send button, tears flow unrestrained down his face, almost blinding him with their intensity.

An hour passes before he feels composed enough to send his next email to Rob and Madge, Penny and Mark and finally to Richard and Janet in Oz.

Hi all,

Thought that it was time that I let you know how things are going. Well I had a great time with this chap called Gee, who I told you about. We visited so many places on my bucket list. He was such a wonderful companion, even though he was young enough to be my own son. But, like all good things, they don't last forever, and he has now left to return to his family. I can't say I won't miss him, because I will.

Being positive I will probably leave Totnes tomorrow (Tuesday) to make for my next destination, Fowey, so I will contact you all again when I get there,

Love to you all,

Henry.

Having to spend the rest of the day in Totnes and not knowing what to do, Henry returns to the bar for a pint and a sandwich. As he stands ordering, a man comes alongside, who Henry ignores, being engaged in his own confused thoughts. That is, until the man suddenly interrupts them and says, "I hope you are going to buy me one as well, my old mucker."

Henry doesn't even have to look at the person standing next to him, to know that his journey has taken a turn for the better. The sound of the voice and choice of words mean that it can only be one person, his oldest and closest friend, who over the years he has confided with (apart from Isabel and his children) more than any other.

Without bothering to look to his side, he says, "Of course I am Rob, particularly as you have come all this way," and then turning to see his friend's beaming face he says, "Oh mate! It's so good to see you, but what are you doing here?" As he finishes speaking, they do high fives before hugging one another.

"Well Henry, I saw your email the other day saying that you had met that chap Gee, but also that he was leaving today, so I thought that you might like a bit of company for a few days. So here I am. I cleared it with the C.O. Who, I have a strong feeling, was glad to see the back of me for a while."

Henry is lost for words for a while, until he says, "Are you sure that Madge doesn't mind, Rob? I mean it's really great to see you, but I wouldn't want to upset her for all the tea in China."

"I'm certain, my old friend. In fact we talked about it and she even said that when I go back, that I was to take your dirty washing with me. She could wash and iron it and then get it back to you, which was the original arrangement before you left. Anyway when you first decided to do your pilgrimage I told you at the time that I would like to do some of it with you, so here I am. What do you plan to do next and where do you plan to go."

Henry can't keep the grin off his face as Rob is speaking, his pleasure plain for all to see. As his friend finishes speaking he says, "To tell you the truth Rob, I was struggling to decide if I wanted to go any further, or call it a day. You see I think I underestimated just how difficult it would be to embark on something like this on my own. Oh! I can do all the arrangements and find my way around, but the difficult bit is motivation. It's a lonely experience, especially after spending so much time with Kate, and then having to start again on my own. But never mind, the great thing is that you are here now, so I won't have to be on my own, for a few days at least. How long do you think you can stay?"

"Well, I was thinking until about Friday. I have to be home on Saturday because Madge's sister Wendy and her tribe are coming over, but if you would like me to stay longer, just say so. It would give me a good excuse to not to see Wendy, or rather her tribe. Wendy is OK in fairness, but I can't say the same for her children who are a pain in the proverbial."

All the time he has been talking, Rob has been wondering just why Henry is having to continue his journey, when the last time he saw him he was so obviously happy living with Kate. Rob seriously doubts that Henry would rather be here now, than being in Goderston with Kate, so concludes in his mind that the decision was hers alone.

"What happened between Kate and you, Henry? You don't have to tell me, but it's obvious that you wouldn't be here now of your own volition. When I saw you last, you and she were like love's young dream."

Henry is not ready yet to face such a direct assault on his motives, and would normally deny the true reasons for him being here. But it is Rob, his old pal from forever, the one person he has always been able to share his worst fears and nightmares with. They have been through thick and thin together. When Isabel became terminally ill, it was Rob and Madge who bolstered Henry's resolve; they who were there when it mattered, who took turns sitting with Isabel when Henry was totally exhausted. They had supported him then, and ever since, so Henry cannot prevaricate in such circumstances.

"It did come as a complete shock Rob, believe me. She just woke up one morning and said that she didn't want to continue our relationship any more, and suggested that I continue my journey before I moved to Australia. I was devastated. Still am, if truth be told. You see I was happy for the first time since Isabel died, and I thought Kate was too. But there was no moving her, so I had no other alternative than to carry on. If I had returned home everyone would know that Kate had given me the elbow, but if I carried on, they would assume that I had done it from choice, before moving to Australia. Please keep this to yourself, Rob. The last thing that I would wish to happen is for anyone to think less of Kate, because I love her and even though I may never see her again, wish her no ill."

"Well, I am as baffled as you Henry. What you have told me doesn't seem to fit with the Kate that Madge and I saw. Are you sure there is no other reason why she would do this? I can understand it if she thinks that you will still go to Australia once your children have gone, so would prefer to face it now, rather than sometime down the track."

"I don't think that can be the reason Rob, because I made it quite clear to her at the time that should they both end in in Australia, that I would go to visit them from time to time, but as far as I was concerned, I saw my future with her in Goderston, or anywhere else, should she prefer it."

Having exhausted the subject of Kate, who Rob can see has upset his old mate, he decides to not push the matter any further, and tries to lighten the mood as he tells him of a little story that he had witnessed. "Did I tell you about the wall that Bill Enwright had built recently?"

"No, I don't think you did," replies Henry. He knows that the person mentioned lives four doors up from Rob, although he doesn't know him very well, only to pass the time of day with. "What happened?"

"Well I don't really know, but I had to pass his place the other day and as I got there, I noticed that there was a new wall at the front of his house. He must have decided to replace the original old wooden fence. So what's unusual about that, you may ask. Well here's the punchline. He parks his car at the front of the house, almost touching it in fact, because the space from the front garden to the house is only some twelve to fourteen feet. As I say, I don't know why, but the builders in their wisdom built the wall as they did. It is about four and a half feet high and in fairness looks very impressive. That was until I looked over it, only to see that they had blocked Bill's car in completely, leaving him no room to get it out. There it sits facing the house with about only three inches to spare front and back. There is no way that he will be able to extricate the car, unless he pulls down the wall.

"I must admit that I couldn't help laughing out loud. Luckily for me, Bill was not at home. Rumour has it that the builders were Latvian, so maybe they didn't understand just what Bill wanted. God knows what happens next.

"As you can imagine, this became the cause of a lot of mirth in the village, and Bill had to stand having his leg pulled endlessly."

Rob can see that the story has gripped Henry's attention, which is what he has hoped would happen, as his friend says laughingly, "OMG I would have given a King's ransom to have seen that. It couldn't have happened to a more deserving person. Bill always was a mean old bugger, it serves him right."

The atmosphere is now hugely improved, so Rob asks Henry again what his plans are for the next few days.

"I would like to get to Fowey next. We all went as a family, just before the children decided that they were getting too old to go on holidays with us. Actually, we all loved the place so much that they changed their minds and came with us for the next two years, so it holds a special place in my heart. I think that if we can get there, it will be a good place from which to visit a number of other places on my list, such as the Eden Project, the Lost Gardens of Heligan, Rick Stein's fish restaurant at Padstow - Oh! And the Minnack Open Theatre, where I have always wanted to go. If we can find accommodation in or around Fowey, we could use it as a springboard to get to them."

"That sounds great Henry, but if we are going to do all of that, I think that it would be best if we drove to Fowey in my car, after which we can use the local bus transport to see all the places you mentioned. After you left on your pilgrimage I got a bus pass as well, so the world's our oyster now. I think that it's a bit late to do anything more today, so what say we start off first thing in the morning. I will get a room here for tonight, and we will make an early start tomorrow, at the crack of dawn. How does that sound."

So it is agreed and the two of them spend the rest of the day visiting places in the local area. They make their way to Dartington where beautiful glass is made, and where there are shops of every description, selling unusual products which cannot be found anywhere else. Rob is quick to draw Henry's attention to this fact, remarking, "It's lucky that it's just you and me mate. If Madge was with us my credit card would be under great strain." But Henry notes with much amusement that Rob selects a beautiful glass clock as a gift for his wife.

After completing their purchases, Henry buying gifts for Penny (six wine glasses) and Richard (an original painting of Salcombe), they both retire to a café for coffee and cake.

"I am really enjoying this Henry. It feels a bit like playing truant."

So the day passes with Henry now feeling completely relaxed. The evening is spent at the pub, which has the folk group performing again, much to their pleasure. After much reminiscing they finally they turn in for the day, agreeing that they will make an early start next morning. Once in his room, Henry Googles places to stay in Fowey, before emailing his children, telling them that Rob has joined him for a few days.

Rob goes online to Madge, explaining the happenings of the day with Henry, and then their plans until Friday.

CHAPTER 25

Fowey

Tuesday 2 July

"I had a look at suitable places to stay in Fowey last night," says Henry, getting out his laptop and pulling up the relevant page. "I found what looks like an ideal B&B. It's at the top of the town, from where it's only a couple of minutes' walk down to the quay. It is a very reasonable cost and even more important is the fact that it has parking spaces, because it's almost impossible to get any accommodation down in the waterfront area that has facilities for cars. Have a look and see what you think."

Proffering his laptop to Rob, Henry resumes his breakfast. After several minutes Rob says, "I agree it looks very nice," at which point Henry says, "Good, I will get onto them now. I would prefer to have somewhere, rather than take pot luck when we get there and not be able to find anything."

He spends a few minutes contacting the owner of the property, and to his delight manages to book for the next three nights.

Breakfast over, they take their leave of the Bay Horse Inn and are soon on the A385 making their way towards the A38, joining it just north of South Brent. By now the sun is a red fiery ball at their backs as they travel west on the A38, crossing the Tamar Toll Bridge at Plymouth. Once over, they are now in Cornwall and as they travel they can see the countryside changing. It is still green and lush, but the further they go the more they see granite outcrops, which appear to be pushing their way up through the landscape. This is the type of rock that typifies the cliffs and bays that extend right the way round this beautiful county. Continuing on the A38 they reach Liskeard, and shortly after branch left to follow the A390 down, to just outside St. Austell.

It is now nearly twelve noon, and Henry is aware that they

cannot book in to the guest house until 3 p.m., but it only takes a few minutes for them to find their way to Fowey. To reach the town they drive down narrow lanes, which have stone walls, either side. Immediately beyond the walls are trees, which hang over the lane, almost blocking out the light. To make matters worse the lane is only just wide enough for one vehicle with only a few passing places. They successfully negotiate this and eventually reach the Bodinnick Ferry car park, which is at the north end of the town.

Henry remembers from previous visits that the only other way down into the town is from the south end, which either means driving down a very steep twisting narrow hill, which has buildings either side, leaving no room for error, or to park at the top of the hill and walk down. The drive from this end of town is one way only, right the way through until the Bodinnick car park - hence Henry's choice of entry.

The day is now perfect, the sun directly overhead, the sky an azure blue with only a few wispy clouds lazily crossing the firmament. As the two of them make their way through Fowey's single one way narrow street, avoiding the few oncoming cars that are brave enough to venture this way, they can see between the houses they pass, that are perched on the riverside, the estuary, which is the almost identical colour of blue as the sky.

Reaching the centre of town they find themselves at the quay, and to their amazement there is a huge cruise ship moored in the middle of the estuary, and they realise this must be the source of the throng of people which are crowding the narrow thoroughfares and shops.

Additionally, people are queuing at the water's edge for boats to take them to various destinations, all talking animatedly as they wait. This normally small community of local people, fishermen, traders and restaurateurs has become a multi-cultural town, alive with people and creeds of many nations for the day.

Entering The Ship public house, they order food and Cornish beer, which they consume slowly, relishing this old building with its nooks and crannies, which haven't changed for hundreds of years. Rob gets talking to a couple of men at the bar, who it conspires, are locals. Before Henry and Rob know it, the locals are regaling them with stories of smugglers who were once prevalent here many years ago, and some not as long ago either, if the nods and winks of the locals are to be believed.

Eventually, they take their leave and find that the town is quieter now, the people from the cruise ship having made their way back to the boat ready for sailing.

Taking the opportunity, the two musketeers decide to take a boat trip up the river and then back down the estuary. This turns out to be a very educational way of discovering the area. As well as the cruise ship, there are a myriad of ships moored on floating piers, making the harbour almost as busy as the town.

The boat takes them up river at first, until the Bodinnick Ferry is reached. As they start to turn their journey takes them to the opposite side of the river, where the boatman's commentary informs them that the pretty white house next to the ferry on the Polruan side of the river was lived in for a number of years by Daphne Du Maurier, the novelist.

As they progress back down the estuary they notice the sides on both the towns of Fowey and Polruan rise almost perpendicularly immediately from the water's edge. This then, thinks Henry, is the reason why the roads are so narrow and the houses cling like limpets, precariously to the face of the cliffs.

They have both enjoyed seeing the area from the river and on arriving back at the quay, they notice that there are other daily boat trips, a couple of which appeal to them, the first of which is up river to Golant, where there is a local market, and the second is across the bay to Mevagissey.

Promising themselves that these are to do another day, they return to the car park, before making their way back up the narrow winding lane. At the top they turn left and carry on following the road signposted, Readymoney. It is only another mile to their destination, which turns out to be a lovely sixteenth-century house in Lostwithiel Street. The front elevation is covered with wisteria up to roof height with roses in full bloom in beds below. The building is of Cornish granite, and the roof is of Cornish slate, as are most of the properties in this area. Agapanthus are growing all around the walls in the front of the house, their blue and white flowers adding further colour to this beautiful house.

THE BUS PASS

They are met by the owner, who to Henry's surprise is a tall, slender, attractive woman who he estimates to be in her early forties. "Welcome to Tregenith House, I am Trudy Warner." She then goes on to show them their room and tell them where everything that they might need can to be found.

While she is talking, Henry is very aware that her speech is not of the local dialect, and asks her how long she has lived here, to which she replies, "Oh, my husband and I moved down here ten years ago. We got fed up with the rat race, and as we had always loved this part of Cornwall, we decided to give it a go. So I run the guest house, while my husband works for himself, doing decorating and small maintenance work. None of it is lucrative, and it is very hard work, but in all honesty we love it and have never regretted moving down here." As she finishes speaking, Henry is vaguely conscious that he recognises her from somewhere, but try as he might, he is unable to recall from where.

He can see the appeal of living in this wonderful place, and had discussed doing something similar with Isabel several times years ago, but the time had never seemed right. But here and now thinking about it, he can see that there never was a right time, and the only way to achieve what you really want is just to go for it.

Their room is large, painted in warm pastel peach with matching curtains at the windows, through which the sun spills. So it must be facing east, thinks Henry idly. It has twin three foot beds and there is another door, which, upon examination, reveals an en-suite bathroom, shower and toilet.

By now totally exhausted after the exertions of the day, they collapse on their beds and within a few minutes are both nodding off.

It is evening before they wake, by which time they are both ravenous. Trudy doesn't cater for evening meals, but recommends Sam's Plaice, a fish restaurant down in the town, near the harbour. This is only a few minutes' walk away, all downhill, and when they get there the place is alive with people thronging both outside and in. Eventually forcing their way in they manage to order a table, but there is a waiting time of forty minutes, so they go upstairs to the bar until they are called when it becomes available. This is obviously the 'in' place for eating in the evening. People are crowded in to every conceivable nook and cranny, all loud with their conversation and dress. The restaurant seems to attract extroverts and extremes from every walk of life. Henry sits bemused by the sheer volume of activity, perfectly happy to sit and stare, while Rob sees it all as a joke, pointing out the more obvious oddities to his friend, which has them both in fits of laughter.

The food, when it arrives, is exquisite, and explains why the restaurant has such a fantastic reputation in the town. Henry has crab salad, while Rob chooses pollock, caught locally, which they wash down with wine.

Once they have eaten, the pressure for table space means that they waste no time leaving, and adjourn to the Ship Inn, round the corner. This too is busy, with every room occupied by people dining, but they manage to get to the bar which is relatively quiet. To their surprise the two local characters that they were talking to earlier in the day are still here.

Rob immediately strikes up a conversation with them again. "Blimey chaps, have you been here all day?"

"Nearly," one of them replies. "We only live up the road and we take the boat out fishing during the night, which means that we only get back usually mid-morning, after which we come here for a pint and a bite to eat, then we crash out in the afternoon. Tonight is one of the nights that we don't go out."

Before long Rob is telling jokes from his never ending repertoire and the bar is alive with laughter. Once again Henry stands silently marvelling at his friend's communication skills, until suddenly George, the older of the two fishermen, makes his own contribution, saying, "Let me tell you of a story about my brother who lives in St. Austell. Every morning he collects his newspaper, and every day on his way back home, there is a house where the rubbish collection bin is still outside. Thinking that the people living there keep forgetting to take it in, he pushes it back into their garden. What he can't understand is why the next day the bin is again outside the house, even though the next collection is not due for another week.

"This goes on day after day for weeks, until one day, on collecting his local paper, there are huge front page headlines about a local brothel which, on looking at the address, he notices is the particular house that he moves the rubbish bin from the path outside, into the front garden. What's more, when he reads the article, he discovers that the prostitutes put the bin outside as a signal for punters, to let them know that they are 'open for business'.

As he finishes, the bar area erupts with laughter, George's story obviously having been heard further than he thought, until Rob says, "I bet the girls must have hated him, doing them out of business." To which George replies, "Oh! You haven't heard the best bit yet. My brother's son works as a fireman, and several weeks after this incident, there was a small kitchen fire at this same property, which he and his crew were called out to. It was quickly extinguished, and as they were leaving, one of the girls propositioned him, saying, 'If you ever want to use our facilities, just let us know and we will give you the same discount rates as we do the police.'"

Once again, as George finishes, there is an even bigger roar of laughter, led from the front by Rob and Henry. Customers and bar staff alike are all falling about in fits of tears.

The story is the catalyst for even more to be told, but by now there are a number of other people who have gravitated to the four of them, and the evening continues in a similar vein, with wine and beer flowing freely. Henry is swept up in the sheer magic of it all, the beer, conversation and companionship reminding him of the 'fishing trips' that Rob, he and the others used to go on.

Eventually it is time to go, so saying their farewells to George and his friend Bert, and all the others who have joined the throng, the two of them wind their way back up the hill to Tregenith House, giggling and laughing like a couple of naughty schoolboys.

During a short lull in their conversation, Henry is suddenly conscious of the fact that he has not thought about Kate for most of the day and pays a silent tribute to his great friend Rob, who has ensured with his presence and wit that this should be so. Having been thus reminded of the fact however, he can't now put her lovely vision out of his mind.

When they get there, the house is quiet with nobody in the lounge, so they make their way to their room, where they both send emails to their respective relatives, before going to sleep.

On Wednesday morning, 3 July, Kate is woken from her sleep by the shrill ring of her telephone. Looking at her bedside clock, she notes that it is half past eight on what appears to be another cloudless sunny day. Idly wondering who it can be at this time of day, she answers, only to hear to her mortification the voice of the senior sister at the breast clinic say, "I am sorry to disturb you at so early an hour, but I am just ringing to inform you that the we have now had time to examine the results of your ultrasound treatment. Unfortunately these have also proved inconclusive, or at least the people here at the clinic just don't have the necessary experience to determine them. Now I don't want you to worry, because as I have already explained previously, there could be a number of perfectly understandable explanations for them, but, as a precaution, I think it best to be on the safe side that we need to send your file to the breast clinic radiologist at Weymouth, for him to have a look at them. I will forward them to him today, so you should be hearing from his office within a day or so."

Kate is too shocked to respond to this for several seconds, until the sister says, "Mrs Challis, are you still there? Did you understand what I was trying to tell you?"

To which Kate replies shakily, "Oh, yes, yes, I am sorry, but it was a bit of a shock. I can't say thank you for the news, but I do appreciate that you are doing everything in the best way that you can to help me."

"Well, as I say, try not to worry. If you have any questions or even if you want to see us again, please do not hesitate to contact us. As I said previously, you should hear from the radiologist within a couple of days, but if you don't, and are worried, please give me a ring and I will chase your file up."

Replacing the phone to its receiver, Kate stands immobile for several minutes, before breaking down uncontrollably in tears.

Despite their exertions the previous day, Henry and Rob wake early, knowing that they have a heavy schedule in front of them. Trudy is already serving some of the other guests with breakfast, and as she moves back and forth to the kitchen, Henry suddenly realises, with a blinding flash of intuition, where he has seen her before. As she approaches their table, Henry asks "I thought that I recognised you yesterday Trudy, didn't you used to be the lead singer in a group in an earlier life. Angie and the Angels."

Colouring slightly, Trudy replies, "Well, fancy you remembering that Henry. Yes it's true, but that was a long time ago."

"How can I forget? My wife and I both loved your music, in fact we saw you a couple of times, once at Hammersmith and also at Wembley Arena. We were both fans of you and your music, somewhere between rock and folk. I still have some of your music on CDs. What made you give up?"

"The music industry can be pretty ruthless Henry, and although I loved doing it, the never ending grind of touring and having to be seen everywhere just took its toll. Finally, when the children came along, I could not continue anymore. This happened about the same time that we had been on holiday down here and when we compared the relentless work ethic that we were doing, with a life down here, it was no contest. Within six months we had packed it all up and moved here, and we have not had a single day's regret since. Thank you for your kind comments and if you are interested, I still perform a couple of nights a week at pubs and halls locally; in fact I am doing a gig at the hall in Fowey, tomorrow, so why don't you come if you are not doing anything."

"Well, whatever we were going to do, we will have to cancel Trudy. You can count us in, can't she Rob?"

"You bet, me old mucker," says Rob.

"So where are you planning to go today, the two of you?"

"Well, we are hoping to get to see the Eden Project," Henry replies. "But we are going to get there by public transport." Once he has said this, he then has to clarify why, which then takes him another twenty minutes to explain, with Rob throwing in his two pence worth from time to time.

As she listens to his story, Trudy is consumed with sorrow at his loss and the events that have led him here. In an effort to cheer him up she says, "Oh! Henry, I am so sorry to hear your story. I hope that things turn out for the better, soon." And then, "I am sure that you will enjoy the Eden Project. There are so many activities going on there now. It's a charitable educational trust, as well as the biomes, which contain trees and plants from all over the world; they have music performances with top artists like Mumford And Sons and Eddie Izzard (I have performed there myself a few times), as well as art courses and many other things."

After asking Trudy instructions for buses and where to catch them, they finish their breakfast, and then leave to catch the local bus that will take them to St. Austell, from where they can then get another to take them to the Eden Centre.

On arrival at the Eden Centre, they are left stunned and amazed at the sheer size and complexity of it all. The whole edifice has been built in a basin left by an old chalk pit. In its place stand a number of huge biomes, each over fifty metres high, one of which contains a rainforest with plants of every description, with a walkway extended high up in the canopy.

The whole project is based upon maintaining green issues that affect the planet, and there are a number of educational courses which explore these issues. It even has its own deep geothermal energy project, with plans to build a geothermal power plant on site, taking energy from the heat in the underground granite rocks.

There is so much to see and they become completely absorbed in this wonderful project, so much so, that Rob is surprised to see that it is now nearly half past three and, even more importantly, that he is ravenous.

Finding a restaurant, they spend an hour leisurely wining and dining, before continuing on. They have, by this time, realised that they cannot possibly complete all the many varied things that this place has to offer, so reluctantly, after another hour's exploration, they decide to call it a day.

Returning by the same way that they came, they reach the guest house at Fowey at six o'clock, where they discuss their plans for the next two days.

"The trouble is there are so many things that we would like to do Henry," says Rob. "We are just going to have to prioritise. Let's see, there are the boat trips, one up the river, the other out of the estuary and across to Mevagissy. Another option would be to get a bus to St. Mawes, from where we could catch the ferry across to

Falmouth. Or we could go across the Bodinnick Ferry and go to Looe or Polperro. The one sure thing though, is that we don't have time to do them all before I have to leave you on Friday. What say you? Oh, and one other thing, we have definitely got to go to the hall tomorrow and see Trudy perform, or 'Angie' as she is known professionally."

"Too right, I wouldn't miss that for the entire world. How about we get to St. Mawes tomorrow and catch the ferry to Falmouth? Once there we could go to Pendennis Castle and have a look around. I think that Looe and Polperro are probably bridges too far. Then on Friday perhaps we could get the boat up the river to Golant, which should be more relaxing, and give us time for a pie and a pint. Or even better, a pasty and a pint.

"Before you leave on Friday, perhaps you could drop me off at Porthcurno, it's a bit of a trek down near Land's End, but I would love to go to the open air Minack Theatre, which is set on the cliffs overlooking the sea. If you could possibly take me it would really help. I will understand if you can't, or don't have time to take me, but it is something that both Isabel and I wanted to do, so I feel that I need to do it, and then I can imagine that she is with me."

Rob readily agrees to all Henry's suggestions, knowing just how much all the places mean to him. After resting for an hour or so, they decide to repeat their experience of the previous evening and eat out again in Fowey. On reaching Sam's restaurant the waiting time for a table is over an hour, so they return to the Ship Inn, where they quickly consume pasties and chips, washed down with Cornish bitter, followed by apple and blackberry crumble.

George and Bert, the two fishermen are not in tonight, but there are several other locals who were in the pub the previous evening, who acknowledge Rob and Henry. Soon they are all gathered at the bar and the evening continues in much the same fashion as the previous one. Rob of course is the fulcrum of the group, the others hanging on to his every word, only occasionally one of them saying something, almost as an offering. Their contribution to be allowed to stay at the party.

Soon, the warmth, the beer and convivial company work their magic once again, and the bar resounds with the sound of raucous laughter, Henry making his own contribution as he relates some of

Malcolm's Mannerisms, which go down a treat.

"But all good things must come to an end," says Henry, as he and Rob bid their farewells to the ever growing assembly. "We need an early start tomorrow, but we will probably be in again before we leave."

So, to the sound of good wishes ringing in their ears, they make their way once again up the steep winding hill, with Rob remarking, "Well it's a good thing that we have had a few sherbets Henry, because I wouldn't like to climb this hill sober."

Before he does anything else, Henry goes on line to book a seat for the Minack Theatre for the Friday evening. He does so, and much to his delight he discovers that the play being staged this week is *Present Laughter* by Noel Coward, performed by the World Theatre Company from Stratford.

Finally, they hurriedly send their diaries of the happenings of the day to their respective families, and their intentions for the next by email, before they put out the light, Henry falling quickly into a deep sleep, before Rob, quietly congratulating himself that he has managed to keep his friend from thinking of his loss of Kate, does the same.

CHAPTER 26

Trudy

Thursday 4 July

"So where are you off to today?" enquires Trudy, as they arrive down for breakfast. After listening to them she says, "Good choice boys, I love both St. Mawes and Falmouth. In fact there is a marvellous venue there, where I have done one or two gigs over the years. I'll tell you what, why don't I prepare some sandwiches and things, a sort of picnic if you like, then you can have them as you travel, in case you can't find anywhere at the particular time that you want to." And brushing away their protests returns to the kitchen. She is only gone for a minute, before she returns half dragging a well-built man, of about the same age as she is.

On reaching their table she says, "This is Wilf, who is the chef for today. I'll get him to do you a picnic before you leave. Oh, I forgot, Wilf is my husband and he has just finished the job he was doing, so I have promoted him for the day."

As he shakes Wilf's hand, Henry has to pinch himself as he considers how much both Isabel and he had enjoyed Trudy's (Angie's) music over the years - a star of his memory. Yet here she is, serving him meals as if there is nothing untoward about it. But as soon as the thought goes through his mind, Henry realises that Trudy is one of the truly greats, because she is normal. No pretentions of thinking she is above the human herd, she is just Trudy, a hard working girl from a normal middle class family, who had the good fortune to be blessed with a beautiful singing voice.

"Nice to meet you both," says Wilf. Trudy told me all about your journey. I suppose most of us have a bucket list and doing something like you are, I guess, would be on most of them."

As he returns to the kitchen, Trudy returns to take their order and Henry enquires how she and Wilf met.

"Oh, he was my roadie almost from the start. When you are thrown together for nearly twenty-four hours a day for months at a time, one of two things is likely to happen. Quite often the tensions of being together over long periods end in tears and bust-ups, spectacularly in some cases. But for me and Wilf the other thing happened. We grew and developed. Problems and disasters that would have finished most other couples only made us stronger. He is my rock, my other self. When I am down he comforts me, when I am happy he laughs with me and when I am uncertain, or have doubts, he encourages me."

For a brief moment there is complete silence, as each of them considers their own lives and the relationships that they have, or have had. The silence is broken as Henry asks, "Whatever happened to the Angels of Angie and the Angels fame?"

"Oh well they were never really a group as such. I used to write most of the songs, and the Angels, who were only backing singers, used to come and go. I would just hire session singers as and when needed. Some of them stayed for a while, but never for any length of time. That is with the exception of Mary Johnson, who was my friend from back in the day at school. We are still good friends and I see her often as she now lives near Truro. What is more, she sometimes accompanies me at gigs, with her daughter Melanie and mine Stephanie. They are still only fifteen but both have lovely voices and enjoy performing."

"Will we be seeing them tonight?"

"Possibly, but it all depends if our daughters have any projects for homework. They both take their GCSEs next year, so we will just have to wait and see. I wouldn't want to do anything that would jeopardise their results."

Finishing their meal, Rob and Henry collect the food that Wilf has prepared for them, and leave to catch the bus into St. Austell. The bus is nearly full with what appears to be pensioners, who from listening to their conversation are going shopping to the supermarket in St. Austell, which is the nearest one to Fowey.

The two friends have to stop themselves bursting into laughter as they hear one old lady confiding to another about her eternally fault-finding sister-in-law. "I suppose Jean means well, but I never met anybody that meant well worse."

THE BUS PASS

There is silence for a while, during which the other old lady's companion absorbs this stunning observation. She is a woman of lesser years, and not wanting to be out done by the first lady, suddenly retorts, for no apparent reason or context, "Of course when I retire, I'm going to be a lady of pleasure."

Finally they arrive at St. Austell, and find the station where they can get their next bus to St. Mawes, which is due to leave within the next few minutes.

The journey goes without incident down the A390 towards Truro, but then after a few miles the bus turns left onto the A3078. The landscape, which has been typical Cornish green rolling countryside, is suddenly transformed into verdant wooded lanes that wind slowly the rest of the way down into their destination of St. Mawes.

Of all the small seaside villages, this town stands out as one of the most beautiful as far as Henry is concerned. The road which runs along parallel to the sea has a predominance of houses, shops, cafes, restaurants and guest houses. Almost every building is painted white, which gives an effect that hurts the eyes when reflected by the hot morning sun.

As in other similar Cornish estuaries that are built on hills, the rest of the town seems to climb up from the quay, houses sprinkled across the landscape. Henry can imagine the view as he looks at them from the quay, high up on the crest of the hill, all the buildings pointing forward with their verandas and picture windows facing out and across the estuary.

There is a Ferry across the Carrick Roads estuary to Falmouth, which is about a mile away by boat. The journey by road in comparison is about thirty miles. As they board and begin their journey, the pilot of the boat gives a running commentary explaining that the Carrick Roads were formed millions of years ago by the action of a glacier which gouged out the basin, leaving the sea to fill it as the tides rose many years later. This resulted in the fact that Falmouth has the third deepest natural harbour in the world, and the deepest in Western Europe. For this reason, Falmouth is the largest port in Cornwall, dealing with the transfer of cargoes and the bunkering of vessels. The port is also busy with cruise ship operators, a fact that is confirmed as the ferry gets near and there are two of them moored at anchor at the quay.

Additionally, there is a further container cargo carrier which appears to be getting ready to leave on the next high tide.

Disembarking, they discuss their options for the day, both realising that their time is limited. Eventually, they agree that they have time to visit the National Maritime Museum, which is only a matter of yards from where they are. After that, if they have time, their second objective will be Pendennis Castle, which is about a mile away.

On entering the museum they are astonished to find the wealth of material that is available for them to explore. The first gallery has an exhibition about the world of smuggling in its heyday in the eighteenth to nineteenth centuries. There are a number of artefacts that the smugglers would have used while carrying out their lucrative, but very often grisly operations.

Another gallery contains works commemorating D-Day, while yet another has installations celebrating the Tall Ships Regatta. There is also a Search and Rescue exhibition where both Rob and Henry climb aboard a Sea King helicopter and meet the crew, as well as visiting a host of other rescues from the past.

Finally they descend down into the Tidal Zone, a natural underwater gallery, and watch cormorants, seals, shrimp, bass and mullet swimming by its twenty-two foot tall tidal windows.

When they both eventually emerge from the museum, they are amazed to discover that it is now two o'clock and, even more importantly, they are ravenous.

Rather than waste more time finding somewhere to eat, they decide to use the food package that Trudy and Wilf have prepared for them, and are delighted to find an assortment of salmon, cheese and pickle, and chicken sandwiches, accompanied by crisps. There are even also a couple of ginger beers to wash it all down with.

Before they set off, Henry suddenly remembers that he has not arranged for his accommodation for the next night in Porthcurno, when he goes to the Minack Open Air Theatre.

Saying a grateful prayer of thanks to their thoughtful hosts, they quickly make their way to the bus stop that will take them to Pendennis Castle, which lies just over a mile west of Falmouth.

THE BUS PASS

Henry having visited the Castle some years ago remembers some of its history, but when they enter he buys a guide which they use to navigate their way round. This tells them that Henry VIII built a gun fort here in the mid-sixteenth century as part of a nationwide programme of defence. Bastion defences were added in the 1590s following the threat of Spanish invasion. These defences were tested during a siege by a Parliamentary army in 1646, Cornwall having sided with Charles I.

The defences were then periodically updated, notably during the Napoleonic Wars, and then again during the Second World War.

As they begin their tour, they suddenly realise just how big the site is, which means that there is a lot of walking involved. But the views looking out into the English Channel are stunning as they stand in the beautiful warm sunshine which appears to make the azure sea shimmer and sparkle.

After visiting some of the many displays, they find their way to the tearoom and sit outside in the courtyard, devouring cream teas. The warmth of the day and the exercise has made both of them sluggish, as indeed it appears to have done to most of the visitors. As they sit, silently contemplative in their own thoughts, they are made aware of a number of older women at the next table, who are discussing their various hobbies and activities.

Henry and Rob are brought out of their reverie as they hear one of the women say, "No, I don't read a lot myself. Well it takes all the pleasure out of it when you have to wear glasses, don't it?"

Rob looks at Henry quizzically, a smile on playing on his lips, but before he can say anything, one of the others, who is evidently talking about another women who the rest of them all appear to know, and who is renowned for having a host of goods on credit, says, "Er goes to sea with a big sail and a rotten mast," a comment which has the rest of them nodding their heads sagely in disapproval.

Smiling to each other, and trying desperately not to laugh aloud at the women who have given them unknowingly such wonderful entertainment, Henry and Rob make their way back to Falmouth by bus, then by Ferry back to St. Mawes. While they wait for the bus to take them to St. Austell, the two friends quickly look at the shops on the seafront, where Henry buys a blue leather handbag, which he gives to Rob, saying, "Please give this to Madge from me Rob, I have never had the chance to thank her properly for all that she has done for me," and brushing aside Rob's protest, continues. "I don't think that I would still be here today without both of your support, so please let me do this small thing to show at least some of my gratitude." Rob, not wanting to do anything to upset his friend, accepts the gift in the spirit that it has been given, and they make their way to catch the bus that is now waiting to leave.

Returning to Fowey at six o'clock they look in on Trudy at the guest house, only to be informed by a woman (who it transpires is Trudy's sister), that both she and Wilf are down at the village hall. Evidently Wilf is preparing the sound system while Trudy and Mary Johnson are having a rehearsal.

This news acts as a catalyst to Henry and Rob, reminding them that they have to be at the hall by just after seven, but that they need to have eaten before then. Quickly changing, they leave and go down to the Ship Inn for a meal.

Even though it is only early evening, the pub is busy, filled mostly with tourists, some with young children, and they have to wait for their food order to arrive. Hurriedly consuming their food, they leave and get to the village hall just as it is opening.

It soon becomes obvious that Trudy, or Angie as she is known professionally, still has a huge following, as the hall fills to capacity. Henry can hear people discussing her and her music, and is thrilled to know that she still has the power to attract such a large gathering.

Suddenly the lights are dimmed, and Angie appears in the spotlight in a blue diaphanous, full length flowing dress, which accentuates her tall, willowy figure, her long blonde hair cascading to her shoulder, emphasising her delicate facial features. Her long aquiline nose and full lips are overshadowed by her blue hypnotic eyes which seem to absorb every member of the audience simultaneously.

Henry is transported back twenty years to The Hammersmith Apollo, to the occasion that he and Isabel had first been to one of Angie's concerts, as he once again experiences the warm feeling of expectation of hearing her once more.

THE BUS PASS

After thanking her audience, Angie begins her performance, accompanied by Wilf, on keyboard and a tall, dark woman, who Henry can only assume to be Mary Johnson on clarinet.

Angie's soft, haunting voice captivates her audience as she goes through the repertoire of songs for which she has become famous, and Henry has to pinch himself to realise that he is not dreaming. Her music is mesmeric, invading her audience with its magic, leaving them with a feeling between contentment and euphoria, like a warm bed on a cold winter's night, or passing a difficult exam. It is not dramatic, or loud, but so much more - compelling and vibrant, one second lilting and warm, the next soulful and sad.

There is an interval, during which Angie moves among the people in the audience, many of whom she obviously knows. As Henry and Rob stand drinking tea, Angie joins them, saying, "Well, was that OK, I hope that you enjoyed it," only to hear Henry exclaim, "Oh, that was so much better than OK. Thank you so much for reviving so many lost memories, an angel must have been looking over my shoulder when I booked your guest house (forgive the pun). Don't you ever want to return to performing again? It seems such a waste of your wonderful talent."

"I am perfectly happy the way things are Henry. Of course I would like to perform regularly, but I have no desire to go back to the old days, which, although exciting, could be pretty bloody at times. No, this way I can have the best of both worlds and keep my sanity at the same time."

As she finishes speaking, her friend Mary joins them and is introduced, to which Henry rejoins, "I am so pleased to meet you. As Trudy will tell you, I am probably one of the oldest fans of Angie and the Angels," only to hear Mary respond, "Yes, she has told me all about you. I am so pleased that we have not been completely forgotten."

The second half of the performance is, if possible, better than the first, as Angie sings completely new songs that she wrote after she stopped recording. Her audience are entranced and completely held in the thrill of the moment as she draws on their unconscious willing approval. There is a certain timbre in her voice that draws Henry like a magnet, so distinctive and yet so appealing. He feels almost lost as he hears it, both joy and sadness confusing his emotions at the same time.

Angie finishes the evening with an audience request spot, and Henry gets the opportunity to hear her sing 'Dance With Me To Love' a number which had been a particular favourite of his and Isabel's.

Congratulating Angie once again, the two of them make their way up the hill to bed for the last night of their stay in Fowey.

At breakfast, Rob regales Trudy and Wilf with some of his joke material, which lightens the atmosphere for Henry, because he is feeling particularly low after such a wonderful happy-sad evening previously. Rob, being Rob, knows how Henry is feeling and does the thing that he does best to lift Henry's mood.

The goodbyes are particularly difficult for Henry, but as they are leaving, Trudy gives Henry some CDs that she has recorded recently, which he obviously does not have in his own collection.

As he thanks her, he says, "If I am ever down here again I would love to come and stay with you. I don't know if that will ever happen, but I would like you to know of the pleasure that you have given me. I still find it difficult to believe that I have met you after so many years, the person who gave Isabel and me so much pleasure."

"The pleasure has been all mine and Wilf's, Henry. You will always be welcome here. Please keep in touch. We would both love to hear how things turn out for you. I mean that as a friend, not as someone you used to go and listen to all those years ago."

So, the last day of Rob as Henry's companion begins as they make their way down to the quay to get a boat to Golant, which is several miles up the Fowey River. The morning is comfortably warm as the small boat, big enough for about fifteen people, makes its way up the Fowey River, with the skipper doing a running commentary, entertaining the passengers with some factual details, which are interspersed with some funny observations.

"This area has two famous people who lived here. The first was Daphne du Maurier's family, who had a second home a mile down river from the village. The second was Kenneth Graham, who in 1907 wrote *Tales of the River Bank* inspired by a boating trip from Fowey to Golant. *The Wind in the Willows* was published in June

THE BUS PASS

1908 and it is believed that this stretch of the river inspired this wonderful tale.

"Only some 220 people live in this isolated spot, in just over a hundred dwellings. There is no public transport that serves the area, but it is still a working village. The village overlooks the tree clad and winding Fowey estuary and is an area of Outstanding Natural Beauty, full of scenic views all year round, where cormorants, egrets, mallards, swans, herons and kingfishers make the river their home."

As the skipper finishes speaking, they arrive at Golant and disembark, after which they have two hours alone to explore the village.

The boat trip and the warm sun has had a soporific effect on the two pals, who meander contentedly through the village, where they first make their way to the parish church, which is of thirteenth century origins. After exploring the church and graveyard, they make their way to the Fisherman's Arms pub, where, as it is now past midday, they decide to have lunch.

Much to both of their chagrin, they are torn between crab salads and Cornish pasties, but, like the two canny old friends that they are, they compromise, having one of each, which they share.

Feeling suitably refreshed they continue their journey through the main street, which appears to be the only street, until they arrive outside a retail art gallery, where they both become absorbed, looking at paintings of the local area. Rob finds a picture of the village which he particularly likes and which is not too expensive, which, to Henry's surprise, he buys.

The village is almost cut off from everywhere and has a quiet solemnity, which they both find very appealing. Inhabitants go about their business in a leisurely manner, not being flustered by traffic, although there are one or two cars, which appear to be driven by elderly people travelling at a speed less than the pedestrians. Its isolation gives the village an air of a lost bygone age, captivating the two friends. Henry feels more relaxed here than since he left Kate, a thought that disturbs him, reminding him once again how much he misses her.

Since he left her, every, place he has visited, his memories have always been of the times that he and Isabel were together, which he subconsciously recognises is his brain telling him the best way to deal with his emotions. But now that the genie is out of the bottle, it is Kate that is foremost in his mind. He imagines her being with him now, as if Armageddon had not happened and they are both still in love with each other.

The thought defies reality for a few moments, until he is pulled out of his reverie by Rob saying, "I think it's time that we made our way back to the boat, me old mate."

Sadly they make their way back to the boat, each knowing that they have experienced something wonderful over the last few days, that they may never have the opportunity to repeat.

The journey back is packed with incidents as the skipper points out various birds, a heron sitting on a branch of a tree which extends out over the river. As they continue to watch, it does its party piece, dropping down to the water and stabbing a fish with its long piercing beak before (it appears to the people on board), bowing to its captive audience. Applause ripples round the boat, which seems to break the spell as the heron flaps lazily back up to its perch.

Arriving back at Fowey, they find Rob's car and start the final leg of their journey together to Porthcurno, which they are both surprised, takes them an hour and a half, going first to St. Austell, then Truro, after which they skirt Helston, before following the A394 to Penzance, finally getting to Porthcurno at five o'clock.

Conversation between them has been desultory, both dreading the parting of their ways, but Henry finally says, "Thank you Rob for everything. These few days have meant a lot to me, and your company has, as always, been fantastic."

Rob brushes the compliment off, saying, "It has been just as good for me too. What are your plans after tonight?"

"I have a couple of options. Ideally, I would like to arrange to visit the Scilly Isles, but, if I can't arrange accommodation on St. Agnes, then I will probably make my way up north Cornwall and go to places like St. Ives, Port Isaac, Boscastle and Padstow."

Finding the guest house where Henry has accommodation for the night, Rob bids his friend farewell, knowing that it will take him

THE BUS PASS

at least four and a half hours to get home to High Wycombe.

Henry is welcomed by what he considers a typical Cornish lady of a certain mature age, as he enters the guest house. "Oh, do come in m'dear," cries Mrs Trevenon. "I will show you up to your room. I am pretty busy at the moment, with people wanting somewhere to stay, so that they can go to the Minack this evening."

"I guess that a good deal of your business comes from that source," replies Henry. "In fact it's the very reason that I am here. I have wanted to come for so long."

Mrs Trevenon ("Call me Jane.") beams and says, "Well, I won't say that it's not welcome, but I do very well with regular visitors, who return year after year, so I'm blessed."

She is a short stocky woman, of fair complexion, with cheeks that are burned red, no doubt from exposure to the weather conditions that are prevalent on this exposed peninsula all year round. Her eyes are the palest blue, surrounded with many laughter line creases. Her hands are careworn, indicating a world where hard work is unavoidable.

As they reach the bedroom, Jane opens the door, which has a large cottage window on the opposite wall through which the sun comes flooding in like a tsunami, eagerly swamping everything it touches. It is now late afternoon and as Henry crosses to the window he can see the sun low in the heavens, burning red like a fiery furnace. Then his eyes are drawn to the horizon where he can see the azure blue Channel lying calm like a sleeping giant. As he lowers his gaze further he can see the rugged granite cliffs defying the oceans might, as they have done for millennia. It is a scene of such majestic beauty, that he can only stand, stare and wonder at.

He is brought back from his reverie as Jane says, "Oh, I am sorry, I should have drawn the curtains, it gets so warm in here," only to hear Henry respond, "Oh, please don't, I find the view absolutely amazing."

The preliminaries over, Jane makes her way back downstairs, after telling him that breakfast is served between eight and nine thirty in the morning. Henry listens to her humming an indeterminate tune as she descends, deciding that he likes Jane Trevenon, with her ready smile and thoughtful ways.

Lying on the bed, Henry falls asleep, as he often does if he sits down or relaxes during the day. He doesn't seem to be able to concentrate for as long as he once used to, he recognises. Waking eventually at seven o'clock, he changes from shorts to trousers, thinking that it might get colder sat outside later on in the evening.

Jane shows him where to find the entrance to cross the field to the theatre, so he makes his way there, collecting his ticket that he has paid for on-line at the ticket office.

The seats are not allocated to any particular place, the only criteria being that there are two types, those for the lower stalls, near to the platform that acts as a stage, or alternatively those for the higher stalls. Henry has selected the lower stalls seats, so he finds one that has no occupants either side of it, although he realises that they will both probably be filled before the performance begins. It is now a quarter to eight and the seats are filling rapidly. Henry finds the whole experience enthralling and is just happy to watch the preparations near to the granite rock stage, the actors making ready for curtain up time.

Because of this, he is only vaguely aware that someone has taken a seat next to him on one side, and only then because he recognises that whoever it is must be female, because he can recognise the perfume that she is wearing as one that Isabel always preferred.

He continues to be totally absorbed by the activities on stage, until suddenly the female beside him says, "Hi Dad, I hope you don't mind if I join you. After all this is one of the places that we all wanted to see when Mum was alive."

CHAPTER 27

The Isles Of Scilly

As he turns to face his daughter, Henry is numb with shock and disbelief, making him unable to speak, because of the lump in his throat, which threatens to engulf him. His eyes filling with tears, he is unable to reply, and there is absolute silence for several seconds as he tries to gain control of his senses.

Eventually he manages to say, in a voice laden with emotion, "Penny love, what and why are you here?" And then before she can reply, the dam bursts, and he is crying tears of joy, while hurriedly rummaging through his pockets for a paper wipe.

"Oh Dad, we have all been so worried about you since you and Kate split up, so knowing that Rob would be leaving you today, I decided, and Mark agreed, that I should take a few days off and spend them with you, visiting some other places that you have on your list." Then, before he can reply, she continues. "I hope you don't mind but I know that the Scilly Isles are on your list, which I can perfectly understand, because if I were in your situation, they would be on mine too.

"However, I digress, what I am saying is that I have booked us return flights on the Skybus in the morning to St. Mary's, and what is even better, is that I have managed to book the Parsonage on St. Agnes until next Friday. I got lucky, because they had just had a cancellation, otherwise I don't think I would have been able to book anything else at such short notice. As you know, the accommodations at the Parsonage are all self-catering, but I managed to get a two bedroom apartment, which will be fine, because I guess, apart from breakfasts, we will be eating out most of the time. So what do you say, Dad, are you up for it?"

Henry has been listening unbelievingly to Penny, while she

explains, overwhelmed by her concern and thoughtfulness, which has also given him time to compose himself.

"If you are sure Pen, then you know that there is nothing that would give me more pleasure. I am sorry that you have had to go to all this trouble love, I never intended to involve you all with my pilgrimage. The only stipulation I make is that you let me pay all the costs you have incurred. David paid me a handsome bonus after I left, so I can certainly afford it."

Penny can see that her father is excited at the thought of seeing St. Agnes again, but also realises, knowing him as she does, that there is no way that he will let her pay for the trip, so says, "Fair enough Dad, now let's enjoy this play that's about to start."

The production is a wonderful experience, everything in fact that Henry always hoped that it would be. The stage is on a flat piece of rock, at the edge of the cliff, and the players enter from behind a large standing stone at the left of the stage. Banners are hung on a number of large stones, but the backdrop needs no such additions, because it is the view of the sea that takes centre stage. The sun hanging precariously on the horizon. A golden burning globe, its reflection casting yellow flickering shadows across the flat azure sea. It is a magical experience for them both.

The play finishes to a rapturous applause, the players taking several bows, and Henry reflects that his long awaited visit has been justified, before reminding himself that Isabel should have been here with him. He quickly overcomes his melancholy as Penny catches hold of his arm, saying, "We had best get to bed if we are to be up and out in the morning," and then, "Where are you staying by the way?"

As they discuss where each of them is staying for the night, it transpires that their accommodations are only some fifty yards apart, so before separating, Henry suggests a nightcap at a pub which he can see as they cross the field. As they arrive the pub is busy with a number of other members of the audience, who have all had the same idea. They discuss their plans for the following day, and Henry can see that Penny is just as excited as he is, at the thought of going to the Scilly Isles again.

Eventually, tiredness begins to take its toll, and they part with Penny saying, "I will pick you up at half past nine in the morning

THE BUS PASS

Dad. The Skybus flight is from St. Just at a quarter past eleven, so don't be late."

The flight is uneventful and leaves exactly on time. The plane is a Norman Islander, which only has a capacity seating for six passengers. It only takes fifteen minutes to the small airport on St. Mary's (the largest of the Scilly Isles), but they are both straining to see out of the windows for places that they can recognise as the plane approaches the islands.

"Look Dad, there's the airport, with the quay in the distance, down to the left. Oh! And there's St Agnes, with the lighthouse in the distance, on the horizon. And isn't that the Scillonian in the Sound?"

Henry too is caught up in his daughter's excitement, and responds in a similar vein. "There's a helicopter just lifting off from Tresco, and if you look left, you can see the isles of Bryher, with Samson in the distance. Oh God Pen, I didn't realise just how much I have missed these wonderful isles."

Landing, they wait impatiently for their luggage to be unloaded, before they board one of several mini-coaches, which will take them down to the quay, so that they can catch a boat which will take them on a short journey of some twenty minutes across to St. Agnes.

It has been several years since either of them has visited here, but they are both amazed as several locals recognise them and welcome them back. Each island has its own boat for transporting people, luggage and other necessities backwards and forwards between the islands. As they unload from the mini-coach on the quay, they can see the St. Agnes boat, aptly named *The Spirit of St. Agnes*, moored up and due to leave in twenty minutes. Quickly climbing aboard with their luggage, they are welcomed by John, the captain, who also remembers them and asks after the other family members, and is suitably apologetic when Henry explains about his loss of Isabel.

Soon, *Spirit* pulls away from her moorings and the short journey begins across to St. Agnes, the furthest south west of the five inhabited cluster of islands. Rounding the Cow and the Calf rocks which stand at the entrance at St. Agnes Porth Conger quay, they pull alongside and tie up before disembarking.

To Henry, returning to this lovely island again after so long is like coming home, so much so that he feels an unexplainable urge, which he resists, to jump from the boat and kiss the land in recognition of the way he feels about this wonderful place.

As is usual, there are a number of islanders waiting with an assortment of tractors, small vans and even an old milk float. This motley collection is gathered here to collect holidaymakers and their luggage, as indeed they are every time there is a holiday changeover.

Suddenly, from out of the crowd, Diane Hick, the proprietor of the Parsonage, is coming toward them, her face wreathed in smiles, as she says, "Welcome Henry and you too Penny, it's been so long since you were here last," and then in a quieter voice, addressing them both conspiratorially, "I was so very sorry to hear of Isabel's death," before reverting back to her original volume. "Which are your suitcases? If you show me I'll load them on to the trailer of the tractor and take them back."

"Well I thought that we would stop off at The Turks Head for a pie and a pasty before we came up to the Parsonage, why don't you join us and then you can get us up to speed with island matters. I am sure there have been a million and one happenings since we were last here."

"That is very nice of you, I would love to, but I can't stay long, because I have two other changeovers today."

So it is agreed and after loading their luggage, they make their way to The Turks Head, which is only some fifty yards further on up the hill, where they are welcomed once again by the landlords Joseph and Paulette, who have been here for many years.

The Turks Head, commonly referred to as 'The Turks' was originally the lifeboat station for the island, the lifeboat, which over the centuries had attended many shipwrecks. Eventually, the station was transferred to the other end of the island, a simple necessary expedient, because the majority of wrecks happened in the western approaches, meaning that the lifeboat, together with its station, which was down next to the church at Periglis beach, could be launched and reach ships in distress much more quickly.

"It's lovely to see you after all these years Henry," exclaims

THE BUS PASS

Joseph. "We were so sorry to hear about Isabel. Diane told us the other night after Penny rang."

Henry and Penny both love this wonderful welcoming pub. It had been so much a part of their holidays over the years. The front has a large picture window, which gives a wonderful light during even the darkest, wettest days. The furniture is all pine tables, chairs and benches and the bar runs two thirds down the side of the room. There is island memorabilia everywhere. Photos taken at the end of the nineteenth and the beginning of the twentieth centuries show the islanders and how they lived. It is immediately apparent that life at this time on the island was harsh, from the clothes that they wore, which were little more than rags, to the expressions on their faces, that spoke of hardship and pain. They lived by fishing, and by growing their own vegetables. The only other source of income was by plundering cargoes of vessels that foundered on the many rocks around the island. Each island had, and still has, its own gig boat, which is a long rowing boat for eight to ten people. Upon hearing a distress signal from a ship in trouble, the islanders would rush to get their own particular boat launched and get to the vessel first. There were salvage benefits that favoured the first boats to attend, although their first function was to save as many lives as possible.

Gig boats were also used to get to ships that needed a pilot to navigate the boat through the treacherous waters, and again this would invariably mean first come, first served.

The gig boats' only function today is a race between the other islands' boats every Tuesday night during the summer months. The gigs are followed by a flotilla of boats filled with supporters and holidaymakers, who encourage their own particular boat and rowers around the course, from start to finish. Henry remembers the times that his family did this, and the pride that they all felt if *Shah*, which was the St. Agnes boat, won or did well.

There are photos of several ships that have foundered around the islands over many years, and the churches' graveyards of all the islands bore testimony to them. The room is a living record of how life was during this period.

In warm dry weather during the summer, meals are also served outside on a small grass area, for patrons who preferred food Al

Fresco. The advantage of eating here was the view across the small stretch of sea between St. Agnes and Gugh, a small uninhabited island which joins the two islands by means of a tombola, or sandbar. There is in fact one dwelling on Gugh, but it is only inhabited intermittently, and then only by people who can afford its exorbitant rent. But it is the source of some fantastic walks, which are often interrupted by seagulls and terns. This is because if they were nesting or bringing up chicks, anyone approaching too close would be dive bombed.

Henry is brought back from his reverie, as they hear all the islanders and holidaymakers start catching up excitedly with each other's news. There are several of them talking at the same time.

Suddenly from the bar next door comes a loud voice saying, "Is that you Henry? It must be, I would know that voice anywhere." And from around the door appears an islander, standing well over six feet tall, with a physique to match. He has long blond hair to his shoulders with a short beard. His eyes are a piercing blue and his complexion is nut brown, earned from years of exposure to the extremes of weather all year round. He wears the obligatory fisherman's blue top, while his legs are encased with waterproof yellow trousers, together with waterproof waders which offer as much protection as possible when the sea is angry. If he had been born in a different age he could have been mistaken as a Viking. All he needs to complete the image would be an axe or spear. His occupation is so obviously that of a fisherman, that it could be no other.

As he enters the bar, Henry rises to his feet and rushes to meet him saying, "Tristan, you old son of a gun, how are you? It's good to see you." They meet and give each other bear hugs, before slapping each other on the back.

Joining the others, Henry says, "You remember my daughter Penny, Tristan."

And before he can say anymore, Tristan retorts, "Of course I do, but I must say she has grown up since I saw her last," and then, "How is Richard? I used to love taking you all out on my boat fishing."

Henry, Isabel and the children had often gone out in Tristan's little boat, the size of a rowing boat, fitted with an outboard motor.

THE BUS PASS

They had many adventures, catching mackerel, pollock, and sometimes crabs, from pots that Tristan had set the previous day. They would get their catch back to the quay, where Tristan would gut and clean the fish so that they could take it home and cook it. What fantastic meals they would make, which tasted all the better somehow because it had been caught with their own fair hands.

As the party continue talking, Tristan included, Diane takes her leave saying that she will get their luggage back to the Parsonage and that they can come up when they are ready.

While they continue to talk, Henry reflects on the other many occasions that he has visited here. There are only some sixty people that live on this island permanently, which means that there are only a few places that visitors can stay. The islands are owned and run by the Duchy of Cornwall, so all the inhabitants lease their properties from this source, which reminds Henry of one memorable occasion, when he and Isabel and the children were staying with Truan and Wendy Hick (Hicks and Leggs are by far the most common surnames on St. Agnes). Anyway, on this particular occasion the Duke of Cornwall (i.e. Prince Charles) decided to pay an unannounced visit, together with his representatives.

They arrived at Truan's house via the back garden, much to Truan's surprise, and as they did so, The Duke of Cornwall asked him, "Would you mind if I came across your lawn?" to which the ever resourceful Truan replied, with rapier-like wit, "Of course you can… it's your lawn."

Henry chuckles inwardly to himself, as indeed he does whenever he recalls this little gem.

Tourism is by far the islanders' largest means of income these days, but Henry remembers that when he and Isabel began coming here in the seventies, most of the Islands grew daffodils for the early London market. There was a labour market shortage at certain times of the year on the island, once the flowers had died off, and the bulbs had to be dug up and dried, and then again later when they had to be planted in September. At such times, the islanders could not manage these activities on their own, so they would offer people from the mainland accommodation and an hourly rate to come and help them.

For those people, who couldn't afford a holiday any other way, this was a means to do so. They would arrive and stay at the camp site, then work on the fields, which were small. To avoid the soil being blown away during storms in the winter the islanders would plant escallonia shrubs around each field, which would absorb the worst of the weather and any soil that got blown, would be stopped by the shrubs. Escallonia is by far the main choice of hedging and is particularly suitable near coastal areas. It is an evergreen and has green glossy leaves with red rose like flowers from early spring to late autumn. Its main advantage is that St. Agnes climate is temperate and usually frost free. The soil is light and rich, but the covering of soil in parts of the island is thin, lying on top of the rugged granite rock of which the island is composed.

When Henry had first begun to bring his family to the island, there was no electricity, so the only means of heat and light at that time was by means of generators, which ran on oil. So this is what most houses used. Henry can still recall those days when they went down to the Turks in the evening, after which they would return in darkness. The only sound that broke the eerie silence was the diesel generators making their distinctive chugging noise as they passed each dwelling, which would make them feel strangely comforted.

It wasn't until much later, in the late seventies or early eighties, that a cable was laid from St. Mary's across the sound, giving the islanders a constant supply of electricity.

Henry is also very aware that fresh water was, and still is, a limited resource on the Island. There are several fresh water wells that the islanders have drilled, but during spells of hot weather, supplies can run low, causing problems. Because tourism has become their major source of income, this remains the islanders' most acute problem, and visitors are asked to limit the amount that they used during times of shortage.

On St. Mary's, the largest of the Scilly Isles, they have installed machinery which converts sea water into drinking water, but the small numbers of people living on the other small off islands cannot warrant this amount of investment.

The only accommodation available on St. Agnes is those where the islanders have either spare rooms to let, or have another building on site, perhaps a barn or an outbuilding in an earlier life.

THE BUS PASS

These often lend themselves to conversion.

There are no hotels on St. Agnes, although there are several guest houses, and only one pub, The Turks, and one post office and general store. The pub serves delicious food all day, while the post office sells almost everything else that visitors might need.

There is a regular boat service to and from St Mary's, where there are more shops and a larger supply of merchandise. The Spirit of St. Agnes makes a couple of trips a day to St. Mary's, but also arranges trips to the other islands. Henry and Isabel had rarely taken these, apart from perhaps a couple of visits to St. Mary's, where Isabel liked to buy the latest version of all-weather wear.

Up until after the Second World War St. Agnes had no recognisable road, merely packed earth paths, which in wet weather turned into muddy quagmires. With the growth of tourism and flower growing, the islanders decided to build their own roads and in 1947 they began laying a concrete surface about five feet wide which went to most of the places where the population lived.

The concrete road ran alongside many of the little fields that were used for flower growing, so there were escallonia trees on each side of the road and this had the effect of softening the look of the road. The escallonia grows some ten feet high, thus casting its shadows across the road, making it cool, even on the hottest days of summer. When the sun goes down at the end of the day, midges and mosquitoes gather in these shady glades, which are soon hunted by elegant swallows, whose main source of nourishment they are. Henry loves to watch these beautiful black and white birds, dipping and swirling following the lanes just above eye level, before swerving at impossible angles to catch their unsuspecting prey.

The effect of the road building was dramatic, opening up a range of options and opportunities for the islanders, making their lives much less onerous and improving their quality of life.

The island is very small, only about a mile wide from the quay to the campsite. The southern part of the island known as Wingletang Down is a heather covered moorland, a beautiful place to walk with some fantastic rock formations including the famous Nags Head, which the islanders often kid visitors is the second pub on the island. Wingletang is uninhabited, that is if you don't count the rabbits or the many special species of birds that stop this way on their migratory journeys. Or even the grey seals that inhabit the rocky sea pools around its coast. But it was here, Henry reflects, that the family would often come, where he and Isabel had their own special rock that they would sit against on the green moss turf surrounding it, and read, or doze, while Penny and Richard would go climbing the many rock formations close by.

As he continues with his memories, Henry is brought out of his reverie as Penny says, "Come on Dad, let's go to the Parsonage and get our luggage sorted out. We can then have a look at all our old haunts. I can't wait to go to Covean and Periglis beaches. Oh, and the Sandbar too. Oh, and…"

"Stop," Henry implores. "You are beginning to sound just as you did all those years ago, when you were a child. Next you will be asking me to do a treasure hunt again."

"What a great idea. Richard and I used to love it when you did them. You would write out clues to find the treasure, which we had to find in its hiding place before we could move on to the next clue, until we finally got to the treasure, which inevitably ended up at the Turks or the café at Covean, where we would have peach melba, or banana split ice creams. They were to die for!"

They talk ten to the dozen as they climb the hill away from the Turks, along the narrow road that has a six foot stone granite wall on their right, over which large ferns appear. Finally, as they reach the summit, they turn, to look back at the stunning scenario that lies beneath them. Their gaze first takes in the Turks and just beyond that Porth Conger where they disembarked. As they lift their gaze they can see across St Mary's sound, from left to right, the islands of Samson, Bryher, Tresco and St. Martins. Finally, as they pan extreme right there is Gugh once again, with St. Mary's beyond hidden in a shimmering haze, caused by the sun rays reflecting on the sea. They have both observed this view many times, but it never ceases to intoxicate their senses, its' magnificence and magnitude making them feel small and insignificant, but grateful to whatever or whoever has created such beauty.

Making their way to the Parsonage, which is past the post office, they collect some hurried provisions, and then make their way up the lane, before turning off right, down to Lower Town.

Henry has a quiet chuckle to himself as he recalls the various place names on the island. There's Higher Town and Lower Town, both of which have only two or three dwellings and he wonders idly to himself how they became to be named in this fashion. Before they get to Lower Town, they pass the school, which all the children of St. Agnes attend until the age of twelve, after which time they transfer to the school on St Mary's for their secondary education. This means boarding on St. Mary's between Monday and Friday each week, then returning Friday afternoon by boat to the island for the weekend.

There are never more than a handful of children on St. Agnes, and there is only one teacher and one classroom in which to teach their range of ages from five to twelve, but it seems to work very well and they have always appeared bright and inquisitive when Henry has had occasion to talk to them. He also knows that some of the children have gone on to University from here, to learn the skills necessary for them to survive, running businesses on the island in today's current environment.

As they pass the school on their left, immediately beyond and above it is the lighthouse, which stands at the highest point of St. Agnes, but after well over two hundred years of service, it no longer contains a light and serves as a day mark.

Now they are here at their destination, because on the lane opposite the Lighthouse lies the entrance to the Parsonage, where once lived the parish priest for St. Agnes, but those days are long gone. There is only one C of E priest who now covers all these islands from St. Mary's.

The Parsonage is a large sprawling building, which lies in spacious grounds, surrounded by beautiful gardens and trees, which meander down the hill. For many years now, the Parsonage has been converted into several self-catering apartments. Because of its location, very little sound penetrates its inner sanctum, giving it a feeling of quiet isolation. Just the occasional tractor on its way up the lane to collect luggage from the quay, or delivering goods that someone has ordered from the shops on St. Mary's, or maybe the farmer from the farm moving some of his cows to a new pasture.

Diane, who has been looking out for them, greets them and shows them to their apartment, explaining where everything can be located and promises to join them at Henry's request one evening at the Turks for a meal.

Quickly dumping their bags, they set off on their first exploration of the island, going first to Periglis beach, where they have spent many warm sunny days shrimping and crabbing in the past, before moving above the beach to sit on the seats facing the cricket pitch.

As they sit contemplating, Henry says, "I played for the island a couple of times, when they couldn't get eleven locals to make up a team, do you remember, Pen? Well I can tell you that the pitch out there is lethal. It's all soft sand which is covered by scrubby grass that gives way when anyone runs on it. Not only that but rabbits dig holes all over it, which makes it even more unsafe, so fielders often twist their ankles when chasing the cricket ball. It's a miracle that no-one has not been seriously hurt over the years. Still, it was great fun and I wouldn't have missed it for the entire world."

Sensing that the moment is right, Penny asks her father, "Dad, I know that it's none of my - or anyone else's - business, so you don't have to talk about it if you don't want to, but what exactly happened between you and Kate, that meant that you left? The reason I ask is because all the times that we spent with you both, you looked so happy together."

Henry says nothing for a few seconds, wondering what to say, because his perception is the same as Penny's. Then he proceeds to tell her about the last dreadful morning that Kate revealed her feelings, resulting in him leaving.

"But I still can't understand it Dad. One of the last things that she said to me, unasked, was that she loved you very much. Are you sure there was nothing else?"

As Henry revisits that last day in his mind, he analyses every word, every nuance of Kate's speech, as he has done many times since, but he is unable to find anything new. Penny sees the distress on her father's face, so doesn't pursue the matter, but determines that she will contact Kate within the next few days to see if she can find out just what the problem is. Thinking further, Penny realises that Henry's possible move to Australia may have been the reason, in which case she knows that the way her father feels about Kate this would never have been a problem. It may possibly be for some silly, insignificant reason that Kate might feel insurmountable, but is in fact easily overcome, if brought out into the light of day. Whatever it is, Penny feels that it's worth a try to speak to Kate, because she has seen the love in her eyes for her father, so there has to be some other cause, in which case as long as love is there, hope is as well. It has to be.

Without a word being said, they resume their tour of St. Agnes, continuing along past the church until they reached the campsite which is full of tents of every size and description. Then on around the coastal path until they come to Troytown Maze, built on this isolated spot by a lighthouse keeper in 1729, a spiralling maze of white washed beach stones on a grassy mound, a few yards from the edge of the beach. The children always headed to this spot when they came here, to follow the maze to see which one of them could get to the centre first.

Looking out to sea, beyond the maze is Bishops Rock Lighthouse, which Henry has been to by means of *The Spirit of St. Agnes*, which makes several trips a week, weather permitting, and whose story he has always found fascinating.

Here stands this man made granite building, forty-nine metres high, built on a rock ledge forty-six metres long by sixteen metres wide, a tribute to the builders who spent years housed on a nearby uninhabited islet, where living quarters and workshops were erected. The men were carried to and from the site as the weather permitted. Working spells were brief as well as being few and far between. All the granite was despatched from the mainland to the island depot, where it was shaped and numbered before being sent to the rock. Henry had been staggered when he investigated how this beacon of light had been built. There had been two other buildings before this one, the first of which had been carried away in a gale, and the second was beginning to show signs of wear, before a second casing was built around it, which remains to this day. Work was completed in 1887, involving a total weight of 5700 tons of granite, at a cost of £66000.

Henry muses to himself, the courage and fortitude of the builders who erected this magnificent edifice that has subsequently saved so many lives. Today, the lighthouse stands proud and clears the horizon, but Henry has seen days when it has been surrounded in mist and fog, or enveloped in waves and spray during gales and hurricanes, when pebbles and rocks have been brought to the surface from the seabed by the force of the wind, and have smashed against the lighthouse windows. Today the lighthouse is on automatic operation, the last keepers leaving in 1992.

While he is in contemplative mood, Henry remembers also while on the trip to the lighthouse, that the boat had stood off a couple of hundred yards. It was low tide, and the skipper was looking to show the people on board the Outer Gilstone Rock. This was the rock on which Sir Cloudesley Shovell's flagship, HMS *Association*, had foundered in 1707, together with four others of the British fleet, returning home from Gibraltar. They were caught in gale conditions and mistakenly thought that they were sailing west of Ushant, but were closing in on the Isles of Scilly instead, a fact that proved fatal, and caused the loss of some 1400 to 2000 lives, the worst incident in maritime history up to that time.

As Henry and his fellow travellers scanned the surface of the sea, they suddenly saw just under the surface, the top of the Outer Gilstone Rock in all its menacing infamy, and Henry experienced a shiver down his back as he looked at it. He now understood just how easily ships could be torn apart and sink within minutes on these treacherous rocks. All these years later, Henry still feels a sense of awe and fear as he remembers the occasion.

As he shudders at the recollection, Henry is brought back to the here and now, as Penny, smiling, says, "Come on Dad, we have got lots more to see," and linking arms with her father they move on round the coast to Wingletang, where they are both intoxicated again with their own special memories.

"I think that we will be spending quite a lot of time here this week Dad. There's that rock that you and Mum used to sit against, reading your books, while Richard and me climbed up those rocks there. Come on let's go to Beady Pool and see if we can find some, so I can make a necklace."

As he looks at his daughter, he is reminded once again how much she looks and acts like his lost wife, and gathers great consolation in the thought, wondering why he has not noticed it much until recently.

Moving on again, but promising to return soon, they reach Beady Pool, so called after a boat from Holland, which had been carrying glass beads and other trinkets to use as bargaining tools with the Indians from the New World when it foundered on rocks just off shore in the seventeenth century. They searched for a while, but without success, although they had found some on previous occasions. They have been shown beautiful artefacts and jewellery by several islanders over the years, which they had made from beads found in the pool.

Carrying on walking in an anticlockwise direction, they find the soft spring grass that takes them to rocks overlooking Covean Beach. This is the most secluded of St. Agnes' beaches, and can only be reached through a narrow track through trees and shrubbery. It was here that they all snorkelled in glorious isolation, and afterwards ate picnics while lazing in the war summer sunshine.

Moving on they reach the Sandbar between St. Agnes and Gugh, which, at low tide can be crossed to enable walking round Gugh, but they decide instead to sit on the beach, both of them reading for an hour. Henry has brought several books with him, while Penny, modern girl, has her kindle. They are perfectly content in each other's company, the sun burning down on them, forcing them to move round to get shelter from the rocks, reminding them to wear sunblock in future.

Looking at his watch, Henry is surprised to see that it is now nearly five o'clock, which reminds him to ask Penny if she would like tea, or ice cream from Covean tea room, before they close for the day. This is a throwback to earlier years, the place they would head for from the beach, after seeing trippers from other islands returning to their boats for transportation back to St. Mary's or wherever. They would know that Covean would be quiet by this time and they could get their own specialties in peace and comfort, sitting outside in the garden. A peach melba for Penny, a banana split for Richard and carrot cake and coffee for Henry and Isabel... fantastic!

Penny laughs as she and Henry repeat the experience from yesteryear.

"These are still just as good as they were all those years ago, Dad. Quite often when you try to recreate a situation like this, the product is not as good as your memory. But these are almost better, don't you think?"

Henry can only agree, wondering why this is so, but concludes that because they love this place so much, their memories will not let them accept less than perfection.

The island is quiet now, all the tripper boats have returned to their respective islands, but one or two will doubtless return this evening, pouring most of their passengers into the Turks, where pasties, chips, crab salads, ale and vino will be consumed with alacrity, while Rick Hicks will entertain them all on the piano, until they join in, singing songs of yesteryear.

Henry remembers with distinct pleasure, the year when Richard, who had played rugby for a couple of years, and knew a few ditties with dubious words and meanings, sang, "I'm climbing up sunshine mountain," which had proved so popular that he had ended up standing on the bar conducting the entire packed room as they joined in the chorus. Penny, seeing Henry smile, asks what he is remembering, and when he tells her, she laughs so much, remember the time with perfect clarity, that they both end up consumed with tears of uncontrollable laughter running down their faces.

They return to the Parsonage, pleasantly tired after the events of the day. Penny Skypes Mark to let him know what they have been doing, and after speaking to her family, hands the iPad over to Henry, so that he can say hello to his grandchildren, who excitedly tell him of the things that they have been doing at school, before asking if they can all come to Scilly next year. Henry is a little taken aback at this, although he remembers that they all came here several years ago when they were young, he wasn't aware that they remembered it. However it becomes very obvious, from the things that they are saying about places on the island that their memories are still vivid, and so he says that he would love to do that, if at all possible, but it would have to depend on the circumstances at the time.

While he has been catching up with his grandchildren, Penny has been emailing Richard in Australia, explaining what they have been doing, the places where they have been and the people they have met who still remember them and come up to speak to them.

"You would love it bruv, it's like we have never been away," she finishes.

They leave to go to the Turks for the evening at eight o'clock, walking down the narrow road, with swallows darting and gliding just above their heads, seeking the midges that are gathered in abundant clouds in the cooling shelter of the trees on either side.

As they reach Higher Town they look west towards the setting sun, which is going down in a fiery red ball on the horizon, its' tongues of flame spreading out across the sea, for all the world looking as if it could absorb it, to leave only a dried out landscape in its place. They have stood at this very spot on countless occasions, but the sheer majesty of this spectacle always left them breathless with its magnitude.

Drawing themselves away they walk on down to the Turks, where people are already spilling out onto the grass area at the front, on this warm summer evening. There is a low murmur of chatter, with spasmodic interruptions of laughter as they draw near. Ordering pasties, which neither of them can ever tire of, they make their way outside to sit under one of the canopies.

There are ten or twelve sets of benches with canopies, all of which have lights running round their perimeters, which give an aura of party time, with people eating and the soft chink of glasses as they are raised in celebration of another lovely day spent on these magical islands. A good number of the people here are from St. Mary's, who have come over on an evening tripper boat, which Henry can see is moored up at Porth Conger.

Eventually the boat leaves at ten o'clock, the skipper being the first out of the pub, an indication to the rest of his passengers that it's time to go, as they follow him down to the quay, like the Pied Piper of Hamlin.

Once the boat has left, the two of them move into the pub, where there is now plenty of space. The only people here now are either holidaymakers or locals, most of the latter who welcome them as if they saw them only yesterday. Recognising several people who are also staying at the Parsonage, they strike up conversations, only to find to their amazement that one couple live fairly close to High Wycombe. Not only that but they also have friends in common who they all socialise with, but seemingly never at the same time. Henry marvels at the sheer coincidence, as they resolve to all get together after they return home.

The tempo of the evening is now dramatically altered, as Rick enters and sitting at the piano begins to play, his audience joining in the traditional tunes of yesteryear. Penny can see the enjoyment on Henry's face as he sings 'Doing the Lambeth Walk', 'Jerusalem', 'There'll always be an England' and many others, until Rick finishes by playing some Cornish folk songs, and is joined by the islanders singing in harmony in true West Country tradition.

By now both of them are feeling the strains of their long day, so they decide to leave. Henry, fortunately, has remembered to bring a torch from the apartment, left there especially for the purpose by Diane. As they leave the all-encompassing light of the pub, they are plunged into complete and utter darkness, their only source of light coming from the torch. They climb the hill, brushing against the huge ferns at each side. Reaching the top, they look back across the moonlit sea to the other islands, and then across to Gugh, where the high tide has now covered the sandbar.

Henry reflects that this view would have looked the same millennia ago, apart from a few yachts which are moored in the bay, and he pays silent tribute to the people who made their homes here since that time. They were a hardy race indeed.

Once they leave the view of the sea, they are immediately returned to darkness, which without the torch they would have found difficult to navigate. All is complete silence, a commodity that is in short supply in today's modern world. They stop for several minutes at the same spot where they had viewed the setting sun. But this time it's for a completely different reason.

Turning their eyes to the heavens, the sky is alive with stars in their celestial heaven. Both Penny and Henry have never ceased to be amazed at how vibrantly clear are the views, as they try to identify various clusters of stars.

"Look, there's the North Star, Dad," which Penny has to point out, or, "Over there is the Frying Pan." They stand entranced as they watch shooting stars flying across the heavens, seeing the sky as it really is, not the version that they normally watch at home, which is polluted by the urban sprawl in which they live.

They both know that there is one more spectacle that they must see before they retire for the night, so they continue on their walk, past the entrance that leads to the lane where the Parsonage can be found, but straight on almost to the end of the island, at

Coastguards, until they can see the Nags Head rock ahead of them. It's not the rock that they have come to see, but rather the light from the Bishop Rock Lighthouse, which as they watch projects its pure beam of light across the night sky, from south to north, then disappearing for a few seconds before resuming its lifesaving trajectory once more. It is a very moving sight, a testament to those brave men who had spent years of turmoil and hardship, living on an islet, little more than a rock, which was open to all the extreme elemental forces that nature could throw at it.

Satisfied that they have accomplished as much as they can on their first day, they return wearily to the Parsonage where Penny Skypes Mark and the children before saying goodnight to Henry, who in turn emails Richard, getting him up to date with their days activities, before going to bed himself.

CHAPTER 28

St. Agnes And St. Ives

Monday 8 July

This then is the pattern of their days. They rise early and have breakfast, before setting out to walk, or read, or just sit on the beach. Surprisingly, Penny seems to be the one who gets most benefit from the inactivity, finding that she is relaxing more each day, which makes her realise just how tense her work lifestyle has made her. She has for years been on a high functioning career course, partly motivated by family needs, but also because of her own inbuilt need to prove herself. As time goes by during the week she questions more and more, the need to work at such a pace.

Mark has a very good job, and unlike her, copes with pressure with alacrity. Nothing fazes him. He does not absorb pressure, just ignores it, or is even unaware of it. He seems to be able to leave work behind when he is at home with his family. In fact he is not ambitious at all, Penny realises, thinking about it. Thinking further about this Penny questions for the first time about her lifestyle. Could she approach it from any other way? Although as a family, the need for two salaries is just as great as it has ever been, what with the mortgage and the costs of getting the children through their education, which may be substantial if they get to university.

The situation with regard to her moving to Australia has still not been resolved, but it is looking more and more unlikely, partly because the company that she works for is finding it more and more difficult to jump through the legal loopholes that are required. But another more compelling reason for her is that she is beginning to have doubts about moving.

She does know several people, mostly women, who run their own interior design companies, most of them quite successfully, and she wonders if this might be the answer. She knows the profit margins that this type of work can generate, which makes her think that she could make very good money working on her own. Also she could cherry pick the jobs to suit her work situation and if her workload became too much she knew enough about the industry to know who to approach if she needed to contract out some work, and still make good profits. Her overheads would be kept to a minimum if she operated from home. This way she could project manage the work, which should give her more time to spend with Mark and the children.

Her mood now lighter, Penny resolves to talk to Mark about it when she gets back. He has always encouraged and supported her endeavours in the past, and has a very analytical mind, which makes him the ideal sounding board.

Whilst all this is happening, as she has done every day since she last spoke to the clinic, Kate answers the phone on Wednesday 10 July in trepidation. All her fears are realised as she hears, "Good morning Mrs Challis, it's the Mammary Radiologist's secretary here. Mr Everard has now had chance to look at the results of your ultrasound, and needs to see to see you as a matter of protocol. We were wondering if you could arrange to be here at our clinic in Weymouth perhaps tomorrow? The reason I am ringing you is because we have a cancellation for ten o'clock, which would fit in nicely with you if you can make it."

Kate is by now thinking the worst and shaking at the images that are going through her mind. After several seconds of undiluted terror she manages to reply.

"Can you give me any indication of the results of my tests?" to which the secretary replies, "I am sorry, but I genuinely don't know what the results were, but even if I did I would not be in any position to tell you. Try not to worry and all your questions will be answered tomorrow by Mr Everard. Can I book your appointment then?"

After another short pause Kate realises that she has no option but to agree and says in a low, soft voice, "Yes, that will be OK. I will see you tomorrow at ten then," and hurriedly rings off before she has time to change her mind.

"Oh Henry, I wish you were here to support and comfort me!" she cries out in turmoil to an empty house. "I know that I sent you away, but I don't know if I have the courage to see this thing through on my own. But I will just have to, I couldn't possibly put you through all this again, after Isabel."

She sits down at the table, her head in her hands, quietly sobbing, until she pulls herself together, saying, "Come on Kate, you can do this," which suddenly seems to do the trick as she has an idea, and picks up the phone to ring David. When he answers, she tells him about her appointment, to which his immediate response is, "Don't worry Mum, I am coming with you."

"Oh darling, that is very good of you, but I can't accept, David," she replies.

There is a silence for several seconds, until David says in a consolatory manner, "Right then, how about if Gina comes with you?"

Kate is very aware of David's concern for his mother, and to his surprise, she replies, "Well if she doesn't mind, I think that is a very good idea."

'Of course she won't mind, Mother. You should know by now that my concerns are hers also. Leave it with me, and I will see that she picks you up a nine in the morning. That should be adequate time to get you there for ten. *And don't worry!*

The week seems to disappear like mist on a hot summer's day, their time spent mostly on St. Agnes, but they go to St. Mary's on Tuesday, choosing the day when it is raining, putting on their wet weather attire, waterproof leggings and tops, before getting on *Spirit*, which has cover at the front for passengers, but is open to the vagaries of the weather at the rear. Even though it is raining and the wind is blowing a force five, churning the sea into a choppy frenzy, the experience is exhilarating, as the skipper fights his way across the sound, the sea being blown from west to east across his bows, threatening to sweep his inconsequential craft onto the rocks on the approach to St. Mary's. The thrill of fighting the elements in this challenging place is both uplifting and scary at the same time. On arrival, Penny insists upon doing some retail therapy, which she assures Henry, is obligatory. Thus they wander around Hugh Town, Penny buying clothes from Foredeck and Seasalt, shops which specialise in clothes suitable for the islands. While she browses here, Henry goes to Gibsons to get a daily paper and look through the selection of books.

Once they have finished, Henry insists upon stopping at the Atlantic Inn at lunch time, where they indulge in crab salads with crusty bread, washed down with Cornish ale and red wine.

This place is yet another warm memory of earlier days spent with Isabel and the children, and Henry is left floundering emotionally once again, but he manages to conceal his feelings from Penny, or thinks he does. But even worse for him is that he gets these feelings of loss in remembered times with Isabel and the children mixed up with thoughts of wishing that Kate was with him now, so that he can show her all these places as well. This leads to him being totally confused, as well as feeling guilty somehow of besmirching Isabel's memory.

As these thoughts flash through his mind, he realises that he needs to discuss his next move once he and Penny return to Cornwall.

"I have been thinking Pen, when we get back to Cornwall that I would like to continue my journey, because there are one or two more places that I would like to see. So, if you could drop me off somewhere, say St. Ives, before you make your way home, it would be most appreciated. I would very much like to see St. Ives, and Isambard Kingdom's ship, the SS *Great Britain* in Bristol, before I return home."

What he doesn't say, but is foremost in his mind, is that he would like to visit David's brother, Geoffrey, before finding his way home, simply because he has never met him. He has no intention of revealing who he is to him, but he knows that he can visit Geoffrey's studio as a customer, wishing to buy things and also see some of the articles that he makes. The moment that Kate told him about Geoffrey, Henry had been intrigued and wanted to meet Kate's youngest son and see his body of work. Although he and Kate are no longer together, he can still go to his studio incognito, if you like.

But none of this does he reveal to Penny.

For her part, Penny is consoled to know that her father feels able to continue his journey alone. Obviously Kate's memory is still very much in his mind, but it is now something that is there only when he is not busy although he has by no means come to terms with her decision. To that end, his journey occupies and blots out large chunks of memory, when he simply doesn't have time for such things. However, once he is in his is room, or eating solitarily, thoughts of her keep returning, giving him no rest, until he is able to renew his quest.

They return to St. Agnes on the afternoon boat in perfect weather, the rain having miraculously ceased, sitting at the back enjoying the feel of wind and sun on their faces.

Arriving early to pick Kate up on the Tuesday, Gina breezes in, saying, "I hope you don't mind, but I thought that it would be best if we got to the clinic with time to spare, rather than be struggling to make it. This way if we are really early we can get a coffee and a cake first." She continues to chatter to Kate, a deliberate ploy that she and David have previously agreed, to take Kate's mind off her coming appointment. It is another perfect summer's day as they drive down the leaf dappled lanes until they reach Dorchester, which they circumnavigate until they reach the A354 which leads them on down to Weymouth.

Arriving at the hospital with only a few minutes to spare, they decide to go to the clinic first, where Kate registers in at reception.

Almost immediately a young woman appears, smiling, saying, "Good morning, Mrs Challis, my name is Gemma Robinson and I am Mr Everard's secretary. May I call you Kate? I spoke to you yesterday if you remember? If you are ready, Mr Everard will see you now."

Kate is swept along with the sheer speed of events and only has time to say, "Of course you can call me Kate," but before she has even finished, Gina is saying, "I am Kate's daughter-in-law, would it be OK if I came in with her?"

"That is no problem at all. If you will follow me I will take you now."

As they follow Gemma through a maze of corridors, Kate

THE BUS PASS

begins to feel nervous, her mind taking her through all the possible scenarios that she might soon be faced with. Eventually they come to an office, where Gemma gives a peremptory knock before entering at the sound of a "Come in."

As they enter they are confronted by a relatively young man, perhaps in his forties, sitting behind a desk facing them. He stands and comes round the desk to greet them, smiling and saying, "Good morning Mrs Challis, thank you for coming at such short notice, but I thought that you would prefer to know the results of your tests sooner rather than later. Come and sit here," he continues, ushering them both to winged back chairs which have a small coffee table in the middle of them. "Oh Gemma, would you be so kind as to get tea or coffee for our guests?"

He is a tall, dark man of slim build, who Kate would consider very handsome at any other time and under different circumstances. As they settle Mr Everard continues.

"Well now, I have looked very carefully at your ultrasound results and without prolonging matters I have to tell you that I have some very good news for you, which is that I can see no evidence of breast cancer. There are two lumps showing, which I can tell by the shape and size are cysts."

Before he has even finished speaking, Kate gives out a long shuddering sigh of relief, with tears filling her eyes.

Noticing her reaction, the radiologist reaches across the table, putting his hand on hers, saying, "Nearly all 'simple cysts' are just that - simple. They are almost never associated with a higher risk of cancer. The only possible exception in which a cyst might indicate a slightly elevated risk for cancer is when other risk factors for cancer, such as a strong family history are already present, but when you attended the clinic originally, they talked to you about this, and eliminated any such risk.

"Because of all these factors I am satisfied, and can say with certainty now that you do not have breast cancer. I could, if you like, arrange for you to come in and have the cysts drained, but quite honestly I would not suggest that this is necessary, because they may go away on their own. If however you feel at some time in the future that they are becoming bothersome, we can then arrange for this to be done. But, what I am also saying is for you to go and live and enjoy your life. We will monitor your progress every two or three years, to put your mind at rest, but if you have any worries at any time, please come and see us."

As he finishes speaking, Gina puts a comforting arm around Kate, saying, "There you are Mum. You have spent all this time worrying about nothing. Come on, let's go and ring David and give him the good news. I think that he has been worrying about it as much as you."

They take their leave of Mr Everard, Kate thanking him profusely, until he replies, "I am only too pleased to be able to give you good news. All too often it is my job to deliver a less hopeful message."

Finding a Costa coffee shop they telephone David, who is delighted, saying, "Well. I think that this deserves a celebration. Why don't we all go out for a slap up meal tonight? I will ring Geoffrey and arrange something and will pick you up at say half past seven? Oh, by the way Mum, will you be telling Henry?"

Kate is suddenly brought back down to earth as she is reminded about Henry. In all the exhilaration she has forgotten completely about him and the real reason that she told him to go. The sudden realization mortifies her, as she is confronted by the fact that if she had waited instead of panicking, it would not have been necessary to treat in the manner that she had.

Putting the phone down, she breaks down and between sobs explains to Gina why she is upset, only to hear her reply.

"Well that's no problem, just get in touch with him and explain and I am sure he will understand."

"Oh, I couldn't do that Gina, not after the way I spoke and treated him when he left. I had to you see, or at least I thought that I had to. There didn't appear to be any other option, and by adopting the method that I did, I don't think that he will ever forgive me, which I can easily understand." Once she has finished speaking, Kate's mood has gone from elation, euphoria even, to desperation and desolation in the space of a few minutes.

The matter is left unresolved, as Gina drives her home.

THE BUS PASS

Wednesday arrives on St Agnes and Henry and Penny catch the boat to Treco, where they visit the tropical gardens, which were started over one hundred and fifty years ago, when sailors started bringing plants and trees from the four corners of the earth to grow here. The Isles of Scilly have a much milder climate than other parts of Britain, which is the main reason that the gardens are so successful here.

After the gardens, Penny suggests a visit to the only hotel on the island, which Henry is only too happy to agree with. It is a couple of miles walk, so their appetites are whetted by the time they get there.

They return to St. Agnes and Wednesday evening is women's gig race night, so they make their way to Porth Conger and on to *Spirit*. This evening's race is from behind Annet the small uninhabited isle that is next to St. Agnes about a mile away. From here the boats line up and at the given signal all race to be the first into the quay at St. Mary's, a distance of about four miles. Along with *Spirit*, other boats are gathered, all loaded with supporters from their respective islands, waving flags and shouting words of encouragement.

Each boat has eight single oar rowing positions and a cox. As the starter's flag drops, the crews make a mighty effort to be in pole position, anything after that being in the wake of the boat ahead, making rowing even more difficult. These are nor the sculls that are synonymous with, say, Henley or the University Boat Race, but rather, they are built for adverse sea conditions, and so, are heavier, unwieldy craft, used originally to fight their way to wrecks in gale conditions, to salvage people and cargoes. A totally different proposition altogether.

It is an honour to row for your own island, something which is often handed down from father to son, or from mother to daughter, and each race is competed for to the crew's last vestige of energy.

Tonight is no exception as the women use every muscle and sinew to get ahead of their rivals. For some years now the St. Mary's boat, *Golden Eagle*, has been the winner more often than not, as has been the men's crew also, a reason not hard to find, because the population of St. Mary's is some two thousand, compared with perhaps a hundred for the other islands, or even only sixty souls on St. Agnes. This whittles down even further when the elderly and young are eliminated, making the chances of winning for some of the smaller islands very unlikely.

But stranger things have happened, as Henry reminds Penny when she complains about the inequality of it all, saying, "The year that we first came to St. Agnes, the men won with their boat *Shah*, and for a couple of years after as well. You see the men were all good and worked as a team. The trouble was they didn't have any other people ready to step into their shoes as they got older. Not only that, but they didn't have anyone else who could replace them if they were injured or ill. They had just enough men who could do the job, but once they were gone, there was no one to take up the challenge, and it was a generation, until some of their children were old enough and good enough, to go forward."

The race is coming to its climax, searchlights from the pursuing supporters' boats illuminating their progress. Foam is being churned up as rowers occasionally miss their stroke. Each skipper of the following boats carrying passengers are giving a running commentary, which resounds across the water. The tide is high and pushing the boats into St. Mary's with *Golden Eagle*, as expected, leading the charge, with the St. Martin's boat a close second and *Shah* lying third but failing fast. However they manage to hold on to this position and that is how it finishes, in front of hundreds of other supporters who Penny is suddenly aware of and who are standing on top of the quay, roaring them home.

Henry and Penny are both physically and mentally drained, having shouted themselves hoarse, but Spirit quickly turns round to head back to St. Agnes and the Turks, where they find the magic elixir to sooth their tired limbs and throats.

But it is Thursday that they both look forward to, in anticipation of a visit to Sampson Island. They have been before, and love the feeling of isolation and tranquillity that this remote island exudes. It is uninhabited, but up until the mid-nineteenth century there were several people living here in severe circumstances. The island has two hills, one at each end, with the middle portion between being just above sea level. The inhabitants were taken off at this time because there was insufficient food and water to sustain them, but the remains of their huts or dwellings can still be found almost at the top of one of the hills, consisting of rock built walls and roof tiles. The main source of sustenance seems to have been sea clams and whatever fish they could catch. The area around the huts is covered with shells supporting this theory.

Today the island can only be visited for a few hours a day. There is no quay or adequate landing place for the boat, so the only way to get onto the island is to wade ashore from the boat over the rocks, a difficult but rewarding operation. Henry and Penny are both aware that they will be left alone on the island, the boat returning at the next suitable tide, so they take a picnic with them, which they can consume later in the day.

On reaching Sampson they wade ashore and explore this small isolated world, finding remains of habitation in the form of huts at the top of a hill, and they both wonder how these people survived for even a few days, let alone centuries.

After looking at the squalor and extreme conditions these people had endured, they look out to sea and the Western rocks, with the Bishop Rock beyond them and are transfixed by the sheer magnitude and beauty of the panorama spread out before them. It is now nearly three o'clock and the sun is high in the sky, its rays burning down on them, and reflecting on the deceptive flat calm sea, causing it to shimmer.

They sit in glorious silence, both lost in their own thoughts, until Henry remarks, "That is probably the most wonderful view I have seen anywhere, Pen," and then, his voice filled with emotion, "I wish your mother were here to see it, I so loved to see her face light up when she saw nature in all its' beauty."

"I know Dad, but if it's any consolation, she did come here with us all, years ago," to which he replies, "Oh, I know love, but I just want her to see it now, I can't bear the thought that we are enjoying all these things and places without her. It's guilt I suppose."

"Oh Dad, you have no reason to feel guilt, she would be so pleased to know that you and I are here now, thinking of her at this place that held so many memories for all of us. She would applaud you, and want you to get on with your life. You know that."

The spell broken, they return down the hill, through the thick undergrowth of shrubs and ferns, to the beach area, in time to see *Spirit* arrive off shore. Taking off their sandals, they wade out and are lifted aboard by passengers who are returning from St. Martin's, who have not been to this beautiful island before, or even realise that it could be visited, asking them questions about things like how do you get here, and what is the island like, or how do you manage without a Starbucks.

Thursday evening is quiet and contemplative, both of them facing the thought of returning to Cornwall the next morning. These few days have concentrated both their minds on issues that have to be addressed. Penny knows she needs to talk to Mark about her future, and also to Kate, although this could be more difficult, but she would at least like to try, for her father's sake. For his part, Henry needs to determine to either go on with his journey, or return with Penny, where she could drop him off on her way home. But neither tells the other what they are feeling, so they suffer their problems alone.

The last evening at the Turks is memorable, the islanders wishing them a safe journey for the following morning and telling them not to leave it so long before they come back the next time.

Addresses and emails are exchanged, and the occasional tear brushed away, but the mood is also one of happiness and laughter, until eventually, they say their last goodbyes and make their way back to the Parsonage, but not before ritually, as they have done every other night, examining the night sky, and finally going to the end of Coastguards to watch the Bishop Rock Lighthouse illuminating the night sky, giving comfort and solace to travellers, as it has done for over a hundred and thirty years.

Diane knocks on the door at half past nine the following morning to collect their luggage, to take down to the quay at Porth Conger. Once she is gone Henry and Penny make their way for the last time down the narrow road, past the school and the church, then on past the post office and then onto Higher Town and the Bulb shop until they reach the crest of the hill, with the Sand Bar to Gugh in front of them and The Turks Head away down to their left.

They stand here for several minutes in total silence, drinking in this wonderful view, each lost in their own thoughts, until Henry says, "Come on Penny love, whatever happens, I promise you that we will come back here again someday. It may be not for a long time, but it will happen, and we will bring Mark and the boys next time."

Penny responds. "Oh, that would be so wonderful Dad, I had forgotten just how wonderful this place is. Let's go, I'm feeling a little weepy at the thought of leaving, so God only knows how I will be when the boat leaves and I see the island disappearing in the distance."

Making their way down past the Turks and on down to the quay, they are met by a small multitude of people all gathered waiting for *Spirit* to transport them back to St Mary's. Diane is still there waiting to help them on to the boat with their luggage, but also to greet their replacements. Tears, hugs and handshakes are exchanged with those islanders that are also gathered here for the same purpose as Diane, and with the sound of, "Don't be so long coming back next time," ringing in their ears the Spirit pulls away from the quay.

Rounding the Cow and the Calf, the boat moves out to cross the Sound and Penny is as good as her word as she dissolves in a flood of tears as she looks back at the island which means so much to her. Henry, as he has done on many previous occasions at this stage, cuddles his daughter to him, thinking of earlier years when she would sit on his lap and he would cover her with his body as she cried inconsolably.

But they are soon at the quay and after unloading they wait for one of the many island taxis to come to take them to the airport. Once there they have plenty of time to get refreshments in the airport café, before they board their flight.

When they get to St. Just, Henry asks Penny if she will drop him off at St. Ives, the next place on his journey.

"Sure Dad, if that is what you want to do, but you can still come home with me now, if you would prefer."

"No love, I have thought about it all this week and decided that I still need to continue for a little while at least. I would still like to visit Bristol to see the SS *Great Britain*, then after that I intend to visit Gee and his family, once I have contacted him to get his address. He was such good company and my saviour when I was feeling low. Perhaps he will let me take him and his family out for a meal as recompense, I owe him that at least." And then in a more conspiratorial voice "I would also like to visit Kate's youngest son, Geoffrey, who lives in Beaminster, who I have never had the chance to meet. I have no intention of introducing myself, I just want to see him. If he is only half as nice as his brother David, then he will be worth the visit. I may also see David, but I'm not sure if I will have the courage to, so I'll see how I feel nearer the time. I got to like him very much, but I don't know how he feels about me now that I am no longer a part of his mother's life."

"OK Dad, I get all that, but just to salve my conscience, let's find you somewhere to stay tonight in St. Ives, before I leave," says Penny, while at the same time determining to speak to Kate soon. She can see the strength of her father's resolve to continue on good terms with David but also she feels that any such move will only bring more heartache for Henry, and she is determined to at least mitigate any further shocks to his system.

Getting out his laptop, the two of them select a couple of likely places to stay. Henry then contacts them and finally books for one night bed and breakfast at The Anchorage, a Grade Two listed building at Bunkers Hill, right in the heart of town, just above the beach and close to all amenities. Local amenities are an essential necessity for Henry, because he is only staying here for one night and has no transport to go very far.

Everything now agreed, Penny drives her father to St. Ives and drops him just above the town, remembering with vivid clarity the last occasion they had stayed here, and the trouble they had experienced, negotiating this lovely little town narrow streets.

Saying their farewells, Penny leaves on her long trek home, while Henry makes his way down into town, soon finding his place of lodgings, where he is welcomed and shown his room.

Wanting to see as much of St. Ives as he can in the short time he has available, after depositing his bag, he finds his way down to the harbour and then wanders leisurely around the fascinating narrow streets, whose shops lure visitors with their multitudinous variety of goods.

But Henry knows that this quaint little town with its attractive shops and houses which climb the hill to Carbis Bay has probably the largest selection of museums in the West Country. He is aware of the Barbara Hepworth Museum and sculpture garden, where sensual sculptures by one of the country's leading twentieth-century artists are exhibited in tranquil gardens.

Closer to Henry's heart though is also one of only four Tate Galleries in the world, put here in recognition of the international importance of art in Cornwall and this town in particular. The gallery holds hundreds of works produced by the St. Ives School, from the late 1800s through to the twenty-first century. In fact the town is still a major attraction for artists, who find the light here so clear and compatible for their labours of love.

Henry goes through turmoil, not knowing where to start first, but eventually his natural inclination of painting draws him irrevocably to the Tate Gallery, where he spends a couple of hours totally entranced by its offerings.

Emerging into the sun, he finds a café, where he has a cream tea, consoling himself with the thought, that when in Rome…

Looking at his watch, he decides that he has enough time to visit the Barbara Hepworth Museum and after a short walk arrives at his destination. He wanders round entranced in this beautiful place, finding a little to his surprise that he can appreciate these beautiful works more than he ever realised before.

Feeling totally satiated spiritually, he leaves knowing that the purpose for which these museums are here are vindicated, because they must have the same effect on many others as they have on him. A very rich, rewarding experience indeed.

As he leaves, the streets are filled to overflowing with holidaymakers, all jostling their way through the town, every road packed from pavement to pavement. The sound of laughter fills the air and Henry is caught up in the sheer exhilaration of it all. This happy feeling reminds him of the times when Isabel and the children and he had been here at New Year's Eve. These had been purely magical times, the town all lit up with banners strung across the narrow apertures, with a number of small bands following the circuitous winding cobbled streets. Then came the most eerily magical time of all, as people came thronging onto the streets, all in fancy dress, their laughter and exuberance making the whole town come alive. There had been so many, thousands it had seemed to Henry, all dressed in different guises. It had been for all of Henry's family an unforgettable experience, as he recalled now, smiling broadly to himself, stopping hurriedly as he saw people staring at him, as if he were 'not quite the ticket'.

By now he is feeling tired, so fighting his way through the crowds to his accommodation he retires to his room, falling instantly to sleep, only to be woken instantly (as it seems to him). But it is in fact over two hours later, as his watch testifies.

After showering he feels ready to face the world again and makes his way down to the beach area, looking initially for somewhere to eat, because by now he is ravenous.

Luckily there are eating places in abundance and he quickly finds the Sloop Inn, which is almost on top of the beach. Once he is settled in, and his food ordered, he is delighted to discover that the inn has a group of musicians who commence their performance, singing local songs of times past, telling of smugglers and their nefarious deeds, then songs that tin miners had sung years ago to keep their spirits up down their dank, dark pits - songs of hope and of the women they loved.

As he eats his meal and sips Cornish bitter, Henry is transported to the long ago, when men's lives were a commodity to be exposed and used by a few who had wealth, gathered at the expense of many helpless souls, unable to extricate themselves from their lives of poverty.

Up to this point Henry has managed to get through the day very well, but his thoughts suddenly drift to Penny, wondering if she has got home safely. This past week has given him the opportunity to renew his parental bonds, although it doesn't quite feel that way to him, their relationship roles being reversed if anything, with Penny looking out for him, while he filled a more subservient role, happy to let her make most of the decisions. It doesn't upset him, but makes him feel strangely comforted to know that she cares so much.

Henry is completely happy here, listening to the music, but is also aware that he needs to contact Traveline to find which buses he needs to catch to get to Exeter the next day, which will be half way to Bristol. He also wants to email Penny and Mark, Rob and

THE BUS PASS

Madge, and also Richard in Australia.

But before any of that, he wants to go to Porthminster Beach, just the other side of the harbour, for this is another place that he brought the family years ago, to watch the surfers riding the crest of the huge waves that this place is known for. The only difference between then and now is that his earlier visit had been in the depth of winter, at New Year. At that time the weather was freezing cold and blowing a force five gale, the water being whipped up into frenzy, the tops of the waves foaming white by the angry sea. The scene was made hauntingly beautiful because of the reflection of a full moon, illuminating the sea in all its heaving savagery. But nothing seemed to faze the intrepid surfers, the only concession they made to the extreme conditions was to wear wet suits. It was a striking but frightening experience to see them paddling out to sea, before turning and rising up on their boards to meet a huge wave which would propel them forward onto the beach with an incredible velocity, or if they were not successful, submerge them beneath its murky depths.

But on arrival Henry finds that the sea today is a mere pussy cat compared to that of his earlier visit, due mainly because it is July, and the weather is warm, even at this time of evening. There are still some reasonable waves, mainly because the beach is funnel shaped, forcing the water into its narrow opening, which a few surfers are taking advantage of; but it does not create the same mesmeric picture by comparison, and Henry is, if anything, slightly disappointed.

Taking his last look at this surfer's paradise, he returns to his guest house, and making his way to his room, contacts Traveline to establish how he is going to get to Exeter using his bus pass the following day.

All his journeys so far have proved to be pretty straightforward, but after discussing his itinerary with Traveline, he is horrified to learn that there is no direct route, rather there are several different terminals, where buses have to be changed. Not only that, but these changes mean that the whole journey will take him nearly seven hours to complete. Starting at St. Ives at nine thirty one, his first bus will take him to Truro, the county town of Cornwall, where he will catch his next bus to Wadebridge. From here he will get his final bus to Exeter, arriving at sixteen twenty-eight.

By now thoroughly depressed, Henry emails everyone with the news of his activities for the day, finishing with his next day's itinerary, making it very apparent just how unhappy he feels about it.

CHAPTER 29

Bridport

Saturday 13 July

Henry is wakened the next morning by his mobile phone playing 'All Things Bright And Beautiful', a legacy from Penny's children, who set it for him one lazy Sunday afternoon, without his knowledge.

On answering it, Henry is delighted to hear Gee on the other end say, "How are you getting on Henry? I have been wondering how you are, and where you have been on your travels since I left you. Come on, spill the beans, I am intrigued to know."

"Oh, Gee, it's good to hear your voice again. Well I've been to a number of places on my list, and am at present in St. Ives, preparing to make my way to Exeter."

Henry then continues to tell Gee about his journey since they parted company. First with his old pal Rob, and subsequently with Penny. Gee is delighted to listen, asking the occasional question, pleased to hear Henry sounding more positive in his outlook.

"That all sounds great Henry, so how is your itinerary looking now? What's next after Exeter?"

"Well, I was thinking of visiting Bristol to see the SS *Great Britain* in the docks, but I'm now having second thoughts, because from Exeter I can make my way up through Dorset, then up to Avebury, Stonehenge, and onto Salisbury before returning home. Just at the moment I feel if I can do that, it will be enough for now. I've been away from my home for nearly three months and I'm beginning to miss it. I never told you Gee, but I did meet a lovely lady at a place called Goderston, which can't be a million miles from you, who I would have been happy to spend the rest of my life with, but it didn't work out, so I'm resolved to return home and catch up with my grandchildren, who I miss. After that, I will probably go out to Australia to see my son for a while. That said, if I have time, I would like to call on you, to see you one last time. You were such wonderful company, when I was in such a bad place emotionally, so I thank you sincerely for that."

"The feeling was mutual Henry, and you are of course most welcome here any time. Just give me some notice before you come, in case I'm not here. I often have to be away to see clients or to collect materials. Oh, by the way, what time do you expect to reach Exeter today and have you arranged your accommodation? Because I know of one or two places that I think you would like."

"Well, I hope to arrive via Wells Fargo at half past four this afternoon, providing highwaymen don't attack, or the stagecoach doesn't get stuck on some muddy road in some godforsaken place. Don't worry about accommodation Gee, I should arrive in plenty of time to arrange something, but thanks all the same."

"OK Henry, if you are sure. But don't forget, if you are this way, drop in and see us. If not, we can still both keep in touch. Please keep me up to date, I am so interested to hear of your progress. I will say goodbye for now, good luck Henry, keep smiling."

"Goodbye Gee, of course I'll keep in touch. Thanks for your call - and your company."

Leaving the guest house, Henry makes his way to catch the No. 14 bus to Truro, which leaves at nine thirty, his mood much more buoyant since speaking to Gee.

Arriving safely at Truro bus station he finds that he has just over an hour to spare before he catches a No. 594 to Wadebridge at eleven forty five. Although his time is severely limited he wanders around the central area of Truro absorbing the sights, smells and character of this bustling market town which is the county town of Cornwall. From preference, he would have liked to spend more time here, visiting the cathedral and other major places of interest, but he reflects to himself that wherever his itinerary led him, he would have always had to make discerning choices about which of those he could visit. It simply was not possible to cover all the places he would prefer in the time available, particularly as his only mode of transport is by local bus.

Knowing that he will have more time to spend when he reaches

Wadebridge, Henry spends as much time as possible before he returns to the bus station, ready for the next leg of his journey.

The route takes the bus along the A39, passing through picturesque little villages, then onto the A30 up to Indian Queens, before reverting back to the A39 and its more sedate pace, through St. Columb Major and on up to its final destination.

Once at Wadebridge, Henry finds that he has a little over an hour available before his final bus leaves at two o'clock. By now he is both hungry and thirsty, so finds a café where he can sit and eat while reading his paper. He has no time at all to look around the town, so doesn't try, enjoying the little time he has available doing the crossword while noting the holidaymakers, the children in particular, who are excitedly requesting their ever patient parents for everything, from ice cream and buckets and spades, to the top brick from the chimney. It is a scene that has never ceases to change or amaze him, bringing back images of Richard and Penny from earlier years.

Boarding the No. 510 bus for the last leg of his journey, Henry is relaxed, surprisingly enjoying the day more than he thought possible. The sun is a searing ball of fire overhead, the heat of which is diluted as the bus passes through tree dappled lanes, which will become snarling and ridiculously congested in a couple of weeks' time, when children break up for their summer holidays, but for now, Henry is at peace with the world, as the bus travels slowly through myriad villages, each one looking like the one previous to it. Eventually, after a mammoth two and a half hours, the bus reaches its destination, the station at Exeter.

The passengers spill out onto the street, Henry being one of the last to leave, and he begins making his way into the centre of the city. He has only gone a few yards, however, when he hears someone calling his name from behind. On turning, to his utter amazement he sees Toby and Avril, from the Mucky Duck.

Toby's face is wreathed in smiles as he welcomes Henry, saying, "I thought that be you Henry, what be you doing in this neck of the woods?" and then, "I was so sorry to hear that things hadn't worked out with you and Kate. Avril and I both thought you were the ideal couple, and whatever happened between you at the end doesn't seem to have made either of you happy. We saw Kate for the first time only the other day, and she seemed very quiet and down, not like her old self at all in fact.

"She hasn't been coming in to the pub. Even Megan and Charlie have only seen her fleetingly, and she won't tell them what the matter is. We are all quite worried for her." Then seeing Henry looking perplexed, Toby continues hurriedly, "Still, it's none of our concern Henry. I just thought that you might like to know."

Henry, totally baffled by what he has heard, says, "I am so sorry to hear that, but I don't feel able to say anything, particularly as Kate so obviously doesn't want to. Suffice to say that I love her and always will. I don't know if it will ever be possible for us to be together again, but it's my strongest wish that one day it may happen. As for what I'm doing here, well I am just making my way home after visiting some lovely places in Cornwall and the Isles of Scilly, which has been a wonderful experience, but I'm now feeling the need to return home. As you have probably surmised, the events leading up to me leaving Kate have left me somewhat bruised and I now have to return home to face the same situation as that when I left, prior to coming on my pilgrimage - i.e. do I move to Australia or stay where I am?"

Toby looks confused for a while, before saying eventually, "Well Henry, it all seems to me, looking from the outside in, that it's a total waste of two people's happiness. Have you tried talking to her recently? Because whatever happened between you, I can assure you it hasn't made Kate any happier, in fact quite the contrary."

"Oh, don't you think I haven't tried Toby? I contacted her several times at first, but she remained adamant. Every time I tried, her rejection was like a hammer blow, until it got to the point where it just hurt too much to try anymore."

"I understand all that Henry, but if you could see the misery and pain that she is so obviously in, I think it would change your mind in an instant."

Not wanting to offend Toby, Henry says in a conciliatory manner, not intending to take any action at all, "Let me think about it Toby. Obviously I hate the thought of Kate being upset and unhappy. The very thought hurts me too, but I don't know if anything I say will resolve it She was very adamant, angry even when we parted. I would sooner not speak to her than make her

THE BUS PASS

that angry again."

"All I ask is that you think about it Henry," says Toby, and then, "Look, Avril and me came in to Exeter today to see our daughter, Theresa, who lives here. We are on our way back home now, so why don't you come back with us? You can have your old room back if you like. You needn't stay very long, just look on it as the first step on your way home."

Henry is dumbstruck at the thought, feeling completely unable to accede to Toby's request, and says, almost defensively, "No, I don't think that I can do that Toby. Kate would probably see me turning up at yours as an unwelcome approach. What I would prefer to do, if you have no objection, is to accept a lift from you to Bridport, where I can probably get a room at the Bull Hotel. There are several places I would like to see around the area before I make my way home, and Bridport would be central for that purpose. Would that be OK? I promise that I will at least come and see you before I finally leave."

Toby does not hesitate, saying, "Of course I will drop you off at Bridport, but I will keep you to your promise of coming to see us, so come on, let's get started, or I'll be late opening."

On the road to Bridport, the conversation is very one sided, as Toby and Avril try to persuade Henry to contact Kate to see if their differences can be resolved. But Henry is very non-committal, not because he doesn't want to talk to her, but is more afraid that if he does, and she still feels the same way as previously, he might find himself in an irretrievable situation.

Getting no response, Toby changes the subject by telling Henry what has been happening in the village since he left, which, it seems, is very little, until he suddenly says, "You will never guess who I saw the other day," and then when Henry is unable to guess, he continues. "Geoffrey, Kate's youngest son, with his wife and daughter. They stopped off for a bite to eat before going to see Kate. I think that it must have been a family get-together, because I looked across the common a little afterwards and David and his family were parked outside her house as well. It was most unusual to see them all together for once. Did you ever meet Geoffrey, Henry?"

"No, I never did Tony. Kate and I talked about going to see

him but the roof fell in, so to speak, before we had the chance."

"You would like him Henry, I'm sure. He is a lovely lad who would help anybody," says Toby. "Which is not something you can say about very many people in this day and age." And then, "Well, here we are Henry, at Bridport. I will drop you right outside the Bull which will save you having to carry your luggage. Now don't forget your promise to come and see us before you go home. Good luck my friend, I have really enjoyed your company these last few months."

As he says thanks, Henry is left once again with an overwhelming feeling of loneliness. A remembrance of wonderful times past, but left with a huge empty void for the future. What will he do and where will he be in say a years' time? Up until this point his life has followed a predictable certainty. True, he lost Isabel, the love of his life, whose presence had ensured lasting love and stability. But after so many years of being alone, he thought that he had found someone who could fill the void left by Isabel. Not a direct replacement, because Kate was different in so many ways, and Henry would not have wanted a carbon copy of Isabel. No, Kate is different. She suffered from the experience of her marriage, which made her wary of any new relationships, but Henry had thought that between them, they had found solace and companionship in each other, which made the break up all the more catastrophic for him.

Brushing all such thoughts aside Henry books into the Bull Hotel, before having a quick walk round his beloved Bridport.

When he wakes the next morning, Henry decides that he will spend the day relaxing after his hectic few days previously, before mapping out his next move. The morning is spent reading the Sunday papers, before walking to West Bay, about a mile away. He wanders idly around the quay, looking down on a myriad assembly of small boats, left stranded on the shore by the outgoing tide. Fishing boats, rowing boats with outboard motors, speedboats, and individual cabin cruisers are all left here, sprawling on the harbour floor, making it look like a like a boat graveyard.

As he scans right towards Golden Cap, the highest cliff in Dorset, he can see a number of people taking a few steps before launching themselves from the surrounding cliffs, suspended by hang gliders. He finds this more than a little surprising, because from where he is standing down on the beach, the sun is shining, its reflection shimmering over the placid sea, without even the suggestion of the merest zephyr of a breeze. But there must be strong thermal currents higher up where the hang gliders are.

Henry watches this spectacle for some time, totally entranced by the sight of the parachute type gliders of various bright vivid colours weaving their magic across the sky. The riders, once they are aloft, all seem to turn back towards the cliff, which Henry can only assume is because they do not want to get swept out over the sea and have to crash land, risking either the loss of their expensive gliders or being drowned, or both.

Stopping at a café near to the beach, Henry considers his options. From a logistical viewpoint, it would make sense if his first port of call were to be Geoffrey's address near Beaminster. He doesn't expect to be there for any length of time, wanting just to meet Kate's' youngest son and to see where he lives. He certainly has no intentions of introducing himself to Geoffrey.

Once he has satisfied his curiosity regarding Geoffrey, he decides that he will then contact Gee and after finding out where he lives he will visit him and invite him and his family out for a meal, in recognition of their few days together.

After that, Henry decides that it will be about time to make his way home, perhaps via Salisbury and Stonehenge. His enthusiasm has never really recovered after he was banished by Kate, but he now begins to accept that the two of them will not be together again. But he also realises that acceptance doesn't relieve the pain and the heartache that he still feels.

Making his way back to the Bull Hotel, he has dinner and spends the rest of the day catching up with his friends and family on email.

CHAPTER 30

Geoffrey

Monday 15 July

"It's me, Penny. Please don't hang up the phone Kate, we need to talk. I know that whatever happened between you and my father is none of my business, but I can't bear to see how unhappy he is now that the two of you are no longer together. Neither do I really understand why, because it was obvious during the time that Mark, the children and I spent with you that you were both infatuated with each other. Is there another reason that you are hiding from him, which explains the change in your feelings towards him. There must be, there can only be. What is it, is there another man in your life. My greatest fear is that you were using him to for your own ends to help David, but in all honesty I don't think that was the reason, because if it were, you couldn't possibly have hidden it from either him or us.

"Your feelings for each other were obvious to anyone who saw the two of you together. Please, please Kate, tell me the real reason that you ended the relationship, so that even if you don't want me to tell him, let me know so that I can at least offer him some understanding of your position."

There is a long silence, after which Penny says, "Kate, are you still there?"

Suddenly she can hear the sound of Kate sobbing at the other end of the line, and says in a soft conciliatory tone, *"There is another reason*, isn't there Kate? Please don't cry love, just tell me so that I can understand. Then I can deal better with Dad."

"Oh Penny, I have been such a fool, but I thought that I was doing the right thing in the long run for your father. You see Penny, I received a letter from the clinic informing me that my breast cancer check-up was due, so I duly attended, after which I came away with nothing further being said. However, after a few days I received a second letter saying that my results were unclear and that they wanted to see me again. As you can probably guess, this was the same day that I spoke to your father when told him that I thought that it would be for the best if he moved on."

"I think I can see where you are going with this," says Penny, interrupting in a soft conciliatory tone. "I guess your first thought must have been something like, 'Henry has already lost his wife to this terrible disease, so how can I possibly let him go through the same thing for a second time."

Before she has even finished speaking, she hears a terrible wail of anguish from Kate at the other end of the line, who continues in a voice filled with stress. "Of course that was my very first thought, but the result was that I panicked and went into a blue funk, not being able to think coherently. All I could think was that I couldn't put Henry through all that again. After all, we haven't known each other for very long, although as you have surmised, my feelings for him are all consuming. On the other hand he told me all about your mother's suffering, and I heard, from the way he spoke, just how much it had taken it out of him. But having said all that, I just panicked and instead of waiting to see the outcome of further tests, I reacted instinctively and the rest you know.

"Obviously I was delighted, over the moon in fact when I was given the all clear, but once it had been confirmed you can imagine how mortified I was that I had driven your father away completely unnecessarily. I will never be able to forgive myself. As for using him, I suppose I did in a way, but not in the way that you implied. In fact, if anything, I used David's needs as a way of keeping your father close to me, rather than the other way round. The first time that I met your father I felt a strong attraction to him. This was before I knew the type of work that he had done all his life. Obviously, once they met, David and Henry got on like a house on fire, which was a complete and unexpected bonus for all of us. David's first concern when I told him that Henry and I had parted, was, (apart from my health issue), Henry, and how it had affected him. He was completely distraught and torn between his concern for me, but also for Henry, because he had come to know and respect him, not only for his management skills, but also as a person."

Penny is herself in tears as she listens to Kate's explanation, but after a short silence she says, "Well, where do we go from here then. I know that Dad would take you back like a shot, although he wouldn't recognise it as taking you back, because he feels you never really left him… and he is right, isn't he?"

"I suppose you are right Penny, but the shame of what I have done to your father has left me feeling depressed, and frightened to contact him and tell him the truth. I did send him an email once, just after he left, to say that I was quite happy for him to send his dirty laundry to me and I would deal with it and return it to him wherever he was going. It was a ploy really to keep in touch with him, so that I knew where he was, and more importantly, how he was feeling, because by this time I was already feeling guilty of the pain and suffering that I had caused him. But he was having none of it. Not because he was angry with me, but because he couldn't stand the thought of contacting or speaking to me on a regular basis, because it would hurt him too much. So you see Penny, I don't feel able to try and contact him now, for much the same reason that he does not want me too. That is, I am frightened that he will reject me or, even worse, not believe me. I'm sorry Penny, but I just can't do it."

Now it is Penny's turn to remain silent, her mind in turmoil, thinking of the right words to use, to keep Kate positive, but although she can see her problem, she cannot think readily of a solution, so for now all she says is, "Oh Kate, I can see and understand how you feel, but I'm sorry, until either of you has enough confidence to take the risk of being rejected, then things will stay the same as they are. Let's not talk any more about it now, but just promise me that you will think about it, and let me know if you can come up with a solution, and I will do the same." And then on a lighter note, "This conversation has at least answered a lot of my queries and doubts, and should make it easier to deal with my father's feelings, although I don't know quite how at the moment. I have no plans to tell anyone else, apart from Richard, who I know has been very concerned for his father, but I'm sure that he will understand completely once I explain."

"Thank you for phoning, Penny, it's been good to share my hopes and feelings. Apart from my family, you are the only other person who knows, but I understand that Richard needs to be

THE BUS PASS

reassured. I will think about all that you have said and get back to you in a day or so."

Penny pauses, thinking what her next move will be. She is heartened and relieved after her talk, because she now knows that Kate still loves her father. Has never stopped loving him in fact, but she can see the next step, which appears almost insurmountable and very difficult to overcome. In essence, how can she persuade, or convince Kate to make the next move, i.e. to contact her father and explain.

She stands motionless for several minutes before picking up the phone again.

"Hi Richard, I thought that you and I need to talk about the situation between Dad and Kate. I know that you are concerned for his welfare, as indeed so was I, but I talked to her this morning, and things are not quite as bad as they appear.

"It transpires that Kate had a mammary check-up, the results of which were unclear, and so she was asked to go back for further tests and investigation. It was at this point that things started to unravel and she began to panic, big time. Her sole thought and concern was for Dad's welfare, so to save him having to go through all the trauma of supporting her, with what she thought she had got, i.e. 'the big C', she decided, without going the whole nine yards with further tests at the clinic, it would be for the best if they separated their relationship. The thought of Dad going through the same turmoil that he had suffered when Mum died was just too much for her.

"Now I know on the face of it that this doesn't make any sense, but she has told me that Dad told her everything about Mum and how much she suffered over those last few months, and she just didn't want him to have to go all through that again. She was totally distraught when she finally realised that she didn't have breast cancer, and that she had sent Dad away in error.

"So this is where we are at now, which sounds fantastic on the face of it, but the real problem which remains unsolved is how they can get back together again. Kate cannot get past the thought of rejection if she speaks to Dad and explains just how and why she did what she did. Now we both know that Dad would be delighted to discover the real reason why she sent him away, although she obviously doesn't know him well enough yet, because even if her condition had proved to be more serious, he would have supported and loved her, because that is who he is. End of."

"Well, I knew that things were not right between Kate and Dad, from reading between the lines of his emails," says Richard, speaking for the first time. "Although he makes every effort to make it appear that he is having a great time, somehow it doesn't ring true. Having said that, it can't have been easy for Kate, and although she panicked, I can see where she's coming from. As for what we can do about it, I'm not sure. Do you know just how long Dad is going to be, before he returns home? I ask the question because I was thinking of arranging a ticket for him to come out and see us, but I can only do so when I can be sure that he is back home and ready. Have you any suggestions that can break the deadlock, Pen?"

"I'm at a loss Richard, because until such time that one of them talks to the other, then it's a stalemate. That being the case, the only course that I can see is for some other person to act as an intermediary," and then expanding on what she has just said, "What if we dropped a hint or gave Dad a few clues to what has happened with Kate, nothing too obvious you understand, then just maybe he might have the courage to call on her on his way home, which I think will be about the end of this week. As far as I know he wants to try to get to Salisbury and Stonehenge, after which he intends to come home."

"That sounds feasible Pen, but it needs to be done with a light touch, because if Dad thinks that he is being manipulated, he will do just the opposite that you expect him to. But it's worth a try Pen, just go careful, the last thing we want to do is drive Dad away from us, particularly at the moment, when he needs our support most."

"OK Richard, let me think about it and I will ring you again when I have come up with something, Take care, and love to you and yours."

After waking and dressing, Henry makes his way down to breakfast, in preparation for his visit to Geoffrey and his family. He is excited at the prospect of seeing Kate's other son and interested to see his studio. But the thing that is driving him most is the fact that he will be able to meet him, without having to reveal who he is and his relationship with Geoffrey's mother. The thought of introducing himself to Geoffrey is just a bridge too far, as far as Henry is concerned.

Luckily, they have never met, because Henry would never have the courage or inquisitiveness to visit him if they had. Geoffrey intrigues Henry and he wishes that Kate and he had visited him before their relationship had finished.

Catching the bus to Beaminster at half past nine, Henry gets off at the sign post to Netherbury, about a mile south of Beaminster.

Although Netherbury is signposted, it is still a mile away from the main road, as Henry discovers once he has left the bus. But the walk is worth it, as he follows a narrow country road, finding himself getting ever deeper into the countryside. Houses of every description are sprinkled sparsely along his path, mostly of origins built many years before. Some are large Georgian houses that must have served the gentry several hundred years ago but also here and there a row of terraced thatched cottages, built, Henry assumes, for agricultural workers employed by local landowners. They would have been basic two up two down houses with no running water, electricity, or any other modern conveniences when built, but now they have all been updated and extended, mostly by people from urban areas, who use them as second homes, which they use to escape to from the hurly burly of their everyday lives.

As he gets ever nearer to Netherbury, the road becomes even narrower, until Henry finds himself in what can only be called a hamlet, a collection of mostly large houses, each standing in extensive grounds. Trees are each side of the road, cutting out the bright sunlight with their huge green canopies. Although he looks very carefully, Henry can find no trace of a shop, pub, or post office, the three main things that constitute a village.

He continues slowly looking for the place where Geoffrey lives, hoping to see something that will give him a clue. Suddenly his thoughts are answered as he sees a large notice board at the end of a small narrow track, which reads 'Geoffrey Challis Studio, centre for Fine Arts, Watercolours, Acrylics and Oil painting and other media, Batik work a speciality. Painting classes held throughout the year. Visitors welcome to come and browse through the studio/shop.'

For some strange reason that he doesn't understand, Henry is now apprehensive about going any further, but quickly gives himself a good talking too, and begins to follow the path. After about a hundred yards he comes upon a clearing in the trees which surround what can only be Geoffrey's home and studio.

The studio is to the left of the house by some forty yards and is set at the extreme rear of the property, with a path leading up to it. The garden is landscaped each side of the path, with beds of roses and other perennial plants randomly spread; among them are a number of fruit trees heavily laden with apples and pears.

As Henry makes his way along the path he can see that the trees peter out at the sides and rear of the plot, and as he nears the studio he can see beyond it to the most amazing view. The ground drops away to reveal a landscape of small fields, surrounded by a combination of dry stone walls and hedges, which continues on as far as the eye can see. Apart from the sounds of birds going about their daily fight for existence there is no other noise. Henry observes also as he makes his way toward the studio that there is a hedge, some six feet high which runs between the house and the studio, and he wonders if Geoffrey had it put there for privacy purposes. This means, thinks Henry, that visitors who are going to the studio do not impact or intrude in any way on anybody who is living in the house. They can come and go without any person in the house even being aware of it.

Henry pushes open the door of the studio, and before even looking at what it contains, he is drawn to the opposite end of the building, which is constructed of glass, through which flows like a moving stream, the natural light from the sun, flooding the studio with its glorious golden warmth. Beyond the end of the building, Henry had an even better view of the landscape that he has seen a few moments ago, and he can see immediately why Geoffrey has opened up the back of the building. The view is, quite simply, inspirational.

Once he has absorbed the view, Henry commences to direct his attention to the room, and is at once surprised to see a figure standing with his back to him at the end of the building. He hasn't noticed him up to this point because his sole attention has been taken up by the stunning view.

As he makes his way towards what, he can now see, is a man standing in front of an artist's easel, he is drawn in an almost mesmeric fashion to him, being vaguely aware of some sort of recognition. The man, thinks Henry, looks almost six feet tall, with short cropped hair, but that is all that Henry can see from the back. He can only assume that this is Geoffrey, but cannot be sure at this stage, so he coughs surreptitiously to make the man aware of his presence.

It is at this moment that Henry receives yet another mind-numbing revelation. As the man turns slowly towards him, Henry takes in the slim build and the ready smile that leaps to his face. But more than that, Henry recognises the stunning clear blue eyes, and for the first time realises who they remind him of.

"Gee, what are you doing here?" explodes Henry, and then as the connection clicks at last. "Or rather Geoffrey."

But then he can go no further, until Geoffrey replies, "Oh! Henry, you have discovered my guilty secret. I would have told you eventually, so I am sorry that you have found it out in this way, before I was ready. How did you find out where I live? Because I deliberately never told you."

"Well I wasn't looking for you Gee, the person that I spent several days travelling with in Devon, when I set out this morning. Rather I was coming to see Geoffrey Challis, the son of Kate, who I fell so in love with, but who I lost for reasons I can't begin to understand. I had no intention of making myself known to Geoffrey, I just wanted to meet him incognito, so to speak, and see for myself how he has transformed his life to become an artist of significant recognition. Although I have never met you (or at least thought that I have never met you) your mother has told me in great detail of where you live, and how you have overcome many trials and tribulations to become so successful, and so I determined to meet you. But I never expected for one minute to meet Gee."

There is silence for a fraction of a second, but before Geoffrey can reply, Henry continues as a more important point occurs to him. "Anyway, I can't believe that meeting you in Totnes was a coincidence, after seeing you here today, so what happened that made your journey there so necessary? And why call yourself Gee, or your daughter Chloe, when her real name is Claudette, for that matter."

An anguished look of pain and guilt spreads across Geoffrey's countenance as he replies. "I am so sorry if you feel that I have offended you Henry, which was never my intention. The truth is much more innocent. You see, when you and my mother parted, despite what you may have thought, she was distraught with guilt and loss, even though it was her decision.

"Once you had left, her first reaction was to contact David in tears, and explain to him what had happened. Her only thought at that stage was of you and how you would manage on your travels. Between them, they talked it over for some time, until eventually David suggested that they could perhaps find someone to keep an eye on you. As you can guess, the 'someone' that they came up with eventually, was me. As for me calling myself Gee, that is in fact the name that everyone uses for me, and have done since I was a small child; it's just a shortened version of Geoffrey, as indeed is Chloe a shortened version of Claudette, so I didn't lie to you Henry."

"But how did you find out how to find out where I was, and why was your mother so concerned for my welfare once she had told me to leave?" complains an exasperated Henry.

"Well that was relatively easy," continues Geoffrey. "You see, you continued to include my mother in your daily emails. I suppose you were so upset that you didn't even realise, but it took a couple of days before I was able to arrange to get to Totnes. We were concerned that you would move on before I could reach you. My original intentions were merely to keep tabs on you, to perhaps speak to you, to try to keep your spirits up, which I could see were very low. But then you did the most unexpected thing, which was to make contact with me and suggest that we spend some time together to look at places of interest.

"I was only too happy to agree, after which there followed three marvellous days, during which I came under your spell in much the same manner that my mother and David had, I guess. You were good company, very funny and informative and I enjoyed being with you. All the things that David and Mum said you were in fact."

"I still can't get over the fact that I am here talking to Gee, who I know and like, instead of Geoffrey, who I don't know, but have heard so many good things about," replies Henry, looking totally bemused. "I had fully intended to visit Geoffrey today and then contact Gee, who I thought lived just south of Crewkerne."

"But I do," says Gee, who by now is beginning to see the funny side of the situation. "Crewkerne is only a few miles north of here. So you see I didn't lie to you, although, as they say, I was a bit economical with the truth. However, I must confess that I was in a terrible quandary when you contacted me and said that you would like to call if you had time. The only regret that I have is that I told you my wife's name was Sally, but I thought that you might make the connection if I told you that it was Sarah."

"But I come back to my original question Gee. If your mother was so unhappy when I left, why did she tell me to leave? There must be another reason, other than the ones that she told me, so come on, and be truthful with me about that."

"I swear to you Henry that I really don't know of any reason, other than those that she gave you. However I do think that you are right, and that there must be something else that she is not prepared to talk about, because it just doesn't add up. I tell you what, why don't you visit her on your way home? It wouldn't be far out of your way, and it might set your mind at rest if you could speak to her in person."

Henry looks thoughtful for a few seconds, running his fingers over his face, as if to try and wake up from a long sleep. "Oh Gee, I'm sorry, but I don't think that I can find the courage to do that. Not after the way she told me to leave. A second helping of that and I think would never recover."

"I can see how that could possibly be disastrous for you Henry. Look, I will be talking to her in a couple of days, and I will explain to her that we've spoken and ask her directly what the real problem is. If she tells me, I promise that I will contact you and let you know. How about that?"

"Would you really do that for me?" asks Henry. "I would be most grateful."

"Of course I would Henry. That and a lot more, after all that we have gone through. Oh, I forgot, before we go any further, let me show you around the studio."

With that, Gee begins to take Henry on a guided tour, starting with examples of his Batik on shopping bags and small pictures. He then shows Henry coloured photographs of much larger pieces that are hung in cathedrals and churches, as well as others in public corporation and municipal offices. Finally there are samples that have been sold to major retail outlets, which Henry recognises seeing when he has browsed through large department stores.

"Obviously I can't produce this product in volumes, but the larger stores are always happy to take whatever I have. I suppose it gives them something completely different and exclusive. Luckily for me, this means that I can get more or less what I ask in monetary terms."

Moving on, Gee shows Henry examples of his glass etchings, most of which seemed to be designed for use as door panels. Henry thinks that they are exquisite, and tells Gee so, which seems to please the younger man out of all proportion, and he says, "Thank you so much for your positive comments Henry. They mean so much to me."

They continue the tour, looking at beautiful Giglee pictures that Gee and Sarah have produced, until they reach an area where ceramics are displayed, which Gee introduces saying, "This is our latest venture and is something that I always wanted to do. So I bought a kiln and all the bits and began to try and make some plates, cups and small decorative items, but, I don't know why, for some reason my efforts were a disaster. I was just about to give it up and put it down to experience, when, without my knowledge, Sarah had a go. You can imagine to my surprise that her efforts were to say the least, stunning. So, she throws the pots etc., after which I then paint the designs. As you can see, it works very well."

Henry agrees enthusiastically as he examines the ceramics which he finds are aesthetically pleasing. Holding some of the items he can feel the love and care that has gone into their production.

Finally Gee shows Henry some of the pictures that he has painted, saying, "I started off doing watercolours, but I also now use acrylics and oils."

THE BUS PASS

Suddenly, changing the subject, Gee says, "Look, I have someone who comes in part time. A young teenage girl who is an art student in a college. Once she arrives, which should be any time now, we could go across to the house, where I can introduce you to Sarah. I have told her all about you and our travels and I know she will be delighted to meet you. If you like you can have a look around while we're waiting."

Henry readily agrees, happy to take the opportunity to spend more time browsing the studio, which he finds fascinating. All too soon, Gees student-assistant, Jennifer, arrives and they leave to go to the house, after he has contacted Sarah, to make sure that she is there.

"Sarah, this is Henry, who I met in Devon while you were in Venice. I told you about him if you remember. Oh, by the way, he knows who I am, and why I was in Devon, so you can talk freely to him."

"I am soooo pleased to meet you, Henry! Gee has told me so much about you, as have both David and Kate. What a wonderful time you both had exploring places that neither of us has seen. So my next job is to get him to take me there. Chloe, come and meet Henry, the man who Daddy met while we were on holiday." Then in an aside to Henry, "I don't think that she will remember you, but it's worth a try."

The same little girl that Henry remembers seeing in the video clip comes running into the room carrying a teddy bear. Arriving breathlessly, her mother asks her, smiling as she does so.

"Where have you been young lady?" to which Chloe, exasperated, replies, "I have been feeding Teddy Mummy, he was very hungry."

As he watches the scene between mother and daughter, Henry is reminded once more just how beautiful they both are. Sarah is simply stunning in an unobtrusive way. She is quite tall and wears no makeup, but her beautiful facial bone structure ensures that she doesn't need it, while her intense green eyes only accentuate her warm soft mouth and ready smile. She is dressed in a purple short sleeved top, with matching purple trousers, which cling closely to her, giving Henry little to leave to his imagination. Her long blonde hair is held by a clip at the back of her head, no doubt to stop it falling over her eyes when she is working.

Chloe's colouring is the same as her mother's, with the same green eyes, but her cheeks are rosy, while her blonde hair hangs in natural ringlets. Her freckles only add to her appeal, and her smile is wide and open as Henry says, "Hello Chloe, it's lovely to meet you, and Teddy of course."

Chloe stands hesitatingly before him, until Sarah says, "Say hello to Henry, Chloe, he knows Grandma Kate and has come to see us."

"Hello Henry," whispers Chloe and then to her mother, "Can I go and finish feeding Teddy?"

"Of course you can," says Sarah, looking at Henry for his silent acknowledgment, and then as Chloe skips out of the room. "I have talked to Kate a number of times recently, and to be honest, from what she says, I cannot for the life of me understand why the two of you parted. You are almost the sole topic of conversation when she rings me, so the reasons she gave you must be false, because she invariably ends up in tears. Although I have tried to get her to tell me what the real problem is, she is very defensive, and I can't get any more out of her. I have no wish to be seen as interfering, so there is little more that I can do. I'm sorry Henry."

"It's OK I understand Sarah, I wouldn't wish for one moment for you to jeopardise your relationship with Kate. No, the sole reason that I came here today, was to invite you out for dinner at the Bull Hotel. Well, it wasn't you, but it turns out it is you, if you can understand what I mean. Gee, Sarah and Chloe, rather than Geoffrey, Sarah and Chloe."

"We would be delighted Henry," interjects Gee. "But I think that dinner would be a little late for Chloe," then turning to Sarah, "I have told Henry that I will speak to my mother and try to get her to tell me the real reason why she told Henry to leave, but don't worry, I won't upset her."

Answering Gees remarks, Henry says, "With regard to dinner, I would like it very much if Chloe could come as well, so why don't we make it lunch instead? If possible I was thinking of tomorrow, because I am feeling the need to get home and see some of my family. I haven't seen my grandchildren for some time, and I am missing them. With regard to your last remark, please don't say anything that may upset your relationship with your mother. Life's too short, and she is the only mother that you have. So, what do you say?"

"Well, I suppose Jennifer could cover the studio," replies Gee. "What do you think Sarah?"

"For me, it would make a nice change. There are things that I need to do, but I don't have anything that can't be left for a few hours, so I would like that very much."

"That's settled then," says Henry, relieved. "I will arrange a table for say one o'clock tomorrow, how does that sound?"

"Fantastic Henry, and now that's been agreed, let me show you the rest of the house."

"I would love that, but I need to be on my way back after that. I didn't mean to take so much of your time."

"Don't worry about that Henry, when you have finished here, one of us can run you back to Bridport," says Gee.

Smiling, Henry replies, "Thank you for the thought, but my pilgrimage wherever possible is by bus, using my bus pass. The walk here from the bus was just wonderful, so if you don't mind, I would like to repeat it."

So it is agreed, and they both give Henry a guided tour of the house, which he thinks is beautiful, and of which they are so obviously proud.

Chloe, not wanting to be outdone, then takes his hand and says, "Come and see my house in the garden," and proceeds to lead him to the bottom of the plot, where Gee and Sarah have installed a large playhouse, painted in yellow, with the roof in red. Chloe insists that he enters the house through its small front door, and as he crawls in she proceeds to show him round the various rooms, all the while talking nineteen to the dozen, her tinkling laughter leading him on, triggering the same response in him as he follows her on hands and knees, trying to keep up. Reaching the rear of the house, he finds himself in a room, which, once he is inside, he has great difficulty in turning, and the only exit route left open to him is to reverse, backing all the way out through the way that he has come.

Chloe of course, finds this all hilarious, her excited laughter made even more so, as she tries to push Henry backwards, only making matters worse.

Henry takes it all in good part, happy to hear Chloe's laugh and see her smiling face. Eventually they both find themselves outside the playhouse, only to find Gee and Sarah in gusts of laughter, tears streaming down their faces.

"She does that to all newcomers," exclaims Gee, amid bouts of uncontrolled laughter. "Sorry about that, but it's so funny."

"Right young lady," says Henry, catching her up in his arms, and throwing her skywards, which only makes her laugh all the more.

They return to the house, and as he prepares to leave, they insist that he first stays to lunch, which consists of cheese and pate, with salad and large crusty pieces of warm bread, spread thickly with butter. Henry has not realised just how hungry he is, and wolfs the food down with alacrity, saying, "This bread is lovely," to which comes the reply from Sarah, "Oh yes, we make it ourselves. I'm glad you like it."

Waving goodbye, and saying, "See you tomorrow," Henry starts his return journey to catch the bus back to Bridport. As he retraces his footsteps he is still stunned by how his morning has developed. To think that he was intending to visit Geoffrey, just to see Kate's younger son, only to find that Gee, the person who he had spent several days with, and who he admired so much, were one and the same person.

His spirits are raised by the thought that Kate had been so concerned for him that she had arranged for Gee to keep an eye on him, that he is almost overwhelmed once again by the love that he feels for her.

As he reaches the main road he only has to wait for twenty minutes before the bus arrives, and his journey gets him back into Bridport, fifteen minutes later.

After looking round various shops and places that he remembers well, he returns to the Bull Hotel and books a table for four people for lunch for the next day.

Back in his room, Henry's mind roams over all the things that people have told him about Kate's reasons for breaking up their relationship. In the cold light of day, he has to admit that there has to be another reason, other than the one she used to dismiss him. If her feelings for him were not the same, then why had she taken so much trouble to ensure that someone (Gee) kept an eye on him and made sure that he was looking after himself. Or, for that matter, why did she contact him herself, offering to continue to do his laundry? Was it just as another means of keeping in contact, to ensure that he was all right. But why?

Whichever way he looks at it, Henry can make no sense of it. But what can he do to try and resolve the situation, if that is at all possible, without contacting Kate. Perhaps there is someone else that he can ask, that might know the answer. But it all comes back down to Gee. He has said that he will talk to his mother, so there is no point trying other avenues until he hears what he has to say.

Henry's mind is overloaded with unanswered questions, as he spends the next couple of hours trying to rationalise what he intends doing next. Coming up with diddly-squat, he decides to catch up on his emails.

To his utter amazement, the first one on the list, which has only been sent a few hours earlier, is from his son Richard, and reads:

Hi Dad,

I haven't spoken to you for some while now, but I have been following your progress nevertheless. Any gaps that I have missed have been filled in by Penny. You seem to be having a busy time since leaving Kate's, which all sounds fantastic. I can remember doing some of them with all of us as a family, which made me feel very nostalgic.

I was sorry to hear that your relationship with Kate broke up. It must have been very traumatic for you, which brings me to the reason I have contacted you. My suggestion is that you get away from your recent bad memories, and come to us for a while, for a complete change of scenery, atmosphere, call it what you will.

So, to save any objections, I have booked you a return ticket to Sydney, departing on Monday 22 July at midday, which I have arranged to be picked up by you on the day of the flight, from the British Airways desk. I know that this is very short notice, but I make no apologies, because I think that if you cab distance yourself from your problems, you will get a better perspective of just how serious, or not, that they are.

I hope that you can understand my concern for you Dad. Just have a break out here for however long that you want to stay. One week, two, a month, or whatever. I will arrange to pick you up from Sydney airport when you arrive on Wednesday 24th.

We are all very excited at the prospect of seeing you once again.

Until then, Love from Richard, Janet and the children.

As he finishes reading his son's email, Henry becomes aware that he is completely overwhelmed by the extreme mixture of feelings that it has generated. His first reaction is one of relief almost. He can fly away and leave his troubles behind him. This feeling is immediately followed by an undefinable ache, a longing for what might have been. He cannot face the thought of not seeing Kate again, although he knows that there is very little likelihood of that happening. But, on the other hand, once Gee has talked to her in a day or so, he may discover some other reason for the way she treated him, which might change things.

For all his doubts, he still clings to the hope that Kate and he can be reconciled, however unlikely that may be.

But he needs to find out quickly, because if it is not possible, he must get home in time to get his flight on twenty-second - only one week away.

Concentrating, he replies to Richard, thanking him for his kind gesture and confirming that he will get the flight, after which he emails Penny, letting her know about Richards offer, telling her he hopes to see her sometime over the coming weekend, before he has to leave for Sydney.

Finally, he E-mails Rob and Madge, getting them up to date, telling them about Richards suggestion, and that consequently he will be home at the weekend, to hopefully see them before he has to leave for Sydney.

He is by now totally confused by the events of the day, and decides to go for a walk to clear his head before his evening meal.

For once, the walk doesn't make things any clearer in his mind. If anything, it makes things even more difficult, the problems appearing to be unsolvable. If, for example, he does A, then the

THE BUS PASS

consequences might be one of half a dozen possible solutions. Likewise if he decides on B, there might be even more solutions. None of them palatable.

No, he will just have to wait to see if Gee can help, once he has talked to Kate.

For the remainder of the day, Henry tries his level best to ignore his problems, and rather, looks forward to seeing Gee, Sarah and Chloe the following lunch time.

CHAPTER 31

Tuesday, 16 July

"I managed to speak to my mother last night, Henry," says Gee as Sarah, Chloe and he, arrive at the Bull Hotel, the following lunch time. "I have told Sarah of our conversation, but I think it would be best if I tell you without Chloe being present. What say we have a pint in the bar first, where we can talk in private? Sarah can keep Chloe happy, and we can join them at the table in a few minutes."

"Of course," replies Henry, more than a little mystified.

"Well," says Gee, as they wait for their pints to be drawn at the bar. "Where to start? I obviously tip toed round the subject of you and her at first, but then suddenly, an amazing thing happened. Without actually cutting to the chase, Mum for no apparent reason began to cry inconsolably. It took several minutes for her to compose herself, before I managed to ask her whatever the matter was.

"Here I will try to tell you in as many exact words as possible, what she said. She began by saying, 'Oh, Gee, I have been so very, very, silly. You see I wasn't quite honest with you when I asked you to follow Henry. Although I was indeed worried about him and how he would get on, on his own, after I told him to leave, the real reason was quite different.

'Some ten days before we parted, I had the usual customary three year letter from the breast clinic, saying that it was time for me to have a mammary examination. All very usual, you might think. But not so, in this particular instance.

'So I went and I didn't hear anything further from them, and so assumed, quite erroneously that everything was OK. It came as a huge blow when I received a letter from them saying that they would like me to go back for further tests. I was absolutely terrified. Not only for myself, but also because I remembered straight away that Henry's first wife, Isabel, died from breast cancer, and that he had been with her right through the process, caring for her until the end. I also knew from the way that he talked about it, of the suffering he had endured as well.

'It was at this moment that I made my unforgivable error. Instead of waiting and saying nothing to Henry (or anyone else for that matter) until I had been able to establish the extent of the problem, I panicked completely, and told Henry to leave, because I didn't feel the same way about him anymore. In fact, as you probably realise from this conversation, nothing could have been any further from the truth. Henry has meant so much to me over the last few months, and I have, through my own foolishness, destroyed our relationship, which can never be corrected.

'The irony of the situation is of course, that after a couple of more visits to the clinic and the consultant, my worst fears, came to nought, and I was given a clean bill of health. So my sacrifice, if you like, was in vain."

As he continues, Gee says, "So there, in a nutshell, you have it Henry. Mum was trying to spare you, quite unnecessarily of course, because she feared that she had breast cancer. I spent ages on the phone, trying to allay her fears that she had lost you, explaining everything that we had done and discussed. But, here comes the rub Henry, old chap; because she feels so ashamed at the way she treated you, she is finding it almost impossible to speak to you. She is frightened that your relationship has been damaged irretrievably, and not only can't bring herself to contact you and apologise, fearing your rebuke, but she fears you contacting her for the very same reason. No matter how hard I tried Henry, I couldn't get her to take the initiative. The only thing that I can suggest you do is to go and see her. But don't contact her first and give her the chance to be out when you call. Just go, that's my advice Henry, for what it's worth."

Henry has been listening to Gee's monologue in a state of shock, barely able to believe his ears. His first reaction is a huge feeling of relief and elation as he realises for the first time that Kate's feelings for him haven't changed. But as Gee had continued he is aware that his problems are not yet over. His major problem is now how to convince Kate that he understands why she did what she did, and that he feels no animosity towards her, because of it.

As Gee finishes, Henry fires a salvo of questions at him, only to see Gee wave them away, saying, "I'm sorry Henry, I've told you all that I know. Now let's go and have dinner, I'm famished."

Henry readily agrees, apologising and thanking the younger man for his help. The discussion has been very encouraging to him, but he can't help feeling about the quandary that Kate must have been in. What a terrible decision to be faced with. Although Henry knew that if Kate had developed breast cancer, he would have supported her and done whatever was necessary to help her overcome the disease. Medical progress has advanced in leaps and bounds even in the few years since Isabel's death.

As they return to the table, where Sarah and Chloe are waiting for them, Henry sees Sarah smiling, as she says, "Good news, eh Henry, I am so pleased for you. But you still have to overcome her feeling of shame and fear of rejection. However I'm sure you can reassure her and convince her that you understand. After all, she thought that she was doing the right thing for you."

"Yes, I agree, but I just wish that she had included me, after all, that is what relationships are meant to be about."

"Oh, I think that you have to look back further to Kate's first marriage, and the terrible experiences she endured. It taught her to stand on her own two feet. Then, after many years she met you, and you were like a breath of fresh air. Can you imagine how she must have felt when she heard from the breast clinic, and realised what it meant to the both of you. Although she was completely wrong not to talk to you when it happened, you can surely see how brave she was to finish with you."

"Of course I am delighted to find out the real reason why she asked me to leave." replies Henry, "But I have an added complication now. You see my son, Richard, has asked me to go to Australia for a break. I think that he was becoming concerned for me, probably because my daughter Penny has kept him up to date with events. In fact he has paid for my air ticket, so I have no other alternative than to go. I leave next Monday, the twenty-second. What this means of course is that if I can't resolve things between Kate and myself, I will not be able to do so until after I return from

Australia, and I don't really want to leave things until then.

At this point in the conversation, Chloe, who is sat in a high chair, exclaims, "Mummy, when are we going to eat, I am so huuungry." Ordering hurriedly to appease Chloe, the conversation carefully ignores any further reference to Kate and Henry, but concentrates mostly on Gee's studio and how he wants to develop it.

Sarah also shows her interest, and Henry quickly realises that they are a strong working partnership and ideas are bandied about. It reminds Henry of his working life when all the creative people in the studio, would get together for 'brain storming sessions' to overcome specific design problems. Brand managers would also have input, based on the fact that they had immediate interface with clients, and therefore knew them better than anyone else. Henry remembers with affection, how useful these sessions were, in building relationships, not only with clients, but also between employees.

As the conversation progresses, Henry chips in with one or two suggestions of his own, which are both carefully considered by Gee and Sarah.

Henry's input suddenly reminds Gee of the work that Henry has done for David, and says, "I went over to Dorchester a few days ago and had a look at the Design Studio. David showed me the new equipment and the systems that you had installed, which has improved both efficiency and quality of the product. In fact, every time I asked a question of either David or the other staff, all I got was, 'Henry says that we have to do it this way.' Your presence is still very much there Henry. David can't speak highly enough of you and the contribution that you have made.

"The employees were also positive. I think that your suggestion to get Malcolm to learn the computer programmes and promote him to studio manager was inspired. He has taken to it like a duck to water, in the best possible way. He supports the other staff, helping them when they dry up of ideas, jollies them along when they are low. They seem to all love him, although your name was spoken reverently as well."

Like all good things, the meal eventually comes to an end, and it is time for Gee and his family to leave. Henry finds himself panicking at the thought, prolonging the moment for as long as he can. Will he ever see these lovely people again, who he has grown to like and respect.

Henry pays the bill, and as they prepare to leave, Chloe comes up to him and says, "Bye, bye, Henry, when are you coming to see us, so I can show you Teddy and his friends?"

To which he can only reply, "Soon, I hope."

Gee and Sarah embrace him in turn, she whispering in his ear, "Faint heart never... well, you know Henry. I look forward to seeing you again very soon. We all love you, most of all Kate."

Henry feels himself welling up, and quickly says his goodbyes before he breaks down.

After they have left, he feels more desolate than ever. In an effort to pull himself together he decides to stroll once again around Bridport, and as he does so he finds places that he has never explored before. This is the thing that he finds so intriguing about this lovely Georgian town. It is like a looking for treasure. Between nearly every shop window there are alleyways which need to be explored. These only lead him on to yet more small paths, which fork suddenly, leaving him not knowing which way to go. He passes second hand shops, which lure him in to their dark interiors, where he is enthralled at the variety of contents. A pair of brass second hand postal scales, or a box of miscellaneous tools, or jewellery, with yet more furniture of every size and description.

Before he knows it, the afternoon has passed in no time at all, so he retraces his steps and returns to the hotel, where he goes to his room to rationalise what steps he needs to take during the next few days.

He is excited at the thought that he might see Kate again very soon. This must surely be his first step if he is to fly to Australia on the next Monday. Anyway, he can't possibly leave it until he returns. No, tomorrow it must be, he thinks. Strike while the iron is hot, that's what they say, isn't it?

However, along with his excitement, there is a seed of doubt. How will she greet me? The indecision only makes him want to hurry the process, to find out once and for all if her feelings for him are still as strong as his are for her.

THE BUS PASS

I will catch the early bus to Dorchester in the morning, and then get the next one that goes through Goderston and hope that she is home, thinks Henry. *I dare not leave seeing her any longer, because of the need to be home by the weekend. But if we can patch up our differences tomorrow, then when I return from Oz, we can hopefully start afresh.*

He can see no further than meeting Kate again, and decides to let the dice fall where they may after he has seen her. The remainder of the day passes slowly, his emotions at fever pitch. He spends the rest of the day in the bar, drinking more than his usual quota, in an effort to make the time pass more quickly.

CHAPTER 32

Goderston

Wednesday 17 July

Rising early the next morning, having slept fitfully, his mind full of images of Kate, he feels drained and tired. At the same time he is excited and can't wait to catch the bus to Dorchester. Leaving Bridport, he takes a final last look as the bus passes through the town, wondering if he will pass this way again. The journey only takes half an hour before arriving at Dorchester, where he boards the bus that will take him to Goderston.

By the time he reaches the village it is half past ten, and as he disembarks he can feel his heart racing in his chest. His mouth is dry and he feels light headed as he makes his way over the stream to Kate's cottage. Not stopping, fearing if he does so, he will not have the courage to go any farther, he makes his way up the front path and raps on the door. There is total silence, apart from the mallard ducks, murmuring their quacks to each other on the stream. He waits several seconds, before knocking on the door again, a process that he repeats several more times before acknowledging that Kate is not at home.

As the realisation hits him, Henry is distraught, not knowing what to do next, but just as he is about to leave he hears a soft cough behind him, and Megan's voice saying, "Oh, it's you Henry, I heard Kate's door being knocked and I thought that I had best see who it was making such a racket," and then in a more welcoming tone, "It's lovely to see you again. Kate said that you might be calling again soon, and if you did, that I was to tell you that she has had to go away for a week or so."

Henry hopes and dreams are shattered in the brief moment that it took Megan to make her speech. Then gathering his thoughts,

THE BUS PASS

Henry says, "But where has she gone? I have to leave to go to Australia next Tuesday, and I want desperately to talk to her, before I go."

He doesn't know if Kate has told Megan the reasons why Kate and he parted, and is loath to ask her, but he has no need to worry, as she says softly to him, "I never knew why Kate and you parted, Henry. She wouldn't talk about it, but I knew that something big was troubling her. You don't get to be best friends, the way that she and I have without picking up the vibes, but it wasn't until two days ago that she finally confided in me, about her health scare. She was in tears when she told me and explained why she told you to leave, but, and here Megan stops for a few seconds, trying to find the right words.

"I can state categorically that her feelings for you have never changed. She wouldn't tell me where she was going, but I think that she just needs to be alone for a while. Give her whatever time she needs Henry and don't worry, she will be there for you when you get back from Australia I'm sure.

"Now, why don't you come round to my place and have a cuppa and a chat, and you can tell me where you have been since you left," she finishes.

The recent events have left Henry completely drained, after finally managing to make the effort to get here, despite being unsure how he would be received, and fearing rejection. He finds that he is shaking, presumably from the shock of the morning's experiences, and is glad to accept Megan's offer which will give him time to relax and compose himself.

Once he has sat down with a large cup of tea and one of Megan's homemade scones, he begins to feel much better and after more encouragement from Megan and Charlie, who has now appeared from his garden, he regales them with stories of his travels since he left. They are enthralled as he continues, only stopping him when he tells them of meeting Gee, and how he eventually finds out that he is, in fact, Geoffrey, Kate's son.

"Yes, Kate told me about that, when she eventually confessed. I was amazed, but on reflection it made me realise just how concerned for you she was when you left."

As he finishes narrating his exploits, the conversation turns to what Henry's next move will be.

"I don't really know now. I was hoping to see Kate today and if things were OK between us, to hopefully stay here until the weekend. In which case, I could leave on Friday or Saturday in time to get home in enough time to see Penny, Mark and the boys before I have to leave for Australia. As it looks now that Kate won't be home by that time, I think that I must make my way back, and catch up with her when I return. However, I think that I would like to stay until tomorrow, so that I can catch up with all the local gossip. By sheer chance I met Toby and Avril in Exeter when I was making my way back to Bridport, so I'll see if they have a spare room at the pub for tonight."

Then turning to Megan and Charlie, "Look, I would be honoured if you would join me at the Mucky Duck tonight for a meal, at my expense of course." Then, thinking aloud, "That would leave me Thursday and Friday to visit Salisbury, and perhaps Stonehenge or Avebury before I go home."

"Thank you Henry that would be lovely," replies Charlie, before Megan can answer. "There is a darts match on tonight, so most of the usual suspects will be there."

As he makes his way across the common, Henry is buoyed at the thought of being here, even though he has not managed to see Kate. He realises also that this beautiful little village has had its influence on him more than he ever realised.

He loves the feeling, almost of intimacy, that living here gives him. Its people are friendly, welcoming and supportive, while the village itself nourishes his very being, and beyond it lies open countryside where he has spent days exploring and walking. It is so much quieter, cleaner and comforting, than the urban living that he has experienced up until now.

Toby looks up from the bar as he enters, a huge grin slowly lighting up his face as he sees who it is.

"Henry my old friend, I am so pleased that you managed to get here before you return home. How long are you staying? Have you seen Kate, because I know she is expecting you."

"Well to answer you in the order that you asked Toby, I am

staying until tomorrow and you are the one who can make that possible if you have a room, and no, I haven't seen Kate, for the very good reason that she has gone away for a few days, where I know not, do you?"

Toby stands, looking puzzled for a moment, before, "I am sorry Henry, but I have no idea where she's gone. She was in here a couple of nights ago with Charlie and Megan, but there was no mention of her going anywhere. As for a room, you can have your old one back for tonight."

"That's great, so give me a pint and have whatever you are having yourself, after which I will go up and send one or two urgent messages."

The two of them spend the next hour talking. Henry telling Toby about his visit to Gee, and the shock he had when he realised that he was Kate's son. Toby responds in a similar fashion as other people who Henry had related this tale to, saying that he thought that this was a good indicator of Kate's feelings for him.

Once upstairs, Henry pulls out his laptop, intending to send Kate an email. To his absolute amazement when he looks, he sees that she has already sent one to him.

With feelings between trepidation and hope, Henry scans Kate's message quickly.

My dearest Henry,

You will have heard by now from Gee the real reason, rather than those that I told you and the things that I did, when I asked you to leave. I was mortified when I received the results from the breast clinic telling me that there was no evidence of the disease. I don't mean that I was unhappy that I hadn't got breast cancer. Rather that I had lost you because I panicked unnecessarily.

If I had waited and kept things to myself until I got the final result things would have remained fantastic between us, just as they had always been. As you have probably realized by now, I am finding it very difficult to come to terms with myself. Through my own foolishness I have jeopardized our relationship and your love, something that has meant more to me than I can say.

All that I can do is ask your forgiveness and hope that one day we can be together again.

I am sorry too, for the subterfuge regarding getting Gee to keep an eye on you on your travels, but I was fearful what you might do after you left. Or rather I was sorry that you found out. But I am sure that you will understand when you realise that I did it for all the right reasons. I was concerned for your welfare because I still loved/ love you.

Oh, Henry, I am so sorry for all the pain that I have caused you. I feel dreadful and am finding it difficult to face the future, so I have decided to get away somewhere for a few days, so that hopefully I can come to terms with it all.

I don't know where I am going to go, but I will just let the car guide me.

Finally my love (I hope that I can still call you that), I understand from Gee that you are leaving to visit Australia on the 22nd, so it is not likely that we will be able to see one another before then. However, please be assured that if you still want me to, I will be waiting for you on your return. Please believe me when I tell you that I love you and always have, but I will understand if you don't want, or feel able for us to get together again. I will understand, but never forgive myself for making you feel that way.

Please, please, please contact me when you get back,

Yours, now and always,

Kate.

By the time Henry finishes reading Kate's message, he is in floods of tears. They run, unchallenged and uncontrollably down his face, until he has to use a tissue to stop the flow.

Here it is then, in black and white. Kate's real reason for taking the action that she did. He desperately wants to reply straight away, but on reflection, decides to do it later on, after he has given it more consideration. The last thing that he wants is to accidently say the wrong thing and upset her even more. No, he needs to get it right.

Henry drafts out a number of replies, none of which he finds acceptable, which only frustrates him more. Eventually he achieves a draft that he thinks is appropriate.

THE BUS PASS

My dearest Kate,

Before you go any further, let me assure you that you have done nothing to reproach yourself for. I understand perfectly why you took the action that you did and for the reasons that you have explained.

I would only say that you thought that you were doing the right thing, i.e. to protect me from your suffering, because I had already gone through the process once with Isabel. However, you obviously misunderstood the depth of my love for you, because it is not possible to differentiate between one and the other. Let me put it another way. I love you too much to lose you prematurely, and by sending me away, that is what you did.

I am beyond grateful that your diagnosis was negative, but regardless, I would have continued to stay to love and care for you whatever the result might have been, because that's life, and there is nothing that we can do about it. Please don't take this as a criticism, because I know beyond any doubt that you acted as you did for all the right reasons, and I love you even more for that.

Just at the moment I am depressed, because I cannot manage to see you before I leave for Australia. But Richard has paid and arranged for me to pick up my ticket, so I have very little option than to go. I recognize how much he cares, even though, right at this moment I would rather be here with you. My love, you never have any need to doubt my love for you, so I will be knocking at your door the minute I get back. But perhaps we could continue to email each other while I am away. It's not perfect, but better than not being in touch at all. What do you think?

I understand also why you feel the need to get away to "Come to terms." with yourself, but I can assure you that it is not necessary for you to suffer any pangs of guilt, or whatever else, because my love for you is unconditional.

Oh, by the way, I called in to see you today on my way home. I saw Megan and she explained that you had gone away, and why.

In the end, I decided to stay overnight at the Mucky Duck, so I invited her and Charlie over for a meal and a pint this evening. The place won't feel the same without you, but it will bring back memories of you, which will make me feel happy.

Please keep in touch while I am away. It will make the time go faster,

Forever yours,

Henry.

He reads it through one more time before pressing the send button, hoping beyond hope that he has judged the tenor of it right.

For the first time since he left Kate, Henry feels happiness within him that will not go away, despite niggling doubts that try to intrude. He continues to feel this warm glow comforting him as he makes his way downstairs to the dining room, where Charlie and Megan are waiting.

As they are eating, Henry tells them of the message that he has received from Kate, which pleases them both hugely, Megan saying, "There, I told you so Henry. Now just make sure that you come back to see us as soon as you get back from Australia." The evening continues with a darts match, which the three of them participate in, albeit not very well. None of them being particularly good at it, or rather neither Charlie nor Megan because they have not played very much, or, in Henry's case, because he has imbibed more than usual, which he consoles himself is because he is more relaxed after receiving Kate's message.

Later, Toby comes out to play darts with them, and is joined by Graham 'Milky' Way. Much laughter ensues as Toby, who is an excellent darts player, challenges all comers to a game at fifty pence each, winner takes all. To make it more even, Toby says that he will play left handed to give them all a chance.

However, this doesn't seem to make any difference at all, as Toby swiftly finishes well before any of the others. But surprisingly for him, Toby laughs and takes the micky out of them. It is so unlike Toby to brag and swagger, until Percy, one of the onlookers, gives the game away, saying, "Didn't you know? Toby's left handed."

"You old bugger," Megan cries, which is taken up by the rest of them, which only makes Toby burst into more fits of laughter before refunding all their wagers to them.

Charlie and Megan take their leave, telling Henry one last time to return as soon as he can. Deciding to have a final whisky for the road, Henry makes his way to bed, feeling slightly inebriated, but very happy.

CHAPTER 33

Blandford Forum

Thursday 18 July

Rising early, and after saying his goodbyes to Toby and Avril, Henry catches the bus into Dorchester, ready for the next step of his journey. To get to Salisbury, he will have to do the reverse journey to that he had taken on the very first day of his travels. This means that the first leg will be from Dorchester to Blandford Forum.

Taking one step at a time he catches the bus. It is only after a short while that it has been travelling, that he remembers with a start, that he has forgotten to go to the design studio to see David. He is full of contrition for this lapse, but consoles himself that he will be seeing him again in the not too distant future.

It is after midday by the time that the bus pulls into Blandford and, disembarking, Henry remembers Bill Whelan, the landlord of the Jack the Lad, telling him to be sure to visit on his way home. Deciding that he has ample time, he determines to stay over for the night, before moving on the following day to Salisbury. So Henry makes his way back to the first place that he stayed at, when starting on his journey. By the time he reaches his destination it is now midday and, as he enters, the first person he sees is Norman, or Sparky, as he is known locally.

"Well, I'll be blowed, if it ain't our old mucker Henry," and then in a loud voice, "Heh Bill, come and have a gander at who's just arrived."

Almost as soon as Sparky has spoken, Bill appears from behind the bar counter, a huge smile on his ruddy face. "Oh. It's good to see you again Henry," and then hesitatingly, "But what are you doing here? I thought that you and Kate were an item, if you know what I mean. The only time that I expected to see you again was here, playing skittles or darts for the White Swan, or there, as one of their team."

Not wanting to divulge too much of his personal life, Henry replies "Well Bill, my son Richard, who is in Australia, recently asked me to go and see him. In fact he made it nearly impossible for me not to go, because he has paid and arranged a ticket for me. Anyway I want to go, because I haven't seen him or his family for several years. Unfortunately it has come at a difficult time for me, but these things happen, so there we are." He ends by shrugging his shoulders to emphasise the point. "But I shall be back shortly. You can't get rid of me that easily, my old friend."

"I think that is a fantastic thing to do. He must think a lot of his old Dad, eh Henry? Now come and have a drink and see the lads. There are only a couple of them in at the moment, but they will all be here tonight. Will you be staying?"

"You bet. I wouldn't miss it for all the tea in China," replies Henry, entering the bar, where he is immediately welcomed by Fred 'King' Cole, Derek and Sparky. Much back slapping and leg pulling ensues, while foaming pints of Badgers bitter are consumed, until eventually the others leave, to resume their various jobs.

After eating a ploughman's cheese salad, Henry makes his way to his room, where he quickly takes out his Lap Top computer, hoping desperately that Kate has replied to his message of the previous day.

He is delighted as he reads.

My dearest Henry,

I was so relieved to get your email, explaining that you understood the actions that I took. You must know by now how I really feel about you. When I read that, it felt as though a great weight had been lifted off of me.

Yes, it is a great shame that we can't see each other for a while (just how long do you think that you will stay in Australia), but I imagine that it will be for at least three weeks, because of the financial cost that Richard has made. Apart from the fact that you will obviously want to catch up with them all. It must be terrible to have grandchildren so far away and not be able to watch them grow and develop. Each time that you see them, must be like meeting them for the first time, although I know that you Skype them regularly.

I was in Totnes yesterday. After Gee told me of both of your experiences I felt that I had better see for myself. It was wonderful. In the afternoon I went to Dartmouth, which was even more beautiful if that is possible. I am moving on today. Where to, I hear you ask? Well I have something in mind so watch this space.

Well I had best go now my love. After receiving your email, I am feeling so much better. One final thing. You need to be sure that when, or if we get back together, you will be able to cope with not seeing your family in Australia very often. I could not bear it if, after some time has elapsed, that you might feel that I was holding you back from seeing them. Of course, you, or we could go regularly to see them, but you need to decide if that would be enough.

Anyway, we can talk about it when you return. I am sure that nothing is insurmountable that a good discussion cannot resolve.

Take care of yourself Henry, and please write soon.

All my love,

Kate.

Henry feels that he is enveloped in a warm glow as he finishes reading Kate's missive. Suddenly, all is right with the world, because he knows without any reservations, where he wants to be and who with, for the rest of his life.

Thinking carefully, so that his reply cannot be misconstrued in any way, he opens a new message.

My dearest Kate,

I can't tell you what a surprise it was to see that you were in Totnes. I feel envious because I am not there, but even more so, because you are.

Regarding the concerns that you have regarding my family in Australia, I would ask you please not to worry about them. As I tried to tell you when I left, as far as I am concerned, my feelings for you transcend all others.

Obviously, that is not to say that my family is not very important to me, of course they are, and I have every intention of keeping in touch and visiting them as often as possible. But I think that this is in accordance with your feelings as well, isn't it?

Your message has raised my spirits too (and my testosterone) and I cannot wait for the day that I return. I shouldn't be wishing my life away, but that is how I feel now.

I am in Blandford Forum today, staying at the Jack the Lad pub, with Bill Whelan overnight. If you remember they play the Mucky Duck at darts and skittles. They are a lovely bunch of lads. Good company too.

I will be moving on to Salisbury tomorrow, where I will probably stay overnight, if I can find somewhere suitable. After that I will make my way home to Wycombe on Saturday. Then I will go and see Penny and Mark on Sunday, before I leave Good Old Blighty on Monday.

Take care my love, and remember that I am thinking of you always,

Love,

Henry.

Henry's evening with the regulars is a roaring success now that normal service has been resumed with Kate. He is so relaxed as he sups a few pints over the course of the evening, with Milky, Abbott, Cliff, Red Rum, Scruffy and Bunter, who are all ensconced in the bar, playing darts, or cards, or pool.

The conversation as usual takes in football, politics and the kids of today. Cliff, seeing an opportunity, says, "Well, my youngster Tony made me laugh the other day. He's coming up fifteen, and he was just getting ready for school, when my wife took one look at him and said, 'You are not going out like that my boy, with your shirt hanging out over your trousers, and your tie all skewwhiff.' As she finishes admonishing him, she advances across the room and proceeds to tuck his shirt in and straighten his tie in a vigorous fashion.

'There, that's better,' she exclaims, before walking away.

"Tony, speaking in a quiet voice that she can't hear, says to her disappearing back, but within earshot of Cliff, 'Who the hell does she think she is?' before smiling to himself as he notices his father watching him, content that he has made a suitable riposte.

The Abbott is the next to chip in, saying, "Last year, about November time, my youngster Wills, who is nine years old, started to prepare his list of things that he wanted for Christmas. This list evolved over several weeks, until eventually my wife had to talk to him about it, saying that she thought that he should now consider the list as complete and that he should not add any more to it. This seemed to work for a while, until my wife spotted him adding more items to his list, and upon questioning him about he said, 'Oh yes Mum, but my list is now complete.' He just didn't get, or didn't want to get the concept of 'complete'

"Nothing happened for a while, until the day in fact that we were Christmas shopping and we went into a large toy store in Salisbury. The reason we went into this particular shop was to buy gifts for other family members' children, not for our own.

"Big mistake! We hadn't been in there very long before Wills spotted something that he would like. I think it was a Lego toy. Boy, did he give us grief, until suddenly my wife realised that this particular toy was not on his list. By now, my boy was in a bit of a state, so without further ado my wife got hold of his hand and proceeded to drag him out of the shop. The funniest thing was as he was being dragged kicking and screaming, he managed one last plea to anyone who would listen, as he shouted repeatedly, 'Get me the Lego, and then my list is complete.'"

Soon, the rest of them are all clamouring to tell their own experiences of their children, each one trying to outdo the other, and the room is alive with laughter.

Henry is sad when the evening draws to its close, and the others start to leave, each one shaking his hand and telling him to return as soon as. He has grown to like and enjoy these warm and friendly peoples company, who have taken him in as one of their own.

Rising early the next morning, and after saying his farewells to Bill and Betty, he makes his way down the hill once again to the centre of the town in time to catch the bus to Salisbury, with their parting remark ringing in his ears.

"Don't be a stranger Henry."

CHAPTER 34
Salisbury

Salisbury will be the last place on his itinerary, before he returns back home to High Wycombe. The No. 184 Damory bus duly leaves Blandford from The Crown Hotel at eighteen minutes past ten, packed full of what Henry can only assume are locals, mostly older women, who all seem to know each other. It soon becomes apparent that they are all on the bus for the same purpose, namely to see a matinee performance of the play *Three Men in a Boat* at the Salisbury Playhouse Theatre.

Listening to their excited chatter, Henry realises that this is a fairly regular outing, and one that obviously has a great impact on their lives. Probably on a par, he thinks, to that when he goes to London to see a play, or a musical at the theatre.

The bus is full of their animated talk and laughter, and Henry begins to envy them, in a desultory fashion. The thought is no sooner there than it is mentally acted upon as Henry decides that he also will go to see the matinee performance. He has not considered what he intends to do when he gets to Salisbury, other than that he would like to have a look round the market on Saturday, i.e. tomorrow. The only other day that there is a market, is on a Tuesday, so tomorrow will be his only opportunity.

So, that's what he will do, he decides. But first he needs to find accommodation for the night. Once this has been achieved he can then try and get a booking for the theatre this afternoon. Then tomorrow he can have a look at the market, after which he could perhaps visit the Cathedral, if he still has any time left before catching a bus to Andover, the first stage of his final journey home.

Pulling up his laptop, intending to look for somewhere to stay for the night, he is pleasantly surprised to find another email from

THE BUS PASS

Kate, which reads:

Hi my dearest Henry,

I thought that I would bring you up to date with my travels. After Totnes, I decided Fowey would be my next port of call. Does that surprise you?

Oh Henry, what a lovely place it is. Just like you, I booked into Trudy's place and fell in love with both it and her. I can understand why you feel the way you do about it.

I can vaguely remember Angy and the Angels, but I was reminded vividly when she played a couple of her CDs for me. She is such a lovely unspoilt person.

I told her about us and how things have changed since you were last here and she was delighted for us and asked to be remembered to you. You obviously made a good impression.

What I can't understand is why I have never been to Fowey before. It makes me realise just why you started your pilgrimage in the first place. When you get back from Australia, I would like us to continue to visit other places on your list, just the way that you have. I am loving every minute of it. The only thing that would complete my happiness is if you were here with me.

I really don't know where I will head to next. I could stay here forever, but I may go to the Eden Project, after which I will probably return home.

Look after yourself my love. Please write soon,

Yours Always,

Kate.

As he reads her email, Henry's spirits are raised visibly, a fact that is made evident to the people around him as they observe the wide grin on his face, which has appeared for no apparent reason.

Pulling himself together, Henry starts to try and find somewhere to stay for the night, thinking that he needs time to consider his reply to Kate. After googling for somewhere suitable, he finds a vacancy at the New Inn, in New Street, which Henry notes from his research is just outside The Close, which is the oldest part of Salisbury. This is surrounded by the city wall and was built in the fourteenth century.

The Close contains the cathedral, the building of which was commenced in 1221 and completed in 1258. It was built on wooden faggots on a gravel bed, with foundations of only some eighteen inches. The Cathedral spire at 404 feet is the highest in the country.

Because of the extreme height of the tower and the very shallow foundations, it has moved several degrees from the perpendicular over the years, causing considerable maintenance to be carried out at various times to stop it from leaning any further.

But the thing that catches Henry's eye as he reads about the city is that the cathedral holds one of the four original copies of the Magna Carta, the document which carries King John's seal, and represents the earliest acknowledgment that future kings must seek approval from parliament (or its early equivalent) before proceeding with anything that might not be approved.

Never again from this date could the monarch ride roughshod over their subjects without seeking approval first from parliament. If he needed funds to fight wars, or for any other purpose, he first had to get permission from parliament.

The status quo has largely remained to this day. King Charles I did try to ignore it, maintaining that he was God's representative and claiming the Divine Right of Kings and as such could do as he liked without reference to anyone. The consequences of this for him were catastrophic, after he lost The English Civil War to Parliament, which was followed by the loss of his head by execution.

So the Magna Carta, Henry considers, is of immense interest and significance, and something therefore that he wants to see.

His reveries are interrupted as the bus arrives at the New Canal in Salisbury. Getting off he finds his way to New Street and the New Inn. Once in his room he decides to reply to Kate, and after running various scenarios through his mind, he begins:

Hello my love,

Thank you for your amazing email. It made me feel as if you are stalking me. In a nice way. Fancy you going to Fowey, not only that but to Trudy's as well.

You are right. She is the most lovely, completely natural person. How she has managed to stay that way after the life that she has led, speaks volumes of

THE BUS PASS

her temperament and nature.

Of course my life would be complete, and it would be fantastic to visit the other places together, just the two of us. I enjoyed those places that I visited, but with you by my side, I would everything that I could possibly want.

The next subject that I wanted to breach with you when we next meet, but that seems so far away right now that I feel impelled almost, to ask it right now, so please forgive me if I am moving thing on too quickly between us.

I don't know if you remember, but on the morning that I left you, I said, and I meant it, that I would be honoured if you would agree to marry me.

Let me clarify what I am trying to say, in my usual ham fisted manner, is that if you do not want to, or do not feel ready to, then that would be OK too. I would be equally happy to continue as we are.

I hope that I have not offended you my love. It's just that I want you to be happy whatever you decide, because when you are happy, so am I.. But I just think that it would be more difficult for you to throw me out again if we are married (joke).

Time seems to be flashing by this week. I have booked a room for tonight at the New Inn, in Salisbury. This afternoon I am going to The Salisbury Playhouse to see Thee Men in a Boat. In the morning I want to visit the large market, which is only here on Tuesdays and Saturdays. My final venue is The Cathedral, after which I will head home about tomorrow lunch time.

Saturday evening I am hoping to take Rob and Madge out to the local pub for a pie and a pint, (or several).

That only leaves Sunday for me to see Penny, Mark and the grandchildren, before I have to leave for the Airport on Monday. Where has the time gone? I am not ready in my mind to go to Australia yet. The thought of not seeing you for weeks is crushing, but I want you to know that I will be thinking of you every second that I am there.

I had best close now, but please let me know how you get on with your travels.

Yours Always,

Henry.

Finding his way to the Salisbury Playhouse, Henry buys a matinee ticket to see *Three Men in a Boat*.

The play is wonderful, so much so that Henry falls asleep, something that he has always considered a compliment to the production of any play, for making him be able to relax. He wakes just in time to see the conclusion of the play, before making his way out, feeling very happy and at one with the world.

After eating at the New Inn, he returns to his room and telephones his oldest friend Rob. Getting him up to speed with events since seeing him last he finally asks, "So you see Rob, I am off to Oz on Monday and am seeing Penny and Mark on Sunday, so I wondered if you and Madge were around on Saturday evening. I would like it very much if the two of you came to the pub for a splosh and nosh on me."

"Well my old mate," says Rob, holding his hand over the phone and shouting out to Madge. "Henry is asking if we would like to go to the pub tomorrow for a meal on him, before he leaves for Australia." Having received a suitable reply from her he replies, "That sounds a great idea Henry, but tell me again, are things are back on track with you and Kate again then?"

"Yes mate, it was all a misunderstanding," says Henry, who goes on to explain about Kate's breast cancer scare.

"Oh, that's great. It had to be something like that, because the two of you were so good together. Congratulations, I am very pleased for you my old mate. Does this mean the patter of tiny feet and sleepless nights?" says Rob, which has Henry laughing uproariously down the phone.

"I don't think so Rob, only if she gets me pregnant," he replies.

Saying their farewells, Henry hangs up, before finally emailing Penny, telling her of his plans and asking if they are available on Sunday, so that he can take them all out for lunch.

Realising that he has a full day ahead of him, Henry is up early, and after breakfasting he leaves the New Inn and quickly makes his way to Market Square where many stalls have already been set up and the vendors are selling their wares.

The market is diverse and fascinating, selling everything from fresh local fruit and vegetables to curtain fabric, carpets from

Egypt, bric-a-brac and antiques, to pictures and frames. There are stalls selling fast food of every persuasion, and all the while there is music blaring out from stalls selling CDs and DVDs. He wanders round, completely absorbed and fascinated by the bartering and bustle of it all, with traders calling out the virtues of their wares.

Looking at his watch, Henry is concerned to note that it is already half past ten. His bus to Andover, the next leg of his journey, leaves at five minutes past twelve, so if he wants to see the cathedral, he needs to go now.

Making his way to Cathedral Close, he goes through the High Street Gate and is met with the stunning sight of the cathedral, with its tall, pencil-shaped spire piercing the sky in front of him. Its stone is of a pale yellow hue, which catches the light from the sun's rays, giving it a golden glow.

Henry looks upwards trying to follow the route of the spire, only to find that it makes him dizzy and disorientated. He spends the next hour exploring the inside of this beautiful building, enjoying its quiet contemplative space, while wondering at the same time of the builder skills, who had assembled such a huge edifice with very little tools, over eight hundred years before. This is a fitting tribute indeed to their sheer bloody mindedness and allegiance to their God.

Asking an attendant, Henry is shown where the copy of Magna Carta is on display and spends twenty minutes examining it. There is also a translation next to it, because it was written in Latin.

CHAPTER 35

Home

Marvelling at what he has seen, Henry makes his way to Bus Stop N at Blue Boar Row in time to catch the No. 8 bus to Andover. Being tired after his hectic morning, Henry falls asleep until the bus pulls in at its destination at twenty eight minutes past one, where, after rubbing his eyes to get the sleep out of them, he hurriedly makes his way to get the No. 7 Stagecoach bus to Newbury, which leaves promptly at thirty five minutes past one.

When the bus arrives at Newbury at twenty-three minutes past two, Henry is once again under pressure for time, before he has to board a No. 1 Reading bus at twenty minutes to three, which gets to Friar Street at three fifty six. By now he is wishing that he had allowed himself more time, perhaps by not stopping over at Salisbury last night, but then reconsiders, recalling all the things that he has seen and done this morning.

He is now on the final leg of his journey as he boards the bus to High Wycombe and home.

As he alights at the bus station, he is delighted to be met by Rob. There is much back slapping and hand shaking as they get into Robs car for the final part of the jigsaw that is Henry's journey.

Arriving at his house, Henry is met by Madge, the other half of the double act that represents his closest and oldest friends.

"I have cleaned and polished all the rooms, washed your bedding, and Rob has given your car a service and a wash and brush up," says Madge, greeting him with a kiss. "The things we have to do to get a free meal."

Henry is at a loss for words, at the thoughtfulness of these two people who mean so much to him. Who have nurtured and supported him for so many years.

THE BUS PASS

"Right I will be round for you at half past seven, on the dot, so get your drinking caps on," says Henry.

As he enters the house, it seems smaller somehow than when he left it, and he feels in a strange way that he is looking at it for the very first time.

Then the realisation of why this is so, comes to him like a bolt from the blue. It's Isabel's magic touch, the touch that could transform their house into a home. Something that has been missing since she died. Only small things, like a bunch of flowers, or an indoor plant adding a touch of colour. Or a glass bowl bought from a stall on the market. Isabel had a happy knack of just making subtle adjustments that would make the house come alive.

It is something which Kate also shares. Her house also bears the light touch that makes so much difference to the indefinable feel of the place. Perhaps it is a female attribute, a throwback to the time when men were hunters and gatherers, while the women stayed behind to cook and make the home comfortable for the returning men.

Suddenly, Henry is forced to consider that since Isabel's death, he has shown no interest in the house, apart from the obvious reason that it is a place for him to live. Oh, he has decorated as and when necessary, but in most other respects it has been a sort of mausoleum to Isabel's memory, but without her gentle nuances of touch. He has changed very little of any significance, and in truth cannot begin to know how.

The evening at The Kings Head with his friends is an unqualified success, spent eating, which is closely followed by drinking large quantities of alcohol. But by far the largest amount of time is spent on catching up with each other's gossip.

"Come on Henry!" exclaims Rob eventually. "I know that things have improved between Kate and you, because Penny emails us, but she doesn't tell us how or why. When I left you it in Cornwall, it didn't seem possible that the two of you would get back together again."

Henry pauses, before relating all that has happened. As he continues, Rob and Madge have little doubt that he is happy for the very first time since Isabel died.

"Well good for you. No, good for both of you," says Rob. "Does this mean that you will be getting married? Although these days it doesn't seem to matter one way or the other."

"I hope so," says Henry quietly. "I have asked her, but she needs to take time to think about it, although she is happy if we just live together. I only asked her, so that she could see that I was serious. But if she doesn't want to, that's OK too. But the main reason that I asked you out tonight was to assure you that whatever happens, I hope that we can still be friends and keep in touch. I also know that Kate feels the same way. We haven't discussed where we will live yet, but I hope that it will be at her house in Goderston. If you remember Rob, we all loved Dorset when we went on our 'fishing trips' all those years ago, you in fact as much as me. So if it happens that way, you will both be welcome at any time."

"Thank you my old mate, of course we will keep in touch. You just try and get rid of us," declares Rob. "Now come on let's have a game of crib, so that I can beat you again."

Henry once again feels comfortable in the presence of his oldest friends, and the evening passes as Rob regales them with more of his stock of jokes and anecdotes. Both Henry and Rob know that it's time to go home, by the infallible method they use to judge these things, as they hear Madge suddenly say, "Oh Rob, I think that wine has gone to my legs again."

Supporting her between them, they make their way home as they have done so many times in the past.

They part with Rob saying, "Have a great time in Australia and give Richard and his family our love," and finally, "Remember, don't be a stranger."

Henry is at Penny's early, eager to see all the family and catch up with their news. As he draws up in his car they all rush out to greet him. "Hi Dad, it's so lovely to see you. Come on in. Mind out boys, stop playing with that ball, before you knock your granddad over."

They all bustle inside, Mark getting beers for the two of them and wine for Penny, while Joshua and Oliver rush outside into the garden to play football.

"Well come on, don't keep us in suspense Dad, how are things between Kate and you?" says Penny. "I know that things have improved because she texted me the other day and told me all about it. Thinking about it afterwards I could see how it happened, and I realised how brave she had been to do what she did. Oh I know with hindsight that she should have waited but unfortunately none of us is blessed with hindsight."

"Everything is going fantastically well you will be pleased to know. In fact the only thing slowing things down is that I am going to Australia for a few weeks, so consequently I won't be able to see her. Never mind, we will still be able to keep in contact on a daily basis, which is something. Now what about you two, how are things. Have you heard any more about going to Australia?"

Penny looks at her father, a smile spreading slowly across her beautiful mouth, her eyes crinkling with excitement and pleasure.

"It's strange that you should ask that Dad, because while you and I were away on the Isles of Scilly, I had time to reappraise and consider my and Mark's lifestyle. I never mentioned it to you at the time because I wanted to discuss it first with Mark.

"To tell you the truth, I don't think that the Australia move will happen, in fact, if it were to transpire, we have talked it over between us, and agreed that we will not be going. After a lot of thought, Mark and I have agreed that I should start up my own interior design company, working from home. I have good contacts in the industry, and would like to develop my own designs from start to finish. The thought excites me. I wouldn't need a large amount of capital, because I could work from home, using the study. The way I see it, is that I do the initial designs and use outside companies who specialise in the building side of it. I would agree costs with them and the client, after which they would deal directly with the client, so that I would not have any major costs. But there is another factor which makes it possible now, because Mark was offered a significant promotion last week, leading a team doing research on a new drug, which could be a break through into Alzheimer's."

"Yes," interrupts Mark, "it's a fantastic opportunity and will hopefully make a difference to people already suffering from it, or even better, reducing the chances of people developing it in the first place. If you remember, I lost my mother to it, and by that I mean that although she only died seven years ago, she was lost to the family some ten years before that. It was a terrible thing to stand helplessly by and watch, without being able to do anything about. So, even though it's too late to help her, hopefully I will be able to help others in the future."

"Congratulations, the two of you," says Henry, genuinely meaning every word, while a small part of him takes happiness from the thought that he will still be able to see them regularly.

Their discussion is interrupted as Joshua and Oliver burst into the room saying, "Granddad, come and play football with us, you can be Liverpool and we will be Manchester United."

Henry is bundled, protesting, outside by the two boys, who put him in goal at the far end of the lawn, before peppering him with shots, amid many shouts of "Goal!" Thinking about it, he wonders how he could possibly score when he was in the only goal, but this is a mere technicality to the boys, as they continue blasting shots at him.

He is saved eventually, as the boys become tired and Mark comes out saying, "Come on you lot, we'd better get going if we are to get to the restaurant in time." Henry has arranged for them all to go to Frankie and Bennie's for lunch, as a treat for the boys, knowing that they love the type of food (with ice cream coming high on the list).

Once ensconced, Penny says rather mysteriously, with a twinkle in her eye, "I think that you are going to enjoy Australia more than you realise Dad, particularly as you know now that all is well between you and Kate. Richard is already planning places for you to go, and things for you to do. Mark and I have been talking it over and we will probably go out next year, during the school holidays. Why don't you and Kate come with us, so that we can all be together?"

Henry is consumed with love for his daughter and her thoughtfulness, and replies in an emotional voice, "I think that is a fantastic idea love. I will ask Kate next time we speak."

Returning after lunch, the afternoon is spent in Penny and Mark's garden, and with the sun high in the heavens, they sit under the awning avoiding the direct heat, but enjoying the gentle breeze that wafts around them. Conversation continues in a desultory fashion, but a comfortable silence is the major contributor. That is until the boys suddenly demand that Granddad joins them in a game of hide and seek, telling him to close his eyes and count to one hundred before he starts to try and find them.

But the game is not much of a challenge, because as soon as Henry gets anywhere near where they are hiding, they give the game away by giggling excitedly. Suddenly unable to stand the tension any longer, they burst forth from their hiding places and instead of rushing away, throw their selves at him, almost hysterical with laughter and excitement. Henry tickles them mercilessly, until they collapse in a heap on the grass, crying, "Again Granddad, again."

With evening approaching, Henry takes leave of them, saying that he still has some packing to do. Emotional hugs are the order of the day, with Penny saying once again, "Enjoy your trip and give them all our love. Take it from me, as one who knows, that you will have a wonderful time. We will see you when you get back, but keep us up to date by email."

So Henry drives home with the sound of their laughter and good wishes ringing in his ears.

CHAPTER 36

Australia Bound

Rob and Madge have offered to take Henry to Heathrow. His flight's time of take-off is at ten to one, but he needs to get there in plenty of time to check in, after which he intends to get perfume for Janet and a bottle of malt whisky for Richard. Hopefully he can find a couple of tops for the grandchildren and some chocolate.

Half past eight is the time agreed that they would leave, so Henry is all packed and ready, and a little surprised when nine o'clock comes and there is no sign of his neighbours. Worrying that something dreadful has happened to them, he decides to go next door to investigate.

He is met at the door by Madge who is obviously upset. When he asks her why, she invites him into the kitchen, where he is faced by a room full of foaming suds. On looking closer he can see that the source of this appears to be from the dishwasher, which is next to the sink and is open. The concentration of foam seems to be emanating from here and he wonders what on earth can have been the cause of it.

"Whatever caused this Madge, I have never seen anything like it!" exclaims Henry, not a little alarmed to say the least, as he fights his way across the room to get closer to the source of the problem.

"Well it's my own fault, you see I had several bowls that needed washing, and so I put washing up liquid in them and then forgot to do anything about them. I suddenly noticed the time and realising that we were late, I put them into the dishwasher and turned it on without thinking. The result is what you can see now. I have already run the dishwasher a couple of times hoping to get rid of the foam, but it seems to be getting worse, if anything."

Just as she finishes speaking, Rob enters the room obviously trying to stifle a laugh, but his eyes give the game away.

"Don't you start Rob," says Madge exasperatingly. "I have just about had enough for one day."

"Sorry love," says Rob consolingly. "But you have to admit that it's funny. Then turning to Henry, "She has had a mare of a time just lately. We had just gone to bed last night. I was reading my book while Madge was doing a crossword. Everything was going fine, until I suddenly realised that Madge had dropped off to sleep. The trouble was that she still had hold of her pen, which had leaked onto the duvet cover. It made a hell of a mess, and everything that she tried to do to get the marks out just made it worse, so it looks as if we will have to get a new duvet cover. Anyway you don't want to hear all of our troubles. Come on, let's get your luggage into the boot of my car, we'll sort it out when we get back."

Heathrow is busy as they arrive at the terminal when Rob and Madge drop him off at ten o'clock. Hurriedly saying farewell, with their good wishes, Henry hurries inside to collect his ticket at the British Airways desk and then check in.

He is so busy that he doesn't have time to consider how he feels, which, on reflection he is grateful for. The next two hours to take off pass quickly, as he shops for the gifts that he wants to take to Richard's family. Then, not liking airline food, he decides to have a meal at one of the restaurants, before he has to go to the gate in preparation for his flight.

The first leg of his journey is from London to Singapore, where there will be a stopover for refuelling, before continuing on to Sydney. He has no love for flying and the twenty-something hours it will take him to get there. If they are anything like they have been previously, it will be sheer purgatory.

Seeing that his flight has been called, he finds his way to the gate, which is heaving with humanity of every description. It doesn't seem possible to him that all these people with their assorted luggage can get on one plane, even if it is a Boeing 747.

Eventually Henry's seat number is called and he makes his way down the tunnel that leads him onto the plane, where he has a long struggle down to the rear. Although Richard has bought him an economy class ticket, he has managed to get a seat at the rear, where the configuration drops down to two seats on the side of the plane. Henry is perfectly happy with it because he has an aisle berth where to some extent he can stretch his legs periodically. Not only that, but because there is only one person inside him, he will not get interrupted so much, by having to let him or her out. Additionally, he himself can get out easily and walk around regularly to keep his circulation going, something that he likes to do.

As the plane begins to fill he wonders idly who will be sitting next to him, hoping that it will be someone who will not be too demanding of his time, because he has never been faced with the situation before. On each previous flight he has always travelled with Isabel next to him and, after she died, Penny. He is frightened that he won't know how to react with a stranger, or in fact, if he can be bothered.

By now it is nearly take off time and Henry begins to hope that the seat beside him has not been filled at all, which would allow him more space to spread out, not only for himself, but also the contents of his hand luggage.

Thinking that he has just enough time to read his emails, he pulls up his laptop, where to his amazement and joy, there is a message from Kate, which he starts to read avidly.

My dearest Henry,

Where to start, I ask myself. Well let me start where you left off, when you asked me if I would marry you.

It's a no brainer really my love. The thought of losing you again is just too painful to contemplate, so the answer is a resounding yes, if the offer still stands.

After your last message and while I was still at Trudy's, I told her the good news, which she was delighted to hear. But better than that, she then offered to perform at our wedding reception free and gratis. I don't know about you my love, but I can't think of anything that I could possibly want more.

The other thing that I didn't tell you, and I hope that you will forgive me for, is that Richard not only left a ticket for you to collect at the desk today, but he left one for me as well. When he told me, through Penny of course, he said that it was there as an option for me, if I had decided by then that the two of us had resolved our misunderstandings.

As far as I am concerned Henry, there are no such misunderstandings, so can you please put my hand luggage in the rack, so that we can get on with the rest of our lives.

Kate.

As he finishes reading Kate's email, which leaved him baffled, Henry is suddenly aware of a figure standing above him, and raising his face slowly to meet hers, he finds the same pair of clear blue eyes that entranced him the first time that he saw her at Goderston.

"Hullo Henry, are you ready for our great adventure?" asks Kate.

"Oh yes my love," replies Henry standing up and embracing her. "I hope it lasts forever."

As they stand together, Kate raises her mouth to his ear and whispers "On a scale of one to ten, I think this is a B, don't you?"

The End

For any comments or to contact for anything else,
please send an email to:
kathandian@btinternet.com

Printed in Great Britain
by Amazon